Praise for *The Nowhere Child*

'The personification of a high-concept thriller, brilliantly executed. Author White raises the bar on psychological suspense, telling Kim Leamy's tale in a stylish voice and with a heart-pounding pace. Read page one, and you won't stop. Guaranteed'
Jeffery Deaver

'Packed with tension, twists and tremendous pace, it's hard to believe that this is the work of a debut author. *The Nowhere Child* is stunning and flawless. I can't recommend it enough'
Thomas Enger

'Beautifully written, perfectly suspenseful and wonderfully dark. I could not put this book down'
Susi Holliday

'Such a clever idea, which grips from the very first chapter'
Ragnar Jonasson

'White skilfully builds an uncertain, noxious world of dysfunctional families and small-town secrets – *The Nowhere Child* is a gripping debut from an exceptional new talent'
Mark Brandi

'*The Nowhere Child* is a fabulous read, populated by such well-drawn and identifiable characters that I felt I knew them. I was desperate to know how the story unfolded. Brilliant!'
Louise Voss

'*The Nowhere Child* lures you in, its teeth disguised in remarkably compelling prose, and gnaws down to the marrow of your bones'
Matt Wesolowski

'I literally could not put this down once I started. A cracking read!'
Michael J. Malone

'*The Nowhere Child* is a well-written thriller that avoids the clichés of the genre. The characters are interesting and believable and the book kept me reading up to the satisfying conclusion'
Phillip Margolin

'*The Nowhere Child* is a page-turning labyrinth of twists and turns that moves seamlessly between the past and the present, revealing the story in parts and successfully keeping the reader guessing until the final unexpected reveal … It's an exhilarating ride and a thrilling debut'
Books+Publishing magazine

'How do any of us know that we are who we are told we are? This gripping read takes you to the very edge of reality'
Jane Caro

'*The Nowhere Child* is a twisty, emotional read filled with suspense and intrigue. The gripping narrative and natural dialogue held me captive all the way through. Dark secrets buried away for years are gradually unearthed, leading to a dramatic, breath-holding climax'
Off-the-Shelf Books

'I read *The Nowhere Child* in one gulp of a sitting. From the emotionally stunning opening until the final heart-stopping resolution, this tale of loss, discovery and what makes a family held me in its thrall first page to last'
Liz Loves Books

'Utterly compelling, emotional and a stunning debut'
Bibliophile Book Club

THE NOWHERE CHILD

Christian White is an Australian author and screenwriter whose projects include feature film *Relic*. *The Nowhere Child* is his first book. An early draft of this novel won the 2017 Victorian Premier's Literary Award for an Unpublished Manuscript, which was previously won by *The Rosie Project* by Graeme Simsion and *The Dry* by Jane Harper, and rights were quickly sold into fifteen countries. Christian lives in Melbourne with his wife, filmmaker Summer DeRoche, and their adopted greyhound, Issy.

THE NOWHERE CHILD

CHRISTIAN WHITE

HarperCollins*Publishers*

HarperCollins*Publishers*
1 London Bridge Street
London SE1 9GF

www.harpercollins.co.uk

First published in Great Britain by HarperCollins*Publishers* 2019
1

First published in Australia by Affirm Press 2018

A catalogue record for this book
is available from the British Library

ISBN: 978-0-00-827653-9 (HB)
ISBN: 978-0-00-827654-6 (TPB)

Printed and bound in Great Britain by
CPI Group (UK) Ltd, Croydon, CR0 4YY

MIX
Paper from
responsible sources
FSC C007454

This book is produced from independently certified FSC™ paper
to ensure responsible forest management.

For more information visit: www.harpercollins.co.uk/green

For my parents, Ivan and Keera White.

MELBOURNE, AUSTRALIA

Now

'Mind if I join you?' the stranger asked. He was somewhere in his forties, with shy good looks and an American accent. He wore a slick wet parka and bright yellow sneakers. The shoes must have been new because they squeaked when he moved his feet. He sat down at my table before waiting for an answer and said, 'You're Kimberly Leamy, right?'

I was between classes at Northampton Community TAFE, where I taught photography three nights a week. The cafeteria was usually bustling with students, but tonight it had taken on an eerie, post-apocalyptic emptiness. It had been raining nearly six days straight but the double-glazed glass kept the noise out.

'Just Kim,' I said, feeling mildly frustrated. I didn't have long left on my break and had been enjoying my solitude. Earlier that week I'd found a worn old copy of Stephen King's *Pet Sematary* propping up the leg of a table in the staffroom, and since then I'd been busily consuming it. I've always been a big reader, and horror is a particular favourite of mine. My younger sister, Amy, would often watch in frustration as I finished three books in the same time it took her to read one. The key to fast reading is to have a boring life, I once told her. Amy had a fiancé and a three-year-old daughter; I had Stephen King.

'My name is James Finn,' the man said. He placed a manila folder on the table between us and closed his eyes for a moment, like an Olympic diver mentally preparing to leap.

'Are you a teacher or a student?' I asked.

'Neither, actually.'

He opened the folder, removed an eight-by-ten-inch photo and slid it across the table. There was something mechanical about the way he moved. Every gesture was measured and confident.

The eight-by-ten showed a young girl sitting on a lush green lawn, with deep blue eyes and a mop of shaggy dark hair. She was smiling but it was perfunctory, like she was sick of having her picture taken.

'Does she look familiar to you?' he asked.

'No, I don't think so. Should she?'

'Would you mind looking again?'

He leaned back in his chair, closely gauging my response. Indulging him, I looked at the photo again. The blue eyes, the over-exposed face, the smile that wasn't really a smile. Perhaps she did look familiar now. 'I don't know. I'm sorry. Who is she?'

'Her name is Sammy Went. This photo was taken on her second birthday. Three days later she was gone.'

'Gone?'

'Taken from her home in Manson, Kentucky. Right out of her second-floor bedroom. Police found no evidence of an intruder. There were no witnesses, no ransom note. She just vanished.'

'I think you're looking for Edna,' I said. 'She teaches Crime and Justice Studies. I'm just a photography teacher but Edna lives for all this true crime stuff.'

'I'm here to see you,' he said, then cleared his throat before continuing. 'Some people thought she wandered into the woods, got taken by a coyote or mountain lion, but how far could a two-year-old *wander*? The most likely scenario is Sammy was abducted.'

'… Okay. So, are you an investigator?'

'Actually, I'm an accountant.' He exhaled deeply and I caught the smell of spearmint on his breath. 'But I grew up in Manson and know the Went family pretty well.'

My class was set to start in five minutes so I made a point of checking my watch. 'I'm very sorry to hear about this girl, but I'm afraid I have a class to teach. Of course I'm happy to help. What kind of donation did you have in mind?'

'Donation?'

'Aren't you raising money for the family? Isn't that what this is about?'

'I don't need your money,' he said with a chilly tone. He stared at me with a pinched, curious expression. 'I'm here because I believe you're … connected to all this.'

'Connected to the abduction of a two-year-old girl?' I laughed. 'Don't tell me you came all the way from the States to accuse me of kidnap?'

'You misunderstand,' he said. 'This little girl disappeared on April 3rd, 1990. She's been missing for twenty-eight years. I don't think you *kidnapped* Sammy Went. I think you *are* Sammy Went.'

There were seventeen students in my photography class, a mix of age, race and gender. On one end of the spectrum was Lucy Cho, so fresh out of high school she still wore a hoodie with *Mornington Secondary* emblazoned on the back. On the other end was Murray Palfrey, a 74-year-old retiree who had a habit of cracking his knuckles before he raised his hand.

It was folio presentation night, when students stood before the class to display and discuss the photos they'd taken that semester. Most of the presentations were unremarkable. The majority were technically sound, which meant I was doing *something* right, but the subject matter was largely the same as the folios in the previous semester, and the one before that. I saw the same graffiti on the same dilapidated brick wall; the same vine-strangled cabin in Carlton Gardens; the same dark and spooky storm drain dribbling dirty brown water into Egan River.

I spent most of the class on autopilot.

My encounter with the American accountant had left me rattled, but not because I believed what he said. My mother, Carol Leamy, was a lot of things – four years dead among them – but an abductor of children she was not. To spend one minute with my mother was to know she wasn't capable of maintaining a lie, much less international child abduction.

James Finn was wrong about me and I was fairly certain he'd never find that little girl, but he had reminded me of an uncomfortable truth: control is an illusion. Sammy Went's parents had learned that the hard way, with the loss of a child. I had learned it the hard way too, through the death of my mother. She went suddenly, relatively speaking: I was twenty-four when she was diagnosed with cancer and twenty-six when it killed her.

In my experience most people come out of something like that saying one of two things: 'everything happens for a reason' or 'chaos reigns'. There are variations, of course: 'God works in mysterious ways' and 'life's a bitch'. For me, it was the latter. My mother didn't smoke or spend her working life in a textiles factory. She ate well and exercised, and in the end it made exactly zero difference.

See, control is an illusion.

I realised I was daydreaming my way through the folio presentations so I downed a cup of cold coffee and tried to focus.

It was Simon Daumier-Smith's turn to show his work. Simon was a shy kid in his early twenties who spent most of his time staring at his feet when he talked. When he did look up, his lazy eye bobbed around behind his reading glasses like a fish.

He spent a few minutes awkwardly setting up a series of photos on the display easels at the front of the class. The other students were starting to get restless, so I asked Simon to talk us through the series as he set up.

'Uh, yeah, sure, okay,' he said, struggling with one of the prints. It escaped from his hand and he chased it across the floor. 'So, I know that we were meant to look for, uh, juxtaposition and, uh, well, I'm not exactly sure I have, you know, a grasp of what that is or whatever.' He placed the last photo on the easel and stepped back to let the class see. 'I guess you could say this series shows the juxtaposition of ugliness and beauty.'

To my complete surprise, Simon Daumier-Smith's photo series was … breathtaking.

There were six photos in total, each framed in the exact same way. He must have locked the camera off with a tripod and taken a photo every few hours. The composition was stark and simple: a bed, a woman and her child. The woman was Simon's age, with a pockmarked but pretty face. The child was around three, with unnaturally red cheeks and a sick, furrowed brow.

'I took them all over one night,' Simon explained. 'The woman is my wife, Joanie, and that's our little girl, Simone. We didn't name her after me, by the way. A lot of people think we named her after me, but Joanie had a grandma called Simone.'

'Tell us more about the series, Simon,' I said.

'Right, uh, so Simone was up all night with whooping cough and I guess she was pretty fussy, so Joanie spent the night in bed with her.'

The first photo showed mother spooning child. In the second the little girl was awake and crying, pushing away from her mother. The third looked as though Simon's wife was getting fed up with her photo being taken. The series went on like that until the sixth photo, which showed both mother and child fast asleep.

'Where's the ugliness?' I asked.

'Well, uh, see in this one, little Simone, ah, the younger subject, is drooling. And obviously you can't tell from the photo, but in this one my wife was snoring like crazy.'

'I don't see ugliness,' I said. 'I see something … ordinary. But beautiful.'

Simon Daumier-Smith would never go on to become a professional photographer. I was almost certain of that. But with his plainly named series, *Sick Girl*, he had created something true and real.

'Are you alright, Miss Leamy?' he asked.

'It's Kim,' I reminded him. 'And I'm fine. Why do you ask?'

'Well, you're, uh. You're crying.'

It was after ten when I drove home through the gloomy landscape of Coburg. Rain fell in fat, drenching sheets against the roof of the Subaru. Ten minutes later I was home, parked, and dashing through the rain toward my apartment building, holding my bag over my head instead of an umbrella.

The third-floor landing was thick with the smell of garlic and spice; the oddly comforting scent of neighbours I'd never actually met. As I headed for my door, Georgia Evvie from across the hall poked her head out.

'Kimberly, I thought that was you.' She was a rotund woman in her early sixties with bloodshot, bleary eyes – 'Heavy Evvie', I once heard a neighbour call her behind her back. 'I heard the elevator ding and looked at my watch and thought, who else would be coming home this close to midnight?'

It was ten-thirty.

'Sorry, Mrs Evvie. Did I wake you?'

'No, no. I'm a night owl. Of course, Bill's in bed by nine so he might have stirred but he didn't complain.' She waved a dismissive hand. 'And if he did I'd have reminded him you're young. Young people come home late nowadays, even on weeknights apparently.'

'Uh huh.'

Nobody had ever actually seen Georgia's husband and there was little to no evidence he truly existed. Of course, he might have just been buried under all of Georgia's crap. From the glimpses I caught of her apartment when she came to her door, I knew that 3E was lined with swaying towers of junk: books, bills, files and over-stuffed boxes. The only window I could see from the hall was covered with newspaper, and although I never actually saw one, I'm sure there were one or two tinfoil hats floating around in all that chaos.

'Well, seeing as how you're already awake …' she started. Georgia was about to invite herself in for a nightcap. All I wanted was to turn the heat up, lounge on the sofa with Stephen King and listen to the soothing, predictable sounds of my apartment – the hum of the refrigerator, the whisper of ducted heating, the quiet buzz of my laptop charger. '… how about a nightcap?'

With a sigh I said, 'Sure.' Ever since my mother's death I've found it near impossible to say no to a lonely woman.

My one-bedroom apartment was sparsely furnished, giving the impression that the place was huge. Even Heavy Evvie looked small sitting in the green armchair by the rain-streaked window of the living room, picking lint from her tracksuit pants and dropping it onto my hardwood floor.

I fetched a bottle of wine from the kitchen and fixed us both a glass. The one good thing about having Georgia over was I didn't have to drink alone.

'What do you think they're cooking up over there, Kim?' she asked.

'Who?'

'Who do you think? 3C. I hear them chattering all day in *Iraqian* or whatever.'

'Oh, 3C. Smells like some kind of curry.' My stomach growled. I had searched the kitchen for something to eat but all I could find were condiments. Wine would have to suffice.

'I'm not talking about their supper.' She lowered her voice to a whisper: 'I'm talking about their *plan*.'

Georgia was convinced the occupants of 3C were terrorists based on two things: they were from the Middle East, and the name on their mailbox was Mohamed. On a number of occasions I'd explained to her that not all people with light-brown skin were terrorists and, regardless, I doubted Coburg, Australia would rate high on anyone's list of targets. But every time, Georgia just shook her head gravely and said, 'You'll see.'

'So what brings you home so late, Kim? I suppose you've been out clubbing.'

'I work nights, Mrs Evvie. You know this.'

She sipped her wine and screwed her nose up at the taste. 'I don't know how you kids do it. Out all hours doing God knows what.'

I finished my wine fast and poured another one, reminding myself to take slower, more contemplative sips this time around. I was only after a warm, foggy buzz that would make it easier to sleep.

'So something weird happened to me tonight, Mrs Evvie,' I said. 'A man approached me at work.'

'Finally,' she said, helping herself to more wine. 'It's about time, Kim. A woman only has a small window to bag a man. Between fifteen and twenty-five. That's all you get. I was seventeen when I met Bill, eighteen when I married him.'

Georgia found a remote control stuffed between the green cushions of the armchair and turned on the television. Tinfoil hat and casual racism aside, all she really wanted was some company.

I curled up on the sofa nearby and opened up my laptop while she flicked through the stations at full volume.

I had intended to casually browse the internet, maybe stalk a high-school friend or purge my email inbox, but my curiosity soon grew too strong. When I opened a new tab and searched *Sammy Went + Manson, Kentucky*, it was as if my fingers were acting independently. It reminded me of the mechanical way James Finn had moved his manila folder about.

The first link took me to an archived newspaper article from 7 April 1990. The article had been electronically scanned in, complete with creases and inkblots. The words bled together in places, making me feel like an old-timey researcher poring through microfilm.

POLICE SEARCH FOR MISSING GIRL

The search for a two-year-old girl missing in the Manson area resumed on Friday with volunteers and law enforcement officers.

Sammy Went of Manson disappeared from her home Tuesday afternoon and has not been found despite a search of the town and its vicinity.

'We have faith we're going to find Sammy and bring her home safe,' Manson Sheriff Chester Ellis said. 'We're currently working under the assumption this is a search and rescue operation.'

Police do not believe the girl's disappearance was the result of foul play, but refused to rule anything out.

> Hundreds of Manson residents searched the extensive wooded areas surrounding the Went residence on Friday.
>
> Search volunteer Karen Peady, a long-time resident of Manson, expressed her fears: 'The nights are cold and there are a lot of wild animals in the area, but the idea she was taken by a man is what scares me the most. It's tempting to think the evils of modern America haven't reached us out here in Manson yet, but there are plenty of sick people in this world, even in a town as small as this.'
>
> Sammy was last seen wearing a long-sleeved yellow T-shirt and blue pyjama shorts. Police are asking for any information that may assist their investigation.

The article was accompanied by the same photo that James Finn had shown me, only this version was in black and white. Sammy's deep blue eyes appeared black, and her over-exposed face was stark white and mostly featureless.

A little more internet research took me to a photo of Jack and Molly Went, Sammy's parents. The picture had been taken in the days directly following Sammy's disappearance, and showed them standing on the steps outside the Manson Sheriff's Station.

They looked desperately tired, faces tense, fear etched in their eyes. Molly Went in particular looked permanently damaged, as if her spirit had left the body to run on autopilot. Her mouth was twisted into a frown so severe it made her look deranged.

Tracing her features on the screen, I compared Molly Went's face to my own. We shared the same long, angular nose and droopy eyelids. She seemed much shorter than me, but Jack Went looked well over six foot. The harder I looked the more I could see myself in both of them: Jack Went's small, pale ears, Molly Went's posture, Jack's broad shoulders, Molly's pointed chin. A little DNA from column A, a little from column B.

Of course, that didn't mean anything. I feel the same way when I read horoscopes – they're designed to allow the reader to see what they want.

Do I want to see myself in Jack and Molly Went? I wondered. The question came to me by surprise and soon my mind was buzzing with more. Hadn't Sammy's eyes been the same deep blue as mine, and couldn't those chubby legs of hers have transformed into long skinny pegs like my own, and if Sammy were alive today, wouldn't we be roughly the same age?

Were Jack and Molly Went still waiting for answers? Did every phone call or knock at the door fill them with hope or dread or some bitter mixture of both? Did they see Sammy's face in every woman they passed on the street, or had they found a way to move on?

The biggest question of all came like a shard of glass to my consciousness: could Carol Leamy, a woman with a background in social work who spent most of her working life as an HR rep for a company that sold and manufactured picture hooks, really, honestly, ever be capable of—

I stopped myself from going any further. The implications were too great and, frankly, too absurd.

The sound of heavy snoring pulled me from my laptop. Georgia had fallen fast asleep in the green armchair, her glass of wine balanced precariously between thumb and forefinger. I took the wine, switched off the television and covered her legs with a fluffy red throw rug. If history was any guide she'd be asleep for a few hours. She'd then wake around three am to use the toilet before waddling back across the hall.

Leaving Georgia where she was, I crept into my bedroom and climbed into bed. When I fell asleep, I dreamed about a tall man made entirely of shadows. The shadow man appeared outside my bedroom window and reached in with impossibly long arms. He carried me away, down a long, narrow dirt path lined with tall trees.

MANSON, KENTUCKY

Then

On Tuesday 3 April 1990, Jack Went emptied his bladder in the upstairs bathroom. His wife was in the shower a few feet away. There was something fitting about watching her through frosted glass. The vague shape of the woman he once knew. That sounded about right.

Molly shut the water off but stayed behind the screen. 'You about done, Jack?'

'Just about.' He washed his hands. 'You don't have to hide in there. You don't have anything I haven't quite literally seen before.'

'That's alright. I'll wait.' She stood behind the screen with her shoulders hunched forward. Her posture reminded Jack of something from his World War Two books – a Holocaust survivor with a broken spirit, or a simple village girl standing in a field of bodies.

Her clothes for the day were hanging on the back of the bathroom door: a pastel-pink sweater with long sleeves and a heavy denim skirt that fell an inch above her ankles. *Pentecostal chic.*

Once upon a time, before Sammy was born, Molly had been warm-blooded and tangible, but lately she seemed watered down. Haunting the halls of their home instead of living in them. She was a remarkable woman in that way: even with the family drugstore doing well enough that she didn't have to work, three beautiful children and the support of her faith, she could still find something to be sad about.

Molly opened the shower screen an inch to peer out. Her shoulders were pinched with gooseflesh. 'Come on, hun. I'm freezing here.'

'I'm going, I'm going,' he said, stepping out into the hall and closing the door behind him.

He found two of his children downstairs in front of the television, engrossed in an episode of *Teenage Mutant Ninja Turtles.* Neither said good morning. Stu, the lumpy nine-year-old, was getting over a cold. He sat under a woollen blanket with a box of Kleenex, staring at the screen with eyes wide and mouth slack.

'Feeling any better, buddy?' Jack asked, placing the back of his hand against Stu's forehead. He didn't reply. The Turtles had him transfixed.

Sammy, the two-year-old cherub, was also watching, but she seemed just as interested in her big brother. Her eyes darted from the cartoon to Stu's face. When Michelangelo made a wisecrack and Stu laughed, she copied him, parroting not just the volume of the laugh, but the rhythm too. When Shredder put some sinister plan into action and Stu gasped, Sammy gasped with him.

Not wanting to disturb the scene of domestic bliss he'd stumbled into, Jack backed quietly out of the room.

His eldest daughter, Emma, was eating cornflakes at the kitchen counter, one arm forming a wall around her bowl, the way he imagined prison inmates would eat.

Is that how she sees this house? He wondered. *A sentence she needs to wait out.* Sometimes it felt that way for Jack too.

'Good morning, sweetheart,' he said, making coffee. 'Coach Harris came by the drugstore yesterday. He says you had PMS *again* so you couldn't participate in gym. Need me to bring you home some naproxen?'

Emma grunted. 'I don't know why two grown men think it's okay to talk about my period.'

'Isn't using your period to get out of gym sort of cliché?'

'It's not cliché, Dad – it's a classic. Besides, Coach Harris is a creep. He always makes us climb the gym ropes so he can "spot" us. That reminds me, I need you to sign this.'

She dug deep into her backpack, pulled out a permission slip and handed it to Jack.

'*For permission to participate in the study of science and evolution*?' he read. 'You need a parent's permission to take a class nowadays?'

'You do when half the kids are fucking fundies.'

He lowered his voice. 'Has your mother seen this?'

'No.'

He took a pen from his breast pocket and signed the permission slip quickly. 'Let's keep it that way. And don't let her catch you saying the F-word.'

'Fucking?'

'Fundie.'

Emma folded the slip and tucked it safely back into her backpack.

While both Jack and Molly were technically members of the Church of the Light Within – Molly through conversion and Jack through blood – Molly took it far more seriously than he did. She attended all three weekly services. That was common for members who found the faith later in life: usually they already had a hole that needed filling.

Jack had started drifting from the Light Within as a teenager and had stopped attending services altogether when Emma was born. He'd justified it by calling it a safety issue: like many Pentecostal fundamentalists, the Light Within handled venomous snakes and ingested different kinds of poison as part of their worship – not exactly a healthy environment for children. So he had stayed home to babysit and let Molly do her thing. He still called himself a Light Withiner to keep Molly from leaving him and his parents from disowning him – although at times neither of those possibilities sounded too bad – but in truth he had long ago lost his faith.

Molly came downstairs, pulling on her pastel-pink sweater. 'Morning, Em.'

Emma grunted a reply.

'Coach Harris told your father you're using PMS to get out of gym. Is this true?'

'Dad's already given me the lecture, so you can cool it.'

'Well, I hope he told you that lying is a sin and your studies are the most important thing in your life right now.'

'Jesus, here we go.'

'Em.' Molly drummed her fist on the kitchen counter. '*Each tree is recognised by its own fruit. The mouth speaks what the heart is full of. When you say His name in vain*—'

'—*you dishonour the faith*,' Emma finished in a tired monotone. '*Words testify to our devotion to God and words are the truth of what we are.* I got it. Thanks.' She put her bowl in the sink. 'I have to go. I'm meeting Shelley.'

She picked up her backpack, clomped across the kitchen in her dirty Chuck Taylors and disappeared out the door.

'Some back-up would have been nice,' Molly said to Jack.

'I thought you handled it pretty well.' He put an arm around her shoulders and tried to ignore the way she stiffened under his touch.

'I worry about her, Jack.'

'She's not a lost soul just yet,' he said. 'Just *a little* lost. Remember what you were like at her age? Besides, I won't be the favourite for long. I read somewhere that when girls hit puberty something is triggered inside their brain and they're reprogrammed to hate the smell of their father. They say it's an evolutionary thing. To prevent incest.'

Molly's face turned sour. 'Just one more reason not to believe in evolution.'

Sammy yanked on one of Jack's pant legs. She had waddled into the kitchen, dragging a stuffed gorilla behind her. 'Dada,' she said. 'Incest?'

Molly laughed. It felt good to hear her laugh. 'Good luck with that one. I have to check up on Stu.'

When Molly left the kitchen, Jack hoisted his little girl into his arms and drew her tight toward his face. His whiskers and hot breath made her giggle and squirm. She smelled like fresh talcum powder.

'Incest?' Sammy said again.

'*Insects*,' Jack said. 'You know, like ants and beetles.'

Went Drugs, the family business, was situated on the corner of Main Street and Barkly, in the middle of Manson's shopping district. The store also provided a shortcut between a large parking lot and Main Street, which meant plenty of foot traffic. People always got sick and business was always good.

When Jack arrived, Deborah Shoshlefski was bagging up a customer's order at the front counter. Deborah was the youngest and most reliable of Jack's shop assistants, a dowdy girl with wide-set eyes that made her seem perpetually surprised.

'Morning, boss. There's a load of scripts need filling. They're on your spike.'

'Thanks, Debbie.'

She rolled her eyes, laughing, and told her customer, 'He knows I hate it when people call me Debbie, so he calls me Debbie every chance he gets.'

Jack smiled politely at the woman as he slipped behind the counter. He barely had time to button on his white tunic before a skeletal hand reached over the counter and grabbed his forearm.

'My joints are hurting something awful, Jack,' an old voice wheezed. Graham Kasey had lived in Manson forever and had seemed ancient even when Jack was a boy. He spoke through loose false teeth in that old-timer death-gurgle that Jack's grandfather had taken on in his final years. 'My bones feel like they're punishing me for something I can't remember. None of the stuff you keep on the shelf is working for me, Jack. Give me something harder than this pussy shit.' He held up an empty packet of Pain-Away, an extra-strength heat rub designed for superficial pain relief.

'Have you seen a doctor, Graham?'

'You expect me to drive all the way to Coleman just so Dr Arter can send me back here with a scrap of paper? Come on, Jack. I know you got what I need.'

'I'm not a drug dealer. And who says you have to go all the way to Coleman? We've got Dr Redmond right here in Manson.'

'Redmond and I don't see eye to eye.'

Jack threw a subtle wink at Deborah, who chortled in return. Graham Kasey was the sort who would rather drive twenty miles to Coleman in his gas-guzzling old Statesman than have Dr Redmond – who was both black *and* a woman – give him a prescription.

'Sorry, Graham. I don't write the scripts. I just fill 'em.'

In the whole time they had been talking, Graham hadn't let go of Jack's arm. His fingers were cold and bony, reminding Jack of dead white caterpillars. 'Don't you know you're s'posed to respect your elders?'

'It's illegal.'

'Oh, illegal my ear. I know how it works, Jack. You can write off anything you keep behind your little counter there. Things get lost all the time. They go missing or get chewed up by rats or they expire.'

'And how might you know that?'

'Well, let's just say it wasn't so damn uptight round here when Sandy ran things.'

At hearing his mother's name, Jack felt hot energy rise in the back of his neck. Went Drugs was opened two years before Jack was born, as the sign above the door – *WENT DRUGS EST. 1949* – reminded him daily. He had bought into it fair and square just four years out of college, but it never really felt wholly his.

It didn't help that his mother – a druggist too and *technically* retired – popped in every other week under the pretence of picking up a bottle of Aspirin or a jumbo-sized pack of toilet paper, only to wander the aisles saying things like, 'Oh, why did you put the antihistamines *here*?' One time she even ran her index finger along the rear shelf to check for dust, like an uptight British nanny.

Graham might have seen a little too much fire in Jack's eyes because he softened and finally released Jack's arm. There were pale marks in the skin where his fingers had been. 'Ah, hell. I'll just take another pack of this pussy shit.'

Jack flashed a smile and clapped a hand against Graham's shoulder. He could have sworn he saw dust rise off the old coot's blazer.

'You heard the man, Debbie,' Jack said. 'One pack of pussy shit for Mr Kasey here. Bag it up.'

'Right away, boss.'

Jack went back to his station to fill some scripts but couldn't quite relax. Graham Kasey had picked at an old scab and now he was irritated.

A grown man with mommy issues, he thought. *Talk about cliché.*

It's not cliché, he heard his daughter say. *It's a classic.*

Jack tried to focus on work, but as he pulled the first script from the spike, he nearly tore it in half. Luckily the important parts were still readable: *Andrea Albee, fluoxetine, maintenance dose.*

He took a small plastic cup and wandered among the towering pill shelves out back, then returned to his desk with Andrea Albee's Prozac and powered up the fat computer on his desk. It buzzed and struggled. A few minutes later a black screen appeared with a green directory. He found fluoxetine on the database and hit the *PRINT SIDE EFFECTS* button for the side of the bottle.

The printer shook and screamed as the list emerged. *Hives, restlessness, chills, fever, drowsiness, irregular heartbeat, convulsions, dry skin, dry mouth.* Just how sad was this Andrea Albee anyway? Was turning her brain numb – and that's exactly what she was doing: contrary to popular opinion, Prozac didn't make you feel happy or *right* – truly worth the side effects?

Deborah poked her head into his station. 'Phone call for you, boss. Wanna take it in here?'

'Thanks, Deborah.'

Her eyes grew even wider than usual. 'You didn't call me Debbie!'

Jack flashed the same smile he'd given Graham Kasey, and Deborah connected the call to the phone on his desk.

'Jack Went speaking.'

'Hi, Jack.' He recognised the voice right away. 'Free for lunch?'

At two pm, Jack pulled in to the parking lot at the east end of Lake Merri and stood waiting against his red Buick Reatta convertible – a car Emma lovingly referred to as his mid-life-crisis-mobile. The lot was hidden from the highway by a quarter-mile of shaggy bushland. It was almost always empty, even at this time of year when the spring weather started to bring people back to the water.

Travis Eckles arrived ten minutes later in his industrial cleaning work van. He got out of the van in a pair of baggy white coveralls and checked his windblown hair in the windscreen reflection. He had a nasty-looking black eye.

'Heck, what happened to you?' Jack asked.

Travis gave the bruise an exploratory poke and winced. 'It's not as bad as it looks.'

Jack took Travis's head between his hands and examined the injury. It puffed out his face, made him look thuggish like his older brother. 'How's the pain? Need some Advil?'

Travis shrugged. 'No. It's alright.'

'Did Ava do this to you?'

Travis ignored him, which was as good as answering in the affirmative.

Ava Eckles was Travis's mother, a wild drunk who liked to talk with her fists from time to time. If the rumours could be believed she had also slept her way through half the men in Manson.

Travis's father was a crewman in the air force and was inside a CH-53 Sea Stallion helicopter when it crashed during a training exercise off the southeast coast of North Carolina in 1983. Everyone on board was killed.

Travis had an elder brother too – Patrick – but he was currently serving time in Greenwood Corrections on an aggravated assault charge. Then there were his cousins, a collection of college dropouts, drug dealers and delinquents.

Some family, Jack thought. But Travis was alright. At twenty-two he was still young enough to get out of Manson, and while being a janitor wasn't anyone's dream job, it was solid work for a solid paycheck. He was crude and abrasive sometimes, but he was kind and funny too. Not many people saw that side of him.

Travis slid the side door of the work van open. *CLINICAL CLEANING* printed on the side in big red letters turned into *CL ING*. He stood aside. 'After you.'

Jack looked over the lake. The evergreens on the Coleman side shifted as a stiff breeze swept through them, but the water was still and empty. They were alone. He climbed into the back of the van and Travis followed, pulling the door shut behind them. It was warm inside. Travis rolled his coveralls down to the waist and Jack unbuttoned his pants.

MELBOURNE, AUSTRALIA

Now

My sister's townhouse was in a labyrinth of identical-looking homes in Caroline Springs. I'd been there at least a dozen times already but I wasn't sure I had the right place until Amy rushed out to meet me.

'What is it?' she called. 'What's wrong? What's going on?'

'What are you talking about? Nothing's wrong. Who said anything was wrong?'

She bent over at the waist and braced herself on her knees, heaving with melodramatic relief. 'When I saw you out front I just … I didn't know you were coming and … I'm sorry. I guess I have a habit of assuming the worst.'

'Yikes. Can't a girl just visit her sister?'

'Not when that girl is you, Kim. You're not exactly the pop-in type.'

I made a big show of rolling my eyes because I didn't want

her to know she was right – which, of course, she was. I'm generally solitary by nature. I feel much more comfortable alone, staying in and reading a book or wandering the aisles of the supermarket for an hour trying to find the perfect brand of linguine.

Amy was five years younger than me, with a warm, round face and full body. *'Bumps in all the right places'*, our mother used to say. It was as if my sister's genes had defined themselves in opposition to my own. Nobody in school ever stopped her to say, 'Excuse me but I think your boobs are on backwards.'

Technically Amy and I were only half-sisters. Her father (my stepdad) met my mother when I was two, and they had Amy when I was five. But blood and DNA aside, there was no *half* about it. Amy was my sister, for better or worse.

Dean had been around long enough to earn the position of official, bona fide *Dad*. Of course, never knowing my real father meant there was no basis for comparison.

'Aunty Kim!' Lisa, my three-year-old niece, had hurried out through the open front door and onto the lawn, two fingers wedged into her mouth. The grass was wet and her socks were immediately soaked through, but that didn't slow her down. She crossed the lawn as fast as she could. I grabbed her under the armpits, hoisted her into the air and turned her upside down. She screamed in delight, giggling until snot came out of her nose.

I set Lisa down on the front step and let her run into the house, her wet socks leaving tiny footprints on the hardwood floors. As usual, the house was a mess. Dishes were piled six plates high in the sink, Lisa's toys were strewn up and down the hallway, and the living-room sofa was covered with coloured crayon, its creases foaming with forgotten chalk and food crumbs.

The television, a brand new fifty-two-inch, was blaring at full volume. Lisa was lured to it like a zombie. She stopped less than a foot from the screen, mouth agape, as if the cartoon characters on the screen were whispering all the secrets of the universe.

In the middle of the living-room floor was an Ikea box, roughly torn down the middle to expose a mad tangle of cheap wood and plastic brackets.

If I spent just one day in Amy's shoes my mind would melt with sensory overload, but she seemed to thrive in the chaos.

'It's a goddamn toy chest for Lisa's room,' she said, picking up an L-shaped bracket and turning it over in her hands, as if it were some mysterious archaeological artefact. 'Or at least it will be a toy chest ... one day. In the far off, distant future.'

'Need some help putting it together?'

'Nah, I'll leave it for Wayne to finish. And I don't even care what that says about me as a woman. Coffee?'

'Sure.'

As she prepared coffee in the adjoining kitchen, she talked about the toy chest for a full five minutes. Shouting over the sound of the percolator, she told me how much the toy chest cost, which section of Ikea she found it in, what it should look like after its construction and the complex series of decisions that led to its purchase. She told me all of this without a break as I waited in the living room. I could have left, gone to the bathroom and come back, and she wouldn't have noticed. Instead I used the time to scan her bookshelves, searching for her photo albums.

In particular I was looking for a fat pink folder with *EARLIEST MEMORIES* spelled out in purple block letters on the cover. The album had belonged to our mother, and should really have been kept at Dean's place, but Amy went a little nutty with photos after Mum died.

The photos were the whole reason I was here. Last night I'd half-convinced myself that I could have been the kid in James Finn's photograph, and I was eager to knock that speculation on the head.

The bookshelf was packed with DVDs, magazines, a framed cast of two tiny feet marked *Lisa, age 6 months,* but there were no albums.

'What are you looking for?' Amy had snuck up behind me. She handed me a cup of black coffee. 'We're outta milk.'

'That's fine. And nothing. I was just looking.'

'You're lying.'

Damn it, I thought. Ever since we were kids Amy could always tell when I was trying to hide something. She had a knack for it that bordered on psychic. The morning after I'd lost my virginity to Rowan Kipling I told my parents that I had stayed over at my friend Charlotte's place. Amy, at all of eleven years old, looked at me over her breakfast cereal and said, 'She's lying.'

Assuming Amy knew something they didn't, Mum and Dean started picking at my lie until the whole damn story came unravelled. It wasn't that I was a bad liar; Amy was just an exceptional lie detector.

Sighing, I came clean. 'I'm looking for the photo album with the baby pictures.'

Amy clicked her tongue, a thinking technique she'd used since she was a kid. The wet *click-click* sound briefly transported me back in time to my bedroom at number fourteen Greenlaw Street. The memory was hazy and fragmented, lacking context like a fading dream. But I could see Amy clearly, at four or five years old, in pink-and-green striped pyjamas. She was climbing into my single bed and I was pulling back the covers to let her in.

As the memory drifted away a heavy sadness remained.

'All the photos are probably in the garage someplace,' Amy said. 'We still haven't totally unpacked the garage, if you'd believe it. Six months later. It's Wayne's job but every time I bring it up he does this big sigh. You know that sigh he does that sounds like a deflating tyre? Like you just asked him for a kidney.'

'So you have it?'

'Why do you want it?'

'This'll sound strange, but it's a secret.'

Amy sipped her coffee, searching my face for whatever hidden tell or psychic signal she usually used to catch me out. Then her eyes lit up. 'Does this have something to do with my birthday? Did Wayne tell you about the photo collages we saw at the shopping centre? Forget it. Don't tell me. I want it to be a surprise. Follow me.'

The garage smelled of old paint and methylated spirits. Amy found a pull-string in the darkness and a fluorescent light flickered on overhead, revealing a cramped concrete room with a low ceiling.

Several rows of packing boxes occupied the space between the far wall and Amy's little red Honda Jazz. We spent the next forty minutes carrying out each box, setting it down on the small patch of unused concrete floor and poring through its contents.

Most boxes contained miscellaneous *stuff*: year-old energy bills, a roll of expired coupons, a tattered apron, a chipped ceramic ashtray with a single English penny sliding around inside, a grocery bag full of magnets that Amy snatched gleefully from my hands saying, 'I've been looking for these.'

One of the boxes was full of my old photography projects, many embarrassingly similar to the ones my students had presented the night before. I found a first-year uni photo-series called *Scars: Physical and Emotional.* Amy had organised the collection into a binder. I flicked through it, cringing; it was more like a high school project than a university folio.

One photo showed the small nick I got on my pinkie toe while climbing out of a friend's pool one summer; another showed the grizzly slice running across Amy's thigh from when she fell off her ten-speed. Here was a nasty burn on my mother's hand, and the fading ghost of an old housemate's cleft palate. Next came several photos showing subjects who looked sad or rejected or angry. It was a pretentious, highly unoriginal project designed to force the audience to consider the scars people carry on the inside as well as on the outside.

'Oh, hey, how's it going with Frank?' Amy asked, leafing through an old school report.

'Eh.'

'What's that mean?'

'We stopped seeing each other.'

'Why?' Amy said in a high-pitched, whining voice.

'No one thing. Just, you know. It wasn't a love connection.'

'You're too fussy, Kim. You know that. And you're running out of time to make babies.'

Amy was aggressively maternal. Reproducing was her sole purpose in life. She and her fiancé Wayne pumped out Lisa as fast as they could and were planning for a second. I, on the other hand, had never once felt the urge to procreate.

We eventually found the family albums in the ninth or tenth box and sat cross-legged on the floor to look through them. Each album was titled with big block letters, written in colours that somehow matched the theme of the photos within. *PERTH HOLIDAY '93* was black and yellow to match the emblem on the state flag. *NEW HOME*, which chronicled Mum and Dean's move from their old place on Osborne Avenue to their smaller but much newer pad on Benjamin Street, was written in blue and green: the blue matched the porch steps of Osborne, the green matched the bedroom walls of Benjamin. The humorously named *OUR*

FIRST WEDDING was written in bright orange – the same shade my mother wore on the big day.

It'd be easy to assume that my mother was the one who meticulously matched each colour and labelled each photo, but it was Dean. Even before our mother died he obsessed over photographing, categorising and recording each and every memory for safekeeping.

Amy grabbed the wedding album the second she saw it. With a sad smile she turned the pages, tracing our mother's face.

At the bottom of the box I found the fat pink baby album, *EARLIEST MEMORIES*, written in the same shade of purple as my childhood headboard. Inside were photos of birthday parties, holidays, Christmases; all lost to time. There was a picture of me in the old flat we lived in before Amy was born: smiling broadly, framed against the ugly yellow wallpaper that lined *every single* room. Another showed my first day of kindergarten, my mother holding my hand and grinning.

A third of the way through I came across a bright, pudgy little girl staring at me through the plastic sleeve. She was standing in the shallow end of a hotel pool, dressed in sagging yellow bathers. She looked somehow contemplative and wise. Below the shot, printed in neat black letters was, *Kim, age 2*. I had a vague memory of that day in the pool, riding Dean's shoulders into the deep end.

The remaining pages were blank. There were no baby photos, and nothing else before the age of three. I hadn't been expecting more. My biological father wasn't a *nice man* – that's how my mother had phrased it on one of the few occasions we discussed him. When she had left him she left in a hurry, a toddler under one arm and an overnight bag slung over the other, with no time and no room for baby pictures. That story sounded worryingly convenient now.

'Are you okay?' Amy asked. 'You look like you've seen a ghost.'

In a way I had. Suddenly the ghost of Sammy Went was haunting each and every childhood photo. Even before I brought up a photo of Sammy on my phone I could see it was more than just a passing resemblance. The deep blue eyes, the dark hair, the tight-lipped smile, the curved chin, the large nose, the small white ears. It wasn't just uncanny; either Sammy was my exact doppelgänger, or I was looking at photos of the same girl.

Why hadn't I seen it before? Was it simply that I couldn't remember what I looked like as a kid, or had I not been ready to see it? Was I ready now?

'Jesus, Kim, what is it?'

'Amy, I came here to compare photos from when I was a kid to a little American girl who went missing in the '90s.'

'Hold up. So you're not making me a photo collage for my birthday?'

I closed my eyes, took a deep breath and started from the beginning. Sitting cross-legged on the floor of the garage, surrounded by packing boxes and the smell of old paint and methylated spirits, I opened up the Sammy Went door and invited Amy inside.

She listened silently with a cool expression that gave nothing away. When I had finished she sat blinking like an owl; buffering. Then she laughed. It wasn't a chuckle or giggle, but a heavy *ha ha*. She put one hand against her belly, threw her head back and cackled, guffawed, snorted. 'So let me get this straight: you think Mum – the woman who bawled her eyes out when the horse died in *The Neverending Story* – was a kidnapper. And you were the kid she napped? She abducted you from someplace in the States and raised you as her own. And never once, not even on her deathbed, revealed the truth.'

'I don't know, I …'

'Maybe she bought you on the black market. Makes perfect sense when you think about it. Oh, or maybe she lowered herself down to your cot on one of those wire harness things like Tom Cruise or trained a dingo to—'

I showed her my phone. She froze, silenced by the photo of Sammy Went on the screen. She took the phone from me and stared, her smile quickly fading. 'Shit, Kim.'

'Yeah. Shit.'

'What did this guy say, exactly?' She was squeezing the phone so hard I thought it might shatter. 'How did he find you? What evidence does he have?'

'I don't know. I didn't really give him time to tell me. I thought he was a nutter.'

After a string of increasingly exasperated expletives, Amy said, 'Do you wanna smoke a joint?'

We left Lisa inside watching TV and sat together on the back step. Amy's yard was small and well-manicured. A blue plastic sandbox had filled with rainwater, turning the sand inside to sludge. The flat grey walls of the houses on either side of Amy's fence blocked out half the sky.

She lit the joint and took a long, deep drag before handing it to me. 'It's a scam. That's what it is.'

'How would that work?' I said. 'He didn't ask me for money or personal details or—'

'Just you wait. He probably stole that photo.'

'Neither of us has ever seen it before.'

'So he, I don't know, took it.'

'Twenty-eight years ago? When I was two? And he's just been, what? Biding his time to pull off the longest sting in history?'

'Is Mum abducting you from a foreign country a more plausible explanation? Something like this, if it was real … Jesus, Kim. It would fuck everything up. We wouldn't be sisters anymore.'

The joint sent me into a momentary coughing fit, but it helped dull my busy mind. 'Don't be ridiculous.'

'Kim, if we didn't have blood connecting us I'd never see you. When you dropped around today it nearly gave me a heart attack. I thought something was wrong.' She took the joint back. 'And shit, I guess I was right after all. You weren't just popping in, were you? You were gathering evidence.'

'Please don't turn against me,' I said. 'Not right now.'

Amy sighed.

Smoke danced and swirled, making my eyes water.

'Wayne will still be able to smell this, you know,' I said.

'If ever I had a good excuse to get stoned, it's today.' She wiped her eyes. I couldn't be sure if it was the smoke that was making her cry, or the situation. She stared off over the back fence. Another townhouse lay beyond it, and another one beyond that.

She shifted her weight and studied her chipped nail polish, looking anywhere but at me.

'What do you want me to do?' I asked.

'Nothing, Kim. I want you to do nothing. Delete that photo off your phone. Delete his number. Forget about the whole thing.'

'I don't think I can do that.'

'I think you have to, Kim. If you follow this thing through, then everything is going to change.'

'Okay,' I said.

'Swear?'

'Swear.'

After leaving Amy's house, I pulled the car to the side of the road and found the number James Finn had given me. I quietly hoped he wouldn't pick up, but he answered on the first ring.

MANSON, KENTUCKY

Then

Emma scanned the forest floor for psilocybin mushrooms. Ideally they should be young, with white bulbs turning a pinkish brown on top. In time they would turn black and curl up at the edges. Shelley Falkner's cousin had told them all about it.

The forest was wet from an early afternoon shower, and smelled of mildew and mountain laurel.

Fifty feet to Emma's left, Shelley Falkner moved around in the thicket like a sasquatch, kicking up dead leaves and snapping off low-hanging branches.

Emma soon grew bored of the mushroom search, so she sat down on the trunk of a fallen sweetgum and searched her backpack for a cigarette. She had to push aside her algebra textbook to find one, which made her think of Manson High, which in turn flushed her system with a familiar brand of anxiety. She was doubly glad she and Shelley had decided to cut class today.

Emma lit the cigarette and dialled up the volume on her Discman until the deep, mournful sound of Morrissey's 'Every Day is Like Sunday' turned the greens of the forest grey. Morrissey was the perfect soundtrack for a town like Emma's. When she thought of Manson, she pictured a beetle on its back, kicking its legs helplessly in the air.

To an outside observer, of course, Manson must have seemed like a quaint, friendly community. It was true that the town wasn't nearly as poverty-stricken as its Appalachian neighbours, and Emma guessed there were slightly fewer hillbillies per capita, but it was a long way from being *A Slice of Heaven*, as the sign on the water tower boasted. The few tourists that trickled through only saw half the picture. They came for the hiking trails, good ol' fashioned hospitality, and to bask in the glory of Hunt House, a grand, centuries-old mansion that stood at the top of Main Street.

But Emma knew what visitors didn't: that locals were only truly friendly to other locals, that if it wasn't in the Bible then it wasn't worth knowing, and that Hunt House was built on the backs of slaves (and supposedly haunted by their ghosts).

'No way,' Shelley called, loud enough that Emma could hear even with her headphones on. 'Em, check it out.'

As Emma climbed down from the fallen sweetgum, Shelley came lumbering through the underbrush, both hands cupped before her as if carrying a baby bird.

She extended her arms to show Emma two handfuls of small white bulbs. 'I hit the mother lode.'

Shelley was a hulk of a girl; not fat exactly, just bulky, with wide, slumped shoulders and a pair of glasses she was forever nudging into place with her index finger. 'This has gotta be them, right? They're just like Vince said.'

She handed one of the mushrooms to Emma, who took it and held it up to the light. It was a creamy colour, with a brown ring on top that reminded her of an areola.

'I guess so,' Emma said. 'It's funny, I always imagined them red with little white spots, like the ones that make Mario super. How do we know for sure they're magic?'

'There's only one way to be sure: we eat 'em. If we start seeing, like, unicorns or something, then we know they're the real deal and Vince ain't *completely* fulla shit. If our throats close over and we go blind, well …'

'Let's take them this weekend,' Emma said, pulling her headphones down. It wasn't that she was particularly *pro-drug* – she had tried smoking a bong once at Roland Butcher's house and nearly coughed up a lung – but she knew she had changed and wanted desperately to *change back.*

It was only last summer she and Shelley spent swimming in Lake Merri; just last spring they spent hiking through Elkfish canyon; only last fall they spent cruising around Manson on their ten-speeds; only last winter they spent skiing the powdery peaks of the Appalachian Mountains.

Now the world had turned grey. Perhaps Shelley's mushrooms would bring back some of that colour.

'Tell your parents you're staying at my place,' Emma said. 'I'll tell my parents I'm staying at yours. I can sneak my dad's three-man and we could hike out to the gristmill, brew the mushrooms into a tea and then—'

Shelley popped a mushroom into her mouth, ending the conversation. She chewed for a moment, a sour expression on her face, as if her cheeks and forehead were being drawn together. Then she swallowed loudly and grinned.

Emma's eyes nearly bugged out of her head. 'You're my hero. What did it taste like?'

'Dirt. Your turn, lady.'

She took one bulb between her thumb and forefinger and moved it toward Emma's mouth, like a parent trying to convince a kid to eat their greens.

Emma moved Shelley's hand away. 'Oh, I think I'll wait a few minutes to see if, you know, you go blind or something.'

Shelley's grin widened. 'Good call.'

A few minutes later Shelley still seemed fine, so Emma closed her eyes and shoved the bulb into her mouth. Shelley was right. It tasted like dirt.

As they waited for the effects of the mushrooms to hit them, they walked aimlessly through the deep concrete channel separating the forest from the outskirts of Manson. The channel was mostly dry aside from a drizzling current of muddy brown water, which was narrow enough to step over in most places. It was littered with cigarette butts, empty bottles of cheap beer and wine, and the occasional split can of baked beans. According to Shelley's mom, a community of hobos used to roam the channel, setting up shelters under the overpass another mile up.

To their left sat the jagged back fences of the houses on Grattan Street. This was the mostly forgotten end of Manson, where the lawns were yellow instead of green, and the faces of the people who lived there were tight and worn. Where the fence slats were loose Emma could see into their yards – long grass; a barking dog; two young boys with dirty faces sitting cross-legged on a trampoline.

Dense woodland foamed to the right, on the other side of the concrete channel. Mid-afternoon sun filtered through the sweetgums and cast a spiderweb of shadows over Shelley's face.

'Are you feeling anything yet?' Emma asked.

'Nuh-uh. Not yet.'

'Me neither.'

They arrived at the large circular culvert that carried the pitiful brown stream under the highway. The concrete tunnel was tall enough for Emma to walk into – although she still hunched with her arms up, afraid of creepy crawlies – but Shelley had to slouch to avoid knocking her head.

Emma held her breath and kept her gaze on the bright circle of light at the end of the culvert. She imagined secret passages leading off either side of the tunnel. One wrong turn could mean blindly wandering the drains beneath Manson for the rest of her very short—

Shelley grabbed her on the shoulder. Emma screamed so loudly it echoed around the curved concrete walls for nearly five full seconds.

'You're such a pussy,' Shelley said, shoving Emma forward and into the light of the afternoon. Emma couldn't argue. As the sounds of Manson came back and a cool spring breeze tickled the back of her neck, she felt more relieved to be out of the dark than she ought to have.

They continued up the channel.

'I have to spend the summer with Dad in California,' Shelley said after a few minutes of comfortable silence. 'Why he chose to move so far away is beyond me, and he only wants me out there to get at Mom. It's like, ever since the divorce they've been in this long, *long* war. But they're the generals; I'm the only one fighting down in the trenches.'

'Mm. You're kind of lucky though,' Emma said. 'Obviously it sucks your parents are divorced, but at least that's sort of proactive. Their marriage didn't work so they ended it. It's smart.'

Shelley baulked. 'That's like telling a paraplegic they're lucky 'cause they get to sit down all day.'

'My parents' marriage has been dying slowly for the past two years and neither of them will put it out of its misery. Wouldn't you rather have your parents separate but happy instead of together and miserable?'

'Ah, but you forgot about separate and miserable,' Shelley said, laughing. 'I didn't know your parents fought a lot.'

'They don't. That's part of the problem. If they fought, maybe they'd sort some shit out. Instead it's like they never finish a sentence. There's a dot-dot-dot at the end of everything they say to each other, never a period.'

'Ellipsis,' Shelley said.

'What?'

'That little dot-dot-dot at the end of a sentence. It's called an ellipsis.'

Emma rolled her eyes.

'Anyway, maybe you're right,' Shelley said. 'Maybe they should get a divorce.'

A nagging sadness fell over Emma then. If her parents really did split then her father would remarry – she knew that. He'd loosen his grip on church ties even further, find happiness and talk bitterly about his fundie ex-wife. But what would become of her mother? Without Jack Went to act as a spiritual buoy, she'd sink deeper and deeper into the Church of the Light Within. Eventually the woman Emma knew might fade away completely.

'Feeling anything yet?' Emma asked.

'Nuh-uh.'

About a quarter-mile into the woods they came across the gristmill, a dilapidated structure surrounded by scrub oak. The sun had dipped behind it, creating a rectangular silhouette reaching out of the earth, like a corpse rising from the grave.

Up until a few years ago the gristmill was still running. Of course even then it made more money from the gift shop and the working tours than it did selling flour and cornmeal.

Emma came here with her mother once. Her dad was visiting his cousins in Coleman and had taken Stu along with him for a boys' day out. Her mother had put it to

Emma to decide how to spend their day together, and she had suggested the mill.

Back then, a wide paved road cut a path in from the highway, wooded on both sides. The road crossed a rattling suspension bridge over a shallow, spring-fed creek. She remembered rolling down her window as they drove over it, sticking her head all the way out to listen to the creek babble below them.

Once inside the mill, they had marvelled at the big pulleys and spinning belts, pounding and churning grain into cornmeal and flour. When the tour was over her mother had bought her a Coke from the visitor centre and they had walked to the south side of the mill to sit in the picnic area.

They had sat in silence, Emma remembered now. It wasn't an awkward silence, but an organic one.

The gristmill was no longer the sort of place mothers took their daughters to marvel at pulleys and drink Coke in the grass. An *economic downturn* – Emma knew the words but had only a vague understanding of what they meant – dried up the mill's funding and what had once been a popular historic attraction soon fell into disrepair. The pulleys stopped pulling, the belts stopped spinning and the windows grew thick with dust. The east wall shifted loose, getting a little closer to collapse with each strong gust of wind.

Shelley shoved the door open and Emma followed her into the mill. It was mostly dark aside from slivers of light falling in through smudged yellow windows. The sour smell of mould hung in the air. Water damage had brought down part of the second floor, exposing a jagged cross-section of wooden beams and twisted metal rods.

The interior wall of the mill was covered with names, scribbled on with different-coloured pens and markers. Emma recognised some of them: politicians and pop stars, and *Rich Witherford*, a colossal asshole from Manson High. Other names she didn't recognise: *Summer DeRoche, Jonathon Asquith, Chris Dignum, Sophie Lane, Angie Sperling-Bruch*. All Emma knew was someone wanted them dead.

That was how the urban legend went: write the name of your enemy on the wall of the gristmill and within twenty-four hours that person will die.

It was an easy legend to disprove; as far as she knew not a single one of the people named on the wall had died – at least not within the allotted twenty-four hour time period. But she doubted that was the point. Writing down the name of your enemy felt weirdly therapeutic. She had written a few names there herself.

She found Henry Micket's name scribbled onto the wood in her own handwriting. Henry was the beautiful track champion at Manson High who Emma had made the mistake of being in love with for a year and a half. He hadn't wronged her in any serious way – in fact she doubted he knew who she was beyond a vaguely familiar face in the halls – but he had broken her heart when he started dating Cindy Kites, another beautiful track champion.

She had written Henry's name on the wall in the heat of devastation and come back later to strike it out with a fat blue magic marker. What remained now was *~~Henry Micket~~*.

It had felt good to write his name down and even better to strike it out. A few strokes of a marker had represented anger, then forgiveness. Seeking once again to express her anger, and perhaps even forgive, she was tempted to write another name on the wall now.

Just for the therapy of it, she told herself. But if that were true, why were her hands now trembling?

'I've gotta pee,' Shelley said, disappearing back out the front door.

While she waited, Emma climbed a flight of groaning stairs to the second floor. Every surface she passed was covered in dust. Remnants from the early-afternoon shower trickled through the dozen or so holes in the ceiling, leaving puddles of dirty brown water on the landing.

She cleared a space with her feet, sat cross-legged on the floor and lit a cigarette.

As her vision slowly adjusted to the dark, she noticed a long trail of carpenter ants marching across the wide wooden floorboards and down through a hole below the window, presumably heading toward a nest inside the rotting walls. The trail navigated around broken glass and debris, a used condom – *ew* – and, at its narrowest point, veered dangerously close to a cobweb. Although Emma couldn't see it, she imagined a fat black spider with gnarly yellow eyes waiting in the shadows.

She stood up suddenly, shaking her head in disbelief. She had to do something about the ants. She set about moving the obstacles that were blocking their path. She kicked away the debris. She found a heavy metal rod and used it to flick away the condom and destroy the cobweb, sending the unseen and wholly imagined spider fleeing into one of the deep cracks between the floorboards.

Emma chewed her lip and waited for her good Samaritan act to pay off.

'What the fuck,' she hissed. 'No.'

The trail had dispersed and was coming apart in places. The ants were disorientated without the broken glass, used condom and cobweb to guide their way. She had removed their landmarks and now their path was lost.

It hurt more than it should have, more than it had the right to, and Emma was suddenly overwhelmed with the urge to cry. No, she wanted to heave and sob.

Dull clarity crept to her then. The magic mushrooms had kicked in. She wasn't hallucinating or seeing weird colours and lights – Shelley's cousin had said that might happen – but all her senses felt heightened. It was as if a fog had cleared and she was suddenly aware of the world around her: her body, the carpenter ants, the gristmill, the forest, Manson, the world, the universe.

Tripping was nothing like she had imagined – certainly nothing like the movies. And it was also nothing like smoking weed. This was subtle and wonderful, and she would spend many years to come chasing this first real high. She would look back on the day she took mushrooms in the forest with Shelley as the last true day of her childhood.

Emma unzipped her backpack and found a black marker inside.

As she walked slowly down the stairs she focused on the dirty floorboards beneath her feet, the crunch of broken glass, the wet slap of a puddle, the slippery page of an old porno magazine, the rattle of a discarded can of green spray paint.

Then she was on the ground floor and scribbling a name on the interior wall of the mill.

('—Emma, did you hear me? Did you—')

She stood back to admire her work.

('—hear what I said? You need to—')

Among the dozens, or maybe hundreds of names, Emma had written *Sammy Went* in neat block letters.

I'm sorry, she thought. *Nothing personal. It's just for the therapy of it.*

('—Christ's sake, snap outta—')

Shelley's meaty hands clapped onto Emma's shoulders and spun her around.

'Did you hear me, Em? Did you hear what I said?'

Emma reached out and tapped the left lens of Shelley's glasses. 'You're beautiful. You know that, right, Shell? Also, can I try on your glasses?'

'Ah, shit. Are you tripping right now? Ah, that's perfect. Just perfect.'

As Emma's focus shifted from the glasses to the face behind them, she saw that Shelley had turned pale. Her mouth was locked in a worried frown, and her eyes were wide and rattled. She didn't look like Shelley.

'Listen, Em. You gotta get it together.'

'What's wrong?'

'There's someone else here.'

'What? Who?'

'I don't know,' Shelley said gravely. 'I heard footsteps out by the visitor centre.'

Emma smiled. 'You're tripping.'

'No, I swear.'

'You imagined it,' Emma said. 'It's the mushrooms. They really are—'

She froze as a shadow moved over the window on the far wall. The glass was cracked, dirty and vine-strangled, but for a brief, startling moment she could make out the shape of a person. Whoever it was slunk away before Shelley had time to turn around and look.

'What is it?' Shelley said.

'I think I saw someone.'

The gristmill door dragged in the dirt as they half-ran, half-stumbled outside. Emma quickly looked back to scan the area where she'd seen the shadow. Nobody was there.

It might have been the mushrooms, but Emma felt quietly terrified.

'I think I want to go home now,' Shelley said.

'Yeah. Me too.'

Step by step, the crunchy leaves underfoot turned to dry soil, to thick grass, to a flat grey sidewalk and finally to the potholed bitumen of Cromdale Street.

Emma knew right away that something was wrong. Too

many of the neighbours were out on their lawns and porches, watching her pass. Roy Filly stared out from his open garage door smoking one of his stinky cigars. Loraine Voorhees rocked back and forth in a rocking chair on her porch, a cup of tea in one hand, a mini fox terrier in the other. Pam Grady, resident neighbourhood conspiracy theorist and long-rumoured lesbian, stood on the curb, hands on hips, face knotted with … was it curiosity? No, it was concern.

Did they know she was high?

The strange energy of the street grew stronger the closer she got to home. As she came over the crest that looked down over her house, she saw her father's convertible parked halfway in the driveway, halfway across the lawn. The driver's side door was wide open.

She walked faster. Something was wrong. Something bad had happened.

Shelley said something, but Emma didn't hear it. She was already running. Her backpack was slowing her down, so she threw it off her back and left it on the sidewalk.

Something bad happened.

As she neared the house, the memory of what she'd written on the gristmill wall swept from her mind as fast and as steady as a receding tide.

MELBOURNE, AUSTRALIA

Now

I've always been drawn to water during turbulent periods of my life. When my dog Shadow died I rode my bike over to Orel Lake and sat on the bank for three whole hours. I didn't come home until I was all cried out and shivering from the cold. When my mother died I sat alone in my car and stared into Bass Strait all afternoon.

Amy had been furious at me when I finally returned to the hospital, but Dean had understood. He knew as well as I that bodies of water have strange powers, and the larger the problem in your life, the larger the body of water needs to be.

The end of a three-month relationship, for example, could be eased by the amount of water that would fit in your bathtub. A simple shower could cure creative block. But the real stuff, the big stuff, the mother-dying stuff and the maybe-your-whole-life-is-a-lie stuff needed someplace expansive, stirring with energy. So I headed to Dights Falls, a noisy weir built across the Yarra River.

I parked the car and followed a narrow dirt track into the bush. Pine needles crunched underfoot. Although I couldn't yet see the river through the trees, the bush was alive with the sound of churning rapids, and the air was wet with spray.

The trees arched and parted the closer I got to the river, finally peeling back to reveal a wide landscape, stunning and simmering. I stood looking over the rapids for longer than I intended, wondering what doors I would open by meeting with James Finn again. He had agreed to have lunch with me, and I wasn't the least bit prepared. I felt mentally off-balance; one nudge from the odd American accountant could send me toppling. Yet what choice did I have but to hear him out?

A lone fisherman was sitting on an outcrop of rocks on the opposite bank. He stood up suddenly, started reeling in his rod excitedly. When he saw his line was empty he deflated, tossed it back into the water and sat back down to wait.

James was waiting at a table near the back of the cafe, nursing a cup of tea and reading from a Kindle. He looked every bit as cold and wooden as when we first met.

'I'm glad you came,' he said when he saw me.

'That's what she said,' Dean would have answered, unable to resist the opportunity. It hurt to think of my stepdad, to wonder what he might think about me investigating his dearly departed wife for kidnapping.

I ordered a coffee and we looked awkwardly at menus, even though the last thing in the world I felt like doing was eating.

'Claire won't let me drink coffee,' James said. 'That's my wife. She knows how wired it makes me. Hence the tea.'

'She's not out here with you?'

'She's keeping the home fires burning.'

I opened the menu, pretended to read it, then closed it again. 'I feel like I should tell you up front that just because I'm here, doesn't mean I believe you.'

'Understood.'

'What I'm saying is my mother's name is on my birth certificate. And I think I would have noticed if she spoke in an American accent.'

'Yet you're here,' he said flatly. 'And for the record, accents can be faked just as easily as birth certificates.'

'Why are you doing this, exactly?'

'I told you,' he said. 'I believe you're—'

'Sammy Went, I know. But why are you so interested in her? What's your angle, I mean? It was nearly thirty years ago. Do you moonlight as a private investigator?'

'Armchair sleuth is probably more accurate,' he said. His fingers drummed restlessly on the table. Up until now he had been nothing but confident, measured and a tad robotic. Now he seemed awkward, nervous and a tad *human*. 'Like I said, I know the Went family. I was in Manson when it happened. Sammy's disappearance just sort of … stuck with me.'

My coffee arrived.

'How did you find me?' I asked.

'Let me show you.' He took a small backpack from the seat beside him and pulled out a manila folder. It was marked, *Leamy, Kimberly.*

He opened the file and handed me a picture of a face with ghostly hollow eyes and a vaguely familiar expression. It wasn't a photograph or a drawing, but something in between: an artist's 3D composite showing a woman with dark hair, a long nose and tightly drawn, lifeless lips. At the bottom of the page was printed, *Sammy Went, predicted age 25–30.*

'I commissioned a forensic composite artist to mock that up,' James said. 'Based on Sammy's appearance and family background they determined that this is what she might look like today.'

The composite looked abstractly like me, but if I had committed a crime and police were relying on it to track me down, I could take my time fleeing to New Zealand.

'I ran that composite through a dozen facial recognition programs comparing it to millions of images online. I got a little over seven thousand hits. I went through each one, narrowed that list down to around nine hundred, and then investigated each one.'

'That must have taken you forever.'

'My mother used to say I have the patience of Job,' he said. 'The sketch matched with a photo you were tagged in on Facebook, which led me to where you teach. I thought about sending you an email, but I had a feeling about you. A hunch.'

'It's a long way to come for a hunch,' I said. 'And this is hardly *proof.* You said it yourself; there were nine hundred faces on your list. And even if what you're saying is true, wouldn't I remember something?'

'Maybe you do,' he said. 'Have you ever heard of Decay theory?'

'No.'

'So, imagine that when a memory is formed, the brain creates a neurochemical trace, so that when you need to, you can retrieve it. Think of it as a big red thread that starts in your consciousness and weaves deep into your mind. When you want to recall a particular memory, you tug on the thread and up it comes.'

As a demonstration, he raised and lowered the teabag in his cup. 'Simple. Makes sense. But Decay theory suggests that when a particular memory isn't retrieved over a long enough time period, the thread fades and weakens, and eventually ...' He drew the teabag from his cup and snapped the string in half. The bag disappeared beneath the milky tea. 'When the thread is broken, the memory just floats around in your brain, untethered, unanchored. You might not think you remember being a little girl in Kentucky, but that little girl might still be up there, in your mind. Maybe she's figured out how to reach you. Maybe that's why you're here.'

I pictured Sammy Went sitting in the middle of a vast black void where all the lost memories find themselves. A red string was tied around her waist, but the other end was slack. She tugged and tugged at the thread, but every time it came back empty, like the fisherman at Dights Falls.

'That's not why I'm here,' I said.

He nodded, tapped the manila folder twice. 'I know. You're here to see proof. The smoking gun. Mind if I use the bathroom first?'

While he was gone I stared at my name on the manila folder. He had left it conspicuously on the table. Did he want me to read it myself? If he was right about it containing the smoking gun, then denial might no longer be a viable option.

Ignoring the file for now, I had a snoop through his Kindle instead. In my experience, a bookshelf – digital or otherwise – usually painted a pretty clear picture of the person who stacked it.

Most of the books in James Finn's digital bookshelf were non-fiction; some history, some war, but mostly true crime. Some of these I recognised – Ann Rule's *The Stranger Beside Me*, John Berendt's *Midnight in the Garden of Good and Evil* and Truman Capote's *In Cold Blood* – but there were plenty more I didn't. There were books about political assassinations, mafia-related crime, celebrity murders, cold cases, serial killings and, surprise, surprise, child abductions.

Oddly enough, seeing all this darkness relaxed me. James's bookshelf had betrayed him as an armchair sleuth with a macabre curiosity for crime.

Unless …

Scanning fast for Sammy Went's name, I wondered if he was secretly a crime writer himself. The awkward, cranky demeanour certainly fit. Maybe he was writing a book about Sammy Went and I was his third act.

When James returned from the bathroom he took a deep breath before sitting back down. 'You ready?'

He opened his backpack. Inside were police reports, maps and files. As he fished through the bag he took out a stack of documents to make room. Sitting at the top of a pile was a list of names under the heading *Sex Offenders in Manson and Surrounding Counties*. About a third of the names were crossed off, which I assumed meant James had eliminated them as suspects. Others were underlined or circled.

The backpack made me uneasy. This wasn't just the curiosity of an armchair sleuth after all, and it didn't look like research for a true crime book, either. This was an obsession.

He took a stark one-page document from the folder and handed it to me. At the top of the page was a small blue logo with *Me-Genes* printed underneath.

'What's Me-Genes?'

'It's a genomics and biotech company here in Melbourne. You send them a DNA sample, pay a small fee and they deliver the results. If you pay a little extra you can have those results fast-tracked.'

The bulk of the document was broken into three columns labelled *Marker, Sample A* and *Sample B*. Each column contained multiple number and letter combinations, many of which matched. I got the sense I'd need a degree in genomics to read it.

But the part that mattered, the part that made my stomach lurch, was printed in big bold letters at the bottom right-hand side of the page: *Probability of sibling match, 98.4 per cent.*

'You're Sample B,' James said.

As I began to understand what I was looking at, my skin rushed hot and my whole body trembled with anger.

'You … You had my DNA tested? How the hell did you even get that?'

'You were drinking a soda when I first met you.'

'Jesus. That's illegal!'

'It's not, actually,' he said. 'I needed to be sure. That's why I came out here.'

I lurched back from the table and stormed out of the cafe, feeling like a worm on the end of a hook, reeling back and forth in the current as I waited for the jaws of a hungry fish.

I marched across the street, swung into my car and started the engine. Glancing in the rear-view mirror I saw James. He had come outside and was watching me with his hands stuffed into the pockets of his jeans. His bright yellow sneakers popped against the grey afternoon. Thunderheads rolled above.

'Goddamn it.' I killed the engine, got out and walked back over to him. 'Who's Sample A?'

'Kim, listen …'

'It says I'm a sibling match with Sample A,' I said. 'Who is that?'

'My wife warned me not to come on too strong. I didn't want to scare you off.'

'Who's Sample A?'

'I am,' he said. 'My real name is Stuart Went. I'm your brother.'

MANSON, KENTUCKY

Then

Chester Ellis, Manson's 64-year-old Sheriff, sat behind his desk reading the *Manson Leader.* His hometown's local rag contained highlights from Tractor Day, photos taken at the groundbreaking of the new Christian history museum and a play-by-play recap of the Manson Warriors game – they suffered a demoralising defeat, as usual, at the hands of the Coleman Bears.

It was set to be another quiet day in Manson. A quiet day in a month of quiet days in a year of quiet days.

He turned each page slowly, scanning the headlines for anything of interest. *Blitz on blackouts: new project to reduce peak energy use*; *Manson athletics club finds a home*; *A new take on old drugs: information sessions help seniors identify addiction.*

He arrived at the personals section and found his own ad at the bottom of the second column: *Prof. & Athletic African*

American man with Christian values. Seeks woman for companionship &/or relationship.

Ellis had lost his wife to brain cancer twenty-one years earlier, but with two sons to keep him busy, dating had been the last thing on his mind. Now his sons were adults, with partners of their own, and Ellis needed … what? He wasn't looking for a passionate love affair. He wasn't even looking for love, although if love happened to come along that would be just fine. He was simply looking for someone to share his life with.

Of course, the ad was largely bullshit. He might have been considered 'athletic' in his college days, but now all that muscle had settled into fat. The 'Christian values' part was a half-truth too. Amelia Turner, who took care of the personals and ran the front desk of the *Leader* on Fridays, had convinced him to add that part.

Sure, Ellis believed in God and tried his darndest not to cuss too much or hate too much, but Christianity was a pretty wide spectrum in Manson. He sat comfortably and conservatively on the casual, love thy neighbour end. But on the other end sat the people he didn't want to attract: folks from the Church of the Light Within.

The Pentecostal *group* – he'd learned the hard way not to call them a sect or, God forbid, a *cult* – worshipped by handling venomous snakes and scorpions. If rumours were to be believed, they also drank strychnine, spoke in tongues and, according to Tom Kirker after a few too many belts of whiskey at Cubby's Bar, drank blood and worshipped the Devil.

One of Ellis's deputies knocked on the door. 'Sorry to bother you, Sheriff. You got a sec?'

'Come on in, Beech. What's up?'

To call John Beecher a *man* felt premature. Ellis was sure he would be a man someday, but right now he was a pale, near-hairless nineteen-year-old with skin that glowed candy-apple red any time he felt nervous, which was often. 'A call just came through from Jack Went. As in Went Drugs. His daughter is missing.'

'His daughter?' Ellis checked his watch. It was a little after four pm. 'She's probably just a little late getting home from school.'

'No, the little one.' Beecher consulted his notepad. 'Sammy Went. Age two. Last seen approximately two hours ago.'

'Jesus. Get Herm and Louis over there.'

'Already on their way, Sheriff. Just thought you'd wanna know.' He looked at the open newspaper. 'Any takers on your ad yet?'

Ellis tucked the *Leader* into the top drawer of his desk. 'Do you remember where we put that book, Beech? That crime scene handbook? Herm and Louis might need it.'

Beecher shook his head.

'It's called "crime scene" something. *Dissecting a Crime Scene* or *Crime Scene Deduction* … There's a chapter in there about missing persons; questions to ask, instructions, suggestions, stuff like that.'

'Oh yeah, like a how-to thing, right? I'm pretty sure I saw that in the bathroom, Sheriff.'

That sounded about right.

Though Ellis's sons were grown men, he remembered how small and fragile they once were. Jack and Molly Went must be going out of their minds.

'On second thought, forget the book. Just give me the Wents' address. I'll call over there myself.'

Cromdale Street was wide and leafy. All but one of the buildings were big colonial-style homes. The exception was number nine: the Eckles' house. Ellis eased off the gas as he passed. He remembered it all too well: the leaning mailbox, the *NO TRESPASSING* sign hung on the fence – which seemed laughably redundant. Who in their right mind would want to trespass on a property like that?

The yard was well-kept – Travis, the youngest Eckles boy, took care of that. But the house was dilapidated and cheaply constructed. Say someone did decide to trespass on the Eckles' yard, and they kicked in the rattling old screen-door – what then? The only things of value were the brass urn that housed Jeff Eckles's ashes and the veteran pension cheques his death brought in once a month.

Ellis drove on down the street.

His deputies had arrived ahead of him and left their cruiser's cherry lights flashing, so Jack and Molly Went's house shimmered in red and blue against the fading afternoon sun. Ellis pulled in beside Jack's convertible and started up the path toward the front door.

'Sheriff,' came a quiet voice from the porch. A slight figure emerged. It was Emma Went, wearing a grave expression. 'She's gone, Sheriff. The sun will be down in a few hours and it'll be getting cold and Mom doesn't even remember if she was wearing a sweater.'

Her tone was heavier than any thirteen-year-old girl's should be. There was something foggy and zombie-like in her movements. Shock, Ellis guessed.

He put a hand on her shoulder. 'Let's talk inside.'

Emma showed Ellis into the living room, where Molly Went was slumped on a big red sofa. She was a good-looking woman, even now, with her hair tied into a messy ponytail, and her eyes puffy and wet. A tubby child of eight or nine sat in her lap. Molly's arms were laced through his, and every few seconds she'd squeeze him like a stress ball. The boy looked uncomfortable but had enough sense to let his mother keep on squeezing.

Deputies Herm and Louis hovered awkwardly. The younger, more athletic Herm was pacing, while the older, calmer Louis rocked gently in place. Both men looked relieved to see the sheriff.

'Herm, start canvassing the street,' Ellis said, trying to make his voice sound commanding. 'Ask if anyone saw or heard anything unusual. Anything at all. No detail too trivial. Check their yards if they'll allow it, and let me know anyone who won't. Louis, pull together a search party. We need to check the streets, the sewer drains, the woods—'

'Jesus, the woods,' Jack Went said. He was standing by the

windows on the far side of the room, drawing back a white lace curtain to peer outside. 'You don't think she could have walked that far, do you?'

'She didn't *walk* anywhere, Jack,' Molly said, squeezing the boy on her lap so hard he made a short, sharp gasping sound. 'Someone took her. Someone came into our house and *took* her.'

'We don't know that, Molly. Please don't get hysterical. It's the last thing we need right now. We have to stay calm. It's only been—'

'*Hysterical*, Jack? Honestly? Our little girl is gone.'

Before excusing Herm and Louis, Ellis took them into the hallway. 'Leave the Eckles' place for now. I'll check in there myself when I'm done here.'

'Not by yourself, you won't,' Herm said.

'I'll be fine. Go on, now.'

The deputies left with purpose, and Ellis returned his attention to Molly and Jack. 'What makes you think she was taken, Molly?'

'Her window was open. Wide open.'

'That doesn't mean anything,' Jack said. 'You leave the window open all the time.'

'I didn't leave it open this time, Jack. I know it.'

'You're talking about her bedroom window?' Ellis asked.

'Sometimes I leave it open to let the breeze in. There's no screen on it or anything, but it's too high for Sammy to reach. Otherwise I'd never … Anyway this time I closed it. I specifically remember closing it.'

'When was the last time you saw her?'

'Around one,' Molly said. 'I don't usually let her nap so late in the day because she ends up staying awake all night, but she was fussy and cranky and I just thought … I closed the window. I remember closing the window.'

'Does the window have a lock on it?' Ellis asked.

She shook her head.

'The latch is broken,' Jack added. 'It's been broken a while, but I wasn't in a hurry to fix it because it's on the second floor and, well, you know. It's Manson. Not exactly the burglary capital of America.'

Ellis nodded. 'And when you came back to check on her she was gone. Is that it, Mrs Went?'

'I came in around two-thirty. Her bed was empty, and the window was wide open.'

Jack paced. 'Look, Sheriff, I don't want to act like an ass here, but she leaves that window open all the time.'

'For Pete's sake, Jack.'

'I'm sorry, Molly, but you do. I don't want to give the impression that the open goddamn window is some integral clue when there's every chance you left it open yourself. The window is on the second floor, remember, so if she *was* taken, then it was by the world's tallest man.'

'Ever hear of a ladder, Jack?'

Jack threw up his hands. 'Look, she probably just wandered downstairs and went outside. Maybe she, I don't know, saw a bird or Grace King's cat, and she followed it, got turned around …'

Molly rolled her eyes. The little boy in her arms dug in closer to his mother.

Ellis smiled at the boy. 'And what's your name, son?'

'Stuart Alexander Went, sir,' he said.

'We call him Stu,' Molly said.

'Well, Stu, do you have any idea where your little sister might be hiding? Is there someplace she likes to play in the neighbourhood?'

Stu shook his head. 'I dunno. Sorry.'

'She's not out there playing,' Molly said coldly. 'She didn't see a bird or Grace King's cat and she didn't wander off on her own. Someone came in her window and took her.'

'What time did you get home from school, Stu?' Ellis asked.

'He didn't go,' Molly said. 'He's getting over a cold. I thought one more day at home might help.'

'Did you see anything strange today, Stu?' Ellis asked. 'Or maybe you heard something? A noise? Anything?'

The boy glanced at his mother, then shook his head. 'I was playing *Zelda* most of the day.'

'What's *Zelda*?'

'One of his Nintendo games,' Jack said.

Ellis felt Emma's eyes on his back, but as he turned to face her she looked at her feet.

'How about you, Emma? Do you have any idea where your sister might be?'

She shook her head.

'Did you notice anything unusual on your way home from school today? Anything at all?'

'No. I-I don't think so.'

It looked like she had something to say.

'You sure? The smallest detail might end up being helpful.'

'I told you; I didn't see anything.'

Nodding, Ellis stood and turned back to Sammy's parents. 'Can I see her room, please?'

Sammy's bedroom was a magical mess of pastel pinks and deep purples. A big toy chest in one corner was bulging with stuffed animals. On the walls hung framed pictures of Sammy's family, some childish drawings, a giant pink 'S' covered with silver glitter, and two movie posters: *Honey, I Shrunk the Kids* and *The Little Mermaid*.

There were more toys on the bed – a couple of dolls and more stuffed animals. Marked against the tangled, unmade bed covers was the vague outline of a small body. Ellis's stomach churned.

He went to the window. It was large enough for a child to crawl through, but far too high for a two-year-old to reach. Even if Sammy had managed to grab hold of the ledge, she'd never be able to hoist herself up. Also, the drop on the other side was close to twelve feet. Considering there wasn't the limp body of a little girl in the garden bed below, it was a pretty safe bet Sammy didn't go out the window – at least not on her own. 'So this was open when you came in?'

'Wide open,' Molly said. 'I checked outside for boot prints below the window or marks from a ladder, but I couldn't find anything.'

Jack shot a glance at Molly.

Ellis put his back to the window and looked across the room, through the bedroom door and into the hallway beyond. 'And this door was closed when you put Sammy down for her nap?'

'No,' Jack said. 'We never close the door. Sammy can't reach the handle and she doesn't like being locked in. Right, Molly?'

Molly kept her gaze on Ellis. 'She was being especially cranky, so I …'

'You shut the door?' Jack said. 'She hates it when you do that.'

'You weren't here and you never are.'

'What's that supposed to mean?'

'Where were you when I called the drugstore?'

'Can we please do this later?'

Ellis turned back to the window and looked out. From this vantage point he had a clear line of sight over to the Eckles' house. Afternoon was slowly shifting into evening, and the darkness creeping in over Manson felt heavy.

A weathered length of cord had been used in place of a latch. Ellis untied it and swung the gate open with an eerie, horror-movie creak. The *NO TRESPASSING* sign rattled in place. He looked up at the Eckles' house, set deep in the yard, and started to walk.

Ellis had crossed this yard some years earlier, flanked by seven armed deputies. They were there to arrest Patrick Eckles for aggravated assault. Patrick had beaten Roger Albom's head in with a pool cue over at Cubby's Bar, and nobody had been exactly sure why.

The porch light buzzed on, exposing a broken screen door and a dusty old sofa. As the front door opened, some base, primal instinct sent Ellis's hand to his holstered .45. He didn't need to produce the pistol; he just needed to remind himself it was there. And it wouldn't hurt to remind whoever answered the door too.

Ellis squinted into the dark of the house. A small woman stepped outside and into the light, can of beer in one hand, cigarette in the other.

'Evening, Mrs Eckles. Mind if I have a quick word?'

Ava Eckles was an unremarkable-looking woman with tangled blonde hair, wiry arms and a fat, protruding belly. She wore black leggings and an old, loose-fitting, pink T-shirt on which Ellis could just make out the words *2% Angel, 98% Naughty*.

'I figured someone would be stopping by eventually,' Ava said, dragging on her cigarette. 'I've been watching your men all going door-to-door. Ours was the only place they didn't visit.'

'I need to ask you about Sammy Went. Jack and Molly Went's daughter from down the street – you know 'em?'

By way of an answer she tossed her cigarette into the yard and lit another one.

'Sammy is missing, Mrs Eckles. Did you see or hear anything unusual this afternoon?'

She folded her arms across her chest. 'Only interesting thing I ever see 'round here is on the TV, Sheriff.'

'Did you notice any unusual cars or people you didn't recognise?'

She sucked on her cigarette and shook her head.

'And you were home all day?'

'Do I look like the sort of woman who has any place to be?'

'What about your boy, Travis?'

'What *about* Travis?'

'Did he see or hear anything strange this afternoon?'

'You'd have to ask him.'

'I'd like to,' Ellis said. 'Is he home?'

'He's working.'

'Is he still at Clinical Cleaning?'

'It's honest work.'

'Won't get no argument from me.'

Ava took a step toward him. She was a foot shorter than Ellis but possessed an unpredictable wildness that put him on edge. 'You sure have a hard-on for this family, don't you, Sheriff?'

'I—'

'Little girl goes missing and you assume an Eckles has something to do with it. It's not enough you locked up one of my sons, now you're looking to lock up the other.'

'We're asking everyone in the street if they've—'

'I think it's time you called it a night, Sheriff. If you stick 'round I'm likely to say something better left unsaid in *polite society*.'

'What might that be, Mrs Eckles?'

She smiled then. Her teeth were small and yellow. 'Well, as a for instance, I might say I don't know what disturbs me more: opening my door to find a cop on my front porch, or opening my door to find a nigger.'

Ellis exhaled sharply. He hadn't been expecting that. Anger and shame rose within like a geyser, but he suppressed it. 'One more question, Mrs Eckles. That work van your son drives 'round in. Does he keep a ladder in there?'

MELBOURNE, AUSTRALIA

Now

There was a space in Dean's driveway behind his Jeep and Amy's Jazz, but I parked in the street in case I'd need a speedy getaway. He still lived in the same roomy three-bedroom house he had shared with my mother. It was painted in heavy browns and reds, but today a misty rain shrouded everything in grey.

My plan for our regular Sunday-night dinner – and the only way I could see to move forward – was to get everything out on the table. Chances were Dean had no idea about Sammy Went, and the news might shatter the way he remembered my mother. But on the drive over I'd decided that wasn't my problem; this was happening *to* me, not *because* of me.

Dean greeted me at the front door with a big hug. As usual, he held the hug for three seconds too long. 'God, Kimmy. You're so skinny. Are you eating enough? Come in out of the cold.'

He was tall and lean and dressed like a sitcom dad from the nineties: white short-sleeved shirt tucked into blue jeans, white sneakers and a brown blazer. The blazer even had patches on the elbows. He ushered me through the front door and into the house. Scout, Dean's thirteen-year-old cat and closest companion, skulked out to greet me. Or to judge me; it was hard to tell.

Amy, her fiancé, Wayne, and my niece, Lisa, were lounging in the living room around a crackling fire. Amy nearly jumped off the sofa when she saw me. She came over with a sad smile and grabbed both my shoulders. 'Everything okay?'

'Everything's fine,' I said.

'No news on the thing?'

I flinched. 'No.'

'What's the thing?' Dean asked, arriving with two glasses of red wine and handing one to me.

'Nothing.' I drank half the glass with one gulp. 'Hi, Wayne.'

'Hello, Kimberly.' Amy's fiancé was the only person in the world who called me by my full name. He wasn't a bad-looking guy – he might even have been handsome if he had any sort of personality. But he talked so rarely and so softly that it was easy to think he was just part of the house, an ornament found at the Sunday market that Dean hadn't yet found a place for.

Dean sat down on the sofa, sipped his wine, smoothed the legs of his jeans and stood up again to tend the fire. He never stayed in one place too long.

'Do you eat walnuts, Kimmy?' he asked. 'They have molecules that block the growth of cancer cells. I want you eating a kilo of walnuts a day. I'm not even kidding.'

'A kilo?'

He disappeared again, returning moments later with an enormous sack of walnuts. He handed them to me, winked and said, 'Farmers' market.'

Everyone is afraid of cancer, but Dean's fear bordered on irrational. Ever since it took his wife he'd been convinced it was waiting to take us all. He wasn't so scared of getting it himself – he drank a little too much, and while he'd never admit it, his clothes occasionally smelled of cigarettes – but he was terrified it might come back to take another of his girls.

He pulled the grate aside from the fireplace and jabbed a burning log with an iron poker. Half the log collapsed into glowing red ash. 'Hey, Wayne, would you mind fetching another log for the fire? They're in the little crate thing on the back deck.'

Wayne stood up, gave a formal nod and left the room.

'So, Kimmy, how's life?' Dean asked.

'Same old,' I lied.

Amy threw me a glance bursting with worry. Luckily, Dean was too engrossed in the fire to notice. 'You know, I was at the shopping centre yesterday and someone was doing pet portraits, and I thought of you. She was making a killing. I was going to bring Scout in until I saw her price list. Forty dollars for three prints, and they're not even framed. Can you believe that?'

'She's not going to take photos of pets,' Amy said. 'She's got way too much talent for that.'

'I'm not saying she should *just* take photos of pets. It would be a good way to make some extra cash with her photography, that's all. She's got that five-thousand-dollar camera just sitting on a shelf gathering dust. You know, sweetheart, I really wish you wouldn't let Lisa drink so much cola. Do you have any idea what aspartame does to a developing body?'

Lisa was standing by the coffee table dunking her hands into Wayne's Diet Coke and licking her fingers. She looked over at the adults with wide eyes.

Wayne came back into the living room cradling a long chunk of wood in his arms. 'Where do you want this, Dean?'

'Take a wild guess, Wayne.'

Dean had prepared a tuna pasta bake that smelled and tasted of nostalgia. He poured more wine, and I had to resist the urge to guzzle it. Lisa sat in the living room watching TV because she refused to eat at the table with the grown-ups. Amy and Wayne sat across from me, the former mournfully staring at me while the latter checked cricket scores on his smartphone.

'Would you rather be stuck on a deserted island alone, or with your worst enemy?' Dean asked. That was his thing. He asked thought-provoking questions at mealtimes to 'stimulate interesting conversation, bring philosophy to the dinner table and to rise above the mundane'.

'If your life was a movie,' he might ask, *'what would the title be?' 'What law, if any, wouldn't you break to save a loved one?' 'What are the three most interesting things about you and why?'*

He rarely repeated a question, and always had his own well-thought-out answer prepared. I happened to like this particular quirk, but Amy, not so much. 'Come on, Dad,' she said now. 'You know I can't enjoy my food when I have to use my brain.'

A memory came to me: sitting in my mother's hospice room, with its yellow wallpaper and the faint smell of shit that we all silently agreed to ignore. Amy had brought in sandwiches, and we were eating them around the bed. Dean brought in some instant coffee from the machine in the hall, turned off the TV – nobody was watching it anyway – and asked, 'If you could send a message to every single person on the planet, what would it be?'

'It's every night with him,' my mother had said. She was breaking her sandwich into pieces instead of eating it. 'Last night we ordered in a large pepperoni and as he's opening the box, he asks me, "What would you change about your life if you knew you would never die?" I mean, what am I supposed to do with that?'

Before she got sick, my mother was a strong, compact woman with piercing blue eyes. By that night in the hospice every part of her had shrunk and yellowed, except for her eyes. They were the same blue all the way to the end.

Had she wanted to tell me the truth? I wondered. *Did that make her last few months even harder than they needed to be? Maybe holding on to that secret was what killed her. Maybe holding in something like that, a secret so big and bad, manifested into—*

'Well, I'd choose to be marooned with my worst enemy,' Dean said as the memory swept away. 'Because bad company is better than no company, and if things got too tense between us, at least I'd have someone to eat.'

Amy looked at me over the table. 'Remember when we were kids and Dad was the strong silent type? I miss those times.'

'Speaking of bad company, what's wrong with you?' said Dean.

Amy had been in a mood all night. She had hardly said a word, and when she did it was short and abrasive. If it had been me nobody would have noticed, but when Amy turned shy it was a big red flag.

'Huh? Oh yeah, I'm fine,' she said.

'She's been like this all week,' Wayne grumbled, still staring at his phone.

Dean leaned forward onto his elbows and studied Amy. 'What's going on, sweetheart?'

Amy glanced at me with an expression that seemed to say both *tell him* and *don't say a thing.*

'Fine,' Dean said. 'Forget my wonderfully thought-provoking and intellectual topic of conversation. Let's talk about the weather, shall we? Or petrol prices, or politics.'

'Let's talk about Esmé Durand,' Amy said.

'Who's Esmé Durand?' Dean asked.

'Do you remember my high-school friend Fiona Durand?'

Dean took a second to think it over. 'Was Fiona the one who wet the bed?'

'That was Michelle. Fiona was the redhead: petite, super cute. She was at Mum's funeral.'

'Was she the one who came home late after your deb and ate the last of my Jarlsberg?'

'That was Natalie. The point is, her mother, Esmé, is single now. Her husband ran off with a woman from his work – he's in finance or something, and she was his boss and, like, ten years older.'

'Quite the scandal,' Dean said, topping up his wine.

'Yeah, so anyway, she's single now.'

'And?'

'*And* she's single, and cute, and I really think you guys would get along.'

'Oh, well, thanks for the offer, Amy, but I don't need my daughter to find me dates.'

'Well, someone has to.'

He quieted then. 'I'm not really looking for that sort of thing just yet.'

'It's been four years, Dad. Do you want to be alone forever?'

Her tone had turned hot and serious. Dean looked like a frightened mouse trying to escape a trap. 'I'm fine, really. I just need to … It's not that easy just to …'

'Mum would have wanted you to find someone.'

'Take it easy, Amy,' I said. 'He said he's not ready.'

Her eyes turned red and wet.

'What's got into you?' Dean asked, his own tone more

serious now – and, if I had to guess, laced with a little anger. 'Why are you crying?'

'Nothing's *got into me*,' she snapped back, dabbing her eyes with her napkin. 'I just don't want you to be lonely.'

'I'm not lonely. I have you guys, and Lisa, and Scout.'

Amy cried harder. Wayne sat and watched her with a stunned, terrified look on his face.

'Darling …' Dean moved to rise out of his chair, but Amy waved him away.

'I'm fine.'

'You're the opposite of fine. What is it? Have I done something? Talk to me.'

'This isn't about you.'

'Then what's it about?'

She took the napkin away from her eyes long enough to glance at me. Then scornfully, bitterly, desperately, she said, 'It's about Sammy fucking Went.'

'… Sammy Went?'

Amy turned to me. Dean turned to me. Even Wayne turned to me, blinking and dumbstruck. It was now or never.

'Sammy Went is …' I took a beat to compose myself. 'A man came to see me. An investigator.'

'Wait, what are you …' Dean was still catching up. 'A cop came to see you?'

'Not a cop. An accountant. He's investigating a missing-persons case. An old one. From 1990. A little girl disappeared. Her name was—'

I froze when I noticed Dean's face, tight and pale. He was

squeezing the hell out of his napkin, so hard his knuckles had turned white. I was hit with a jarring clarity: *He knows.*

He had heard the name before. Maybe not for a while, maybe not for years, but all that time he had been waiting to hear it again. She told him. She told him and she didn't tell me.

This new information felt like a sledgehammer to the stomach, and for a second I was sure I was going to spray my half-digested pasta bake all over the dining room, *Exorcist*-style. Instead I lurched forward and braced myself against the table.

Dean shot around the table, tossing his napkin down.

'No,' I said. 'Don't come near me.'

Amy looked from me, to Dean, and back to me again. 'Kim ...'

My head reeled. In an effort to steady myself I knocked my half-empty glass of wine off the table. My knees began to give way. I would have collapsed if not for Wayne, of all people. He tucked a fast arm under mine and kept me vertical.

'How much do you know?' I asked Dean.

Amy kept looking back and forth, as if she were watching the world's saddest game of ping-pong. 'What are you talking about, Kim? He doesn't know—'

'Slow down, Kim, please,' Dean said. 'We need to just slow down and talk this thing through.'

'How long?'

But I didn't give him a chance to answer. Now I was certain I was going to vomit. I threw myself back from the table and dashed to the bathroom.

As I kneeled by the toilet and looked at the remainders of Dean's pasta bake, I wondered if this might be the last Leamy Sunday dinner. I tried to stand, but a rush of vertigo drove me back down against the bathroom tiles. There came a knock on the bathroom door. It was Dean.

'I'm coming in, okay?'

The urge to vomit again was stronger than the urge to tell him *no*. Seconds later I felt his big hand against my back.

'Here, drink this.' He put a glass of Coke in my hand. I sipped it, then handed it back. My head was pounding.

'When your mother got sick all we talked about was how we were going to beat it,' he said, easing his back against the wall and sliding down to sit next to me. 'Then, when it became pretty obvious we weren't going to beat it, we started to talk about what comes next.'

Using a few squares of toilet paper, I wiped my lips then flushed the toilet.

'You have to understand, Kimmy – and this is going to sound pretty dark – but I wanted to die with her, and I told her as much. She made me promise I'd live as long as I possibly could, and that I wouldn't become one of those men who die of a broken heart within a few months of their wife's passing. That was especially important to her. You know why?'

'Because of us,' I whispered. 'She wanted to know Amy and I were being looked after.'

'Bingo. All she ever wanted was for her girls to be safe, healthy and happy. In the end days, when the hospice staff were upping her meds little by little and we could all read the writing on the wall, we talked about …'

'Sammy Went?'

'She made me promise, Kimmy. She wanted the secret to die with her.'

Tears came to his eyes, and for a moment the anger inside me slipped away. The only other time I had seen him cry was when my dog, Shadow, died. Shadow – named after *Shadow the Sheepdog*, my favourite Enid Blyton book – had an enlarged heart. The vet told us the kindest thing to do was put her to sleep forever. Dean was tasked with taking her for her one last ride in the old Datsun. When he came home with an empty collar in his hands there were tears streaming down his face.

We sat in silence for a minute. I studied the dull-green bathroom tiles. The grout was grey and lumpy. I imagined Dean on his knees, laying all those tiles one sheet at a time. My mother would have brought him a sandwich and insisted he stop for lunch.

'You know what I see when I think about the past?' he said. 'A deep, vast ocean. Memories are the fish, I suppose. When I'm wading in the shallows I can reach in and pull one out if I want to. I can hold the memory in my hands, look at it, then drop it back into the water and let it swim away.'

He stared at the bathroom wall, tears falling freely down his face. 'But the deeper you go, the darker the water becomes. Soon you can't see your feet anymore. You can't see the fish either, but you can *feel* them moving around you, brushing past your legs. Those fish belong *out there*, in the deep part.

They're … sharks, Kimmy. Sharks and monsters. They should be left alone. Do you understand what I'm saying?'

Silent, I climbed to my feet once more and was relieved to find my balance had returned. I stepped over Dean's long legs and left him there on the bathroom floor. Closing the door behind me, I walked downstairs and out into the cold night.

Into the ocean, I thought.

MANSON, KENTUCKY

Then

'Sammy … Sammy … Sammy!'

Hundreds of people were calling her name. The procession of search volunteers stretched from the concrete channel and through the woods, cutting a jagged line all the way to the firebreak. They marched slowly, three feet apart, eyes down, searching the underbrush as they called out.

'Sammy! *Sammy*!'

One in every dozen searchers was a cop. Travis knew there weren't that many cops in Manson – as an Eckles he had reason to know these things – so he assumed the extra patrollers had been bussed in from Coleman or Redwater.

There was more action down on the water. Travis took a break from the search and stepped over to the lookout above the lake. He counted seven dinghies on the water and even more divers. Each diver towed a small coloured buoy behind them.

As hard as the searchers in the forest were praying to find the little girl, Travis guessed the men in the water were praying they wouldn't.

A grizzly thought came to him: *that little girl is dead.*

If they pulled her tiny body out of the lake, it would break Jack's heart, and *that* would break Travis's.

Joining the search was a good cover – it seemed like half the town had turned out to help – but Travis was here with one mission: he wanted to see Jack. The drugstore was closed and Travis doubted it would be open again for some time, and he didn't dare call the house. Even under the most mundane circumstances he wouldn't dream of calling Jack at home and risk getting caught out by Jack's wife. And he certainly wouldn't dream of it now.

He hiked up the search line, trying to catch a glimpse of someone familiar. It was almost noon, but an eerie fog had rolled in overnight and was refusing to leave.

Travis spotted Fran Hapscomb, the apple-shaped woman who worked at Canning Gas & Go. Travis filled his work van up at Canning once a week, and Fran was always up for a good chat. She knew Travis was an Eckles as well as anyone, but she thought of him as one of the *gooduns.* This of course meant she thought of his brother, mother and most of his cousins as *baduns*, but, hey, she was only human.

Travis waved at her. She waved back and grinned. Then, remembering that she was searching the forest floor for a missing two-year-old, she adopted a more suitably troubled expression.

'Hello, Travis,' she said in a mournful tone to match her face. 'Ain't this just tragic? You hear about this happening in the city, but in Manson ...' Shaking her head she looked out over the forest, and they both listened to the calling volunteers.

'Have you seen Jack?' Travis asked her.

'Jack? You mean Jack Listi from the hardware store? Oh, he wouldn't be out in these hollows with that bum leg of his, as much as I'm sure he'd like to help. You know he calls that limp an old football injury, but if you ask me he's got the gout. I have it on good authority he's moving through two cases of Rolling Rock a week, and it's only him out there on that farm. So either he's feeding it to the cows or—'

'Not Jack Listi, Jack Went. Sammy's dad.'

Colour rose in her cheeks. 'Oh, Jack *Went*, of course. He was down in the parking lot by the lake earlier, handing out supplies to searchers. He gave me this.' She flashed a bottle of water in Travis's direction and then clutched it to her bosom as if it were a secret treasure. 'Do you know Jack Went?' she asked in a tone that he took as mildly suspicious.

'No,' Travis said. 'Well, yes and no. We're neighbours.' *Neighbours with benefits*, Travis thought, and felt his lips curl up into a smile.

She suddenly brightened. 'Don't you live on the same street Sammy was taken from? Did you see anything? It musta been like a circus after it happened.' She leaned forward, clearly looking for any shred of *inside info*.

'Pam Grady lives right up the street from the Wents,' Travis said, lowering his voice dramatically. 'On the afternoon it happened she says she saw a tall blond man in a dark-coloured sedan. He was parked outside Jack and Molly's place just watching the house.'

'Oh my Lord.'

'Pam says he was wearing dark glasses, and the weird thing is, she says he didn't seem like the type who'd kidnap a little girl. He was even wearing an expensive suit.'

'A suit?'

'Pam thinks – and this is between you and me – but she thinks he worked for the government.'

'No!'

Travis nodded and touched the end of his nose with an index finger.

Sure, he was playing with Fran, but everything he had told her *was* true – technically. Pam Grady really did claim she saw a tall blond man in a dark sedan across the street from Jack's place on the afternoon Sammy went missing. But Pam Grady also claimed the moon landing was fake, and that George Bush was secretly dusting Manson with harmful chemicals through the long white trails left behind by airplanes. Besides, how could Pam tell the blond man was tall when all he did was sit in his car?

Still, Fran behaved as if Travis had given her a wonderful gift, and he sensed she'd be chewing on that nugget of gossip for the rest of the day.

He said goodbye to her and hiked back down the trail, away from the search area. The path was trampled, wet and muddy.

'*Sammy … Sammy … Sammy!*' came the voices from all the way up the search line. It occurred to Travis that yesterday only a handful of people knew this kid existed.

'*Sammy … Sammy!*'

He scanned the underbrush while he walked, half-expecting to see a tiny, bloody hand reaching out from behind a log, or a wide-eyed corpse staring up at him.

Nightmare fuel, he thought, and then, *Please, God, don't let me be the one who finds her.*

If Travis Eckles was the one to find the body … Boy, oh, boy, would *that* give Fran Hapscomb something to chew on.

Not one of the gooduns after all, she'd say. And it wouldn't just be her. He could see the *Manson Leader* headline now: *Eckles Boy Finds Body: Too Convenient for Comfort?*

A mobile workstation had been set up at the north end of the parking lot. A long silver trailer had been towed in with *Church of the Light Within* printed in big white letters on the side, each 'T' in the shape of a crucifix. Travis doubted they'd asked Jack before deciding to help out.

A large marquee had been erected beside the trailer, under which a handful of long-sleeved fundies hovered around a foldout table. On the table sat three rows of bottled water, some snack-sized bags of potato chips, a dozen or so PB&J sandwiches (individually wrapped) and a stack of colour photocopies, each featuring the same photo of Sammy Went.

Sammy looked like an angel in the photo, dressed all in white. She had Jack's eyes: glowing blue and deep like tiny planets.

A small green-and-blue Copy Hut logo was featured at the bottom of every copy. No doubt Jerry Lawson gave them a discount to include the logo. *All advertising is good advertising,* Travis thought cynically.

And while he was being cynical, the idea of handing out photos of Sammy to search volunteers seemed morbidly redundant. Was there more than one missing child out there? He imagined one of the volunteers moving aside a fallen tree branch to find a shivering, scared little girl underneath. The volunteer might then hold up the Copy Hut photo of Sammy, compare it to the little girl on the forest floor and call out, *False alarm, this one's not her.*

A mousy woman emerged from the group under the marquee and wandered over to Travis, a bottle of water in one hand, a plastic tub of sandwiches in the other. He recognised her as Becky Creech. Her older brother was head honcho at the Light Within.

'Hello,' she said. 'You're Travis Eckles, aren't you?'

He was so distracted by Becky's ankle-length pale-blue skirt that he didn't stop to wonder how she knew who he was. She wasn't bad looking for a fundie, although it was hard to tell under all that baggy fabric. Her hair was tied back behind a set of perfect ears – Travis always had a thing for a good set of ears on either sex – but her smile seemed forced.

'If you're looking for something to do, we need someone to run sandwiches up the search line,' she said. 'They'll be breaking for lunch soon and it's best they hold their positions.'

She held up the tub of sandwiches, and Travis noticed a small messy scar between her thumb and forefinger. A snake bite. The Light Withiners messed around with rattlesnakes out there on the church compound. If you saw a fundie walking around the streets of Manson, it was a pretty safe bet they'd have a snake bite or two.

'Everything alright over there?' called a loud voice. Reverend Dale Creech had just stepped out of the trailer and was walking toward them. Dale was tall and handsome, with a striking chin and thick dark hair. Travis knew he must be crazy – all the fundies were – but something about Dale's smile set him at ease.

'Travis Eckles,' Becky said. 'This is my brother, Dale.'

They shook hands. Dale's hands were soft.

'Good to meet you, Mr Eckles,' Dale said. 'Although I wish it were under better circumstances. May God help us find that little girl.'

'Amen,' Becky said.

Search volunteers and lookie-loos – and Travis suspected those two groups weren't mutually exclusive – milled about the parking lot in small clusters, talking in serious whispers. Travis hoped to find Jack's face among them but came up empty, though he did manage to spot Jack's red convertible parked by the lake.

Travis walked over to the car. Jack had left the top down, and Stuart, his nine-year-old, was sitting in the back seat playing a Game Boy.

'Hi, Stuart,' Travis said.

The boy looked up with sad, soulful eyes, and that grizzly thought returned: *this kid's little sister is dead.*

'I'm Travis, from up the street. Do you remember me?'

The boy nodded. 'They're all looking for my sister, you know.'

'Yeah.'

'I wanted to help look but Dad says I'm too little.'

'Well, your dad is a smart guy,' Travis said.

'Travis?' Jack was walking over from the lake.

He looked terrible. His face was gaunt and pale, and although it was impossible, it looked as if he'd lost twenty pounds in the last twenty-four hours. His yellow shirt had been buttoned wrong, creating a gaping hole that reminded Travis of a strange, floppy mouth.

'Jack, hi, God,' Travis said. He had an almost overwhelming urge to reach out and kiss him, witnesses be damned. He wanted to cradle his head and tell him everything was going to be alright. Instead he stood stiffly with his arms by his side.

'What are you doing here?' Jack said.

'I was worried about you.'

Jack glanced at Stuart, who had returned his attention to the Game Boy. He then ran a hand through his hair and sighed. 'Just go home, Travis.'

'I wanna help.'

'You can help by getting out of here.'

'Can I see you later? We can just talk. Whatever you want.'

Travis reached out and touched Jack on the forearm. At that moment Kathryn Goodman – who wrote features for the

Manson Leader – looked over. She was standing with a group of volunteers, taking down names and quotes. She chewed on a pencil, eyes flicking from Jack to Travis and back again.

Travis imagined another headline: *Eckles Boy in Torrid Love Affair with Father of Missing Girl.*

Jack shook his arm free and took a step away. 'I need to get back to it.'

Travis checked that Kathryn Goodman had turned back to the volunteers. 'I want to be here for you, Jack,' he said.

Jack winced then waved a dismissive hand at Travis as he turned to his son. 'Stu, come get something to eat.'

Jack helped Stuart out of the car, and they both walked away without another word.

The fog was starting to clear by the time Travis hiked back to his van, which he had parked on the shoulder of the highway, just outside the entrance to the lake. Still, the search conditions weren't getting any better. Grey stormclouds rolled on the horizon; the fog would soon be replaced with an afternoon downpour.

When he got to the van, Travis found Sheriff Chester Ellis with his face pressed against the rear window, hands cupped around his eyes to get a better look inside. While there was nothing to see in there aside from cleaning equipment, it still made Travis nervous. Cops always had that effect on him, but he suspected even the most law-abiding citizen would be alarmed to find the Manson sheriff – not a deputy or a patrolman but *the sheriff* – sneaking a look at their shit.

'Can I help you out, Sheriff?' Travis said when he was close enough.

Startled, Ellis turned around. 'Travis,' he said. 'Travis. Hi.'

'Looks like you were just admiring the Dyson Cyclonic Vacuum Unit. Not as good as the old SuckDuck, if you ask me. That thing's practically a robot.'

'Oh, ah …'

'Or maybe you were checking out the Lagger Max Pipe Cleaner? It uses an optimised hydro mechanics nozzle, and while I don't exactly know what optimised hydro mechanics are, I've never met a drain it couldn't unclog. Mustn't be able to see much peeking in the back window though. Here, let me help.' He went to the side door and slid it open.

I've got nothing to hide, old timer, he thought, but for a terrible second he imagined Sammy Went's dead body tumbling out onto the road. Thankfully, he found the bed of the van cluttered with equipment – hoses, nozzles, vacuums and chemicals – but no corpses.

Ellis's storm-lit face was grave. 'I'm sorry, son. I guess I was being a snoop.'

'It's fine, Sheriff,' Travis said. 'I'm used to it. And I know things in Manson are pretty damn tense at the minute.'

'That's putting it mildly,' Ellis said. 'Did your mom mention I came by your house?'

Travis nodded. 'Didn't sound like she gave you the warmest greeting.'

Ellis shrugged. 'I suppose not.'

'Sheriff, I don't mean to sound rude or nothing, but why were you waiting by my van?'

'I was on my way back to the station when I saw it, thought I'd stop and have a word if you were around.' He hiked up his dogshit-brown pants, uniform of the Manson Sheriff's Department, and took a deep, contemplative breath. 'There's a couple questions I've been meaning to ask, and I figured no time like the present, right?'

'Is it about Sammy Went?'

He gave a curt nod. 'Yes, son, I'm afraid it is. You know what canvassing is, Travis?'

He shrugged.

'When something like this happens, usually the police will go door to door looking for information. Sometimes it helps. Maybe someone saw something strange or heard a scream; something like that. You with me?'

He nodded.

'I had my deputies canvass your neighbourhood the night Sammy went missing. Had them ask if anyone noticed anything unusual, and a couple of them – well, most of them, actually – mentioned your name.'

Surprise, surprise, Travis thought. *Something bad happens in Manson and an Eckles is the first to be blamed.*

'We got reports that you spend a lot of time out front of the Wents' house,' Ellis continued. 'At all hours, people said. They said you walk past the windows late at night and look in. They said you *lurk*.'

'Lurk?' Travis's mouth suddenly felt dryer than a fresh

towel. Of course he walked past the Wents' house at all hours; of course he lurked. But it had little to do with Sammy and everything to do with her father. 'You know Pam Grady said she saw a tall blond man in a dark-coloured sedan parked across the street from—'

Ellis held up a hand to silence Travis. 'I'll level with you, son. I put about as much stock in what your neighbours said about you as I put in Pam Grady's men-in-black theory – which is to say, none. The truth is, people are quick to find someone to blame. Hell, I think they even *need* to find someone to blame. And if that someone is from your family, well, all the better.'

'Yeah,' Travis said. 'I've noticed that.'

'The trick of it is, I wouldn't be doing my job if I didn't follow up on every lead, no matter how unlikely. So here I am, asking: where were you Tuesday afternoon between one and two-thirty, when Sammy went missing?'

Sucking her father's dick, Travis thought. 'Work.' he said.

Ellis took Travis's answer down in a pocket-sized notepad. 'Cleaning, right? And where was that?'

'The company I work for contracts all over Manson.'

'Where were you on Tuesday?'

'Tuesday I would have been at Manson Business Park,' Travis said.

'Which business?'

'Clinical Cleaning has contracts with a lot of the companies there.'

'Which one were you cleaning on Tuesday?'

'Um …'

'I'm sure your company keeps logs, right? I can check with them if you're having trouble remembering.'

'No,' Travis said. 'I was at Miller & A.'

'Miller & A?'

'Miller & Associates. It's an accounting firm.'

'And you were there between one-thirty and two. Great, I'll give them a call.'

'Wait, sorry, between one-thirty and two, I was out.'

'Where?'

'Lunch.'

'You pack your own or eat out?'

'I can't remember.'

'You can't remember?'

Travis swallowed an invisible obstruction in his throat. Ellis hiked up his trousers once more and said, 'Like I said, just doing my job.'

'I think I got a burger.'

'Where from?'

'Huh?'

'Where did you get the burger from?'

'... Wendy's.'

'Wendy's. Good. I'll swing by there to confirm, and maybe pick myself up a Frosty while I'm there.' He scribbled in his notepad then looked up. 'And who gave you that shiner?'

It took a moment for Travis to cotton on. 'Oh right, the black eye. It's nothing. I ran into a door. Dumb, I know.'

Ellis looked at Travis for a long time – at least, it felt like a long time. Finally he closed the notepad and slid it into his breast pocket. 'That's all I need, son. Thanks for your cooperation.'

'Yeah. Right. Anytime. So I'm free to go?'

'Why wouldn't you be?'

At that, Travis slid the side door shut, climbed into the van and pulled onto the highway at a respectable, law-abiding speed.

Travis' mother was sprawled out on the sofa watching TV, not yet passed out but well on her way. It was barely two pm and already the blinds were drawn. Travis didn't bother to open them. This was the kind of house meant to stay dark.

'What's new, honey-pie?' his mother asked.

Travis was surprised to realise she was still in the early stages of getting drunk. Usually the charming, fun-loving Ava Eckles had long since been drunk under the table by two, replaced with the sad, regretful Ava Eckles – the *how could your daddy go and leave us the way he did* Ava Eckles. As if Travis's father had any more choice in his death than John Lennon had about being shot in the back.

'Hi, Mom.'

'They find her yet?'

'Huh?'

'That little girl?' she said. 'Weren't you off helping them look?'

'Oh, yeah; no. There's no news yet.'

'No way they're finding her alive. What's it been, three days? Can you imagine what she looks like now, all muddy and pale and chewed up by bugs? Tomorrow it'll be worse, then the next day. The flesh will get to stripping away and even her clothes will be rotted off. That's if he left any clothes on her.'

'Who?' Travis asked.

'Oh, you know, whoever. The nut that took her.' She paused to drag on her cigarette, never taking her gaze off the TV. A soap opera was playing. *The Bold and the Beautiful* or *Days of our Lives* or *The Young and the Restless.* They all looked the same to Travis. 'It was only a matter of time, you ask me.'

'A matter of time before what?'

'Before Manson caught up with the rest of the world in rape and murders per capita.' She took another drag of her cigarette and erupted into a coughing fit. 'What if it takes them a year to find her? She'll be nothing but bones and dust.'

She reached between her feet and pulled a fresh can of beer from the cooler. If Ava Eckles was good at one thing, it was getting her drunk on. During the few sober hours she spent awake, lurching from room to room with squinted eyes and a pounding head, she prepared for the day to come. She emptied the ashtray and laid some magazines out on the coffee table, along with a sandwich, some potato chips and a fresh packet of cigarettes. And, most important of all, she set the freshly stocked blue cooler of beer by her chair. The refrigerator was less than twelve feet from the sofa, but twelve feet started to feel like fifty after her sixth or seventh beer, and a hundred after her thirteen and fourteenth. With the cooler beside her she could unplug the phone, settle onto the sofa with her stories and drink herself into oblivion.

Practically an expert on getting sauced, Travis thought. *And she damn well should be after all the practice she's had.*

Ava wasn't always such a white-trash cliché. She'd always had a wild temper, for sure, but she only started thinking with her fists when she started to drink, and she only started to drink after Travis's father died. Travis was just thirteen when his father's helicopter came down. Since then Ava's lifestyle had been funded, and justified, by that veteran's death pension.

Travis got through it as best he could, but Patrick had never fully recovered, and Ava seemed in a hurry to join her husband in the grave.

'Why aren't you at work?' she said. 'You get fired? If I don't get rent the start of every month you're out on your ass, you know that.'

'I didn't get fired,' he said. 'I just didn't feel like cleaning today.' He sat down next to her on the sofa. 'Can I have one of those?' A beer would calm the nerves Sheriff Ellis had filled him with.

'That depends. You paying?'

'Come on, Mom.'

'If you wanna keep a friend, never borrow, never lend,' she said. That was one of her favourites. 'Besides, I'm only charging you cost. I ain't making no profit.'

Travis found a dollar bill in his wallet and dropped it on the coffee table.

'I ain't got change,' she said.

'It's fine. You keep it.' He cracked open a can of beer and drained the whole thing. The buzz hit him right away. He found another dollar in his wallet, dropped it on the coffee table and pulled another can from the cooler. This one he drank in small sips.

A pleasant fog was starting to drift over his mind and numb his worries when he heard the familiar *creak* of the front gate being opened.

'Go see who that is,' Ava snapped.

Sighing, Travis climbed off the sofa with a grunt and went to the window. He pulled the blinds and squinted into the bright grey day. When the man walking up the porch steps came into focus, Travis nearly pitched forward into the glass.

'Holy fucking shit,' he said.

'Watch your mouth,' his mother said, cracking open a fresh can. 'Who is it?'

'It's Patrick,' he said in an unbelieving tone. 'Patrick's home.'

HARTFORD COUNTY, CONNECTICUT

Now

The 787 descended through a clear blue sky, made an easy landing and began a slow taxi toward the terminals. The American flag danced and fluttered against a flagpole beside the runway.

When I reached the baggage claim area I switched on my phone. There were six missed calls from Amy and a single text message from Dean: *Where are you?* They had no idea I had left the country. Dean's words were still echoing inside my head: *'The deeper you go, the darker the water becomes.'* Even if Dean knew the full story – which I doubted – he would never sail into that ocean with me. Not if it meant ruining my mother's name.

Feeling tired and angry, I turned my phone off again.

Stuart and his wife were waiting for me outside customs. Claire was a small-framed, pretty woman. She practically lunged at me when I arrived: threw her arms around my neck and pulled me tight. That particular brand of erratic intimacy would usually alarm me, but there was something warm and genuine about Claire, and I liked her instantly. Or maybe I just needed a hug.

'It's so good to finally meet you,' she said. 'This whole thing is just so, *wow*, you know. I hope you don't mind that I invited myself along.'

'Of course not.'

'That accent,' she said. 'I love it.'

Stuart shook my hand formally and took my suitcase. 'I can't quite believe you're here,' he said.

'Neither can I.'

'I wasn't happy with how we left things,' he said. 'Tact isn't exactly one of my specialties.'

'I can vouch for that,' Claire said.

Stuart and Claire lived in Grundy, an hour's drive from the airport. Grundy, Claire told me, was a bedroom community for New York and Stamford, and was teeming with college kids. Beyond that we didn't talk much on the drive. It was my first trip to the United States, but the landscape, fast food joints and, somehow, even the smell were infused with nostalgia. I guess that's what happens when you grow up watching American TV.

We took the scenic route into town so we could drive past the head of the Pequannock River. Stuart told me the word *pequannock* was Native American – Pauguseet, to be exact – for either 'broken ground' or 'place of slaughter'.

Their home was a small California-style bungalow just outside the town limits. It reminded me of a Christmas card. The spare bedroom was cosy and warm. I was exhausted from the long flight, and all I wanted to do was fall into bed and sleep a solid, dreamless sleep. But I was determined to get into a decent sleeping pattern, so I forced myself to stay awake.

Stuart picked up Chinese for dinner and we ate around a small table in the kitchen. After the appropriate amount of smalltalk and preamble, I blurted, 'I talked to my stepfather.'

'About Sammy?' Stuart asked, dropping his chopsticks.

'About everything.'

'What did he say?'

'… He already knew.'

Stuart looked ready to jump out of his seat. 'What do you mean he knew? How much did he know? Kim, are you saying he confirmed it?'

'Easy, Stu,' Claire said.

'He didn't confirm it, but he didn't deny it either,' I explained. 'I don't think he knows that much – or if he does, he's not going to tell me.'

Claire took my hand. 'God, Kim, that must have been difficult.'

I nodded. 'It was. It's why I came here.' I looked Stuart in the eye, no easy task for me at the best of times. 'I need to know why the woman who raised me went into your home twenty-eight years ago and took your sister away.'

'That's what I want too, Kim.' For a moment he looked as though he might cry. 'Our first stop will be Martha, West

Virginia. That's where our – sorry, *my*, sister lives. At least that's where she was living the last time we spoke. We don't see each other much, but I'm sure she'll want to meet you.'

'I didn't realise you had a sister.'

'I have two,' he said with one cocked eyebrow.

I thought about Amy.

'From Martha we drive right through to Kentucky,' Stuart said. 'We arrive in Manson, turn up on my mother's doorstep and no doubt give her a heart attack.'

'What about your father?' I asked.

Stuart and Claire exchanged an uneasy glance. Stuart then looked at his noodles. 'Dad lives in Wyoming now. I called, left a message, but I'm not even sure it's still his number. You know how tragedy forms a bond within some families? It was the other way around for us.'

I met his eyes. There was hope in them, and that worried me. Was he hoping I'd be the glue that bound his family back together?

'All up you're looking at around fifteen hours' drive,' Claire said. 'You'll be sick of each other by the time you get to Manson.'

'You're not coming?' I asked Claire.

'As much as I love a good road trip, I'm going to stay here and hold the fort. I think it's important for you two to get to know each other.'

That's what worried me. Claire was naturally warm and so far had made an excellent buffer. The idea of spending so much time with anyone, especially someone I'd only just met, made my inner introvert tense. To Stuart, I was a long-lost little sister, but to me he was still a stranger.

'How much do you remember about what happened?' I asked Stuart.

'Not much.'

His lips drew tightly together, and I got the unnerving sense he was holding something back. I'd originally pegged him as kind of a dick, then a troubled man with a sad backstory and an obsessive mind, but neither of those were the whole story. The term *tip of the iceberg* seemed to have been coined with Stuart Went in mind. 'Most of what I know about the case, I learned later,' he said. 'By talking to my parents, reading police reports. Stuff like that.'

'Were there any suspects?' I asked, spooning rice into my bowl.

'Everyone's favourite suspect was Travis Eckles.' He stumbled over the name, hesitated, then continued. 'Travis lived up the street from us and was from a pretty rough family. Others thought that Mom did it. Thought she lost her temper, maybe. Shook Sammy or struck her and killed her accidentally.'

'Why would anyone think that?'

'People usually blame the parents first, and for good reason, apparently.' Stuart said. 'My mother lost her temper every now and then, same as everyone, but she never hit us.'

'Does she still live in Manson?'

'She'll die in Manson,' Claire said with a slight roll of the eyes.

'Even after people accused her of killing her own kid?'

'Mom would never leave her church,' Stuart said. 'She's … I was sort-of raised Pentecostal. Mom was big into the Church of the Light Within. Dad, not so much.'

'What's the Church of the Light Within?'

Stuart looked at Claire, who raised a curious eyebrow. I'd always been both awed and frustrated by couples who could communicate telepathically like this. 'You didn't tell her?' Claire asked.

He stiffened, turned to me and asked, 'Do you know what snake handlers are?'

'No.'

'Some churches handle venomous snakes and think God will protect them.'

'Wait … So your mother was a snake handler?'

'No,' Stuart said. 'Not *was. Is.* We don't talk much about it anymore, but as far as I know she's still a member of the church.'

'And you grew up with that?'

'Well, yes and no,' he said. 'There were never snakes in the house or anything like that. All that stuff happened at the church. Mom tried to convert us and Dad tried just as hard to keep us away from it.'

'He's not religious?'

'He was raised under the Light Within but pulled further away the older he got. Mom got into snake handling through his side of the family, believe it or not.'

'That doesn't sound like much of an environment for a kid.'

He shrugged. 'I guess Dad always thought she'd come to

her senses, and Mom always thought the same of him.'

'But it's a trick, right?' I asked. 'The whole snake-handling thing? They don't actually handle snakes, do they?'

'There's no trick. The snakes are a little lethargic at times – underfed, probably – but they're not drugged or defanged. That would go against the principle.'

'Do people ever get bitten?'

'Oh, sure, plenty. Anyone who's been doing it long enough has been bit. There've been a few deaths too.'

'Stuart lost his uncle Clyde to snake bite,' Claire said.

Nodding, Stuart said, 'He wasn't my actual uncle, we just called him that. But, yeah, apparently Clyde would grab whole handfuls of rattlers and pull them in tight to his chest. One night he got bit. Right here, in his shoulder. He refused to be treated and died two days later. It would have been a horrific way to go: a bite from a rattler destroys nerves, tissue, even bone.'

'Why did he refuse treatment?'

'Because he didn't *need* treatment. God was going to save him. But I guess God was busy that day with starving kids in Africa, or something.'

Abstractly, the shadow man from my nightmare popped into my mind. 'But why snakes?'

He sighed – the sound a man makes after being asked a question for the hundredth time. 'Because they're nuts, Kim. And because of Acts 28:1–6 from the Bible: *And when Paul had gathered a bundle of sticks, and laid them on the fire, there came a viper out of the heat, and fastened on his hand. And when the barbarians saw the venomous beast hang on Paul's hand, they said among themselves, "No doubt this man is a murderer, who hath escaped the sea, yet vengeance suffereth not to live."'*

It sent chills up my spine.

'And Paul shook off the beast into the fire. When he should have swollen, or fallen down dead suddenly, instead no harm came to him. The barbarians changed their minds, and said that he was a god.'

What am I going to find in Manson? I wondered.

We had an early start in the morning, so Stuart turned in after dinner. I stayed up and shared a wine or three with Claire. I needn't have worried about my jetlag; Claire kept me awake with good company. Her softness perfectly complemented Stuart's rough edges.

'Can I ask you something, Claire?' I said, after consuming enough Dutch courage. 'How do you think Stuart would feel about me going on this trip alone?'

'Why wouldn't you want him to go with you?'

'This is all so overwhelming, as you can imagine, and I just want to go at my own pace.'

Claire thought it over for a moment. 'Can I show you something?'

She led me through the back door and out into the yard. At the edge of their property was a large shed. Claire unlocked the door and let it swing open. Darkness lay beyond. 'The light switch is on the left.'

'What's in there?'

'Something my husband doesn't want you to see,' she said. 'But something I think you should.'

Curious and a little nervous, I stepped inside and found the switch. The lights flickered on and, strobe-like at first, illuminated the interior of the shed. Only, it didn't look like a shed; it looked like a police squad room. Set against the far wall was a row of whiteboards, each with various names and notes written in different-coloured textas. Photos had been stuck to the boards, each marked with a name and, from what I could tell, their connection to Sammy Went.

Scanning left to right over the faces, I began to read: *Deborah Shoshlefski, Went Drugs employee, Sammy's one-time babysitter, alibi unknown; George Gregson-Rull, convicted in '97 for the murder and possible rape of Melissa Jennings and Rachel Kirby, both age four, connection to Sammy unknown, alibi unknown; Ava Eckles, neighbor, alibi unknown …*

The list went on, but my gaze drifted past the photos to a large map of Manson pinned on the wall. Marked on it were search areas and walking trails. One area was circled in red and marked, *Gristmill.*

It overwhelmed me. 'Why did you show me this?'

Claire hovered in the doorway, pulling an oversized cardigan tight across her chest. She spoke softly, in carefully measured sentences. 'This is a gentle reminder, Kim. You've been dealing with this a little under three weeks. But this has been Stuart's life.'

The only window in the room was collaged with dozens of photos of Sammy Went. Until now, the only photo of

Sammy I'd seen was the one Stuart had shown me back in Australia. Suddenly here she was at different ages and angles. Sammy Went as a newborn baby; her first Christmas; a vacation to Cumberland Falls; asleep in her mother's arms. All my long-lost photos, found.

This is me, I thought.

Smiling sadly, Claire took my hand in hers. It was official: she had a mother's soul. It made me think of Amy.

'You've never been far away from him,' she said. 'Even during the happiest times, there's always sadness in him because Sammy should have been there. Finding you has been his life's work. Take him with you. You'll need him – I think you know that. But more than you need him, he needs you.'

MANSON, KENTUCKY

Then

Jack Went was thinking about the little things: Sammy's scuffed and lonely toothbrush beside the bathroom sink, a half-eaten PB&J left on her high chair by the kitchen table, her tiny, *tiny* pair of rubber boots sitting beside the front door.

He was on his way home after a fruitless day spent searching the lake and surrounding woods. Sammy was about to spend her fourth night away from home.

He was still thinking about the little things when a blue pickup truck came fast into Glendale Street, cutting him off and nearly sending him careening into the brick wall of a preschool.

He slammed on the brakes and felt rage, hot and unstable, course through his veins. But anger was better than the dread that had clung to him all day. He could do something with anger. He could get out, walk through the fresh smell of burned rubber and beat the living shit out of the pickup driver.

As he got out of his car and started across the street, where the blue pickup had pulled over and was now idling, his hands formed into fists and his ears thrummed with his own heartbeat. His system flushed with adrenalin.

'What the hell kind of driving is that?' He shouted. 'You trying to get someone—'

He paused when the pickup door swung open and he saw the driver. She was a small, compact woman in her forties, dressed in a clean white blouse and with heavy make-up around the eyes. All of five-foot-two, she had to jump down from the driver's seat, arms spread wide for balance. She landed with a pained grunt and started toward Jack, her eyes wide and unblinking like a fish's. 'I'm so sorry. Oh my Lord, are you okay?'

Jack took a deep breath. He was silent for a few beats. He had to concentrate on repressing the primal, violent thing inside. If he spoke too early it might come out as a scream. 'I'm fine.'

'I don't know what happened. This car is a rental and I'm not used to driving something so big and I guess I got a little pedal-happy and, oh my Lord, are you hurt?' She spoke with an accent, English or Irish if Jack had to guess.

He managed a thin smile. 'Well, nobody got hurt. That's the main thing.'

'Thank God! My heart's still racing. Are you sure you aren't hurt?' She paused, studying Jack's face. 'Wait, I know you!'

'I don't think so,' Jack said.

'I saw you on the news. You're him. You're that little girl's father, aren't you?'

He nodded and gave a look of vague sadness that by now felt rehearsed.

The woman took a step backwards. She looked spooked. She glanced back at her pickup, then once more at Jack. 'Well, if you're sure you aren't hurt …'

'I'm fine,' he said for the second time, walking back to his car. He climbed in, pulled sharply away from the curb and kept on driving down Glendale, leaving the blue pickup on the side of the road and the woman watching after him.

As Jack stepped into his house, the collective emotional weight of his family clapped down around his head. He hadn't slept. It felt like his body was coming apart. He could imagine pieces of himself falling off as he crossed the downstairs foyer – an ear, a couple fingers, his left arm.

He heard someone clanking around in the kitchen and wondered, *Could that actually be my wife?*

Since Sammy's disappearance, Molly had done nothing but cry and pray, the two most useless things to do in an emergency. If his wife had quit crying and praying long enough to get the kids fed, it would be a major improvement. At least food was tangible and real.

More likely it was Emma making the noise in the kitchen, whipping up her famous grilled-cheese sandwiches. At all of thirteen, his daughter was really stepping up to the plate. She had taken over motherly duties with Stu, making sure he was washed and fed, and when he had awoken last night from a nightmare, it was Emma who padded into his room and climbed into bed beside him.

But Jack found neither Molly nor Emma in the kitchen. Seeing his nine-year-old son in a *Kiss the Chef* apron would have surprised him less than who he now saw shuffling from hotplate to oven, dish rag over one shoulder.

'... Mom?'

Sandy Went sucked something red from the end of her finger, closed her eyes and nodded gently, happy with the taste. 'Do you have any garlic? Real garlic, I mean, not that stuff that comes in a tube.'

'What are you doing here, Mom?'

'Making dinner for your family.' She came to him with a hug. Jack's arms stayed flat by his sides. 'I'll come by in the morning to make breakfast and take care of the kids too, and I'll leave lunch for them before I head to the store.'

The rage that had begun when the pickup ran him off the road started bubbling once more, creeping over his body and settling in his jaw. 'I've closed the drugstore.'

'Nonsense,' she said. 'What, you think I'm too old to button on the old white tunic?'

'We're fine,' Jack said through thin lips.

'Oh, honey, you're a long way from fine. You need to concentrate on finding Sammy. But, in the meantime, life goes on. I'm here to sweat the small stuff for you, Jackie.'

'Nobody asked you to do this.'

'We're family,' Sandy said. 'It's what we do. And you're wrong about that. Molly called me. She said you ain't praying.'

The rage tightened his neck and shoulders. His wife was closer to his mother than he ever would be. As sure as Jack had pulled away from the Church of the Light Within, Molly had run headlong toward it, jumping in with both feet. 'I have to check on the kids.'

In the living room the Disney version of *Robin Hood* was playing. It had been Stu's favourite film for a couple of years, but over the past twenty-four hours it had become like an obsession. He'd played it on a near-continuous loop, the quality of the VHS getting a little worse with each screening. Jack didn't know what it was about the movie that Stu loved so much, but guessed the repeat viewing had something to do with knowing how it ended.

The doorbell rang.

'What now?' Jack muttered under his breath. There had been a steady stream of visitors in the past seventy-two hours, offering endless thoughts, prayers and casseroles.

Jack answered the door. A man with a vaguely familiar face stood on the other side. He was fat, both hands stuffed into the pockets of his elastic-waisted jeans. He had a wispy white goatee and wore a white fedora.

As Jack's mind adjusted – like walking from sunlight into a dark room – he slowly began to recognise him. *If he were twenty years younger and about a hundred pounds lighter, and if you took that ridiculous fedora off his head, he'd look just like …*

'Buddy?'

'Hi, Jack,' he said.

'God, Buddy Burns. How long's it been?'

'Twenty years, or close to it,' Buddy Burns said. 'I've seen you 'round the town on occasion, but never had the nerve to say hello.'

'The nerve? Why not?' Buddy took his hands out of his pockets and folded them before his big gut. 'I've never felt right about how we left things, Jack. I wanted to reach out, but my pride always got in the way. But when I heard about little Sammy, I just …'

'Why don't you come inside,' Jack said. 'How about a beer?'

Buddy flinched.

'Right, sorry, no alcohol. How about a Coke instead?'

Before Jack drove away from church for what he knew would be the very last time, feeling lighter with each mile that spun away under his old Ford, Buddy Burns had been his best friend. They lived in each other's pockets back then. They'd go hunting, fishing, hiking, or just sit on the bed of Buddy's old pickup and talk. They spent hours talking. About God, life, death, love, the universe, the theory of evolution.

It wasn't exactly a church rule not to drink alcohol, but it was definitely frowned upon. Still, Buddy would pack a cooler full of beer, and that added an element of youthful rebellion to the relationship.

The last night they spoke to each other they had been parked out by the lake. He and Buddy had kissed, and not for the first time. The only difference now was that just as things were heating up, Jack had asked Buddy to leave the church. 'We can get out together. We can drive south and start from scratch, worship in our own way.'

Buddy had turned cold suddenly, called Jack a faggot and left him to walk the six miles back into town alone.

'Five kids?'

'Yes, sir,' Buddy said with a proud nod. 'I don't mess around.'

'You certainly don't.'

They sat together on a low wooden bench in the back yard.

'Molly talks highly about your wife,' Jack said.

'They do get on.'

Jack sipped his Coke and looked up at the house. The lamp in Sammy's bedroom was on. He couldn't see Molly but knew she was in there, balled on the floor among the toys, crying or praying or a combination of both.

'How is she?' Jack asked, catching himself by surprise.

'My wife?'

'Mine. Before this, I mean. You must see her at the services.'

Buddy nodded uncomfortably. He removed his fedora, turned it over in his hands then put it back on his head. 'She's reaching out to God, and from what I can tell, God is reaching back. That's all any of us can hope for.'

A cold breeze picked up and stirred the leaves along the

back fence, and Jack thought about Sammy. *Are you cold, baby, wherever you are?*

'What have you got for me, Buddy?'

'How's that, Jack?'

'We haven't spoken in decades. You didn't just drop by to give me your thoughts and prayers – as appreciated as they may be.'

Buddy stood and stepped from one foot to the other, like a child stalling before handing a report card to their parents. 'Gosh, Jack, now that you mention it, there is something I … Well, I don't know exactly how to tell you this, and I hope you understand that it can't get out that it came from me …'

'What is it, Buddy?'

'Honestly, Jack, you need to promise you'll keep the source confidential. If my wife found out, or the church …'

'Buddy Burns,' came the shrill voice of Jack's mother. Sandy was walking across the yard, drying her hands on her apron. 'Had I known you'd be dropping by I'd have made more food.'

Buddy blinked rapidly and Jack saw something strange on his face. At first he might have described it as awkward surprise, but that wasn't quite it. Buddy Burns looked *frightened*.

'Hi, Sandy,' he said, tilting his fedora with a trembling hand. 'That's alright, my wife'll have dinner ready for me and the girls when I get home. Speaking of, I should get a move on.'

'Just a second, Buddy,' Jack said, then turned to his mother. 'Can you give us a minute, Mom?'

Sandy Went's eyes narrowed as they moved between Jack and Buddy. Then she smiled. 'Of course. But don't be too long or your dinner'll get cold.'

Jack waited until his mother was back in the house to speak again. 'What were you saying?'

But it was too late. Buddy was spooked. 'Another time, Jack.'

Jack remained in the back yard a minute, watching Buddy Burns waddle up the garden path and into the house. *I was in love with that man once upon a time*, he thought.

Not ten seconds after Buddy left, Emma appeared. She wore one pink latex cleaning glove and held the other. 'Phone for you, Dad.'

He was up off the wooden bench so fast he nearly pitched forward into the garden. 'News?'

She shook her head. 'Doesn't sound like it.'

'Who is it?'

'He didn't say. But, Dad,' she paused to look back inside the house, then lowered her voice. 'It sounded like he was crying.'

He knew it was Travis before he even heard his voice.

'I know, I know,' Travis said. 'Spare me the lecture, okay? I wouldn't call if it wasn't important.'

Emma was right: Travis sounded emotional, his voice crackly and wet. Nevertheless, Jack would certainly *not* spare him the lecture. 'What are you thinking?' he whispered down the line. 'You don't call me at my home. Period. But in the middle of this …'

His mother poked her head through the door. Jack had taken the call in the upstairs bedroom for some privacy, but apparently he wasn't going to have any.

'Everything okay, hun?' she asked.

'Everything's fine, Mom.'

She hovered a moment, looking puzzled. Then, with a deliberate sigh, she stepped back out into the hall and closed the door.

He heard chatter, laughter and music on the other end of the line. 'Where are you?'

'Cubby's,' he said.

He could picture Travis in Cubby's Bar, standing by the scuffed payphone near the restroom doors, twirling the telephone cord into an anxious knot with his fingers.

'Sheriff Ellis thinks I did it, Jack.'

'Did what?'

'Took Sammy.'

Jack raced to catch up. 'What? No, he doesn't.'

'He does, Jack. He's been sniffing 'round and asking questions.'

'Jesus, Travis, he's asking everyone questions. He's just investigating, that's all.'

'He asked me where I was when she went missing.'

Jack drew in a tight, nervous breath. 'What did you tell him?'

'Nothing. And that just made it worse.'

'What do you want from me, Travis?'

He fell silent again, and for a long time Jack thought he might hang up. Then, 'I don't want anything from you, Jack. I was calling to warn you.'

'Warn me? About what?'

'The cops may be coming round to ask you some pretty uncomfortable questions soon. I didn't want you to be caught off-guard.' He took a sip of something Jack assumed was beer. 'I'm sorry, Jack, but I have to tell Ellis about us.'

The sounds in Jack's world suddenly dulled, like someone had dunked his head underwater. '… What did you say?'

When Jack was thirteen, he and his friends hiked to Paw's Bluff, a ledge in Elkfish Canyon jutting out thirty feet above the pristine, and freezing, waters of Lake Merri. A lethal combination of hormones, peer pressure and a few swigs of cooking brandy swiped from his mother's kitchen had given Jack the courage to jump. The fall itself had been thrilling, but the icy November water had attacked him from all sides like thousands of tiny steel teeth. Worse was the sudden evacuation of oxygen from his body.

Until now, nothing had compared to that experience. Travis's threat – or was it a *decision* – sucked the air out of Jack, and he found himself gasping in shallow breaths, telling himself to calm down, relax, count to ten. He had to get back control over his body and over the situation.

'It's just self-preservation,' Travis said. 'Ellis is gonna keep coming after me until I give him an alibi. You remember where I was when your daughter went missing, don't you, Jack?'

Jack closed his eyes as the memory flooded in: Travis on his knees, mouth and hands around Jack, Jack biting hard into his bottom lip to keep himself from screaming. 'How much have you had to drink?'

'You're not my dad, Jack.'

The sound came rushing back into Jack's world. He could fix this. He had to fix this. 'Stay where you are.'

He was relieved to see Travis's Clinical Cleaning van parked in the lot at Cubby's Bar, and was more relieved to see Travis sitting in the front seat, a beer in his hand.

Jack got out of the car and knocked on the passenger-side window of the van, half-expecting Travis to hide the beer. He didn't bother. He finished what was left in his can, took a fresh one from a cooler on the seat beside him and leaned across to open the door.

Jack got in. Empty beer cans swam in a messy pile on the floor of the van. Jack counted them. 'Four?'

'Five, including this one.' Travis cracked open his fresh can as if to punctuate his sentence. He fished around in the cooler, found it empty. 'Damn. This is the last one. We can share.'

Jack cracked his window to let some fresh air into the van. 'I'm fine, thanks.'

Travis eased deeper into the seat and rested one hand on the wheel. He glanced over at Cubby's. 'Wanna go grab a drink inside?'

'No, Travis.'

'No surprise there.' He circled the beer can in his hand, crushing the edges between his thumb and forefinger. 'I don't know why you came all the way down here, Jack.'

'We need to talk.'

'There's nothing to say. It's the only way forward. If I don't come clean—'

'That's not going to happen, Travis.'

'And when they send me off to Greenwood, what then? You want me to end up like my brother?'

A deeply horrible question popped into Jack's mind: *How far am I willing to go to keep this secret? Does Cubby's have CCTV? Would anyone have recognised this car already?*

'Say something for Christ's sake,' Travis said. He looked desperate, but Jack saw something that gave him hope.

This isn't a decision yet, he realised. *This is something he wants to be talked out of.*

'Travis, if there comes a time when Ellis lays formal charges, I'll step forward. I'll explain everything. I won't let anything bad happen to you. I promise you that.'

'Ain't you tired of hiding, Jack? Ain't you tired of fighting it? Don't you just wanna start living sometimes?'

'How long you think we'd last in a town like this?'

'We could move away, be together, be out in the open and—'

'My daughter is missing, Travis.'

'I know. Shit. I mean after. When you find her.'

'That's not what I want,' Jack said. 'I've always been clear about that.'

'Yeah. You've always been clear about exactly what you want from me.' He chugged the last of his beer, crushed the can and dropped it onto the floor of the van. 'So you wanna get in the back or do it up here in the front seat?'

'Jesus, shut up.' Jack looked around.

'Isn't that what you want from me?' Travis said.

'You're acting like a child. Go ahead and tell Ellis. I'll deny it, and who do you think people are going to believe? The married druggist with three kids and a wife, or an Eckles?'

'Who do you think *your wife* will believe?'

Jack was suddenly aware of the weight of his wedding band.

A bus pulled up at the top of the parking lot. Printed in big white letters on its side was, *The Booze Bus*. Underneath, in smaller letters was, *Hop on for our famous Kentucky bar crawl.* A group of a dozen rowdy men in button-up shirts, which Jack took to be a stag party, filed out of the bus and loudly milled about by the front door of the bar. Jack guessed this wasn't their first stop.

Travis put a hand on Jack's leg. He wanted to swat it away. He wanted to strangle the boy. The rage grew hot inside his belly. Instead, he kissed him, and Travis kissed him back.

Seconds later they were a tangle of limbs. Travis unbuttoned Jack's jeans, slipped his hand under the waistband of his underwear and—

'*Hurrk!*'

Jack froze. 'What was that?'

He looked left. One of the men had wandered toward

them and was leaning against a black pickup truck, vomiting hard. His skinny legs wobbled like a newborn foal's.

'*Hurrrk.*' The man moaned. Spat. Then, turning to gather himself, he spotted them in the van. He smiled broadly and walked up to them. 'Don't let me interrupt,' he said, pausing to hiccup and wipe vomit from his chin with the palm of his hand. 'Who am I to stand in the way of young—?'

Now he really saw them: two men in the cabin of the work van instead of one man and one woman. He ran the equation in his head and made a sour face. 'Couple of queers,' he muttered, then started back across the street toward Cubby's.

Jack grabbed the door handle.

'Don't,' Travis said. 'He came in on the Booze Bus. He's an out-of-towner. He didn't recognise us.'

But it was too late. Jack was already out of the van and following the skinny man across the parking lot.

'Hey, hold up a second, buddy,' Jack called. 'What you … What you think you saw wasn't what you …'

The skinny man turned around, eyes unfocused. He laughed. 'Hey, pal, whatever floats your boat.'

'No, what I'm saying is—'

'Jack.' Travis was out of the van too now. 'Leave it alone. This guy just wants to go back and get his drink on, right, buddy?'

'Plenty more room for it now,' the skinny man said, patting his belly.

A couple more guys from the stag party spotted their skinny friend.

'Everything alright over there, Don?' one of them called. He was a big man with wide shoulders and a barrel chest.

The skinny guy, Don, waved back at them. 'Everything is fine and dandy, boys. Emphasis on the *dandy*.' He burst out laughing, bracing his hands on his knees and heaving with delight. Turning back to Jack, he said, 'Get it? *Dandy*?'

Jack took a step toward him.

Skinny Don put his hands up in mock-surrender. 'I don't wanna wrestle with ya, mister,' he sang. 'Got a wife at home who would be none too happy about it.'

'Jack, stop.' Travis had caught up to him and clamped a strong hold on Jack's arm. 'Let it go.'

Now Skinny Don's friends were crossing the lot toward them.

Good, Jack thought. The rage had taken hold now. He might have to explain what he was doing here later, when he stumbled home broken-nosed and bloody, but that was a distant concern. Now he wanted a fight. Fight away the pain and the panic, the fear and the hatred. Fight away the church and Molly and his mother and Buddy and Travis and Sammy.

Where are you, Sammy? Where the fuck are you? Get your ass home right now, you hear? Get your ass home right NOW!

He shoved Travis away, sent him stumbling backwards, arms pinwheeling for balance. For a moment Jack thought he might go over, but at the last minute he steadied.

'This is a mistake, Jack,' Travis said, in a fiercely sober voice – impressive considering the amount of beer he'd consumed in the last hour.

The two men from the stag party arrived. The barrel-chested man clapped a hand on Skinny Don's shoulder and asked, 'What's going on?'

'I went and got myself in the middle of a lover's quarrel,' Skinny Don said.

'That's not what—' Jack took a step toward Skinny Don, but the barrel-chested man blocked his path. The third guy – a vaguely handsome, bookish type – watched wide-eyed, with a catch-up expression.

'We got a problem here?' Barrel Chest asked.

Jack's neck flushed with heat.

'No problem,' Travis said, putting himself between the two men. 'There's no problem. It's a misunderstanding, that's all.'

Barrel Chest looked at Travis a second, then shifted his gaze to Jack. He shook his head, turned to walk away and muttered, 'Faggots'.

'What did you say?' Jack said – only he didn't really say it. It sounded like Jack, and came out of Jack's mouth, but something else was talking: something dark and furious. The rage.

The Devil, he thought vaguely.

Barrel Chest turned. 'Run on back to your boy-toy before I do something you'll regret.'

Jack felt the edges of his lips curl up in what he expected was a frightening grin.

'Careful now,' Skinny Don said, giving Barrel Chest a playful poke in the side. 'Looks like this guy might be *into it*. What we call brawling, his kind calls *making love*.'

Barrel Chest sized Jack up, spat, and then cracked his knuckles. 'Fine. Let's get it over with, then. From the look of you this won't take long.'

Skinny Don jumped from one foot to the other, laughing like a hyena circling a kill.

A few more men from the stag party had come out of Cubby's now. They were lingering around the bus, laughing and singing. A few of them were looking over at Jack. He didn't care. The more the merrier.

'Jack, please,' Travis said.

But Jack was already strutting toward Barrel Chest, cracking his neck to the left, then the right. And here came Barrel Chest, strutting toward Jack, hands clenching into fists.

About six or seven stags crossed the lot: Barrel Chest's backup. Jack knew then that he was going to be on the losing end of this fight. Even if he managed to land a few good ones on Barrel Chest, and he was confident he would, there'd be no winning against all those men, drunk or not.

It didn't matter.

Don't go fooling around with a shoving dance now, Jack told himself. *Go right in there punching.*

He pivoted on his front foot, cocked his fist and—

'I know you.' It was the third guy, with the vaguely good looks and catch-up expression. 'Yeah, yeah, hold up. I know this guy.'

'No you don't,' Jack said.

'Yeah, I do. I saw you on the news over breakfast this morning. Yeah, I know you. I know this guy.' He turned to the other stags who had just arrived. 'I saw this guy on TV this morning. His kid got kidnapped or something. Right?'

Barrel Chest softened. 'What's he talking about?'

'Nothing,' Jack said.

'Oh yeah, I saw that too,' one of the other stags said. He was a short, stocky man with a heavy brown beard, but no hair on his head. 'Ah, jeez, mister, that's some bullshit right there. I've got four of my own and ... ah, jeez.'

'Missing kid, huh?' Barrel Chest muttered sheepishly. 'Look, buddy, why don't we just call this a night?'

'Does the kid's mother know you're here?' Skinny Don asked. Jack smelled puke on his breath.

All eyes were on Jack. He knew how it looked. No, not how it looked. He knew how it *was*.

'No,' Jack said. 'She doesn't. And I'd like it to stay that way.'

Some chatter ran through the stags. Some of them gazed around stunned; others smiled smugly.

'For the record, this isn't what it looks like,' Jack said. He was directing his words at Barrel Chest. He seemed to be leader of the pack. 'Like your buddy said, my little girl is missing and ... and ...' He turned to Travis. 'And I think this man had something to do with it.'

Travis deflated but didn't seem the least bit surprised. It was as if some part of him had expected Jack to betray him.

'I was out here interrogating him,' Jack said.

Barrel Chest looked over Jack's shoulder to Travis, then to his friends.

Skinny Don asked Travis, 'Is that true?'

'I'm gonna go.' Travis walked back to the van.

Skinny Don moved on him. 'You some sort of sicko?' he spat. 'You like to mess around with little girls, is that it?'

'I don't want any trouble,' Travis said. He looked over at Jack with eyes full of heartbreak.

Skinny Don tugged at the back of Travis's coveralls, yanking him backwards. Travis turned and shoved at him, but Skinny Don danced around from one foot to the other, laughing his hungry hyena laugh again.

Travis took a few steps toward Jack. Then another few. 'What do you want me to have done, Jack? Tell me and I'll confess right now.'

Jack glanced at Barrel Chest, who seemed baffled.

Stay back, Travis, Jack thought. *Don't you make me do it.*

'You used me one way, Jack. You may as well use me the other.' He was close enough to whisper now, less than a foot from Jack.

The stags circled in, eager for a show.

'What are you gonna do about it, mister?' Skinny Don said.

Barrel Chest put a hand on Skinny Don's shoulder to calm him. 'Take it down a notch, Don.'

'It's a good question,' Travis said. 'What *are* you gonna do about it, *mister*?'

'Back off,' Jack said.

'What are you gonna do about it, Jack?'

'Back. Off.'

'You can't have it both ways. You can't have *me* both ways. You can't hate me and love—'

Jack punched him in the face. Travis spiralled backwards, dazed and whimpering. His nose was bloody – broken, probably. He fell to one knee as if he might propose marriage, collecting the blood in his hand and watching it drip through his fingers. Two teeth had broken off at the gum.

Sagging, Travis said, 'I really didn't think you'd do it.'

Jack hit him again.

It was after midnight when Jack got home. He didn't bother turning on any lights. He knew his way well enough. Instead, he went into the living room, collapsed onto the sofa and began to cry.

He heard footfall on the stairs. Molly appeared in the hallway, a slight silhouette in a white nightgown. *Like a ghost*, he thought.

'Jack?'

'Did I wake you?'

'I don't sleep anymore.' She switched on the light, eyes widening as she took in the mess on the sofa. 'What happened to you?'

'It's okay,' he said, even though it wasn't. 'It's not my blood.'

'Does this have something to do with Sammy?'

He shook his head.

She might have flown into a rage then, demanding answers and quoting scripture. Instead she went to him. She wiped his tears, sat beside him on the arm of the sofa and took his head into her hands.

'I made a mistake, Molly,' he said. He leaned into his wife. She smelled natural and familiar. Her skin was soft, much softer than Travis's. She gently stroked his hair for the first time in years.

'You want to talk about it?' she asked.

'Not really,' he said.

Molly didn't press him any further.

SOMEWHERE IN PENNSYLVANIA

Now

I inched down the passenger-side window to let a rush of fresh air into the Prius.

'As soon as the internet came about I started looking into it,' Stuart said. 'We didn't have it at the house back then so I'd have to access it from my high-school library. I'd look for information about other missing kids, or convicted child-killers who might have had something to do with what happened.'

We were cruising along a lone stretch of highway. Beyond the white oaks and Norway maples that flanked the road were endless fields and an occasional lonely farmhouse. The world seemed larger out here – certainly larger than my comfortable little corner of Melbourne. As the sun climbed on the horizon, exposing more and more land, it felt like we were being absorbed, less like driving *through* the country, than *into* it.

'Back then there was a cap on the amount of time they'd let you stay logged on,' he continued. 'So I'd work myself into a frenzy for my thirty-minute window, printing out any information I could find. When my time was up I'd collect my stack of reading material, sneak it home in my backpack and hope to God my parents never found out.'

'Would that have been so bad?' I asked. 'Your behaviour seems sort-of normal under the circumstances.'

He shrugged. 'They would have shipped me off to a psychologist, probably.'

That might not have been such a bad thing either, I thought.

'So you've been investigating since high school with no break?'

'For a brief period in college I tried to forget about the whole thing by smoking a lot of grass, but that only helped for a while. I was addicted. To the investigating, I mean, not the grass. Still am, to tell you the truth. This *thing* – drive, urge, compulsion, whatever – was out. And you can't put the toothpaste back in the tube. Then I met Claire, and she helped me keep my obsession on the right side of unhealthy … for the most part.'

'Sounds like love.'

'There's no way I would have found you without her.' This was the most animated and emotional I'd seen him, and for the first time I felt an enormous amount of empathy for the man.

If I lost Amy I might act the same way, I thought.

'How did Emma deal with it?' I asked.

'She had a funeral for you.'

'I ... Uh ... What?'

'Yeah. She filled a wooden crate with a bunch of your old toys and books, and buried it out behind her place. She invited the whole family, but I didn't go.'

'Why not?'

'It felt too much like giving up.'

I imagined Emma Went mourning her little sister while, on another continent, I might have been riding my bike down Oliver Street, or sitting in the living room watching TV with Amy, or walking with Dean, or having my hair brushed by my mother.

'Did you ever think about not telling me?' I asked. 'Not just for my sake, but for your family's? If they found a way to let go, then—'

'Have you ever read "Enoch Arden"?' he interrupted.

'No.'

'It's an English poem from the nineteenth century. We had to study it in high school. It's about a sailor, Enoch Arden, who gets shipwrecked on a desert island for ten years. When he finally makes it back to his family, he stops outside his home to look through the window. Inside he sees that his wife has remarried. She's happy, having found a way to let the past go. Enoch sees this and decides not to enter because he knows his wife is better off without him. Then off he wanders and dies of a broken heart.'

My hands were trembling.

'Mr Baily had us write an essay about it,' he said. 'Explaining why Enoch made the decision he did and, more importantly, if he made the right decision.'

'And did he, do you think?'

He laughed. 'Obviously not. If I were Enoch Arden I would not have hesitated for a second. I would have broken down the front door and got in a fight with the new husband. Maybe that makes me selfish. What do you think?'

'About Enoch Arden?'

'About ... *this*. Do you wish I hadn't told you?'

'The jury's still out on that,' I said. 'I like to think of myself as a take-the-red-pill sort of person, but honestly, I'm scared.'

'Scared of what?'

'Of what this might do to my family. Amy and Dean are the only constants in my life, the only relationships that ever felt long term.'

Stuart fell silent. He leaned forward to switch on the radio. I assumed that marked the end of the conversation. I didn't mind. The melodic hum of the engine and muffled chatter of talkback soothed my itchy brain.

We followed the wide scenic highway across Pennsylvania and down into West Virginia, skirting around rural towns, travelling long stretches of farmland and wilderness, passing through cornfields and tobacco plantations. We didn't talk a lot, but the more time we spent on the road, the more comfortable the silence between us became. Gradually, I felt like we were finding our rhythm.

After driving long enough to form a perfect imprint of my backside in the passenger seat, we arrived in Martha, West Virginia. It was a hardscrabble town lined with vacant houses, dilapidated concrete buildings and corrugated metal sheds. We pulled into the Big Wind Motor Inn – a five-storey cube that rose from the earth like a giant, mustard-coloured sore thumb – around eight pm. We each booked a room and agreed to meet for breakfast before heading off to see Emma.

My room was a standard single. The bed was soft and the heating worked. I took a long shower and spent much of it sitting on the tiles watching my bellybutton fill up with water. Afterwards I sat on the bed and flicked through the TV channels, watching local news and feeling every bit the stranger in a strange land.

My phone chirped. Dean was calling. I flicked the mute button and watched his name on the screen. A crisply focused image came into my mind: Dean staring at his phone with a dejected expression, one hand moving over his face, tears welling up. Sighing, I answered.

'Hi, Dean.'

'Thank God,' he said. 'I was getting pretty sick of talking to your voicemail.'

'Sorry. I've been busy.'

'Where are you? When I couldn't reach you I went to your building. Your neighbour, the big woman, she said she hasn't seen you. So I called your work and your boss told me you'd taken a few weeks off?'

'I just needed some time.'

'Amy's going out of her mind,' Dean said. 'I understand you not answering *my* calls, but there's no need to punish your sister for—'

'How much did you tell her?'

'About what?'

'About Sammy bloody Went.'

'I didn't tell her anything, Kim. And don't think she hasn't been asking.'

'I have to go, Dean.'

'Wait, Kimmy, I get that you need space. You can take as much as you need. But please tell me you're not planning on going to the States.'

'No,' I said. 'I'm already here.'

There was silence on the other end of the line. 'Kim, don't go back to Manson.'

'Why not?'

'There are things you don't know.'

'Like what?"

'… I can't. I promised your mother.'

'Tell Amy I love her.'

'Kim, wait—'

I hung up and turned off the phone, then I found a bottle of wine in the minibar and turned the volume up on the TV. The noise was supposed to drown out the thoughts screaming in my head. It didn't help much, but the wine did.

Some hours later I fell asleep thinking about family, old and new.

Huge plastic eagles stood on either side of a large wooden sign that hung over the entrance of the trailer park. The sign read, *Elsewhere Park*. The eagles had been painted with the stars and stripes.

Stuart drove slowly through the sprawling park, navigating a complicated series of streets and cul-de-sacs. When he'd told me Emma lived in a trailer park, I'd envisioned broken homes, overgrown lawns, old people on rocking chairs with thousand-yard stares, and savage dogs barking on the ends of chains. But Elsewhere had the quaint energy of a summer camp.

Kids were playing, kicking balls and riding bikes. People were walking their dogs. We had to stop to ask for directions twice, and each time we were met with kind, friendly faces.

'What you're gonna do is keep on down this street until you hit a bright red Fleetwood,' one man told us, leaning an elbow on the window and stuffing a pipe with tobacco like a Tolkien character. 'That's Kate Fenton's place, but then again, who knows how it'll come out when her divorce is final. Anyhow, when you reach Kate's Fleetwood you're gonna take a left and keep an eye out for an eggshell-white bungalow. That's old Nigel Ryan's place, and no doubt he'll offer one of his trademark waves as you cruise on by his porch there. When you're past Nigel's place, you're gonna want …'

Emma's mobile home was a large beige Fleetwood with a burgundy trim below a shingled roof, sitting at the end of a cul-de-sac that sloped downwards into a shallow, spring-fed stream. All in all, it didn't seem like a bad place to raise a brood of children. Emma had three teenage boys.

The driveway was empty, but Stuart swung the car around and parked in the street, facing the direction we came in. I smiled to myself, comforted by the familiar manoeuvre.

'Planning for a speedy getaway?' I asked.

'With Emma you never know,' Stuart said, without a trace of humour.

The front door of Emma's trailer was wide open, the screen door shut. Stuart took the steps ahead of me and rang the bell. A moment later a skinny woman appeared, looking grey and distorted through the flyscreen.

'Yeah?' she said.

'It's me, Em,' Stuart said to the silhouette behind the screen. 'It's Stuart.'

'Stu?' She pulled back the screen door with one hand and took a cigarette from her mouth with the other. She beamed. 'Holy shit, what are you doing here?'

Emma was forty-one but looked fifty. Her bleached-blonde hair was tied back in a loose ponytail. Her face was tanned and leathery. She wore an oversized Burger King polo shirt.

'I was in the neighbourhood,' Stuart said.

'In the neighbourhood, my ass. Come 'ere.'

She tossed the cigarette to the ground, stubbed it out with her sock, and gave her younger brother a hug. With her hands still clamped on Stuart's shoulders, she stood back to look at him.

'It's been too long, Piss-Shit.'

Stuart shook his head and turned to me. 'That's what she called me growing up. Sweet, right?'

Emma grinned through small crooked teeth. 'So who's your friend? Are you planning on introducing us? I'm guessing Claire isn't in the picture anymore.'

Stuart blushed. 'No, Claire and I are still married. This isn't … This is …' He paused, searching for the right words.

'Spit it out, Piss-Shit,' Emma said. Her smile faded when she noticed his grave expression.

'Em … This is Sammy.'

Emma flinched. 'Nice to meet you, Sammy. We had a sister called Sammy. Stu's probably filled you in.'

'No, Em, this is *Sammy*.'

A heavy silence followed. Emma glanced from me to Stuart and back again. 'That's not funny.'

'It's not supposed to be funny. This is her. I found her. I-I finally found her.'

'Fuck you.' The words fell out of her mouth as a whisper. 'Fuck you, Stu.' Tears welled in her eyes.

Now Stuart was crying too, which shocked me. I hadn't thought him capable of showing such emotion outdoors, where anyone could see. It was easy to imagine him sobbing into a pillow when he was alone in the house, or crying softly into a stream of hot water in the shower, but not on the doorstep of a trailer in Elsewhere.

Emma grabbed me by the shoulders, and for a moment I thought she might attack me. She looked wild and alive. 'Is it true? Are you my little sister?'

I stood there blinking. 'Possibly … probably …' I said. 'I don't know; *yes*.'

'But your accent?'

'Australian.'

'Christ.' Her knees gave out. She fell on the stoop and sobbed. I kneeled beside her and discovered that I was crying too.

'It's okay,' I whispered, mostly because that was what you were supposed to say to people when they cried. 'It's alright.'

'I thought you were dead,' she said. 'All these years and … Fuck me.'

'Shh,' I told her, and I slung my arms around her shoulders. We cradled each other for what felt like an hour – but was probably more like a minute or two – before one of her sons poked his head out from behind the screen door in a panic.

'Mom? What's going on?'

Emma wiped her eyes and climbed to her feet. She kept one hand clamped firmly against my arm, as if she were scared of letting me go. 'It's okay, baby. I'm fine. I'm great, actually.'

'Why is everyone crying?' the boy asked.

Emma laughed. 'These are happy tears, Charlie. Now get out here and meet your aunt.'

MANSON, KENTUCKY

Then

Stepping into the Manson Sheriff's station felt like stepping into the Devil's butt crack. The radiator had malfunctioned overnight, which wouldn't be such a terrible thing if it hadn't malfunctioned in the *on* position. Even with every window in the station open it still felt like a sauna.

On the walk to his office, Ellis stripped to his day-old undershirt and wiped sleep from his hot, heavy eyes. He had slept a total of four hours in the last forty-eight. And that was just the beginning of Ellis's problems.

It had been five days since the girl disappeared. Five days of searching, organising, brainstorming, detecting and God knew what else. Five days of apologising, over and over, for being no closer to finding her.

Deputy Beecher stepped out from the break room with pit stains as big as dinner plates and black bags under his eyes.

'I called Barry, Sheriff. He's got a job over in Redwater and can't get to the radiator till midday at the earliest.'

'You look like a corpse, Beech,' Ellis said. 'Have you been home?'

'I got a couple hours in the holding cell. You know, it's funny, that room used to creep me out. But right now, being locked in there with that little cot and a pillow don't sound half-bad.'

'You've got that right.'

'So what about that radiator?' Beecher said.

'Well, I suppose in the grand scheme of things, a busted radiator don't seem like our biggest problem.'

'Normally I'd agree with you, Sheriff, if not for the press conference.'

'Oh ... *oh shit*. That's today, ain't it?'

'Louis reckons we should drag all our chairs out onto the lawn so at least the reporters have somewhere to sit without sweating.'

'That's fine,' Ellis said. 'Rustle me up some Aspirin, would you, Beech?'

'Got a headache, Boss?'

'Not yet.' But he was pretty sure he'd have one by the end of the day. It wasn't the investigating that put the pain in his head so much as all the politicking that went on with it. Everyone had a problem and expected Ellis to solve it, and every solution seemed to create a fresh problem.

The press conference was the perfect example. What should have been a simple item to tick off the list was about to be derailed. Every molehill was a broken radiator away from becoming a mountain. What if the weather didn't hold? What angle might the media give *that* story?

Manson Police fail to organise their way out of wet paper bag.

It wasn't just the damn radiator, either. Amelia Turner from the *Manson Leader* had called the station late last night for a 'special favour'. She needed two seats reserved for her at the press conference, right up front: one for her and one for her sixteen-year-old daughter, Beth, a budding photographer.

Special favours were all well and good, but Ellis was expecting media from all the surrounding counties to attend – maybe even some heavy hitters from NBC or CNN. What if Amelia Turner didn't get her seats right up front? Would she tell her colleagues at the *Leader* that he didn't even have the power to hold two seats?

Or worse, would she blab about the personal ad? *Prof. & Athletic African American …*

Oh, brother.

The bigger and biggest problem, of course, was that he had nothing to give the media. There was no news and there were no leads. The point of the conference was to ask the public for help, but the reporters would want *something.* He imagined himself opening a lion's cage and climbing in at feeding time, with nothing to give them but the flesh on his back.

He pictured tomorrow's headlines – not just the *Leader*'s, but state-wide: *Incompetent sheriff turns up no leads*; *Search for Sammy in doubt due to clumsy investigation*; *Press conference rained out.*

'There's something else, boss,' Beecher said. 'We got a call last night from Clara Yi over at Greenwood Corrections.'

'Yeah?'

'Patrick Eckles is out.'

He had heard that Patrick was being fast-tracked for release. Terms like *model inmate*, *good behaviour* and *proof of rehabilitation* had been thrown about, and it was only a matter of time before he came home. 'When?'

'Wednesday,' he said. 'A day after Sammy was taken. Which is, you know, good timing for Patrick.'

Good timing indeed. Patrick being under lock and key at Greenwood Corrections was about as good an alibi as he could hope for. One week earlier and maybe everyone would be pointing fingers at him instead of his little brother.

'Feels like only yesterday I put that kid in cuffs,' Ellis said. 'It's a pretty early release.'

'Maybe he found God in there,' Beecher said.

Ellis snorted, walked into his office and found the telephone blinking; there were seventeen messages on the machine. He poured himself a coffee and sat down at his desk to listen to them.

The first was from a deputy over in Coleman. The Coleman Police Department had been helping out with manpower and running leads out of town, and for a nanosecond Ellis thought they might have something he could throw at the hungry media. But the deputy in Coleman had no news. *Whoever said no news is good news can go jump*, he thought, pressing the button for the next message.

Beep.

Next was a message from Doris Wong, a neighbourhood gossip who had somehow got a hold of Ellis's personal extension. 'I might have gone and done your job, Chester,' Doris Wong's message went. 'There's a black man of medium build with low, baggy pants just walked down my street. He looked damn *suspicious*.'

Beep.

The following two messages were also from Doris Wong, who called back each time to add a small, yet apparently significant detail. 'Oh, I forgot to mention, *the perp* was wearing a baseball cap. The cap was blue, and he was wearing it frontways. Some of 'em wear 'em backwards, but not this one.'

Beep.

'Me again, Chester. It's been nearly fifteen minutes since my last call so I'm still here watching out the window, wondering why you haven't sent a patrol car to bring me in and talk to a sketch artist while the details are still fresh in my—'

Beep.

'Oh, uh, hi, hello.' A woman's voice, pleasantly nervous. Ellis couldn't place it. 'This is weird. I'm sorry. My name is Sue Beady and, uh. Well, I'm about five-three, a hundred fifty pounds on a good day, coming up on my fifty-third birthday and I don't care who knows it. Uh, what else? I'm sorry. This is just so weird. I don't usually do this sort of thing.'

Ellis propped the phone between his shoulder and cheek and found a pen that worked. He jotted down the woman's name and measurements. He wasn't sure why, but investigations were about details and these were definitely details.

'I've got sandy blonde hair, brown eyes and, hell, I don't know, the rest can be a surprise, I suppose.' She laughed. It was a beautiful laugh. 'Shoot, I haven't even ... Here I am describing myself and you've probably got no idea why I'm calling. I read your ad in the *Leader.* "Professional" and "athletic". "Christian values". All that.'

He dropped his pen and grabbed the phone with both hands, pressing it against his ear. Heat rose in his cheeks.

'Now, I don't exactly go to church each Sunday,' Sue Beady's message continued. 'But I live by the Ten Commandments and try to break as few of them as I can. I wasn't so great at the honour thy father and thy mother part, but God never had the displeasure of meeting Frank and Carla Beady, let me tell you that much and may they rest in peace. Anyhow, if you feel like taking a five-three, hundred-fifty-pound stranger with sandy blonde hair out to dinner, why don't you go ahead and give me a call.' She gave her number. 'And if you don't, I promise I won't take offence. You have a fine day now.'

Beep.

There were more messages but nothing of consequence, and if there had been, Ellis might not have even heard them. Sue Beady's soft, beautiful voice was still ringing in his ears.

The press conference was scheduled to begin at ten am. By nine-fifteen the lawn in front of the station was bustling with reporters, news producers, camera operators, photographers and plenty of other people scrambling around doing whatever it was they did.

The parking lot was overflowing with news vans, each with its own acronym: CNN, NBC, STKV, WKYP, GRMTV. The list went on. More vans were on their way in, pulling up onto front lawns and parking over sidewalks – traffic rules be damned. The line reached all the way up to Francis Avenue and halfway around the corner.

On top of that, half the town had turned up. Ellis hadn't counted on this many people being here, but he understood it. That little girl had come to represent all the kids in Manson, and what happened to her, whatever *that* was, had come to represent all the *bad things*. Things like serial killers and sex predators. Things from faraway places like Frankfort and New York and Detroit.

The *bad things* had reached Manson.

While Ellis stood on the front steps and watched the great droves of people drift in, Deputy Beecher sidled up beside him and said, 'There ain't no way we have enough chairs for that many rear ends, boss.'

'That's alright, Beech. People can stand.'

Beecher had arranged a series of foldout chairs into angled rows. He had even placed small *Reserved* signs on two seats in the front row for Amelia Turner and her daughter. There was no podium, but all things considered, Beecher had done alright.

'This is fine work, Beech,' Ellis said.

Beecher turned cherry-red. 'I'd make one hell of a wedding planner.'

'It's not too late for a career change,' Ellis said, and he half-meant it.

Sammy's family – Jack and Molly Went, their teenage daughter, Emma, and nine-year-old, Stu – arrived a little before ten. The press exploded around them.

The Wents looked colourless; black-and-white figures moving through a coloured landscape of reporters. Molly's face was slack and dried out, Jack looked as if he hadn't eaten in days and there was—

A bandage?! Ellis thought. *A bandage on Jack Went's right hand?*

As if reading Ellis's mind, Molly slipped her arm under Jack's and took hold of his hand, concealing it from view.

They walked together in sadness, but it was little Stu who was hardest to watch. He was fragile and pale; a living body with no spirit left inside.

Ellis had to mind himself not to cry. If Sammy represented what could happen when the bad things came to Manson, Stu Went was a ringing symbol of Ellis's guilt and failure. That boy's childhood was bleeding away like warm bathwater down a drain. He needed that hole plugged. He needed hope, they all did, and Ellis had none to give.

His hands began to tremble, so he stuffed them into the pockets of his trousers and found the folded square of paper marked with his speech notes for the conference. He took it out and unfolded it. His handwriting barely took up half the page. All the empty space below felt like an accusation.

'It's time, boss,' Beecher said.

The press conference felt more like a firing squad. With no leads or answers to offer, Ellis didn't fool anyone into thinking their local sheriff was up to the task of finding Sammy Went. There were plenty of tough questions, but the one that stung most came from Manson's own Amelia Turner. From her reserved seat in the front row, armed with a silver tape recorder that she aimed like a pistol, she had asked, 'How confident are you in your ability to solve this case, Sheriff?'

He had stumbled vaguely through an answer he couldn't quite remember, and supposed he'd read all about it in tomorrow's edition of the *Leader*.

He returned to his office and collapsed into his chair, feeling like a dusty old tool hanging in a shed someplace. He glanced at the notepad on his desk. He had printed Sue Beady's phone number neatly at the top of a blank page. It wasn't the right time to be chasing a date, of course, but it had been a dark few days. He needed a little light. So he punched the number into his phone with clammy fingers and got her machine.

'Uh, yes, hi, hello,' he told her answering machine. 'This is Chester Ellis. You called and left a message and, uh, I got your message and now I'm leaving you one.' He paused to slap his forehead. 'There's a fancy Italian place in Redwater called Barracuda's. Well, I don't know how fancy it is, come to think of it, but they make fancy pizzas. And if you were free sometime, I'd love to take you up on your offer. Ah, you can call me back if you like. You have my work number. Or you can call me at home. The number is—'

She picked up. 'Chester, are you there?'

'Yes, ma'am.'

'How does Sunday sound?'

'Ma'am?'

'For dinner at the fancy pizza joint,' she said. 'Too eager?'

Ellis took a breath. 'No, not too eager at all.'

'Good. There is one condition though.'

'What's that?'

'Don't call me ma'am.'

Ellis smiled. 'It's a date.'

Seconds after Ellis had hung up with Sue, Beecher came into the office wiping sweat from his brow. 'We may have something, boss.'

Ellis pulled his cruiser into the north end of the parking lot by the lake, where the search for Sammy was still in full swing. Some of the volunteers were chatting by the big marquee beside the Light Within trailer. The church had maintained a presence here since the day after Sammy's disappearance. They might be a bunch of kooks, but Ellis was happy with any help he could get.

They parked. Ellis and Beecher got out and walked up to meet Deputy Louis.

'Found something, Louis?' Ellis asked.

'Maybe, boss. One of the divers spotted something out by Willow's Point. Might be nothing, but I thought you ought to hear it from the horse's mouth.'

He led them to the boat ramp, where a short woman was

hoisting her diving gear onto the bed of a pickup truck. Her wetsuit had been thrown over the truck's side mirror and was dripping wet. Between loads from the ramp to the truck she took hungry bites of a sandwich.

'Officer Beaumont, this is Sheriff Ellis and Deputy Beecher,' Louis said. 'Beaumont's one of Coleman's finest and knows her way around a scuba tank, so she's been helping us with the search on the lake.'

'We're going to owe Coleman PD about a million solids when this is all through.'

'Don't mention it,' she said. 'And call me Terry.'

'What have you got for us, Terry?'

'I was in the water out around Willow's Point. As you can probably imagine, trying to find a body in Lake Merri is something like trying to find a hymen in a whorehouse.'

Beecher stifled a laugh.

'Willow's Point is a long way from any in-roads – not an ideal place to dump a body unless you want to carry the thing over your shoulder for six or seven miles.'

'Unless you got a boat,' Beecher said.

'Either way, the shape of the lake narrows significantly there, and there are plenty of jagged rocks to catch and snag. If that little girl went into the water and the fish have left enough of her for us to find, I figured Willow's is as good a place as any to look.'

'Did you find something?' Ellis asked.

'In the water, no. Out of it, maybe. This time of year the silt can be a real bitch and visibility was low, so I was spending a lot of time on the surface wiping down my mask. One of those times I noticed a man watching me from the bank.' She tossed a strap over her equipment and went around to the other side of the truck to tie it down. 'He didn't look like a hunter or a hiker, and he didn't have any fishing equipment with him. My dinghy was the only boat on the water, and, like I said, that area is miles from any access roads. So, right away I thought it was kind of … off. Then he waved me in, like he wanted to talk, you know.'

'Did you talk to him?'

Terry slammed the back door of her pickup, latched it shut and nodded. 'I swam within fifteen or twenty feet, but I wasn't going any closer than that. I usually dive with a partner, Dave, but his wife is due with their third and she won't let him leave the house unless it's for a box of Ding Dongs. So I kept my distance. Just in case, you know. This guy in the middle of nowhere like that gave me the creeps. When I was close enough, he asked if I was with the search group looking for the little kid that went missing. When I told him yes, he asked me if we'd found anything yet.'

Ellis waited. 'That's it?'

'Do you remember Virginia Schorbus?' Terry asked.

'Name rings a bell.'

'Virginia Schorbus went missing from Redwater back in, jeez, musta been '81 or '82. It was a big case. A buddy of mine worked on it, and he told me there was this fella who was always around asking questions, helping out with the search. He even cooked meatloaf for the victim's parents.

Nobody thought anything of it at the time, but a couple months later they find Virginia's body buried in this same fella's back yard.'

'Oh,' Beecher said. 'That gave me chills. Why would he do that?'

'He might have been keeping tabs on the investigation,' Terry said. 'Or he might have got off on the, you know, power of it all. Anyway this was going through my brain when this man on the lake started asking questions. So, I called over to him and asked what his name was. Without another word he turned around and walked back into the woods. Almost as if *I'd* spooked *him*.'

'How long ago was this?' Ellis asked.

'Couldn't have been more than twenty, thirty minutes. I came right back as soon as it happened.'

'Did you get a good look at him?'

'I don't wear my glasses out on the lake,' she said. 'My diving mask is prescription, believe it or not. But he had dark hair. Might have been somewhere in his late thirties or early forties. Can't say for sure.'

'Could you describe him to a sketch artist?'

'I could try,' she said.

'Can you show us where you saw him on a map?'

Beecher unfurled a map of Manson on the hood of Terry's truck. He and Ellis held a corner each to stop it blowing away as Terry marked the spot with a small red 'x'.

'What do you think, Beech?' Ellis said. 'In the mood for a hike?'

Before he had time to answer, a high-pitched whistling noise erupted from the woods. Birds shot out of the trees. The whistle lasted five or six seconds, and was followed by a series of short, sharp toots.

'What the heck is that?' Beecher asked.

Ellis looked to the trees. 'One of the searchers found something.'

Ellis, Beecher, Louis and a trail of search volunteers moved quickly through the woods, ducking around towering trees. They trudged through the smell of decaying vegetation, of damp earth, woodfire and rain. Every thirty or forty seconds the whistle started up again, and Ellis would adjust his direction accordingly.

Around a quarter mile in from the lake they came across Harry Barr. Along with being a Light Withiner, Barr was a dispatch assistant for Easy-Time Towing Company and, from what Ellis heard, a wannabe novelist. He wore his hair in a long braided ponytail. When he saw them, the whistle fell loose around his neck. His cheeks were red from blowing.

'Over here,' he called. He had marked a patch of earth with a small yellow marker flag, but Ellis couldn't yet see what Harry had found. 'It's right here, by this bush.'

When they got within twenty feet of Harry, Ellis had Louis keep the volunteers back. He and Beecher approached with caution. The grass around the marker flag was damp and trampled with footprints.

'I'm afraid to say those boot prints are mine, Sheriff.'

Ellis kneeled by the flag and scanned the forest floor.

Nestled at the foot of a swatch of bottlebrush was a stuffed gorilla. It was sopping wet, scuffed with dirt and mud.

'Think it's hers, Sheriff?' Harry asked.

'We'll see if her family can ID it,' he said, but in his gut he already knew it was Sammy's. It had to be. She'd been here. She'd been right *here*.

Ellis rose with a creak and a grunt then scanned his surroundings. Ancient Virginia pines encircled them, blotting out the sun in places. 'No two-year-old wandered this far from home by herself. Someone brought her out here. She must have dropped this on the way.'

The only logical reason he could imagine for bringing a little girl all the way out here was to murder her. He was sure Beecher and probably even Harry were thinking the exact same thing, but all three of them had the good sense not to say it out loud. Whoever dragged Sammy out here was looking for privacy, and Ellis had an idea about where they might have found it.

The jagged silhouette of the gristmill rose ahead of them. It was a depressing place, full of sharp edges, graffiti and broken glass.

They approached from the south. Fifty feet before the mill sat a low grey building with all the windows boarded up. In chipped white letters above the entrance were the words, *VISITOR CENTER*. Except the V and both Rs had long since disappeared, leaving only faded outlines. Ellis saw that the lock was broken. It had been struck with something heavy, like a rock or a crowbar. The wood around it was splintered inward in a jagged starburst pattern.

'Kids, maybe,' Beecher said, but his skin had flushed red.

'Maybe,' Ellis said. He pushed gently on the door and it swung open with a creak. Light crept in through the boarded windows, splashing strips of yellow across an empty room. All the shop fittings had been removed, leaving pale white imprints against the floor.

'What do you make of this?' Beecher asked. He'd found several neat mounds of broken glass and dirt behind the door, as if someone had swept them up. 'Kids don't usually tidy up, do they?'

Ellis removed his flashlight to get a better look at the shape against the far wall. It was an army-green duffle bag. Beside it was an unrolled sleeping bag, inflatable pillow, propane lamp and a large plastic jug half-filled with water. 'Someone's been sleeping here.'

'Think it's the guy the diver lady saw?'

'Hard to say.'

Ellis scanned the duffle bag with the beam of his flashlight and a terrible thought occurred. *You could fit a toddler in there.*

Tucking the flashlight under one arm, he unzipped the bag slowly, praying not to see the lifeless eyes of a dead child staring back at him. Thankfully, there were no dead children in the bag. There was a woollen blanket, matches, a dozen tins of tuna and a brown paper shopping bag. Inside the bag were comic books: *X-Men*, *Batman*, *Wonder Woman*.

'Want me to radio it in?' Beecher asked. 'Tell them we might have a crime scene.'

'No,' Ellis said. 'We're gonna leave everything exactly how it was. Maybe whoever these belong to will come back for them. Get on the horn to Herm and Louis. Tell them I want their eyes on this place.'

While Beecher called Herm and Louis over for stakeout duty, Ellis walked over to check out the gristmill. He shoved the door aside and stood silent just inside the entrance. Towering shapes shifted into dusty old belts and pulleys. The exposed ribcage shape of the half-collapsed second floor shifted into focus.

The concrete beneath his feet was wet in places, littered with broken bottles, used condoms, and a sopping wet porno magazine. The air smelled of piss.

He climbed the stairs. They creaked and groaned under his considerable weight. He saw himself falling through them to the lower floor, consumed by rubble and debris. Thankfully he made it to the second-storey landing unharmed.

The upstairs windows were strangled from the outside by vines. What little light came through them cast jungle-party shadows across the mill floor. There was nothing up there aside from more debris.

On his way back downstairs, he noticed one of the walls was covered with writing. He scanned the sea of hand-scribed names with his flashlight: *Stephen Rumbold, Catherine Dixon, Margie Foss, Ellia Fleming, Patricia Carrasco, Jerry Baker, Robert Ammerman, Trinity Hinkle, Karen Garland ...*

Beecher appeared in the doorway. 'On their way, boss. Find anything else?'

Ellis gestured to the wall with his flashlight. 'What do you make of this, Beech?'

Beecher stepped into the mill and joined Ellis by the wall. He looked at the names. 'Oh, this is one of them urban legends, Sheriff.'

'How do you mean?'

'You're s'posed to write the name of your enemy on this wall and within twenty-four hours they'll be dead.'

'How do you know that?'

'My kid brother told me. He comes out here with his buddies sometimes.'

'Your brother know anything about that?' He shone the flashlight over the porno mag.

Beecher chuckled.

'Well, I'll be,' Ellis said, stepping closer to the wall. His joints might not be worth a damn anymore and his hearing was on its way out, but he had the peepers of a sprightly young man. 'Take a look at this, Beech.'

'What is it, boss?'

Saying nothing, Ellis drew his flashlight up to illuminate a single name among hundreds: *Sammy Went.*

MARTHA, WEST VIRGINIA

Now

We sat together in the living room of Emma's mobile home, around a fake brick fireplace that housed a gas heater. Every wall in the house was lined with framed photographs, but I didn't notice Sammy Went in any of them.

Emma's boys – Charlie, twelve; Harry, fifteen; and Jack, eighteen – sat stuffed together on one sofa, studying me like an interview panel. They were all handsome boys. Emma deemed the eldest two old enough to drink, so they shared a can of Pabst. Charlie was stuck drinking chocolate milk.

'I got a DNA sibling test and we matched,' Stuart said. He was sitting in an armchair by the window. 'The timeline adds up, Kim's childhood photos match Sammy's and her stepfather essentially confirmed it.'

'What does *essentially confirmed* mean?' Emma asked. She sat beside me, holding tight to my arm and smoking.

'He didn't deny it,' I said. 'Dean, my stepfather, didn't meet my mother until I was two. But sometime after that she must have confided in him ... told him I wasn't ... biologically hers.'

'Was she the one who did the, you know, the kidnapping part?'

'We don't know,' I said.

'What did she say when you confronted her?'

'I didn't. I couldn't, I mean. She died four years ago.'

Emma frowned. 'Well ain't that a bitch.'

The truth was I wasn't even sure I'd have confronted her if she were alive. Dean's collusion was enough to break my heart, but at least he had an excuse to lie, weak though it may have been. He was simply protecting his wife, and keeping a promise. But Carol Leamy knowingly took me away from another family. It would have taken nearly everything I had to ask her the question, and more than I'd have left to cope with the answer. If she'd been alive when Stuart approached me, I might never have called him back.

'Have you talked to the cops?' Emma asked. 'The FBI has a file on Sammy too, right? If what you're saying is true, they'll want to know about this.'

'We haven't contacted anyone yet,' Stuart said.

'Why not?'

He looked at me. 'Because we're going at Kim's pace. And that reminds me, boys, we need to keep a lid on this stuff for now, okay?'

Jack, Harry and Charlie all turned to Stuart in unison with slack expressions and O-shaped mouths, as if they'd rehearsed it.

'What I mean is, don't mention any of this to your friends at school and, you know, don't tweet about it or anything.'

Emma turned to me. 'Have you considered organising a press release?' she asked.

'A press release … No.'

'Honey,' she said. 'I can't even imagine what you're going through and I can't imagine what sort of damage this shit has already done, but you have to understand: you're not going to be the only one with questions. And I'm not just talking about the cops. What we've got on our hands here is *a story*. Everyone's going to want a piece, and you'd be smart to keep that in mind. This thing is going to get away from you, and fast, if you don't hold on with both hands.'

Control is an illusion, I thought.

She released my arm, looked me in the eyes and then took my arm again. 'We don't have to think about it right now, but it's a mistake not to think about it at all. You hear me?'

'Uh huh,' I said.

'What do you think happened?' she asked.

Stuart answered for me. 'Her kidnapper was passing through town, maybe visiting someone in Manson, when she spotted Sammy out someplace with Mom or Dad. At the playground on Wilton Street, maybe, or shopping in Home Foods. She may have recently lost a child or had a history of mental illness that—'

'I was asking Kim.'

They both turned to me. My mouth felt dry and the beer wasn't helping. 'I don't know. This is going to sound naive, but the mother I knew just wasn't the type of person to do something like this.'

'But she is the type of person to lie about it your whole life,' Emma said. 'My point being, you don't really know what type of person she was.' She turned to her brother. 'Remind me: did any eyewitness accounts mention seeing a woman near our place around the time of the abduction?'

Stuart shook his head. 'No female suspects. You know, aside from Mom.'

'Do you go back to Manson much?' I asked Emma.

'Oh, I escaped Manson when I was nineteen and have only been back a half-dozen times since. That's what they call it in Manson. You don't *leave*, you *escape*. That was ...' She paused, counting on her fingers around her cigarette. 'Six years after it all happened. I moved to Cincinnati with Karl Asbrock, fellow Mansonite. That's Jack's daddy.'

The washing machine was on in the next room. When it switched cycles the walls of the trailer rumbled.

'Things didn't work out between me and Karl. After the divorce, I guess I drifted for a while. Enrolled in college, dropped out of college, met Ron – that's my *current* husband. Then I pumped out a couple more of these devils.' She gestured to the boys on the sofa. 'The rest is history, I suppose.'

Afternoon sun flowed in through the window, illuminating hundreds of dust mites caught in the air.

'Ron isn't around a whole lot,' she said, lighting another cigarette. 'He drives trucks, which I sort of hate. But it's probably the key to our long-lasting relationship. Absence makes the heart grow fonder, right?'

'And you're working at Burger King now?' Stuart asked. I didn't pick up any condescension in his voice, but Emma must have.

'We can't all be *accountants*.' She described his profession with the same pinched tone she might have used if he were a rocket scientist or brain surgeon or the King of England.

Stuart raised his hands in defence. 'What did I say?'

To me, Emma said, 'I just work the breakfast shift. Ron makes good money driving trucks, but if I didn't work too, I'd drive myself crazy, right?'

I finished my beer. Emma stood to get me a fresh one without even asking if I wanted a second. I liked that very much.

She sat back down beside me, cracked open her own beer and smiled. 'So what the hell happened to you?' She chugged her beer and belched softly. 'Where did you grow up? What did you do? Are you married? Kids? You obviously weren't kept in a dungeon and fed fish heads all your life.'

'Ha. No.'

'Well, catch me up, girl.'

Buzzed from my one-and-a-half cans of Pabst, I gave her the highlights of my life up until the point Stuart entered it. It didn't take very long. I told her about growing up in Australia, about my mother, about Dean, about Amy.

When I told her about my mother's death she sighed deeply. When I told her I wasn't married and that I didn't have kids she just shrugged. 'All that stuff is overrated, anyway.'

'Gee, thanks, Mom,' Jack, her eldest, said with a wry smile. Emma belched again by way of a response, which got all her sons laughing.

The doorbell rang.

'That'll be the pizza,' Emma said. 'Say, Sammy – sorry, *Kim* – do you mind? I didn't get a chance to hit the ATM today.'

Stuart threw Emma a disapproving look.

'It's fine,' I said. 'I've got it.'

We talked for hours. We moved to the kitchen table to eat pizza and drink more beer, and pretty soon it was fully dark outside and Elsewhere was slowly turning in for the night, one trailer at a time. The kids skulked off to watch their screens and Stuart put himself to bed in Jack's room, no doubt worn out from the emotional outpouring at Emma's front door.

Then it was just Emma and me at the kitchen table. The pizza boxes were empty and we were five beers in apiece. Heavy metal music drifted across from a neighbouring trailer. Dogs barked, crickets chirped and a light wind strummed against the screen door.

It turned out Emma and I had a lot in common: we both hated it when people cracked their knuckles, had a strong aversion to feet and enjoyed Gillian Flynn novels. And we both got tattoos when we were younger that we now regretted. Mine was an owl with red glowing eyes under my right arm, hers the name of her first husband encased in a red love heart on her right breast.

Several times throughout the night I had wished Amy were with us. My phone was still racking up missed calls from her and Dean, and it was getting harder to ignore them.

A few minutes before midnight Emma said, 'Yep, I'm drunk enough. That's for damn sure.'

'Drunk enough for what?'

She climbed to her feet, nearly pitched forward in a drunken daze, then caught her balance at the last second. 'Drunk enough to show you something I couldn't share with you when I'm sober. At least not this early in our ... *relationship*.'

Emma fetched two torches from under the kitchen sink, handed one to me and quietly led the way to the end of the cul-de-sac.

'Where are we going?' I asked, switching on my torches and zipping up my parka. There was a chill in the air and a light mist was rolling in over the trailer park.

'You wouldn't believe me if I told you,' Emma said, stepping over a rusty guardrail and starting down a grassy slope on the other side of the cul-de-sac.

I followed her by torchlight as we moved through knee-high witchgrass and soon arrived at a narrow stream.

'We can cross just down here,' she said as we came upon a treacherous bridge made of large, flat stones spaced a few feet apart across the water. 'Watch the third stone. It's unstable and slippery as all fuck. Wait till I'm across and I'll light up the path for you.'

Laughing, drunk and more than a little baffled, I lit Emma's path. I worried that her beltful of beer might send her careening into the stream, but it had the opposite effect; it gave her enough drunken confidence to take each stone with self-determined agility.

When she arrived safely on the other side of the stream, she held her feet together, stretched out her arms and bowed. I tucked the torch under one arm and clapped enthusiastically.

'Thank you, thank you,' she said, bowing once more. 'Now it's your turn.'

She dropped the beam of her torch over the stone path, and seconds later I was halfway across the stream, trembling with delighted terror. 'This better be worth the trip.'

When Emma didn't answer, I angled my torch toward her and saw that she was frowning. She put her hand up to shield her eyes from the light. 'Take it easy with that thing.'

'Sorry,' I said.

'This way,' Emma said. 'Careful, it's steep.'

We climbed an embankment and started along a grassy ridge. To one side was Elsewhere: hundreds of rectangular black shapes, some with lights on. To the other side was a sprawling industrial complex: factories with tall chimneys pumping out white smoke. The chimneys made the air smell like gas.

'Is it much further?' I asked loudly into the wind. The cold was sobering me up and I wasn't sure that was a good thing.

'Not far. Just up ahead. There, see?'

We arrived at a young cherry blossom struggling against

the wind. A foldout chair had been erected beside the tree, surrounded by empty beer cans and cigarette butts.

'What is this place?'

'This, my long-lost sister, is your grave.'

I shone the torch in her face to check she wasn't joking, but I needn't have. I could tell by the stiffness of her voice. Turning my beam back to the cherry blossom I noticed a rain-soaked toy in a glass box at its foot – a stuffed gorilla.

'I read this thing online about grieving,' Emma said. 'I was always reading about stuff like that online to, you know, figure out a way to get past it all.' She looked over at the blinking factory lights. 'This one thing I read was about how to grieve without a body. It suggested a mock funeral, where you put a bunch of the person's stuff into a box or crate and bury it. So that's what I did. It felt silly in a way, but ... I don't know. I guess it sort of helped.'

Kneeling beside my own grave, I shone the torch over the stuffed gorilla – waterlogged and droopy, one eye missing. I would have liked to photograph it. When I reached out and touched the glass box, a rush of sadness welled up inside me. Had I been alone I might have let it out: sobbed into the wind.

'This gorilla was hers, wasn't it?' I asked. 'Mine, I mean. Sammy's.'

Emma nodded and lit a cigarette. 'I saved up and bought it for you on your first birthday. You dragged that thing with you everywhere until ... It spent a year and change in an evidence locker. Fuck, sorry. Here I go again.' She was crying. She finished the last of her beer, crushed the can and dropped it beside the rest. She sat down in the grass beside me. 'Do you remember *anything*?'

'I don't think so.'

She wasn't happy with my answer.

'I wish I did, Emma. I wish I remembered you. And Stuart.'

'Not exactly something you had a lot of control over.'

'I know. But I feel guilty for living my life and going about my business when you and Stuart were out looking for me.'

'I wasn't looking for you,' she said. 'In the beginning I was, but then I was burying you, grieving you. I spent the best part of two decades trying to forget you ever existed.' She flicked her cigarette into the air. It went sailing out over the ridge and landed in the stream below us. It sparked a moment, then faded. 'I'm the one who should be apologising. I gave up on you, Sammy. *Kim*. Whatever. Stuart never did. We fought a few good ones about that. I told him he was in denial. He told me I was a bad sister. I guess he was right about that one.'

She fished around in her pocket and found her keys. One of her many key rings was a mini Swiss army knife. She extended the blade, used it to pop open the glass box and handed me the stuffed gorilla. 'You should have this. It's technically still yours.'

Emma climbed to her feet and started back toward the stream without a word.

All the boys were bunked together in Harry's room, so I took Charlie's. I was too exhausted to care that my feet dangled over the end of his bed. There was a rotating nightlight attached to the bedhead that slowly spun stars and planets in an arc across the ceiling.

I drifted off to the sound of Emma's excited chatter on the telephone, the hiss of another can of Pabst being opened, and the spark of her cigarette lighter. I fell asleep clutching the stuffed gorilla tighter than I'd like to admit.

That night, I dreamed of the shadow man again.

I woke with a throbbing behind my eyes. Sunlight spilled in through the window. I'd forgotten to switch off Charlie's nightlight, and now the planets and stars were barely visible against the bright morning ceiling.

I climbed out of bed, dressed, and found Stuart waiting nervously in the kitchen. It was early, but Elsewhere sounded wide awake and alive outside.

'Morning,' I said. 'What's up?'

I could tell something was wrong right away. He was pacing back and forth by the window, pausing occasionally to draw back the curtain and peer outside.

'I'm sorry, Kim.'

'What for? What's going on?'

He drew the curtain back once more, winced at what he saw outside, then closed it again. 'She called them. Emma called them, God damn her.'

'Called who?' I was already on my way to the other window. I pulled back a yellow curtain with frayed seams to look outside. The first thing I saw was a hefty middle-aged man in a light-blue parka hoisting a TV news camera up onto his shoulder.

I craned my neck to see a well-dressed woman standing at the end of Emma's driveway. She was shivering against the early morning chill and trying desperately to flatten her hair against the breeze.

There were more media people up the street; parking news vans, preparing sound equipment and erecting tripods.

My first thought was that something dramatic must have happened in the trailer park overnight to draw all the media – a murder perhaps. A microsecond later, when the rational part of my mind caught up, I thought of Amy and Dean, and Lisa and Wayne, and how control is an illusion.

There would be no more walking at my own pace. It was out of my hands now. I felt like an old, unravelling sweater. Someone had taken a thread and run away with it.

No, not someone, I thought. *Emma.*

She was out in the street, I noticed then, wearing a pretty pink shirt and tight black jeans. She was being interviewed by a reporter in his fifties with a striking mop of white hair.

'Everyone,' Stuart said from the other window. 'She called everyone.'

MANSON, KENTUCKY

Then

Nobody talked on the way home from the press conference. The atmosphere inside her mother's Taurus was tense. From the back seat, Emma watched her father's hands on the steering wheel. He had removed the bandage from his right hand. The knuckles beneath were torn and bloody, and she had a fair idea how they got that way.

Jack drove slowly. He was never exactly a speed-hound – especially with his kids in the car – but today he was noticeably less gas-happy than usual. He wasn't in a hurry to get home, Emma figured. Neither was she. Two aunts from her mother's side had descended on the house late last night and a third was due this morning with Emma's cousin, Todd. Anne, Pauline and Tillie. Her dad called them the Brides of Dracula. Emma might agree but for one fact: vampires could only enter a house when invited.

Manson passed by outside the window: houses, parks, stores, lakes, gullies, ditches, fields, sewage drains.

Sammy could be in any of those places, Emma thought. The press conference had not inspired her with confidence. The cops had nothing. Emma had nothing – except her father's torn-up knuckles.

'Hey, Dad, would you mind pulling over?' She asked, leaning forward.

'You feeling sick, honey?' Molly asked.

'No. I just feel like walking around for a while. If that's okay?'

Jack looked at Molly, then into the rear-view mirror. 'Everything alright, Em?'

'Not really,' she said.

'Yeah. I guess that was a pretty stupid question.'

He flicked on his indicator and eased the car to the side of the road.

Molly swivelled around in her chair to look into the back seat. 'Don't be out too long,' she said.

'I won't.'

'I mean it, Emma. Be home long before dark. Promise.'

'I promise.'

Stu tapped Emma on the arm and asked, 'Can I come?'

'Not this time, buddy,' Emma said and stepped out of the car, feeling instantly lighter as she shut the door and watched them drive away.

The late morning was clear and blue. Her scuffed Chuck Taylors slapped against the bitumen. She walked to the concrete channel, then along it for a quarter-mile. Occasionally she'd turn to glance at the overgrown yards on Grattan Street, but mostly she kept her eyes on the ground in front of her.

She had a cigarette in her pocket but didn't feel much like smoking it. She'd taken up smoking to add a little darkness to her life, but now she had all the darkness she could handle.

She climbed up the embankment at Lytton Street and headed toward Shelley Falkner's place. *Her second home*, she used to call it. But it felt like years since she had visited. In truth it had only been two weeks, but that was during the pre-dark times. She had only been fourteen days younger, then, but it felt more like forty years.

Shelley lived in a two-bedroom apartment on Elgin Avenue, directly across from Canning Gas & Go. Shelley's running joke was that her apartment could fit inside Emma's house nearly three-and-a-half times; six if you included the front and rear yards.

Emma knocked. Mrs Falkner – *'How many times I gotta tell you to call me Nicky?'* – came to the front door and stared at Emma a moment, dumbstruck.

'Oh, Emma!' She snaked her arms around Emma's shoulders and drew her into a tight, maternal hug. Mrs Falkner was tall and broad, just like her daughter.

'I'll call Shelley,' she said, turning to face the interior of the apartment. 'Shelley! SHELLEY!'

Shelley came up the hallway, paused when she spotted Emma standing on the stoop, and then took small, slow steps toward her. 'Em. Jesus. Are you okay?'

Emma tried to nod and tell Shelley, yes, she was okay. Instead she burst into tears. It was the first real cry she'd had since Sammy disappeared, and now the finger was out of the dyke.

'I'm sorry,' Emma whispered. 'This … This isn't why I came over here.'

'Shut up,' Shelley said, pulling Emma into her arms.

'We've been praying for you and your family,' Mrs Falkner said. 'If there's anything we can do … Do your folks need anything? Do you? I just don't know what kind of world we live in when—'

'I'll take it from here, Mom,' Shelley said.

Shelley's bedroom was as messy as you'd expect from a thirteen-year-old, but there was a cosy, nest-like quality to the disorder. The walls were lined with *bad art*. There was really no other way to describe it. Big canvases splashed with oil paint, depicting eyeballs, skulls, a horse looking down over the planet with a single tear rolling down its long white cheek.

One would assume the art was Shelley's – it had a certain broody, teenage quality. The truth was even sadder. They were her father's, a frustrated artist living a life of quiet desperation as a travel agent in California.

Shelley knew the art was bad, but she didn't hang it ironically. Family was family, for better or worse.

'I'm practically a celebrity at school now,' Shelley said, drawing her knees up to her chin. 'It's by association, of course, but you know me: I'll take it.'

They sat together on the floor. Emma glanced around and thought about the sleepovers she'd had here, the long afternoons spent talking, the studying, the gossiping, the seances. *The child inside is dead*, she thought.

'They want the gossip, is all,' Shelley said, a twang of stiffness in her voice. 'It'll all go back to normal when Sammy comes home. They'll be back to the shoving and the teasing.'

Emma smiled for Shelley's sake. 'What gossip did you give them?'

'Lady, I don't have any gossip to give.'

'Yeah, listen, I'm sorry I didn't return your calls, I just—'

'Stop. After what you've been through, what you're *going* through, Jesus, Em, I'm just …'

'Don't,' Emma said, noticing that Shelley's eyes were wet behind her glasses. 'You'll get me going again.'

'Oh please, this is just allergies. I'm your emotional rock.'

Emma reached out her hand and Shelley took it. 'What else are they saying at school?' Emma asked.

Shelley hesitated, pressed her big glasses against her face with an index finger. 'Ah, you know what they say, Em. Manson High is like a hotdog stand: full of lips and assholes.'

'What are they saying, Shell?'

Shelley took a deep breath. 'That your mother sacrificed Sammy to the Devil. I told you. Lips and assholes.'

Emma wasn't surprised that the kids at school blamed her mother's church. The Light Withiners were already downright bonkers, but their beliefs had still been exaggerated and embellished by too many trips up and down the grapevine.

People thought they drank blood, worshipped Satan and sacrificed animals – and children, apparently – at the Devil's alter.

That doesn't rule out your mom, a nasty, snake-like voice whispered in her mind. *You remember how angry she got at Sammy that time when she thought nobody else was home.* Emma tried to silence the thought, but the voice was persistent. *Sammy came along and your mother darkened and your family started to pull apart, and wouldn't things have been easier if Sammy were never born? And don't you think your mother knew that too?*

Shelley watched her for a moment. 'Is there any news?'

Emma shook her head and let a beat of silence pass before asking what she had come here to ask. 'Shell, I need a favour.'

'Anything.'

'There's some stuff going around about Travis Eckles. Have you heard anything?'

'Sure. Those who don't suspect your mother suspect Travis. Why?'

Emma shrugged her shoulders. 'He called the house last night.'

'Travis?'

'I answered the phone. He didn't say who it was and when I asked him he didn't tell me, but I recognised his voice. I'm almost positive he was crying.'

'Crying? What did he want?'

'To talk to my dad. I don't know what he said, but Dad went out after the call and … You can't tell anyone else about this, okay?'

Shelley crossed her heart and raised a two-finger salute. 'Scout's honour.'

'Dad came home late, and his hands were all split open and raw, like he'd been in a fight.'

'Jesus. What happened?'

'I have no idea. Dad isn't saying anything and I haven't worked up the guts to ask him.'

'You think it has something to do with Sammy?'

'It has to, right? Dad must have found something out about what happened.'

'If your dad had any evidence the cops would be all over it, wouldn't they?'

'That's what I need your help to figure out,' Emma said. 'There's someplace I need to go, but I don't think I should go alone. Will you be my back up?'

'Anytime and always,' Shelley said. 'What did you have in mind?'

They stood outside number nine Cromdale Street, before the rain-clogged gutters, the torn bug screen, the weed-strangled lawn, the *NO TRESPASSING* sign.

Shelley had worn her Doc Martens – good for kicking if the need arose. 'You sure about this, lady?'

But Emma was already untangling the old length of cord that served as a latch on the front gate of the Eckles' property. The gate swung open with a *creak* and Emma walked through, flanked by Shelley. Their walk became a march across the lawn, up the rotting porch steps and right to the front door. Without hesitation – there was no turning back now – Emma lifted her hand to knock, but before she had the chance—

'Are you girls lost?'

Ava Eckles was sitting on a worn brown sofa on the porch, sucking down a cigarette. She looked like death with her pale skin, beady, yellowed eyes and near-skeletal arms.

Perhaps Emma's aunts weren't the only vampires in Manson.

'Oh, hello, Mrs Eckles.'

Ava squinted at Emma. 'I know you.'

'Yeah, I live down the street. I'm Emma Went. This is Shelley.'

'*Emma Went.*' The words seemed to leave a bad taste in her mouth. 'What are you doing on this side of the fence, *Emma Went*?'

'I want to talk to Travis,' she said. 'Is he home?'

Ava's teeth shone yellow against her pale lips. 'Uh huh.'

'May we see him?'

'Why?'

'We just want to ask him a few questions.'

'Like, "Did you murder my little sister?" Those sorts of questions?'

Emma exchanged a glance with Shelley, who seemed smaller than ever before. She had always felt safe with her imposing best friend, but around the Eckles even giants lost their courage.

'No,' Emma said, but it was a lie.

'Look, nobody deserves to lose nobody – 'specially not a child. But everyone's saying my boy had something to do with what happened to little Samantha, and that ain't right neither.'

'*Sammy*,' Emma corrected. 'Her name is Sammy.'

'Little girl, I don't give two shits what her name is. And if you really think my boy has it in him to lead your sister out into the woods and slit her up the belly or whatever it is you're envisioning, do you really think it's a good idea to come here? Into the lion's den?'

Shelley pushed her glasses into place and asked, 'Is that what you think happened, Mrs Eckles?'

Ava shrugged her shoulders. 'Don't matter what people think on this side of the fence, now, does it?'

'I thought I heard voices.' A tall, slender man appeared from behind the rusted screen door. He had thin, slightly feminine features and short-cropped, jet-black hair. Emma didn't recognise him at first. 'Mom, are you scaring the Jehovah's Witnesses again?'

'We're not Jehovah's Witnesses,' Emma said. 'I'm—'

'Jack Went's daughter, I know. Sorry, I was making a joke. A bad one, apparently. I'm Patrick.'

He extended his hand to shake; his fingers were warm and stiff. He smelled fresh and washed, and wore a button-up shirt tucked into fitted black jeans. 'Why don't y'all come on inside. I just put a fresh pot of coffee on.'

'Oh yeah, do go on inside,' Ava Eckles said, her lips making loose wet sounds against the butt of her cigarette. 'Into the lion's den.'

Patrick Eckles held the front door open. 'You'll have to excuse my mother. I can assure you her bark is much worse than her bite. That's not to say she don't bite, but you get what I mean.'

Saying nothing, Emma and Shelley stepped into the house.

After leading them through a dimly lit and narrow corridor, Patrick invited Emma and Shelley to sit at the kitchen table. Emma's idea of how an ex-con was supposed to look, act and talk was subverted the day she met Patrick. He spoke in full sentences and was devoid of any home-drawn skull tattoos.

Clean dishes were piled high on the dish rack, and the room smelled like lemon-scented floor cleaner. Patrick crossed the floor, took three coffee mugs down from a cupboard and held them out for Emma to examine.

'Do you have a preference?' he asked.

Printed on the face of the first mug was *World's Most Okayest Employee*; on the second was *Cancel My Subscription Because I'm Tired of Your Issues*; on the third was *Coffee Makes Me Poop*.

Emma flashed a humouring smile. 'Surprise me.'

'I'll take the poop one,' Shelley said, which made Patrick throw his head back and laugh.

He filled the mugs with fresh coffee, added cream and handed Emma *World's Most Okayest Employee*.

'So, Patrick, when did you get …' Emma couldn't choose between *home* and *out*.

Patrick rescued her. 'Wednesday. Two years ahead of schedule, thank you very much. You see, girls, if you say please and thank you and try not to jam a shiv into your cellmate, prison really ain't so bad.'

Emma and Shelley exchanged a nervous glance.

'Another bad joke,' Patrick said. 'I wouldn't know a shiv from a cheese-knife.'

'We'll take your word for it,' Shelley said.

'I was just sorry as hell when I heard about what happened to your little sister,' he said to Emma gravely. 'I know how it feels to miss family. Everywhere you go it's like you're forgetting something. Are there any leads?'

Emma shrugged. 'A few.'

That was a lie. Sheriff Ellis had made that pretty clear at the press conference, but Patrick didn't need to know that. Of course, he'd probably figure it out himself if he watched the evening news.

'Don't take this the wrong way,' Patrick said. 'But what are you girls doing here?'

'We want to talk to Travis,' Shelley said. 'Is he home?'

His face suddenly grew very serious. He crossed the room again and slid the kitchen door closed. When he returned to the table he spoke in a low, deliberate tone. 'My little brother had nothing to do with what happened.'

'Who says he did?'

'Half of Manson,' Patrick said. 'The sheriff too. But all that has more to do with his surname than it does any evidence. I'm sure when word gets out that I'm back in town more than a few people'll think I had something to do with it.'

Emma sipped her coffee slowly. It was hot. That was good.

She imagined scalding hot coffee could be used as a pretty effective weapon. 'What makes you say that?'

'I'm an Eckles,' he said. 'Even better, I'm an ex-con.'

Shelley stood up and helped herself to some more sugar. 'Where is your brother?'

'Upstairs.'

'Can we talk to him?' Emma asked.

'He's resting. Licking his wounds.'

'What wounds?'

He put his elbows on the table, leaned forward and looked Emma directly in the eyes. 'Black eye, split lip, fractured jaw, two teeth broken off at the gum.'

'... Did my dad do that to him?'

Patrick eased down into his chair and sipped his coffee. 'Why would your dad do something like that?'

'Because he found out Travis has something to do with Sammy's disappearance.'

'Did he tell you that?'

'He didn't have to,' Emma said. 'What else would they fight about?'

'Love,' Patrick said. 'As so many of these types of things are, it was about love.'

MANSON, KENTUCKY

Now

Manson appeared suddenly as we came over the crest of a hill, a bumpy landscape of buildings under a phlegm-grey sky. At its centre stood an imposing white water tower with giant red letters painted across its face. I couldn't yet make out the words but Stuart knew them by memory: '*Welcome to Manson. A small slice of Heaven.*'

The town was heavily wooded on two sides. Beyond the woods lay a sprawling collection of rich green ridgelines and valleys. On the way into town we passed a huge road sign that read, *Jesus is King.*

West Virginia had acted as a decompression chamber into Kentucky, this strange and seductive new land of endless wilderness, enormous food portions, country music and Christian talkback radio. There was a nervous energy in the air that seemed to thicken the closer we got to Manson, and

I couldn't shake the image of a lobster in a pot of water, gradually being brought to boil.

'We made it,' Stuart said.

'You sound surprised.'

'After what happened at Emma's place, I thought you might call the whole trip off.'

'I thought about it. Not for me so much as for my sister. Amy, I mean.'

Stuart looked as if this was the first time he had even considered how this might be affecting *my* family. And now that he had considered them, did he feel guilt? Regret? Mild curiosity? I remembered our conversation about 'Enoch Arden' and decided he probably didn't.

'You handled that well back there,' Stuart said. 'All those reporters. It can't have been easy.'

'It wasn't,' I said. 'But it's like I've fallen off a cruise ship exactly halfway between two islands, and at this stage there's no use treading water – know what I mean?'

He nodded. 'Got to swim toward something.'

'Exactly. Got to swim toward something.'

A little after two pm we booked two rooms at a hotel about two kilometres from the town centre. The Manson Comfort Inn was surprisingly expensive, but boasted spectacular views of the surrounding wilderness.

As we walked from the front desk to our rooms, which were at opposite ends of the hotel, Stuart asked me if I'd mind him heading out on his own for the afternoon.

'Sure,' I said. 'Where are you headed?'

'To see Mom.' He tugged awkwardly at his ear. 'I figured I should go alone first. Sorry if that's weird or whatever, but with this stuff about to hit the news and all the insanity that's about to kick off, I just ... I don't think it's a great idea to spring you on her.'

Of course I didn't mind. In fact I was relieved that Stuart had chosen to walk ahead and scout the terrain, so to speak. It had felt wrong turning up at Emma's place without warning. Besides, I wanted some time alone.

I sat down on the bed and took out my phone to check my voicemail. There were sixteen messages and counting. The first was from a junior producer with a slow and appealing Southern drawl. After explaining who he was and who he worked for – Phil Wride, KLTV *Action News* – he asked me to call him back to discuss the possibility of 'financial compensation for exclusivity.'

Financial compensation, I thought, remembering that I paid for the pizza at Emma's place. *Is that why she called the media?*

The next message was from a cop. 'Howdy, Ms Leamy. This is Detective Mark Burkhart over here with the Manson police. I'm wondering if you could make some time to swing by the station for a chat. It seems that everyone from WKYP to CNN knows who you are, so it's about time I did too.'

He left a number to call him back, but I was in no hurry.

The third voicemail was from Amy. 'Kim, where are you? We need to—'

I moved the phone away from my ear. The media back home in Australia were probably reaching out to her and Dean right now for a quote. Maybe the police were already involved too. I knew she'd be desperate to hear my voice. She'd want me to tell her everything was okay, and that no matter what, we were, and forever would be, sisters. By screening her calls I was fulfilling her fears about me. *'If we didn't have blood connecting us I'd never see you,'* she'd said in the back yard of her townhouse a million years ago.

But I couldn't. Not yet. So I turned off my phone without listening to any more messages and stuck it in the bedside drawer alongside the Gideon.

I found a beer in the minibar and – perhaps unwisely – switched on the TV.

I flicked through the stations looking for something warm and comfortable like a sitcom, but settled on an old episode of *Antiques Roadshow.* An elderly British man had just discovered his old vase was worth somewhere in the neighbourhood of two thousand pounds. He showed as much enthusiasm as someone admiring a well-cooked roast potato.

The beer dampened the noise in my head, until *Antiques Roadshow* cut to a commercial and the words *WKYP News Update* slid right to left under a fast-paced, oddly unsettling news theme. The titles dissolved to reveal a suited man with a serious expression. 'This is your *WKYP News* update and I'm Richard Looker,' he said, shuffling a stack of papers and stacking them into a neat pile. 'Topping our seven o'clock news report tonight: a stabbing in Lexington has left one adult dead and one juvenile injured; police are unable to rule out arson in a Clark County factory fire; and, closer to home, a potential answer to a mystery that has plagued a family for nearly three decades. Here's Beth Turner.'

The news cut to a wide shot to reveal a woman with puffy dark hair. I'd seen her earlier that day outside Emma's trailer. 'Thanks, Richard. As some viewers might remember, two-year-old Sammy Went disappeared from her home in Manson back in 1990, and the case has remained unsolved ever since. Until, quite possibly, today. Mounting evidence is pointing to Kimberly Leamy, a woman from Melbourne, Australia, in fact being Sammy Went. Ms Leamy was unavailable for comment.'

In the past few weeks I'd experienced a number of surreal moments, but this had to be the strangest so far: first, hearing my name mentioned on a newscast, and then seeing my own face appear on the screen, hurrying from Emma's trailer, past a huddle of reporters and into Stuart's waiting car.

'Are you Sammy Went?' a voice behind the cameras called.

'No ...' I said. 'No comment.'

Beth Turner barrelled the camera lens and said, 'While local police are yet to release a statement, Sammy's sister, Emma Went-Finkel, believes she might have finally found her long-lost sister.'

Suddenly Emma was on the screen, standing in Elsewhere in her pretty pink shirt and tight black jeans, without a trace of a hangover. 'I'd be lying if I said I'd fully accepted it,' Emma said. 'I feel relieved, exhausted, confused ...' Her glance moved between the camera and the WKYP microphone tucked under her chin. 'It's been a rollercoaster, but I'm just happy to have my little sister—'

I switched off the television and stared at my reflection in the black screen. My face had changed. The difference was subtle, and I'm sure noticeable only to me, but it was there nonetheless. My eyes were more sunken than usual, my cheeks more gaunt. A combination of stress, freeway food and lack of sleep, I told myself. But that was only part of it. I was *changing*; transforming into Sammy Went on the outside as well as in.

Will I become a completely different person? Or just a half-person – not quite Kim Leamy and not quite Sammy Went, but someone in between, like Stuart's composite sketch?

Stuart was quiet over dinner. He sat staring out the window at the blinking lights of Manson.

'How was your mother?' I asked.

'She already knew. A reporter called her this morning. Emma called her too, I'm guessing. I asked her how she felt and sort of expected her to scream at me to bring the car around so she could come and meet you right then and there.'

'But she didn't.'

'No, she didn't,' Stuart said. 'Mom can be cold sometimes. It's like a switch. She's all about keeping things in.'

'Apple doesn't fall too far from the tree, I suppose,' I said with a dry, buzzed smile.

'Are you talking about me or you?'

'Touché.'

'I guess it does run in the family,' he said. 'Emma's the exception. She'll shout her feelings from the rooftops if she thinks someone will listen. Social media was invented for people like our sister.'

I caught the waiter's attention and ordered another round of drinks for the table. Stuart raised an eyebrow. While he didn't say it, he clearly thought I was drinking too much – and by American standards he wasn't wrong.

'I called Claire,' he said.

'How is she?'

'Worried,' he said. 'They ran a promo on CNN and it's already all over the web. She asked me how you were.'

'What did you tell her?'

'That I hadn't really asked. She didn't like that.'

I laughed.

'Dad called,' he said.

'He did? What did he say? Will he come to Manson, do you think?'

'I said he called, I didn't say I picked up.' Stuart sighed uncomfortably. 'He left a voicemail. I'll call him after dinner. Just need a couple more of these first.'

He gestured to his scotch and soda. Maybe he wasn't worried about *my* drinking after all.

'Your family is …' I was feeling tipsy and confident and oddly childlike, so I went ahead and finished my thought, '… fractured, isn't it?'

He nodded. 'You noticed.'

'Do you think your family would still be together if none of this ever happened?'

'No,' he said flatly. 'The Wents were well on their way to being fractured even before the vanishing.'

A silence fell over the restaurant. The floor was briefly empty of staff, and there were only a handful of other diners.

'I used to believe that when I finally found you, it would repair the family. I thought we weren't complete because we were missing a piece, so I figured finding and returning that piece would fix everything. But life doesn't work that way, does it? Emma runs off to the media and Mom is … Well, Mom is Mom.'

'I'm the missing piece,' I said, turning the thought over in my mind. 'In a weird, sort of abstract way I've always felt like that. I've always been looking for the rest of the puzzle and thought when I found it, everything would be *fixed*. We're similar in a lot of ways.'

'I've noticed,' Stuart said. 'Hey, Kim?'

'Yeah.'

'How are you?'

I smiled. 'You can tell Claire I'm fine.'

I awoke in my hotel room at four am, sopping wet. The sheets were soaked through, and for a dazed, sleepy moment I wondered if my room was leaking. Or maybe I left the thermostat set too high and sweated through the covers. But the room wasn't hot, and the thermostat was set to a comfortable sixty-nine, which, after taking too long to work it out in my head, came out around twenty degrees Celsius.

When the sharp smell of urine hit my nostrils I was struck with a sudden, jarring clarity. For the first time since I was a kid, I had wet the bed.

MANSON, KENTUCKY

Then

Travis woke to voices in the house. Female voices by the sound of it, though that didn't make much sense. It was probably just the TV, but he decided to get up anyway. Easing himself off the bed, he pulled on a day-old pair of underwear and shuffled over to the mirror on the back of his bedroom door.

The man in the mirror was a mess. His right eye was completely swollen shut. Stale globs of blood had settled at the base of each nostril, and the stitches over his split lip were knotted with lint and something yellow. Jack had done a number on him, that was for sure. The worst of it, and the one thing Dr Redmond couldn't patch back together – *'You'll have to see a dentist for that, Travis, and he might be fool enough to believe you got this falling down a flight of stairs, but I sure as heck ain't,'* – were the two teeth that had completely broken off at the gum.

Since visiting Dr Redmond he had decided to refine his story. Falling down a flight of stairs was something battered wives told the police when they came knocking at the door.

Is that what I am? He wondered, picking a piece of pillow lint from one of his stitches. *A battered wife?*

No, a mugging was a better lie. When Sheriff Ellis came knocking, Travis would tell him three guys in ski masks jumped him on his way out of Cubby's Bar. All of this would be a moot point, of course, if just one of the men from the booze bus sang, and he'd be downright surprised if one of them didn't – or hadn't already.

You're a fool if you think this story isn't going to get out, he told his reflection. *Chances are it's already out there, and people are already coming to the wrong conclusion: Jack Went found out it was Travis who took that little girl and dealt out some fatherly justice.*

'If only they knew,' he said aloud.

He was drawn to his bedroom window by the familiar creak of the front gate.

A crack of anxiety pulsed through him when he saw who it was: Emma Went and her hulking friend Shelley Something. They were on their way out.

He rushed into the hall and nearly ran into his brother coming up the stairs.

'I was just coming up to talk to you,' Patrick said.

'What was Emma Went doing here?'

Patrick frowned. 'Those stitches are coming apart. Have you been playing with 'em?'

'What did she want, Pat?'

'Your dressing needs changing too. Come on.'

Patrick led him into the bathroom. Travis sat on the lip of the tub as his brother peeled the bandage from his nose and dropped it into the wastepaper basket. It was red and sticky. He dabbed some rubbing alcohol on a cotton pad and cleaned up Travis's face.

'Does it hurt?' Patrick asked.

'Like a motherfucker.'

'Did you fill the prescription Redmond gave you yet?'

'Not yet,' Travis said.

Patrick placed a new bandage over Travis's nose with gentle precision. 'I've gotta tell you, kid, it's hard seeing you like this. The old me would have dragged that old bastard out onto his front lawn and kicked the shit outta him.'

'He's not *that* old,' Travis said. 'And that didn't work out so well the last time.'

His big brother fell silent for a moment. It was strange having him back in the house again. He loved the hell out of Patrick, and Ava was a lot easier to deal with when he was around, but he was ghostly and different. Prison had changed him, and not in the way Travis had expected. He might have understood if Patrick had come home with the posture of a broken man; if he woke to sudden nightmares or felt anxious and overwhelmed in open spaces. Instead, Patrick walked upright and proud. He had quit smoking and hardly drank anymore. Had prison truly *reformed* him?

'It wasn't entirely Jack's fault, you know,' Travis said.

'Let me guess: you were asking for it?' He sat down next

to Travis on the tub. 'Emma wanted to know what happened. Like the rest of Manson, she assumed the fight had something to do with Sammy.'

To think of what had happened outside Cubby's as a *fight* was fiction. Jack had beaten Travis, and Travis had let him do it. So why didn't he hate Jack for it?

'What did you tell her?' Travis asked. When Patrick hesitated, he asked again. 'Pat, what did you tell her?'

'The truth.' Those two simple words landed like grenades.

'You didn't,' Travis said in a pleading tone. 'What gives you the right, Pat? Tell me you're lying, tell me—'

'You're a suspect in a kidnapping and Jack Went is your only alibi. It's time to stop protecting him and start protecting yourself.'

'I am,' Travis said. 'It won't just be Jack's life that'll change, it's mine – yours too. And Mom, shit, can you imagine what she'll say when she finds out what I am?'

'Not *what* you are, Travis. *Who* you are. And trust me, Mom sees more than she lets on.'

'You had no right. You had no—'

'I never told you what happened in the bar that night, did I? When I hit Roger Albom with that pool cue?'

Travis fell silent. He shook his head. He had probed his brother about it a few times but Patrick had always been evasive, insisting it was nothing more than a dumb bar fight.

'I was playing pool with some buddies,' Patrick said. 'Roger Albom and a couple girls had next dibs on the table. When I was done I handed him the cue but he wouldn't take it. He said, "No thanks. Fag genes might run in the family."'

'… So, what, it was my fault you went to Greenwood?'

'Of course not,' Patrick said. 'It was my choice to do what I did. And honestly it wasn't so much what Roger said. It was that he represented all the shit you're going to have to face, just for being who you are.' He rose from the tub and put a hand on Travis's shoulder. 'I'm heading out for a while, kid. Later.'

'Yeah,' Travis said. 'Later.'

When Patrick was gone, and Travis had heard the front gate creak open and shut, he skulked around the house feeling sore and depressed. His mother was passed-out in the living room, a beer can clasped in her left hand and the TV remote in her right.

She has the right idea, sleeping away the day, Travis thought. On his way back to bed he passed Patrick's room. The door was slightly ajar. He would have kept on walking, had he not spotted something that gave him pause. He pushed open the door and stepped inside, sure that the thing on the bedside table couldn't possibly be what he thought it was.

Patrick's bedroom was exactly how he had left it on the day he was marched out the front door by the sheriff's deputies. A single bed stood before a giant Sex Pistols poster, one corner dog-earing. Tacked all around the poster were smaller band photos cut from various magazines, featuring The Ramones, Dead Kennedys, Circle Jerks, Black Flag. On the back of the door was a rusty yellow sign saying *RESTRICTED AREA*, presumably stolen from a construction site.

The only thing that was different – and the very thing that had drawn Travis inside – was the presence of a Holy Bible.

Before going to prison Patrick had been a proud atheist, and as far as Travis knew that hadn't changed. Yet here it was, a bedside bible.

He picked it up. It was worn and well-used. A handwritten inscription on the inside cover read, *Patrick, in your hands you hold the original gift that keeps on giving. With love, B.*

'Who's B?' he wondered aloud, letting the Bible fall open to a page marked with a fat envelope. A passage on the page had been highlighted: Acts 3:19. *Now repent of your sins and turn to God, so that your sins may be wiped away.*

He opened the envelope. Inside were multiple letters, each one written by the same person.

Becky Creech?

He had seen Becky just yesterday with her brother, Dale, at Sammy Went's search party. She had known Travis's name.

He sat down on the bed and unfolded the first letter. It was dated October 7th 1987.

Dear Patrick,

I hope you don't mind me writing you in prison. You don't know me, but if my math is right we're around the same age, and if I hadn't been home-schooled I'm sure we would have shared a few classes at Manson High (Go Warriors!).

I'm writing to you on behalf of The Church of the Light Within. From the outside, the Light Within can seem sort of radical and, let's face it, insane! But it's really

full of kind, honest, God-fearing people who just want to be a part of something bigger. If you've ever thought about being part of something bigger, or even if you just want to talk, write me back.
With love, Becky Creech

P.S. I've enclosed a photo.

He checked the envelope for the photo, but it was gone.

Had Becky Creech been trying to convert Patrick? Worse, had she succeeded?

He flicked to the next letter, this one dated November 3rd 1987.

Dear Patrick,
I was so pleased you wrote me back, and thanks for the compliment – I'm glad you liked the photo. Maybe you can send me one?

Let me try to answer a few of your questions.

Yes, we handle venomous snakes. No, we don't eat their hearts or drink their blood. No, we don't secretly worship the Devil (that one's my favourite Ha Ha!). Yes, sometimes people do get bit.

When God moves on you to take up a snake, there are two reasons you will get bit. One, so that God can save you from your suffering. Two, so God can take you home to Heaven. It might be a snake that takes you, or it might be cancer or a car wreck or a plane crash, or it might be old age.

However it happens, we believe everyone has an appointment with death, and that death brings us back to God.

'Death brings us back to God.' I've always liked the way that sounds.

Now I have some questions for you: Were you born in Manson? What did you do between finishing high school and right now? (Spare no detail!) What's prison like?

That last one's a big one, I suppose, so maybe you could split your answer into two parts. Part one would be all the literal stuff like food, your cell, the other inmates, things you do in your spare time – like do you really make license plates or is that a myth?

Part two would be all about how it feels. I know a little bit about feeling trapped. My walls aren't concrete, and I don't sleep in a cell with bars over the windows, mind you. My walls are made of guilt. Wow, that sounds quite dramatic, don't it?

I want you to know that I don't sit in judgement of you, Patrick, nor will I ever. You're there because you sinned, but to sin is to be human. Growing up Pentecostal means you spend a lot of time hearing how unworthy of God's love you are, but it wasn't until recently I started to understand what that was all about. See, if we didn't have sin in our heart then what would be the point? Worship would be too easy then, wouldn't it?

A youth pastor (the funny and funny-looking Dave Flenderson) once told me that moral behaviour requires sacrifice. That's what it all comes down to. See, I might have wanted to scream at Erin Taylor for calling me an 'effin' fundie B-word' last week in the parking lot of Home Foods, and you might have wanted to beat that man over the head with that pool cue, and that's okay. It's actually normal to want to do those things, but it's by not doing them that we earn God's love.

With love, Becky

Travis flicked ahead and found a letter dated March 3rd 1988.

Dear Patrick,

I want to tell you about Clementine. She's a two-year-old cane rattler. Now, a lucky rattler might live for twenty years out in the wild, but a two-year-old in our church is practically a senior citizen. The average is ten months. The stress often takes them earlier than that.

Clementine is a cranky old thing, and she's been known to take a bite of a Light Withiner from time to time. But never EVER has she bit the hand that feeds her. That is, until the day she bit the hand that feeds her. My hand.

Let me back up a bit.

Our church is in the middle of a huge plot of family land just outside the town limits. The land is wooded aside from a clearing where the church stands and an unsealed road that leads to it. When I say the land is mostly wooded, I mean WOODED. The forest is thick, deep and dark. If you looked at our property from above you'd see forty hectares of green and not much else.

Light Within services are held three times a week – Tuesday nights, Friday nights and Sunday afternoons. On the first Sunday of every month I have to stay back and feed the snakes, which all live in a big wooden hutch out by the treeline. It's one of my chores.

Yes, I'm twenty-six and I still have chores.

The snake hutch is actually more like a shed. It's a small concrete shelter with no windows and a painfully low ceiling (as in, I thump my head against it every ... single ... time!). The hutch is always sweltering inside from the buzzing heat lamps.

We keep mice by the tanks in small plastic tubs with holes punched in the top. The mice are alive, by the way. When my father was in charge we'd buy them frozen, which was only half as gory. But when my brother, Dale, (Reverend Creech now, which I'm still getting used to) took over the 'family business', he started breeding them himself to save money. He says the trick is not to name them.

Feeding the snakes is easy. Open lid of terrarium, drop in mouse, close the lid and repeat. On the day I got bit, I was thinking about other things – talking to myself or humming or something. I was distracted. Then I got to Clementine's tank and bang! She clamped down on my hand. Hard. Deep into the webbing by my thumb. It was as if she'd been waiting for me.

My hand was bleeding pretty fierce, but we keep a first-aid kit back in the church, along with a few vials of antivenin (although you better keep that to yourself:

most snake handlers don't like people to know they have antivenin on hand because, heck, we shouldn't need it if God's watching over the bite, right?). As it turned out, I didn't need it either. I don't know how much you know about snakes, but there's such a thing as a dry bite (when there's no venom released), which is the kind Clementine gave me. Dry bites hurt, yes-sir, but they won't kill you.

Now, this is where it gets a bit crazy, so stay with me. Clementine in her cage lashing out violently like that reminded me of you. It felt like a (excuse the highbrow word) metaphor. The bite represented what happened in Cubby's Bar and I suppose the webbing of skin between my thumb and forefinger represented the upside of Roger Albom's head. Clementine's tank represented your prison cell and her life represented your sentence. Heck, even her flat, broad face reminds me of yours (no offence, I think Clementine is a fox!).

All of a sudden I couldn't stand the thought of Clementine being locked up. So I bundled her up inside a hessian sack, took her outside and walked into the woods. I didn't want to release her too close to the church. When Dale noticed her missing he'd go out looking for her (and did, by the way, to no avail).

I took her deep into the forest and found a quiet place where the sun was pouring in through the sweetgums. I put the sack on the ground, pulled back the edges and took a step back. Sure, I could have taken her out of the sack myself, but I wanted it to be her choice.

She didn't seem to want to leave. She poked her head out of the sack a few times (can you imagine seeing a huge American forest after two years of living in a glass tank!) but snuck back into the sack each time.

I waited.

Nearly an hour later, when the sun was coming down and a chill was rising, when my mother would be looking out through the kitchen window and wondering why I wasn't home yet, Clementine made her move. She slid her front half out of the sack. She basked there a moment in the setting sun, and I could have sworn I saw her smile.

Then she was out of the sack and slithering away into the underbrush. She didn't turn to look back once. I watched after her a while then started back toward the church. It wasn't until then I realised I was crying. I'm crying as I retell the story here too.

Clementine's not an 'outdoor snake' but I bet she'll do alright for herself, and I have to tell you, Patrick, it felt pretty good to set something free for once. Clementine lashed out at the world that imprisoned her. How she lives her life on the outside is her choice, but I pray she goes forth with forgiveness in her heart. I pray the same for you, Patrick.
With love, B.

Compulsively, Travis flicked forward through the letters. Had his brother become a fundie? Would he start handling snakes and drinking poison or whatever the hell they did out there at the compound?

He plucked another letter from toward the bottom. It was dated February 1st 1989.

Dearest Patrick,
A quick note to tell you how excited/nervous/exhilarated/terrified I am about our 'special visit'. After all the hoops we've had to jump through for forty minutes alone, part of me assumed this day would never come.

I can't say I'm going to be an electric eel between the sheets, but I can tell you I'm ready, darling. And I can say my love for you is deep and true and raw and total. I'm ready for you to know me. All of me.
With love and anticipation, B.

There was one final letter, dated December 10th 1989.

You said it would get easier, Patrick. But it gets harder each day. Sometimes I pray my light will go out. Then I remember, you are my light. You are the light in my heart and the light at the end of the tunnel. But I don't know how much longer I can survive. Come home, Patrick. Come home and take me away from this place. Come home and rescue me from these people.
With love, all of it, B.

Travis checked and re-checked the letters, but found no answers to the many questions that were now thumping around inside his head. What exactly had happened between this letter and the last? Who did Becky Creech need rescuing from? What was the nature of this relationship?

An Eckles and a Creech? It was almost laughable.

The only other clue – if you could even call it that – was the title of a bible verse marked hastily in pen at the bottom of the final letter: Matthew 24:29-34.

He turned his attention back to Patrick's bedside bible, leafing back and forth through its pages until he found the verse in question. Again, a section of the text had been highlighted. Travis read it three times. It felt eerie, and troubling: *the sun will be darkened, and the moon will not give its light; the stars will fall and heaven will be shaken.*

MANSON, KENTUCKY

Now

I woke before dawn from a dream about a fruit tree casting a long shadow across a freshly cut lawn. While there was nothing in the dream to suggest this, I knew I was standing in Sammy Went's back yard. Birds were chirping somewhere in the distance, and for a moment, I felt safe.

Having hardly slept the night before, I was groggy and disorientated. After washing my bed sheets in the tub at three am, I had hung the *Do Not Disturb* sign on the door. Never had I meant those words more. I'd lain down on the stiff modern sofa, pulling myself into a tight, mortified ball. Sleep came and went sporadically. Each time I woke I checked the sofa, and each time I was relieved to find it dry.

I had actually wet the bed. Had I had too much to drink at dinner, or was this something deeper?

When I was thirteen I hid my first period from my mother: not because I was embarrassed or ashamed, although I'm sure that was part of it, but because I was worried it would make her sad. I didn't want her to think I was becoming a woman because I, myself, was afraid of becoming a woman. Now, I was afraid of becoming a child again.

I dressed and took a cup of coffee out onto my private balcony, where I sipped it slowly and took in the view of the woods. They were deep and vast.

While bodies of water made me feel calm, heavily wooded areas seemed to have the opposite effect. They were dark and full of monsters, powerful and wild, brutal and primal. They filled me with the sudden urge to … photograph them?

I had packed my dusty Canon SLR mostly on instinct, not expecting to use it. But I took it from my backpack now, flicked it on and framed up a snatch of wilderness. The mountain range was less ominous through the camera lens.

When Sammy disappeared, had Molly Went spent days, months, years, looking into the same forest I was capturing now, wondering if her little girl was out there? Of course, Sammy hadn't been half-buried in the woods, bloated and rotting with deep bruises around her neck where the *bad man* hurt her. Instead she had been spirited away to Australia, where she was nurtured, loved, fed, clothed, mentored and about a hundred other things.

It felt good to be taking pictures again. The Canon filtered my reality and, in a very small way, allowed me some control over it. I wondered if that was what had drawn me to photography in the first place. With my camera slung around my neck, I felt ready to take on Manson.

Keeping the water tower in view, I walked toward town, stopping here and there to take pictures. A long concrete channel running under the highway, carrying a wide stream of murky storm water. *Snap*. A dead crow by the side of the road. *Snap*. A motorbike with jacked buckhorn handlebars zooming past, its driver a heavy woman in her sixties. *Snap*.

Perhaps naively, I had half-expected to suffer flashbacks when I finally reached Manson; a certain tree or river or corner or hill might trigger a repressed memory, and I would suddenly be transported back to age two. But nothing about Manson was going to be that easy. There was no sudden rush of nostalgia or jarring realisation that, yes, this was where I was meant to be.

Perhaps those memories – only partially formed in the mind of a toddler – were simply too deep to access, and the thread Stuart had told me about could never be repaired. Sammy was there, red string tied around her waist, tugging and tugging from the dark and pulling the string back slack each time.

Or perhaps it was the town itself. Manson had clearly changed a lot in twenty-eight years. There was sadness in that. Time moved on, and I could keep up or fall behind, but I could never go back. The life I might have led as Sammy Went, born-and-bred Mansonite, simply didn't exist.

What did you expect to find here? I asked myself.

I spent the next hour aimlessly wandering the streets and taking pictures, starting at the busy town centre before circling outwards until the houses were further apart from one another and the lawns were wider.

I came upon Cromdale Street by accident. It would be nice to imagine that divine intervention led me there – that an invisible hand had nudged me in the right direction. More likely it was a coincidence. I recognised the street name from the articles I'd read about Sammy Went. I knew she was taken from a house on Cromdale, but I didn't know which one. Walking up and down the street, I willed a memory to form – or if not a memory, a feeling. I'd have settled for an *inkling*. But nothing came.

The house at number nine caught my attention, and on my third pass of the street I stopped out front and looked over the old wire fence. It was the only place on Cromdale that looked unchanged in thirty years. The ramshackle house was half-boarded up, set back from the street across a tangled and overgrown yard. The homes to either side were well kept and relatively modern, but number nine looked like a sombre time capsule.

I brushed mud and dirt from the mailbox, and found the name *Eckles*. I was about to take a photo when I spotted the old woman. She was sitting on the front step of the house, so still she had completely blended into her surroundings. Her skin was stiff and yellowing, like a mannequin that had been left out in the sun. She was staring at me. A chill ran down my spine. I lowered the Canon and kept moving.

After heading back into the town centre, I stopped for a second coffee and to flick through the pictures I'd taken so far. The coffee shop had just opened, and I had to wait for the manager to flick on all the lights before she came to the counter to serve me. When she did, she froze, blinked at me a couple of times behind a pair of large glasses, then smiled.

'Sorry,' she said. 'What can I get you?'

The menu loomed above me with an overwhelming number of options. 'Can I just have a black coffee?'

'Sure,' the woman said, stared at me for a couple more seconds, then set about making the coffee. She was large-framed and in her forties, with the hunched posture of someone who had spent their life fighting against their height. I wasn't quite as tall as her, but taller than average, so I knew a little bit about how she must have felt.

When she returned to the counter with my coffee, the big woman nudged her glasses into place with an index finger and said, 'I know who you are.'

'Oh?'

'I saw you on the news,' she said. 'But I remember you too, from the old days. From before. I was a friend of Emma's. How is she?'

'I don't know,' I said honestly, fastening a plastic lid over my coffee cup as fast as possible so I could get the hell out of there. 'How much do I owe you?'

'It's on the house,' she said. 'Welcome home, Sammy.'

Was I home? Was I Sammy?

Sipping my coffee, I walked back along the shoulder of the highway toward the hotel. It was still early so there wasn't much traffic about. My Canon swung left and right while I walked, feeling strangely heavier now.

I came to a dusty, old wooden sign that read *Gristmill & Visitor Center, ¼ Mile.* I'd taken this same route on my way into town, yet somehow hadn't noticed it before. Below it was an arrow pointing along an old dirt road curving off into the woods. Trees arched inward and over the entrance, nearly concealing the trail from view. What I could see was narrow and overgrown with knee-high grass.

For the life of me I couldn't tell you why I chose to enter the trail. Perhaps an invisible hand was guiding me after all.

The road opened a little as I got deeper, but an imposing wall of trees on either side dulled the sounds of the highway and made me feel closed-off from the world. The air was filled with the smell of damp earth and pine needles, and a light breeze whispering through the branches made me feel uneasy.

I like to consider myself an outdoors type. I'm no Bear Grylls, but I spent much of my youth hiking, swimming and exploring. But Australia seemed very far away right now. There we had the bush, which was as yellow as it was green. It may have been filled with dangerous creatures, but it was familiar. This place wasn't *the bush*; it was *the forest*. Forests were dangerous places from fairytales, where children were abandoned by their parents and captured by witches.

Dean was wrong when he said the past was like an ocean, I thought. *It's more like a dark forest filled with monsters.*

The further I moved through the trees the more consumed by them I felt; yet, I didn't turn back.

I came upon a grand, old suspension bridge. It was obviously built to support the weight of passing cars, but judging from the graffiti and unrepaired weather damage, that was a long time ago. The boards flexed and groaned as I crossed.

Across the bridge and twenty metres further down the trail, I arrived at …

Nothing.

If there had ever been a gristmill here it was long-gone now. In its place was a large rectangular area of stripped-up earth. The sounds of the forest quietened as I walked to its centre. The soil below my feet was black. Nothing had grown here for years. It felt as though ghosts were watching me.

This is a bad place, I thought, grabbing my camera and snapping a few shots. Dead earth. *Snap.* Fallen trees. *Snap.* An eerie light falling in through the branches overhead. *Snap.*

Something was different.

The sense of control I'd felt while photographing the mountains was gone. The filter had slipped away, and now my environment was just as ominous through the lens of the Canon as it was in reality.

I switched off the camera and walked briskly back toward the suspension bridge.

I came to take on Manson, I thought. *And Manson won.*

MANSON, KENTUCKY

Then

Emma held her head under the bathwater for as long as she could, trying to block the sounds of the world. The frosted bathroom window was turning white to grey as the sun came down. Another day was ending.

During daylight hours it wasn't too hard to imagine that Sammy was simply off playing – at the swing set in Atlas Park, maybe, or rummaging in the sand down by the lake. But when night fell, her absence grew more obvious. Kids her age weren't supposed to be outside after dark. They were supposed to be having baths, watching cartoons and being put to bed.

Emma rose from the water, dried herself and dressed in one of her mother's oversized terrycloth bathrobes, being sure to pull the straps tight – she had caught cousin Todd staring at her chest at least a dozen times since his arrival.

The Brides of Dracula were poring over old photo albums in the living room.

'Come and join us, Emma,' Tillie said. She was the youngest aunt. 'We're reminiscing.'

'Maybe later,' Emma said. 'Where is everyone?'

'Your brother is in the basement playing video games with Todd,' Pauline, the eldest aunt, said. 'Your mother is resting and your father is AWOL.'

'Dad isn't AWOL. He's out looking for Sammy.'

The aunts glanced at each other. They no doubt had their theories about why Jack had come home late with torn-up hands, but they didn't know the half of it. Their heads would collectively explode if they had any idea that Jack and Travis Eckles were …

What? Emma thought. *In love?*

As Emma left the room, Pauline called after her. 'Don't go clomping up them stairs, now. Let your mom rest.'

The master bedroom was still and empty, but Sammy's bedroom door was shut, a light creeping out from beneath. Emma knocked.

'What?' her mother said from behind the door.

'It's me, Mom. Can I come in?'

'Oh, of course.'

Sammy's bedroom was just as she had left it, only cleaner. The big toy chest bulged with stuffed animals in a sea of pastel pinks and purples. The framed family portraits seemed to hold greater significance now. Molly had taken one down from the wall and was turning it over and over in her hands.

'Sorry I snapped,' she said. 'I thought you were one of my sisters.'

'Were you sleeping?'

'Hiding, more like it.'

'Mind if I hide in here with you for a while?'

Molly smiled sadly. Her skin was blotchy and dry. She scooted over on the bed to make room for Emma.

'It smells like chemicals in here.'

'I did the carpets,' Molly said. 'I want everything to be perfect for when she comes home. I did the same when I was pregnant with you, you know? I cleaned the house from top to bottom.'

Emma looked at the photo in her mother's hands. Her father had taken it. It showed Molly and the kids roasting s'mores around the fireplace of a cottage in Cumberland Falls. Sammy was in Molly's arms, happily chewing on her fingers and looking away from the camera.

'Remember that trip?' Molly said. 'It was only this time last year, but it feels like a million years ago. We were all so happy.'

Emma remembered the trip well, but there was nothing happy about it. Sammy had been teething and cranky, which had made her mother unbearably tense. Moments before Jack had called her over to have her picture taken, Molly had been pacing, bobbing Sammy wildly in her arms and saying things like 'What do you want from me?' and 'I can't help you,' and 'Take her for me, Jack, she's driving me crazy.' The photo showed a moment, but not the story.

Was Molly remembering around the bad parts, Emma wondered, or blocking them out completely?

Molly traced Sammy's face in the picture and smiled. Her lips looked sickly and pale. 'Do you remember Matthew 19:14?'

'Remind me,' Emma said.

'Jesus said, *Let the little children come to me, and do not hinder them, for the kingdom of heaven belongs to such as these.*'

Molly pressed the photo against her chest.

'Is that where you think Sammy is?' Emma asked. 'In heaven?'

Her mother looked at her for a long time, but said nothing. Instead, she laid her head on Emma's lap and closed her eyes, and only flinched for a second when Emma began to stroke her hair. She wanted to tell her mother what she'd found out about Travis, but it would be a long time before she could find the words.

They remained still and quiet on the bed that way for the next hour. It was the longest they'd spent together since before Sammy was born. They might have stayed there for much longer, had Tillie not burst into the room.

'Molly, phone call for you,' she said, panting from her rush up the stairs. 'It's the sheriff. It sounds like news.'

Sheriff Ellis was standing in the dank brown lobby of the station. There were big circles of sweat under each of his arms, and dark rings below his eyes. Lately, everyone in Manson looked exhausted.

'Molly, Emma, hi. Thanks for coming in,' he said. 'Where's Jack?'

'I couldn't get a hold of him,' Molly said. 'What's this about, Sheriff?'

'Follow me.'

He led Emma and her mother into the conference room, a wide space with a coffee machine gurgling in one corner. A fluorescent strip light buzzed overhead. On a long table sat a cardboard box marked *EVIDENCE.*

'Take a seat,' Ellis said. He remained standing as Emma and Molly stuffed themselves into hard plastic chairs. 'As you know, we've been coordinating a line search of the woods. One of the volunteers found something. We'd like you to tell us if it belonged to Sammy.'

He opened the evidence box and took out a small plastic bag. Sealed inside, worn and muddy, was Sammy's stuffed gorilla. It took a moment for Emma to accept the reality of what she was seeing. Emma bought the toy for her sister on her first birthday, and Sammy had dragged it with her everywhere she went. It didn't make sense for it to exist in this space without Sammy.

A terrible and terribly childish thought rushed to the front of her mind: *Sammy is truly alone now.*

Emma expected her mother to burst into tears or, worse, fall on the floor and start praying. But she did neither. She picked up the bag and stared at the gorilla with a stony expression. 'This is filthy. I need to wash it. It's not safe for a child.'

'Mom.'

'Is it your daughter's?' Ellis asked.

'It's hers,' Emma said.

He reached for the gorilla. Molly's fingers clutched at it a moment before letting him take it. She followed the toy with her eyes until it was safely back in the evidence box. 'I'll see to it you get this back just as soon as possible, Molly. You have my word.'

'What does this mean?' Molly said. 'Is she out there, in the woods? Is Sammy out there?'

'There's more,' Ellis said. 'The toy was found not too far from the old gristmill. We searched it and found evidence of some sort of squat.'

'A squat?'

A foggy memory drifted into Emma's mind like a bad smell. It wasn't wholly formed yet, but it had something to do with the mill. Emma knew she had been there the day Sammy disappeared, but a combination of shock and psilocybin meant she couldn't remember much.

'We believe whoever took Sammy kept her out there overnight. Maybe for longer.'

'Why?'

'Well, we don't know. It's isolated. Private. They might have taken her there to keep her safe and quiet until they could work out a ransom demand.'

'You don't need to sugar coat it, Sheriff,' Molly said. 'If someone was going to call about a ransom they would have done it by now. If someone took her someplace isolated and quiet, it was for a very different reason.'

Emma flinched. So far she had been successful in blocking certain scenarios from her mind. Call it denial or blind hope, but Emma believed strongly that whoever had Sammy at that moment – *and someone did have her, she didn't wander off into the woods and get lost* – would be taking care of her. But that was childish and dumb and what happened that day at the mill with Shelley?

Magic mushrooms ... carpenter ants ...

'In any case,' Ellis said, clearing his throat uncomfortably. 'We're keeping this detail out of the media. We're hoping whoever stayed in the squat will return for their things so we can question them.'

'Whoever took Sammy is halfway across the country by now,' Molly said. 'Sammy's either with them, or she's—'

'Mom, stop.'

'Do you have *anything*?' Molly said. 'Any leads? Suspects? Anything at all?'

'We might have a suspect,' he said. 'One of the search divers spotted a suspicious-looking man over near Willow's Point.'

'What man?' Molly said.

Ellis went to a table in the corner, piled high with reports, files, photographs, notepads and Post-its. If a cluttered desk was a cluttered mind, then God help Sammy. Ellis found a police sketch and put it on the table before them. The illustrated face looked like a hundred people in Manson. He was neither thin nor fat; there were no disguising scars or tattoos; he had dark stubble or a light beard, and hollow black eyes.

Were those eyes the last thing my sister saw? She wondered.

'Who is it?' Molly said.

'We don't know, but we will. We sent a copy of this sketch to every police station and news outlet from here to Redwater. There's still hope, Molly. But there is something else.'

Molly raked her fingers through her hair and made a sound somewhere between a sigh and a whimper. 'What?'

'This is going to sound a little nutty,' Ellis said. 'But there's an urban legend surrounding the gristmill, I'm not sure you've heard it. If you write someone's name on a specific wall, the legend says, then that person will die within twenty-four hours.'

That foul smelling memory began to crystallise then, and all at once she knew exactly what Ellis was going to say. *A black marker moving across the wall. Writing a name. Writing* her *name. Shelley's scared, wide eyes. The figure in the window.*

'Someone wrote Sammy's name on the wall,' he said.

'What? *Sammy's* name?' Molly said. 'That's ridiculous.'

Ellis reached into the evidence box, took out a Polaroid photo and slid it across the table for them to see. It showed Sammy's name, just as Emma had written it on the dirty wall. She felt sick. What was wrong with her?

'It's an urban legend,' Emma said. 'It's not real. People who write those names don't *actually* want the person to die. It's dumb kids' stuff.'

'It's probably someone's idea of a sick joke,' Molly said. 'Written after Sammy went missing. Teenagers, probably.'

'I had the same thought,' Ellis said. 'But with the squat and Sammy's toy being found in the area, it's something we have to take seriously. Can you think of anyone who might have written this?'

'Sammy is two,' Molly said. 'She doesn't have that many enemies.'

'Do you recognise the handwriting?'

Molly took the Polaroid in her hand and studied it a moment, then shook her head. 'No.'

On the way back to the car Molly gnawed her fingernails. Emma had never seen her do that. They slid into the Taurus but Molly didn't start the engine. 'Just tell me why, Emma?'

'… What?'

'Tell me why, then we never have to discuss it again.'

'Mom, I don't—'

'You think I don't know my own daughter's handwriting?'

Emma suddenly felt very cold. 'It was supposed to be a joke.'

'Please don't lie to me, Emma. Not about this. Lie to me about anything else but not about this.'

'I was high,' she said. 'Shelley and I cut class the day Sammy went missing and ate magic mushrooms in the woods.'

'Jesus.' It had been years since Emma heard her mother take the Lord's name in vain.

'I was high; it was dumb. That's why I wrote it. I'm sorry.'

But that wasn't the whole truth, was it? When people got high they ate too much and watched stupid movies and said things like, *If you can drink a drink, why can't you food a food?* They didn't wish their sisters were never born, and they certainly didn't wish their sisters were dead.

'Are you going to tell the police?'

'No.'

'Are you going to tell Dad?'

'Tell me why I shouldn't.'

Emma started to cry. 'Because it would break his heart.'

'I don't understand why you're like this, Emma,' Molly said. 'What's your deal? What's *wrong* with you?'

'What's *your* deal, Mom? What's wrong with *you*?'

'This isn't about me.'

'But it is, and it has been for a long time. I don't know if you're depressed or going through a mid-life crisis, and I don't know when we all silently agreed to ignore it, but you've changed.'

'You've never respected my faith.'

'It's got nothing to do with the Light Within, Mom. It's Sammy. You changed when she was born. You went into labour as one person and came home from the hospital as someone else.'

Emma waited for her mother to fly into a rage, to start quoting scripture. She waited for a fight, but a fight didn't come. Instead, Molly started the engine, turned up the radio and drove them home without another word.

MANSON, KENTUCKY

Now

Stuart was eating breakfast in the hotel restaurant when I returned from my walk, feeling defeated. His eyes expanded when he saw me – having hardly slept the previous night, I must have looked terrible – but he chose not to comment, and I was thankful for it. Instead he hailed the waitress and ordered me some coffee.

'My grandmother called me last night,' he said, dispensing with such pleasantries as *Good morning* or *How did you sleep?* 'She wants to meet you.'

'Okay,' I said.

'Mom called last night too; late,' he said sheepishly. 'How would you feel about seeing her alone today?'

'You don't want to come?'

'She asked me not to be there when you two meet.'

'Why?'

He shrugged. 'She might have talked to Emma. We sort of had it out over the phone. The conversation began with her telling me I'm a control freak and ended with me telling her to go fuck herself.' He rubbed sleep from his eyes. 'Welcome to the family, I guess.'

The waitress arrived with my coffee and I avoided looking at her. It felt as though the entire hotel staff knew about the wet sheets hanging in my bathroom.

'Are you eating?' he asked.

'I'm not hungry. I'm not feeling great.'

I felt sick, actually. I was about to *meet my mother.* I was running different scenarios in my head: Scenario A involved a tearful reunion wherein Molly threw her arms around me and cried, 'My little girl has come home.' Scenario B saw Molly taking one look at me, deciding she was much better without me in her life and promptly slamming the door in my face.

'Was there a fruit tree in your yard growing up?' I asked. 'Right at the back of the yard, up against the fence. A lemon tree, maybe?'

He thought it over. 'Um, yeah, there was. God, I haven't thought about the lemon tree in years.' He smiled. 'Dad and I used to pee on it. He said it was good for the growth of the lemons. Do you remember it?'

'Just a weird dream I had last night. Remember what you told me about Decay theory back in Australia?'

He nodded.

'Is there any way of connecting back with those memories, do you think? Even after the thread is broken?'

'I don't know, Kim.'

The image of Sammy Went returned, alone in the nowhere place deep in my mind. She was curled up with her knees under her chin, sitting in a graveyard of dead memories: things that might have once been important to me and were now long forgotten. She tugged at the red thread around her waist, resigned to finding nothing at the other end.

Stuart wiped his mouth with a napkin even though he'd hardly touched his food. 'Hey, Kim, I feel like I need to warn you. Mom can be sort of … intense. She wasn't always, but over the years she's … She can be intimidating, is all, and …' The more he spoke the more he stumbled on his words, like a helpless puppy scratching at the door before a storm. I reached across the table and touched his hand – something completely out of character for me.

'What are you trying to say, Stuart?'

He exhaled with relief or resignation – I couldn't tell which. He then stiffened, bringing his hands up to the table and folding them neatly, once again the robotic, measured man I had met in Australia. 'I just don't want her to scare you off.'

He didn't want to lose me. He had found me once and didn't want to have to do it again.

A strange sort of deja vu snuck up on me. I'd had this conversation, or one like it, before, only not with Stuart. It was back at Amy's house, when we'd smoked a joint together.

You're not going to lose me, I wanted to tell Stuart, but it was suddenly very important that I tell Amy first. I stood up fast enough to make my head spin, but my nerves had temporarily subsided. 'Excuse me. I need to make a phone call.'

When I reached the elevators I turned back. Stuart was sitting at the table where I'd left him, staring at his plate. He looked as though he'd just seen a ghost, and once again I got the sense he was holding something back.

'... Kim?'

'Hi, Amy,' I said.

I was sitting at the edge of the stripped hotel bed, phone slapped hard against my face.

'We've been trying to call. Reporters have been calling us. Not just Aussie ones, Americans too. And the Federal Police have been in touch with about a million questions, and—'

'I leaned away from you,' I interrupted. 'I leaned away from you both. And I should have been leaning on you.'

'You're damn right you should have,' she said. She started to cry, so I started to cry. Not since my mother died had I spent so much time crying.

'Can you just forgive me and be my friend again?'

'... Fine,' she said.

Tears rolled down my cheek and I fought to keep them out of my voice. 'I need a favour.'

'Okay?'

'It's a big one,' I said. 'Amy, will you come out here, to the States? I know it's hard with Wayne and Lisa, but I just ... I don't think I can do this without you.'

She sniffed, no doubt trying to keep the tears from her voice too. 'We're already on our way to the airport, Kim.'

'What?'

'I'm in the car with Dad. We were coming whether you liked it or not.'

'I love you, Amy. And Dean.'

'We love you too.'

A sense of dread washed over me then, a sudden, abstract feeling that I might not ever see my family again.

I read an article about clairvoyance a long time ago. It suggested that when a tragedy occurs it can send ripples of energy back through space-time, like tossing a stone into a still body of water. The article suggested that some people could sense those ripples of energy long before the event took place. If I believed in those kinds of things I might be more worried. But I didn't, so I choked back the fear, said goodbye to Amy and went out to meet Stuart in the parking lot.

Molly Went lived in an apartment in a part of town called Old Point. On the car ride over, Stuart explained that she'd never wanted to leave the old house – the one Stuart grew up in, and that Sammy disappeared from – but his father had insisted.

'It was all part of letting go, I suppose,' Stuart said. 'And intellectually I agree with him. Whether you were dead or not, you were always going to haunt that place. But part of me never really forgave them for selling up.'

'Do you ever go back there?' I asked, remembering my walk down Cromdale Street.

'Sometimes. They've redone the driveway, extended the house, put up new trees and cut down old ones. For all intents and purposes the house doesn't really exist anymore.'

I wondered if part of him saw me the same way. Biologically I was his sister, but I had changed too. I had been renovated, perhaps beyond recognition.

'For a while after the sale went through, I had a recurring dream. Sammy would finally come home, but nobody would be there to greet her. The house was empty, cavernous. We'd all packed up and moved away.'

We drove in silence for a while.

Old Point consisted of one long, potholed road that ran beneath several sets of dangling traffic lights. There was hardly anyone around so the lights seemed redundant. We passed narrow shop fronts, old houses, and a junkyard behind a barbed-wire fence.

Stuart pulled up outside a cheap and charming apartment building with a grocery and liquor store on one side, and a Methodist church on the other. He pointed to a rickety balcony on the second floor. 'That's her place, see? The one with its own forest.'

The balcony was overflowing with potted plants, a set of noisy wind chimes and a wall-mounted statue of Christ. It was the balcony of someone who had downsized their home but not their possessions. A red balloon had got tangled up in the telephone wires nearby and was drifting back and forth in the breeze, like an anchored boat caught in a gentle current.

'She's in 2A,' he said. 'You'll see her name on the buzzer. M Hiller.'

'*Hiller?*'

'Her maiden name.'

'Oh. Right.'

There was so much I didn't know about this woman; the woman who gave birth to me, who held me and nursed me and loved me, presumably, for the first two years of my life.

'Want me to hang around?' Stuart asked. 'I can keep the car running. Just in case.'

He had intended it as a joke, but I didn't find it the least bit funny. 'I'll just meet you back at the hotel.'

'Well, good luck.'

Astonishingly, he leaned across and gave me a hug. It was stiff and awkwardly brief, but it was a hug nonetheless.

Waiting on the curb outside the apartment building, I watched until the car turned a corner and disappeared. Then I walked up the steps to meet my mother.

MANSON, KENTUCKY

Then

A little after midday, the sheriff's police cruiser thumped along the highway under screaming sirens. Ellis drove. Beecher sat beside him, eyes dancing on the road ahead. Nine minutes earlier Deputy Louis had radioed in with an update. The man from the sketch had returned to the gristmill.

'How you feeling, Beech?' Ellis asked.

'Fine. Good. A little nervous.'

'You remember how to use that thing?' He gestured to Beecher's sidearm.

'It's been a while since I took it out to the range,' he said. 'But I remember which end to point at the perp.'

God, let this be the end of it, Ellis thought. But even if it wasn't, it felt good to be out of the office and doing something real.

He killed the sirens, eased the cruiser onto the shoulder of the highway and came to a stop by a fading *Gristmill & Visitor Center, ¼ Mile* sign. The road was blocked in parts by fallen trees and flood damage. They'd have to walk the rest of the way on foot.

Ellis and Beecher climbed calmly and quickly from the cruiser, took up protective vests from the back seat and strapped them on. Beecher's was too big. His skinny arms dangled through the loops, and he looked younger than ever.

They walked briskly down the trail, but as they neared the mill they peeled off into the woods.

Deputies Herm and Louis were nestled in a hunting blind two hundred feet from the mill. Everyone had agreed it was a long shot that the man would return, especially after his sketch hit the news. But the way Ellis figured it, if he himself had left a load of potential evidence someplace and then saw his own face splashed across the television, he might just be scared enough to return to the scene of the crime.

Looks like I might have been right, Ellis thought.

'You two look like real cops,' Herm said when Ellis and Beecher reached the blind.

'Where are we at, boys?' Ellis asked.

'Our man hasn't moved, Sheriff,' Louis said, lowering a pair of binoculars.

'And he matches the sketch?'

'Caucasian, short-cropped dark hair, forties. Dressed in blue jeans and a military jacket. We didn't get a good look at his face, but he's in the mill as we speak.'

'The mill? Not the visitor centre?'

'Nope. If he's come back for his stuff, he's sure taking his sweet time.'

'Any chance he spotted you?' Beecher asked.

'Unlikely. We're under heavy camouflage and a long way out. We're also downwind, so none of these farts Louis keeps ripping should have given our position away.'

'It's not my fault,' Louis said. 'Diane's going through a spicy phase. It's s'posed to speed up your digestion.'

'It smells like something crawled up your ass and died,' Herm said.

'*Shhh*,' Ellis said as he took up Herm's binoculars and directed them through the woods. He adjusted the lens until the gristmill shot into focus, emerging from the landscape of trees and shrubs like an ancient temple. It, and the visitor centre beyond, were deathly still. 'Did you see the girl?'

'If we had, we would have led with that, Sheriff,' Herm said. 'What's the play here?'

'Beech, Herm, you're with me. We'll go in quietly. Louis, you hang back.'

'Oh, man, because of the farts?

'In case he gets past us,' Ellis said, handing him the binoculars. He unholstered his .45 and Beecher did the same.

Herm had brought a shotgun. He cocked a shell into the chamber and smiled. 'Lock 'n load.'

Ellis raised an eyebrow.

'Sorry, I've always wanted to say that.'

There was a nervous energy in the air. His men were excited – and who could blame them? They were doing the kind of thing you imagined before joining the force, creeping toward a dank and draughty building to catch a bona-fide bad guy. This was a manhunt.

Under different circumstances Ellis might have been excited himself – or nervous, or scared, or anything. But he wasn't. He was tired. That's all. His emotional bank was dry, and all he wanted was for this case to be over and done with. He longed to go back to paperwork, speed traps and the occasional small-time dope bust.

'We go in calm and careful,' Ellis said. 'If this guy does have Sammy, we'll need him to lead us to her.'

Louis spat. 'If that guy's leading us anywhere it's to that little girl's body.'

'We don't know that,' Ellis said. 'Discharging your firearm should be a last resort, understand?'

'Okay, Sheriff,' Beecher said.

'Having said that, don't take any chances, boys.'

Ellis started toward the mill, but Beecher called him back. 'Just a sec, Sheriff. This is gonna sound corny as hell, but do you mind if we do a little prayer first?'

Ellis couldn't help but smile. 'It certainly couldn't hurt, Beech.'

The four of them bowed their heads as Beecher prayed. 'Lord, we commit ourselves to your care on the mission that now awaits us. When we pass through the waters may you be with us, when we pass through the rivers may they not sweep over us, when we walk through the fire, may we not be burned …'

Ellis said a silent prayer of his own – not to God, but to Sammy Went, wherever she was. *Please don't let this old place be where any of us die,* he asked her. *Even though it might well be where you did.*

Predictably, Sammy didn't answer.

'Amen,' the men said.

A little before one pm, Sheriff Ellis and Deputies Beecher and Herm approached the gristmill. The front door hung loose from its hinges. Herm, biggest of the three, lifted and pushed it inward, then stepped back quickly to allow Ellis and Beecher to enter. At first all Ellis saw were shadows, but soon the jagged cross-section of wooden beams and steel posts drifted into focus.

The men moved slowly into the building, stepping over broken bottles and empty cans. There was no sign of their suspect, but it was practically guaranteed he heard them enter. Ellis had expected the man to run, giving his position away immediately. Instead he was hiding. That suggested he possessed a calm that scared Ellis proper.

As he moved deeper into the mill, Ellis turned to briefly glance at the name wall. In the low light he could see hundreds of names, but he only read one: *Sammy Went.*

They arrived at the bottom of the staircase. Ellis gestured for his deputies to continue searching the lower level. He was going to check upstairs. Beecher glanced at him with a nervous expression before moving deeper into the ground floor.

Ellis climbed the stairs. The light was dimmer on the second floor.

He checked behind a large old steel vat and found nothing but rat shit. He climbed onto a low catwalk. In the old days, mill staff would have used the catwalk to add corn to the machines. Now it was threatening to collapse at any second, like the stairs that had brought him up here.

Though the catwalk was only three feet from the floor, it gave him a good vantage point to look out over the mill. He saw nobody, but there were plenty of shadows to skulk in and corners to hide behind.

He continued on past a bank of smudged yellow windows and glanced briefly outside. Below him, and past a tangle of vines, he saw Deputy Louis holding his gun in both hands, eyes trained on the mill.

After completing a full circuit of the second floor he was satisfied the man was not up there. Had he managed to escape, or was he downstairs?

He was suddenly shaken by strong instinct to find and protect Beecher.

Ellis started back to the staircase. He made it halfway across the floor before noticing several boot prints on the dusty floor. He was pretty sure he hadn't walked this way. He unfastened his flashlight to examine them.

These are fresh, he thought. *Very—*

Footsteps pounded across the floor behind him. He turned in time to see the man thundering in his direction. It was too dark to see his face, and all Ellis had time to do before the man slammed against him was shout, 'Stop!'

Ellis flopped backwards and hit the floor, hard. He had

landed in something wet. He closed his hand around the handle of his .45, only to realise that it wasn't his sidearm at all. He had apparently holstered his gun when he reached for his flashlight.

That mistake might kill you, old man, he thought. The man was on top of him, hands clenched tightly around Ellis's throat. Ellis swung the flashlight toward his attacker who knocked it from his hands. It rolled away, flickering bright flashes against the underside of the catwalk.

'Leave us alone,' the man said through groans of effort. 'Why can't you just leave us—'

Ellis pushed against the man's face but he was too slow and too weak and too tired. He was going to die here. He was going to die in a puddle of piss with his .45 safely in its goddamn holster.

As he began to slip into unconsciousness – *or am I shuffling into death?* – the man leaned forward, and for a moment his eyes were caught in the dim light falling in through the dirty windows. Ellis didn't see evil in them. He didn't even see madness. He saw something he recognised: fear.

Then he didn't see much at all. Ellis's eyes rolled into the back of his head, and the sounds in the mill became distant. Now there was only his own wheezing gasps. The man's short grunts. Footfall up the hallway. Three shots.

Gunshots!

The man's grip loosened, and Ellis could breathe again. The body atop him fell limp and slumped to one side. Ellis lifted himself up onto his elbows and looked around, blinking, drawing in shallow breaths. Deputy Beecher stood at the top of the stairs. His pistol was still raised.

'You alright, boss?' Beecher said, his voice small and shaky.

Ellis could hardly hear over the ringing in his ears. He tried to answer, but the words got caught in his throat. He tried to stand, but his legs weren't yet ready to work.

Beecher walked up, slid an arm beneath Ellis's and hoisted him up. 'You hurt?'

'I don't know,' Ellis said. 'I–I don't think so.'

Beecher fetched Ellis's flashlight from beneath the catwalk and shone it over the man's face.

MANSON, KENTUCKY

Now

The apartment buzzers loomed before me. Never had I been more nervous about pressing a button. After briefly – and seriously – considering running away, I summoned some courage and buzzed Molly's apartment.

The flat, round speaker hissed with static, then Molly spoke. Her voice was light and cheery, once again subverting my expectations. She had neither the voice of a stranger nor one that was overly familiar. She spoke just three short words, sharp and confident: 'Come on up.'

There was a buzz, and the front door of the apartment building clicked open.

Down a narrow hall, up a dimly lit flight of stairs and out onto the second floor landing, I watched my feet one after the other, willing them to keep moving.

As I neared Molly's apartment door it opened, and a

big man stepped out. He was in his late sixties but looked powerful enough to rip a tree from the ground. He had a charming smile that lit up when he saw me.

'As I live and breathe,' he said, closing the door to Molly's apartment. 'Molly told me you were coming. I'm Dale Creech.'

He stuck his hand out and I shook it.

'Nice to meet you,' I said. 'I'm Kim.'

'I love that accent,' he said. 'How are you finding it all? I can't even imagine what it must be like to come back here after all these years.'

'Emotional rollercoaster does not even begin to describe it,' I said.

He glanced back at Molly's door. His smile faded and was replaced by a look of casual concern. 'I know we've only just met, but can I give you some friendly advice?'

'Okay.'

'Molly is having a tough time with all this. She struggles, and sometimes she might come off as … Give her a little time, is all I'm saying. Be patient with her.'

Creech was the second person to warn me about Molly today. It did nothing to help my nerves.

'Well it was lovely to meet you,' he said.

We shook hands again. He smiled and started toward the stairs. I waited until he was gone before finally knocking on Molly's door.

A weathered woman with a kind, sad face answered. Her hair was white-grey and pulled tight back from her face, which was a sprawling roadmap of deep wrinkles and worry lines.

Molly was in her early sixties – I had to do the calculations quickly in my head – but she looked much older than that. What shocked me most was her weight. Granted, the pictures I'd seen of Molly were close to thirty years old, but in each one she'd been slender – a little curvy perhaps, but a long way from overweight. But the woman who answered the door was enormous. If not for her face, and in particular her eyes, which I recognised from the photos, I might have thought I had the wrong apartment.

'Hello, Kim,' she said. Her voice was as light and pleasant as it had sounded through the intercom speaker. 'I'm Molly. It's a pleasure to meet you.'

She took my hand firmly and shook it. I hadn't expected her to pull me weeping into her arms the way Emma had, but hadn't this woman spent the last twenty-eight years searching for me? Mourning me? A handshake felt desperately formal.

'Come on in,' she said.

Her apartment was smaller than my place back in Australia, and filled with too much furniture: three sofas, two armchairs, a long dining table, cabinets and bookshelves. The floors were lined with overlapping rugs, each with a slightly different pattern, so that it felt like walking across a Magic Eye image. It reminded me of Georgia Evvie's place back in Australia. Come to think of it, Molly reminded me of Georgia too.

In contrast to the rest of the apartment the walls were stark and white, except for a small wooden crucifix.

'You have a lovely garden out there,' I said. From inside, the balcony looked even more like a jungle.

'Mmm, my pride and joy. Do you have a green thumb too?'

'No.' Remembering the rich colours of my childhood garden – the greens, reds, pinks and, most of all, the bright-purple deadnettles below my bedroom window – I almost added, *My mother, on the other hand, had about the greenest thumb you could imagine.* Luckily I held my tongue.

'How are you finding our little town?' Molly asked in her casual, just-making-conversation way.

'It's nice. Really American, if that makes sense.'

Molly's formal tone had put me on edge. The carpet might as well have been made of eggshells. For a long time neither of us spoke.

As I hadn't yet been invited to sit, I hovered, shifting awkwardly from one foot to the other. When a stovetop kettle whistled in the adjoining kitchen and Molly went to fetch it, I seized the opportunity and sat down on one of the three large sofas.

Molly returned with a pot of peppermint tea, which smelled strong and fresh. She poured us each a cup.

'I heard you met my daughter,' Molly said.

'Emma, yeah. She seems lovely.'

'Stu told me she could have carried herself better. Said she hurried off and called the media the first chance she got.'

'It's fine. I mean this whole thing is … Everyone reacts differently. My first reaction, after denial that is, was to keep it all to myself. Emma just went the other way. I have a little sister too, back home. If she got taken away from me … *God*, I have no idea what I'd do.'

'*Words testify to our devotion to God, and words are the truth of what we are.*'

'Pardon?'

'When you say His name in vain you dishonour Him.'

'Oh,' I said. 'I'm sorry. Old habit, I guess.'

She shrugged and sipped her tea. 'Have you talked to my ex-husband?'

'Stuart's been in touch, I think.'

Molly looked at me with a crooked, sly smile. 'Jack's a queer, you know.'

My muscles tightened the way they do when an older relative says something casually racist or homophobic. 'Actually, I didn't know that.'

'Just one more thing Stu has been keeping up his sleeve, I suppose.'

That Jack Went was gay was news to me, but what surprised me more was the contempt in Molly's voice. I wondered: was she angry as a scorned ex-wife, or was she offended because of her faith?

As if reading my thoughts, she continued, '*If there is a man who lies with a male as those lie with a woman, both of them have committed a detestable act. They shall surely be put to death.* Leviticus 20:13. I know that's not *politically correct*, but I take my cues from God, thank you very much.'

When I'd thought of Molly, I hadn't exactly envisioned the mother from *The Brady Bunch*, but I hadn't pictured the mother from *Carrie* either. An inconvenient truth was dawning on me: I didn't much like this woman.

She looked deep into her cup like a psychic reading tea-leaves. She might have been seeing the past in there, or she might have been seeing the future: neither impressed her. 'Listen, dear. I don't know if this is going to be good news or bad news for you. I don't know what you're looking for here, and I don't know what you left behind. But Sammy got put in the ground a long time ago, and you and the rest of us best let her rest down there.'

'I don't understand.'

'You're not my daughter.'

I said nothing.

'I'm ashamed to say Jack ain't the only sinner in the family,' she continued. 'I tried to guide my children toward the light, but Jack led them just as surely into darkness. Sammy's death forced them to make a choice: let God's light lift them above it all, or drown in the despair. Jack chose perversion, and you might have noticed Emma has a complicated relationship with alcohol. Now, Stu ain't a big drinker, and as far as I know he ain't no fag, but he's got just as much of the Devil in him.'

She leaned back and rested her tea on her considerable gut. Late-morning sunlight fell in over the balcony and cast long shadows against her face. She flashed me a smile. For a moment I was reminded of the witch from *Hansel and Gretel*. I could suddenly picture Molly Went née Hiller stirring an alchemic cauldron and sprinkling in some eye of newt.

'Stu lies,' she said. 'That's his sin. To others and to himself. He's a passionate man. Charming when he wants to be. Persuasive when he puts his mind to it, which is why I asked him to give us some time to talk alone today. He's caught you up in his web of bull-S-H-I-T and for that, I'm sorry.'

'Look, this is hard,' I said. 'At first, I had the exact same reaction, but … See, I …' My words became clunky, foreign shapes in my mouth. They tumbled out and meant mostly nothing. 'See the thing is …'

'Better to remain silent and be *thought* a fool, dear, than to speak out and remove all doubt.'

She flashed her witch smile once more.

I didn't very much like this woman at all. Abductor of children or not, Carol Leamy's heart was full of light and love. Molly's seemed full of darkness. But was it my disappearance that put the darkness there in the first place? Had I left an open wound to fester and become infected and turn into … this?

'Your son tested my DNA—'

'—My son wanted so desperately to believe his sister was still alive that he cooked the whole thing up.'

'I saw the test. The probability was 98.4 per cent. You're in denial, I get that, but—'

'—Oh, denial's nothing but a five-dollar word. I knew you weren't my daughter before you stepped through that door. You know how?'

Because Sammy Went got put in the ground a long time ago, I thought, but kept my mouth shut. I had become flushed with anger, and it was making me feel shaky. If I kept on talking I might burst into tears, and a woman like Molly would see that as weakness. I didn't want to give her that. I didn't want to give her anything.

'Do you know anything about snakes, dear?'

'Not much, no.'

'But you know they defecate, right?'

My lips tightened. 'Yes. Of course.'

'They defecate plenty,' she said. 'My faith brings me into contact with snakes, and their little turds too. The reverend of my church has us collect those snake turds up in plastic baggies. Can you guess why?'

'Almost certainly not.'

'People with rodent problems come to the reverend having tried everything: traps, poison, cats. He gifts them a baggie of snake turds to dole out anyplace they'd seen a mouse or rat, and *bam*. The rodents clear out. See, when a mouse gets one whiff of that unmistakable sweet, beefy odour of snake turd, they think there's a predator around and hightail it. The funny thing is, most mice ain't never even seen a snake before, but a voice deep inside tells them it's trouble.'

She was beginning to strike me as a crazy person.

'Now how do you think they know that?' she asked.

'Instincts,' I said.

Molly touched her nose. 'Instincts. The Lord stuck 'em in Adam, and Adam passed 'em on to us. Instincts are like a little piece of God you get to carry 'round with you. I know you're not my daughter for the same reason rats know to avoid the smell of snake turd. Get it?'

'Yeah, I get it.'

She grinned. 'Not such a fool after all then, are you, dear?'

MANSON, KENTUCKY

Then

On his way home from the grocery store, after heading south down Rennie Street, taking the left onto Barkley and the right onto Cromdale, Jack found himself outside the Eckles' house.

He watched the upstairs window for a long time, hoping to catch a glimpse of Travis. But it was empty. He saw himself putting the car into park, walking across the lawn and knocking on the front door. He saw Travis coming out to meet him on the porch, accepting his apology – *and you owe him one, Jackie Boy, you must know you owe him one* – and he saw things returning to normal. As normal as they had been before, at least.

But that was another reality. In this reality that boy would never forgive him, Molly would never love him, Buddy Burns was old and Sammy was gone.

Gone. The word bit into his mind with sharp teeth and refused to let go. *Missing, taken, abducted* and *kidnapped* at least gave a whiff of a happy ending. They were bad words, but they weren't final. *Gone* was ugly. *Gone* meant Sammy wasn't coming back.

The Brides of Dracula were talking in a huddle when Jack walked into the kitchen to put away the groceries. All three fell silent when he entered, giving him the distinct impression they'd been talking about him.

Go ahead and talk, Jack thought. *Gorge yourself on the rich, sloppy gossip you've found here. Gorge until you make yourself sick.*

Molly's sisters did more than love gossip: they consumed the stuff as if their lives depended on it. Back in Arlington, Virginia, a neighbour's brief affair or a friend's overdependence on pain medication might have been considered *solid goss*. Their sister becoming a Pentecostal snake handler must have kept them well-fed for months. But now they were playing in the big leagues.

He hated them, and it was easy to do. Each had a hand in bullying and belittling his wife over the years, fostering a fractured ego and creating a mind ripe for religious conversion. It was wrong to blame them for everything, but in this moment it felt right enough.

Pauline broke the silence. 'You've got more important things to worry about than getting groceries,' she said. 'Just put it on the list and Todd'll take care of it.'

Jack liked getting groceries. It was one damn task he could complete. 'Have you seen Molly?'

'She's out in the garden with Stu,' Tillie said. She was a nasty woman, but of the Brides of Dracula she was perhaps the most tolerable. 'You want a coffee? You look like you could use one.'

He shook his head.

'Meatloaf for dinner sound okay, Jack?' Anne asked. She was more softly spoken than her sisters but had the scorned, quiet rage of a middle child.

'I'm not hungry. But thanks.'

'I'll make a plate for you,' Anne said, glancing at her sisters.

Pauline's son, Todd, was sitting in the living room watching a rerun of *Roseanne*. Pauline had dragged him here from Virginia because she was too scared to get on a plane and too fussy to drive long-distance by herself. Jack felt sorry for the kid. He had hardly said three words since his arrival, and his bags were still packed in the upstairs guestroom, ready for a quick escape. And who could blame him? This was a bleak place, and there seemed to be nothing but dark days ahead.

Gone, Jack thought sadly.

He found Molly sitting on the low wooden bench in the back yard. She was watching Stu play in an old red sandbox that he hadn't touched since he was four or five. Stu seemed to be regressing. Jack feared he might start speaking in baby talk and wetting the bed again. It wasn't normal, but none of this was.

When – *if* – Sammy came home, there would be fractures to mend, but for now the Wents were treading water.

He joined Molly on the bench.

'Any news?'

'No,' she said. 'You?'

'Nothing.'

Stu was digging slowly and methodically in the corner of the sandbox, as if unearthing a dinosaur fossil. As Jack watched him, he thought about the stuffed toy in the woods, the unknown man spotted in the area, Sammy's name written on the gristmill wall: all questions without answers. The mystery of it all made him want to punch something.

'Your mother called,' Molly said. 'She reopened the store. She thinks you should fire your shop girl.'

'Debbie?' He smiled wanly. 'If she has to work for my mother too long she'll probably quit.'

'She said Travis Eckles came in to get a prescription filled. Said he was in bad shape. Black eyes, busted lip … You did that to him, didn't you, Jack?' She took his hand gently in hers. 'I heard the rumours about him too, but it's by resisting sin that we earn God's love.'

He said nothing. They were seated barely six inches apart, yet the space between them seemed insurmountable.

His wife deserved to know the truth, of course, and had deserved to know for a long time. But now was not the time. Besides, where would he even begin?

'Do you remember that Christmas Eve in, God, it must have been '75 or '76,' she said. 'Before Emma. We were staying overnight at my parents' place on that uncomfortable foldout sofa with the metal bar that ran down the middle. You remember that thing?'

'My back sure does.'

'My sisters had been driving me crazy, as usual, and they had me so … *worked up* that I couldn't sleep. I must have been tossing and turning because around two or three in the morning you woke up and asked me what was wrong. I started in bitching about Tillie or Pauline or Anne, or all three of them, and I said that I just wanted to get up and leave. Spend Christmas Day together. Just the two of us. You remember what you said?'

He smiled. 'I said, *okay*.'

Molly squeezed his hand. 'So we did. We crept around the house, packed up all our stuff and we just left without leaving a note. We drove halfway through the night and ended up getting a room at that filthy motel.'

'The Blue Dolphin Inn.'

'You remember the name?'

'I remember everything about those early days,' he said. 'The *us vs them* days.'

She looked at him sadly. Her expression reminded him of the knowing way Travis had looked at him on Friday night, seconds before Jack's fist connected with his face. It was starting to feel like the whole world knew something Jack didn't.

'We lost our way, didn't we?' she said. She put her head on Jack's shoulder and closed her eyes. The gesture disarmed him, and if he had let go, he might have cried. 'What the heck happened to us?'

You found the Church, and I found Travis, he thought. *We were both awakened by those discoveries.*

'Molly, I need to tell you something ...' Jack started.

'Where's Stu?' She swung her head up from his shoulder and jumped off the bench. 'Stu's gone. Stu! Stu!'

The sandbox was empty aside from a small plastic shovel and a mound of sand.

'I closed my eyes for thirty seconds, I—Stu! STU!'

'Molly, relax. He must be—'

But she was already running headlong toward the sandbox, her bare feet slapping hard against the concrete path that led into the yard. 'STU!'

Their boy emerged seconds later from behind the big lemon tree that kept watch over the garden. He was zipping up his fly. 'I'm right here, Mommy.'

She dropped to her knees and grabbed him by the shoulders. 'Where did you go? Why were you hiding? Don't you do that, Stu. Don't you hide from me! You hear?'

'I was just peeing on the lemon tree,' he said. 'It makes the lemons grow faster, right, Dad?'

Stu giggled, and for a moment Jack worried that Molly might strike him. Instead she drew him into her arms.

'Don't you do that to Mommy. You scared me.'

'Sorry.' He was crying now too.

'Hush now,' she said. 'Hush.'

Jack watched his wife cradle their son beneath the lemon tree for a long time, until the doorbell rang. He went inside and looked down the hall. Sheriff Ellis was standing in the front doorway. The Brides of Dracula were consuming him.

Jack sat Ellis down on the armchair by the window and closed off the living-room doors. Molly sat with Emma on the sofa across from him. Before they could start, Tillie came in with four glasses of iced tea, hovered, and then reluctantly slunk out the door.

'What is it, Sheriff?' Molly asked. 'Is there news?'

He cleared his throat and glanced at Emma, who had turned pale. 'This might be a bit sensitive for young ears.'

'She can stay,' Jack said. Then, to Emma, 'If you want.'

Emma nodded. Jack sat next to his daughter and put his arm around her.

'There was an incident today,' Ellis said after a sip of iced tea. 'I wanted you to hear it from me first. The man in the sketch we put out, our person of interest – he came back to the gristmill. My deputies were keeping a close watch on the place.'

'Was Sammy with him?' Molly asked, sitting forward urgently.

Ellis shook his head. 'I'm afraid not. We approached him and there was an … altercation.'

'Altercation?'

'He attacked me,' Ellis said. 'If you noticed I was walking with a limp when I came in, that's because he got in a few good ones before we could … subdue him.'

'What's he saying? Is it him? Did he take Sammy?'

'We didn't get a chance to question him,' Ellis said, eyes moving between Emma, Molly, Jack and his own feet. 'He was shot and killed during the altercation.'

Molly gasped.

'Well, who is he?' Jack said, standing, pacing. 'Maybe he left Sammy with a friend or family member.' His belly churned with anger. If this mystery man was the one who took Sammy, the chances of finding her were blown away when he was. It would be easy to project his rage onto Ellis, to accuse him of fucking up the investigation. It would feel good. But it wouldn't be fair. The old man in the faded brown uniform was doing the best he could. Nobody in Manson had been prepared for what happened.

'We're trying to confirm his identity as we speak,' Ellis said. 'Since the sketch ran on TV we've been getting a lot of tips. One came from a psych nurse in Redwater. She believes the man could be one of her outpatients. An ex-veteran named John Regler.'

'*Believes*?' Jack said. 'Is it him or not?'

'We contacted the army barracks and we're expecting a fax in the morning containing Welt's photo and record. My gut tells me it's him. The nurse had been eager to get a hold of Welt because he missed his last appointment and she's worried about him. He's pretty messed up by the sound of it.'

'Messed up?'

'Something called *post-traumatic stress disorder.* He's also schizophrenic.'

'Jesus,' Jack said.

Emma burst into tears. Jack and Molly went to her.

'Is it because of the name?' she said between sobbing gasps. 'Did he read Sammy's name on the gristmill wall? Is that why he did this? If he was crazy maybe he read it and—'

'Of course not,' Molly said, shooting Emma a tight, unreadable look.

'No,' Ellis said. 'In fact, if he really was John Regler, we have reason to believe he had nothing to do with Sammy's disappearance.'

'What?' Jack had emotional whiplash.

'We're double-checking his hospital records, but we believe John Regler attended a support group on April 3rd, the same day Sammy disappeared.'

Emma heaved with relief and fell into Jack's arms. He held her tight.

'I'm sorry it's not better news,' Ellis said, setting his half-finished glass of iced tea on the coffee table and climbing to his feet. Jack hadn't noticed the limp when Ellis first came in, but he noticed it now. 'Jack, would you mind walking me out?'

'We need to talk about Travis Eckles,' Ellis said when they had reached his cruiser, far enough from the house that not even the Brides of Dracula could hear.

A cocktail of anger, fear and shame rushed up Jack's spine. Had Travis talked to Ellis after all? How much had he said?

'He was mugged on Friday night in the parking lot outside Cubby's Bar, by three masked, ethnically ambiguous men.'

Jack said nothing.

'A mugging in Manson. Do you believe that?'

'This town is changing,' Jack said.

'But here's another thing: a man named Joe Holt made a report to Coleman police about a fight he witnessed in that very same parking lot, on that very same night. He said, and this is a direct quote, "The fella with the missing kid beat the hell outta the kid who took her."'

'I have no idea what he's talking about, Sheriff.'

'Listen, Jack, I'm happy to go along with whatever reason you give about how you tore your hands up. Travis hasn't raised any formal charges, and Joe Holt had a bellyfull of bourbon that night. All I ask is that you share.'

'Share what?'

'Tell me what you know. You're a smart guy. One of the smartest I know. I find it hard to believe you'd beat down a kid based on rumours, which, as far as I know, are the only things tying Travis to Sammy's disappearance. So what do you know that I don't?'

'Like I said, I have no idea what that man is talking about.'

Ellis looked hurt, and for a moment Jack felt deeply sorry for him. 'Okay, Jack.'

Shaken and desperate, Jack went into his bedroom and shut the door behind him. Molly's handbag was slung over the edge of her side table. Jack grabbed it, turned it upside down and emptied the contents out onto the bed. A purse, loose change, a sanitary napkin, a pocket-size bible, and …

Bingo, he thought when he spotted her address book. He flipped it open, leafed through to the B section and found Buddy Burns's number. He picked up the phone by the bed and dialled.

On the second ring, the voice of a young girl answered. 'Burns' residence.'

'Hello. Is your Dad home?'

'Yes, sir. May I ask who's calling?' she asked, her voice deliberately sweet. He pictured a Pentecostal cliché: a pretty young thing in a long-sleeved sweater and skirt running nearly to the floor, her hair in tight braids, her fingernails nice and clean.

'It's Jack Went.'

She gasped. 'You're Molly's husband.'

'That's right,' he said. 'You know Molly?'

'Yes, sir. From church. Has Sammy come home yet?'

That stung. 'No. Not yet.'

'We've all been praying for her, praying she'll come home quick smart; praying this whole thing ain't punishment handed down by the Lord praise his name.'

'Punishment? For what?'

'For Molly sharing her bed with a non-believer.'

This poor girl doesn't stand a chance, Jack thought sadly. He wanted to school her – actually, he wanted to reach through the telephone and slap her across the face – but instead he said, 'Why don't you run along and get your dad for me now?'

She did. The line can't have been quiet for more than thirty seconds, but in that silence Jack went to a dark place. What if that little girl was right? What if God – the God he'd been raised under and genuinely believed in until he was a teenager – was punishing him? Not just because Jack had lost his faith, but because of what he had done with Travis Eckles and with Buddy Burns, and with a handful of anonymous men from Coleman to Harlan County.

Hadn't God slaughtered Egyptian firstborns because their king was stubborn? Didn't he kill David's baby to punish him for his adultery with Bathsheba? Hadn't he sent bears to maul the children who made fun of the prophet Elisha?

Nahum 1:3, Jack thought. *The Lord is slow to anger but great in power; the Lord will not leave the guilty unpunished. His way is in the whirlwind and the storm, and clouds are the dust of his feet.*

Buddy came on the line. 'Jack?'

'Hi, Buddy. Sorry for calling out of the blue like this.'

'No, no, it's fine. It's good to hear from you. Any news on Sammy?'

'No news yet,' he said. 'But listen, Buddy, the other day when you came by the house, you started to tell me something. Do you remember?'

Buddy fell silent, and now Jack conjured a vision of him standing in place of his daughter, perhaps turning his fedora over in his hands, perhaps blinking nervously the way he would right before they'd kiss – but instead of Buddy *now* he imagined Buddy *then*. He had been lean, once, with high cheekbones and strong, protective shoulders. He hadn't been handsome, but he had been good-looking; soft and masculine at the same time.

'Yeah, Jack, I remember.'

'What was it you wanted to tell me? I got the sense that it might have been important. I also got the sense you didn't want to say anything in front of my mother.'

He took a deep breath and told his daughter, who was presumably lingering close by, 'Hey, sweetie, go on upstairs to your bedroom for a minute okay? … Don't look at me like that. Go on, now … You still there, Jack?'

'I'm here.'

'I'd prefer not to go into it over the phone.'

'Could you meet me?'

'I don't know, Jack.'

'Please.'

'… Where?'

'Our old place?'

Buddy paused, perhaps startled by a rush of memories. Jack wondered if those memories disgusted Buddy or turned him on.

'I can be there in an hour,' he said finally.

It was dusk when Buddy pulled his Ford Bronco into the lot by the lake. Jack's was the only other car there, yet Buddy parked at the far end, thirty feet away. Jack watched him climb down from the driver's seat and waddle over, fixing that goddamn fedora on his head. Buddy took a packet of cigarettes from his pocket and lit one.

'For the record, I gave these up a decade and change ago,' he said. 'But on the way here, I found myself pulling into the Gas & Go to pick up a fresh pack.'

'Thanks for meeting me, Buddy.'

Buddy inhaled deeply and looked over the lake.

They walked to a low stone wall and sat down beside each other, their backs to the lake. A cold breeze came off the water, carrying the faint smell of fish and garbage. This was the same parking lot where Jack had been meeting Travis to make love; the same parking lot where Jack had asked Buddy to leave with him all those years ago.

'The last time we were here you made me choose,' Buddy said. His tone was grave and nostalgic, as if they were standing on a train platform saying goodbye forever. 'You made me choose between the Church and, well … you.'

'That's not how I remember it, Buddy.'

'It's how it happened, Jack.' His voice cracked and for a moment the old Buddy Burns, the man Jack once loved, spilled out.

'We can get out together,' Jack had said. *'We can drive south and start from scratch, worship in our own way.'*

Before walking the six miles back to town alone that night, Jack had looked out over the lake and thought about swimming to the middle and sinking under.

'It wasn't meant as an ultimatum,' Jack said.

'But you know that's what it was. We both did. What we were doing … What we did …'

'What about it?'

'It was against His will.'

The Lord will not leave the guilty unpunished, Jack thought. 'I don't want to argue with you, Buddy. I don't have any fight left in me.'

'My point is, I chose the Light Within, and for better or

worse I stand by that decision. But me coming out here, telling you what I'm about to tell you … it could bring everything down. Everything my life is built around.'

'What are you talking about, Buddy?'

'I'm choosing *you* this time.' He dragged deeply on his cigarette, stubbed it out on the wall and dropped the butt in his breast pocket. 'There are dark days ahead, mark my words.'

'It's about Sammy, isn't it?' Jack felt hot and impatient. The longer Buddy drew this out, the more anxious Jack became. His bowels gurgled with nerves.

'It happened after the last healing service,' Buddy started. 'I know it's been a while since your last service, but I'm sure you remember what those healing sessions are like.'

'Jumping,' Jack said.

The Light Within held these so-called healing services four times a year. Worshippers gathered in great numbers to pray for a cure to this or that – cancer, emphysema, multiple sclerosis, dementia, depression, you name it. The Reverend, Roy Creech in Jack's day, would strut up and down the aisles calling on God to instruct him who to heal. He might carry a handful of rattlesnakes, speak in tongues, or place a hand on a truebeliever's forehead and order the Devil out.

Oftentimes, the placebo effect was strong enough to drive a Parkinson's sufferer from their wheelchair, or for someone near-blinded with cataracts to proclaim they could once again see. The placebo effect was no good for cancer though. Or inborn blood diseases or genetic abnormalities. In those cases, it was God's will that the sick remain as they were.

'The line of people looking to be healed went all the way out the back door and into the parking lot,' Buddy said. 'Your Molly was one of them.'

'Molly? When was this?'

'A few months back. Late March, I think.'

'She was sick? I don't understand.' He wouldn't put it past Molly to ask God for help with her health instead of her husband – who just happened to be a damn good druggist – but aside from a cold here and there, he couldn't remember her being sick.

'Creech called on a few people first,' Buddy continued. 'Sherman Harcourt with the diabetes, Helen Mitchel with her son in San Francisco addicted to heroin. Then he called on Molly.'

'What did she say was wrong with her?' Jack asked. 'I know she suffered a migraine or two over Christmas but—'

'This wasn't no migraine.'

A strange sense came over Jack then. He wanted Buddy to hurry up and get to the point of the story, but he also wanted him to close his mouth and tell him nothing. A nagging intuition told him he might be better off not knowing.

Buddy dragged on his cigarette, holding it with trembling hands. The sun had sunk on the horizon, and his features were darkening. 'Reverend Creech asked your wife what she needed God's help to heal. She told him the Devil was in her.'

'Why would she think that?'

'She could feel his influence, Jack. She could feel him tugging on her, whispering in her ear. She said the Devil must be in her, 'cause how else could she explain how she felt about her little girl?'

'Sammy? She was talking about Sammy?'

Buddy nodded. 'Molly felt nothing for her, Jack. I'm sorry to have to tell you that, but she stood in front of Creech and the Church and God himself, and said as much.'

Now that Buddy mentioned it, Jack had noticed a change in Molly around the time Sammy was born. But hadn't it started to go bad before then?

'She was ashamed,' Buddy said. 'So ashamed. She fell right to her knees and begged Creech to help her, begged for an exorcism right there and then. She desperately wanted to love that little girl. Let me be clear about that, Jack. She might not have been able to, but she *wanted*—'

'Jesus Christ,' Jack said, and Buddy flinched. 'The Devil has nothing to do with it. Why didn't she see a doctor? Why didn't she talk to me?'

Then he remembered sitting beside Molly's hospital bed, holding a newborn Sammy in his arms. Molly was telling him … *what?* Something about not feeling right, about this time being different from when Emma and Stu were born … about … *She did tell you*, he thought. *At least she tried to. And what did you do? You hushed her and told her it was probably just the damn pethidine.*

'What did Creech tell her?' Jack asked, conjuring an image of the man placing a bible on his wife's head and calling on Christ to drive the Devil away.

'Nothing, then,' Buddy said. 'He moved past her and went

on to Dolly Base and her arthritis. But afterwards, when the service was done and a few of us had stayed back to help sweep up, I heard them talking.'

He fell quiet. He took the fedora from his head and turned it over in his hands. Jack wanted to toss that damn hat into the lake.

'What were they talking about?'

'If anyone knew I was here telling you this—'

'Oh, for Christ's sake, Buddy.'

'They'd turn against me, mark my words.'

'What did Creech say?' Jack's nerves were shot now, replaced with hot rage – the sort that had consumed him that night outside Cubby's.

'He said the Devil wasn't in her …' Buddy said.

'Well, that's good, isn't it?'

'You didn't let me finish. Creech told Molly what she thought was Satan whispering in her ears, was in fact her instincts.'

'Instincts? I don't understand.'

'He said the Devil wasn't in *Molly*, but it might well be in her little girl.'

MANSON, KENTUCKY

Now

I stepped out of Molly's apartment and started walking in the direction of my hotel, head down, my mind like an overflowing glass of water. Since meeting Stuart in Australia, since confronting Dean about my mother, since Emma, since Manson, more and more water had been poured into the glass, and I hadn't yet had a chance to empty it. Now that I'd met Molly, the glass seemed ready to shatter.

I was barely five metres from Molly's building when an approaching car sounded its horn and slowed down. The driver-side window rolled down, revealing a grinning man. He was somewhere in his late forties, with a thick red beard and a colourful shirt. He rolled to a stop. 'Afternoon, ma'am.'

'Hello.'

'You're Kimberly Leamy, aren't you?'

'Kim,' I said cautiously.

'I'm Detective Mark Burkhart.' He found his badge and produced it for me. 'Can I offer you a coffee, Kim?'

'How did you know where to find me?'

'Well, ma'am, I'm a cop, and Manson ain't exactly New York.'

I couldn't see that I had much of a choice, so I climbed into his cruiser and as we drove across town, he asked, 'Have you had a chance to come up for air yet?'

'A few times,' I said. *But each time I get dragged back under*, I thought.

'We used to climb that thing as kids,' he said, gesturing to the looming water tower. 'We weren't supposed to, but half the fun was waiting for the sun to go down and keeping one eye out for the cops. Of course, in those days we didn't have these ugly things to contend with.' He pointed to four wide barbed-wire fences blocking each leg of the tower. 'They added the safety guards in '86, when Daryl Wixey fell backwards off the ladder from about halfway up. Broke his back in two places. Probably would have died if he didn't fall right – and he only fell right because he'd had a skinful of vodka.'

Burkhart rolled down Main Street and pulled in to the police station parking lot. 'Daryl falling off the water tower and nearly dying was about the biggest thing to happen in Manson when I was growing up. That is, until the disappearance of Sammy Went.'

The coffee at the Manson Sheriff's Department was shockingly delicious. I'd been expecting something black and stale from a filtered pot, but Burkhart brewed up two cappuccinos from a giant silver beast of a coffee machine, complete with steamed milk.

We sat in the station's break room, my back to a line of vending machines, Burkhart's to a noticeboard filled, not with *Wanted* posters as you might expect, but with fast-food brochures, a *Game of Thrones* calendar and a motivational poster with *Don't do something permanently stupid when you are temporarily upset* printed in different shades of red and blue.

Burkhart took a small voice recorder from his breast pocket and placed it on the table between us. 'You mind?'

'It's fine.'

He pressed a red button and the recorder chirped once. 'Ready when you are.'

So I started from the beginning. I told the detective and his voice recorder about Carol Leamy, about Dean, about my sister, about my childhood. There were no hidden clues or secrets for Burkhart to glean, but that didn't seem to bother him. He watched me silently, patiently, only speaking to urge me on or send away a deputy looking for a snack.

Talking about my Australian family made me long for my mother. I couldn't wait to see Amy and Dean, of course, but what I really wanted was five more minutes with Carol Leamy. My memories of her were being coloured more and more every day. When she took me Christmas shopping as a child, did she spend the whole time looking over her shoulder? When we took daytrips to the beach, was she watching out for police? When she dyed her hair blonde, was it vanity or was it a disguise?

When I reached the end of my story, I asked, 'What now?'

'I'll take statements from Jack Went, Stuart, Emma, Molly, everyone. Your sister and stepfather too. We'll coordinate with Australian police for that.'

'You might not have to. They're coming here.'

'Even better,' Burkhart said. 'Our goal will be to create a timeline of events starting with your disappearance. We'll want to do our own DNA test too, I'm sure you'll understand.'

'Of course.'

'We'll get some pictures of Carol Leamy on the local news, see if anyone recognises her from the good ol' days ...' He leaned back in his chair and stroked his beard. 'What was she like?'

'She wasn't the kidnapping type, if that's what you're asking.'

'So, what, you think she mighta had help?'

I said nothing.

The hum of the vending machines filled the small break room, and for a moment I was transported back to my apartment in Australia, to the hum of my refrigerator, the buzz of my laptop charger on the desk in the corner. Home seemed a long way away and a long time ago, and I wondered if I'd ever get back there. It was an odd, abstract feeling, similar to the one I'd experienced when I last talked to Amy. It was something more than a bad feeling – more like a premonition.

'Come on,' Burkhart said. 'Every man and his dog has a theory. You must have one too.'

'Have you ever heard of the Hicks babies?' I asked.

Burkhart shook his head.

'Back in the sixties – in Ohio, I think – there was this Dr Hicks guy. He would take babies from poor mothers and sell them to couples who, for some reason or another, couldn't have kids of their own. He even forged fake birth certificates.'

'A baby black market,' he said, disbelieving. 'So your theory is that the kidnapper sold you to Carol Leamy, who raised you in Australia.'

I shrugged my shoulders.

'Well I suppose that's as good a theory as any,' he said.

It was also the only theory I could think of that might redeem Carol, at least a little. Buying an unwanted child was a lot more forgivable than stealing one that was loved.

'How about you?' I asked Burkhart. 'You said every man and his dog has a theory about what happened that day. What's yours?'

Frowning, he drummed his fingers lightly on the table. 'Mine's a work in progress.'

'Do you remember much about when it happened?'

'Oh yeah,' he said. 'I live over in Coleman now, but I grew up right here in Manson. I was seventeen when Sammy went missing. Still living in Old Commons with Ma and Pa Burkhart. Everyone *had* a suspect and everyone *was* one.'

'Like who?'

'Well, Molly for one. Jack too, probably. Everyone looks at the parents in cases like this. Travis Eckles, who came from a rough family and lived close by. Dale Creech, Reverend of the Light Within.'

'Dale Creech? I just met him. He seemed … nice.'

Burkhart laughed. 'Nice and weird. I mean, all fundies are. You have to be at least a little weird to play with venomous snakes and expect God to protect you, right?'

I thought about Molly.

'It was just a rumour. One of many. People are quick to assume all priests take a special interest in little kids.' He finished his coffee, stood up, and slid some change into one of the vending machines. 'You want anything?'

'No thanks,' I said. 'Did the police ever question Creech?'

'They questioned everyone in town, basically. I've been going through all the old reports. Creech had an alibi backed up by a dozen members of his church. Not that that says much. The Light Withiners were tighter than a duck's asshole – excuse the language.'

He entered a code, retrieved a chocolate bar from the machine and returned to the table. He opened the chocolate wrapper with slow and dedicated precision, as if performing an autopsy. 'Now, where were we?'

'Dale Creech?' said Stuart.

We were twenty miles outside of Manson, driving down a narrow, unsealed road through a dense forest to visit Stuart's grandmother. Sandy Went lived, he had explained, in the middle of assfuck nowhere.

'Did you know him well?' I had to speak loudly to be heard over the bumpy road.

'Mom did,' Stuart said. 'I spent some time investigating the reverend. He's creepy, sure, but he had a tight alibi and no motive.'

'Would anyone from the Church talk to us about him?'

'I doubt it. The Light Within are—'

'Tighter than a duck's asshole?'

He laughed. 'I was going to say they were a close-knit community, but duck's asshole works just as well. If any of them knew anything they'd likely keep it to themselves. Nobody goes against the Church, lest they be shunned.'

'What about your grandmother?'

Stuart only shrugged.

'What's she like?'

'She's nothing like Mom,' he said. 'If that's what you're worried about.'

'Molly wasn't *that* bad,' I lied.

'Yes, she was. Mom's broken. She should have got out of this town like the rest of us did, but instead she sat and stewed in everything. Guilt. Sadness. Accusations. But she'll come around; just give her time.'

It wasn't as easy as that. I'd lost a mother then discovered I had another one. Deep down I think I'd hoped Molly would fill the void Carol left in my life – that I might find a *mom* to replace my *mum*. Now the whole thing seemed terribly unfair.

Sandy Went lived in a large old farmhouse at the end of a long driveway. Stuart parked the car nose-out (his standard getaway position), and we started toward the front door. He had warned me his grandmother didn't see so well anymore, and if I wanted to be heard I'd have to speak up real loud, but at ninety-one, he said, Sandy's mind was still as sharp as ever.

A slim woman came out to meet us. She studied me with narrow, suspicious eyes and said, 'Well, you look like a Went, that's for sure.'

Stuart laughed. 'This is Kali, Gran's nurse and resident ballbreaker.'

They hugged, and she planted a kiss on both of his cheeks. Then she turned to me. 'You want tea, coffee, bourbon?'

'No thanks,' I said.

Kali showed us into the house and busily waved us down the hall. It was cavernous and spotless. 'Sandy's right through there, out on the back porch.'

We went out the back door onto a deck that looked over an expansive garden. A slight elderly woman sat silently in an old porch swing. Pale-grey cataracts covered both her pupils. She must have heard us shuffling toward her, because she cocked her head at a curious angle. 'Stu?'

'Hi, Gran,' he said.

She reached out and found his hand. 'It's been too long, boy. Is she here?'

'Gran, this is Kim,' he said, waving me closer.

Sandy reached out for my hand, and when I gave it she squeezed it and pulled me down next to her. 'An absolute pleasure, Kim. Tell me, how's my garden looking? My eyes are about as useful as tits on a bull nowadays.'

'Oh. It's nice. Really pretty.'

'No offence, darling, but I'm gonna need a little more than *nice* and *pretty*.'

Looking out over the garden, I paused to take in the scene. 'Well, the deadnettles look sort of saggy, but not in a sad way. They're wet, covered with little drops of dew. They seem happy.'

Sandy Went smiled and lifted her chin. Her hair was tied back into a loose ponytail. Her face was creased with wrinkles. She sniffed the air. 'How about the coral bells?'

'Which ones are they?'

'At this time of year they should have dainty little pink flowers, most likely lining the slope at the rear of the garden.'

She pointed to the exact right place, where dazzling pink flowers had been tightly packed in a planter made from recycled wood.

'Oh yeah,' I said. 'They look like they're in full bloom, and there's a little black-and-brown bird digging around back there, looking for worms.'

Grinning now, she reached out and found my hand again. She pressed it once more, but this time didn't let go. We sat together on the porch swing in silence a moment, holding hands and listening to a gentle breeze move across the garden, stirring the coral bells and sending the black-and-brown bird skyward.

Stuart leaned against the porch rails and watched us with a hint of a smile.

'Stuart told me you went to visit Molly.'

'Yes,' I said.

'She didn't exactly welcome you with open arms, I'm guessing.'

'No. Not exactly. She doesn't believe I'm ... She believes her daughter died a long time ago.'

'Well, in her defence, we all did. It was easier to assume Sammy's light went out. That might make me sound like a horribly dark woman, but it's the truth. I used to pray she was dead, I'm ashamed to say. Because if she was dead, her suffering was over. She was with God and that was a lot better than being held in a basement dungeon someplace, or being tortured or forced into unspeakable acts.'

Stuart flinched.

'Those were the only options I could see,' Sandy continued, holding tight to my hand. 'Torture or death, and of the two, death seemed a little more appealing. I never considered that she might be cared for, that she might be given a good life. Were you given a good life, Kim?'

'Yes, Sandy,' I said. 'A very good life.'

She turned in my direction, but I must have appeared as a dark-grey silhouette to her. 'Molly might come around, and she might not. She might be too far gone.'

'When was the last time she came to visit, Gran?' Stuart asked.

She released my hand, found a handkerchief in the pocket of her cardigan and used it to dab her eyes dry. 'I haven't seen your mother in, oh, nearly four years.'

'You don't see her in church?' I asked.

She shook her head. 'Well I don't see *anyone* much these days, but I left the Church way back in '94. I still hold the Light Within close to my heart, but its numbers have dwindled over the years. In the old days, you couldn't swing a cat in Manson without hitting a fundie or two on the head, but last I heard there were less than a dozen members left.'

'Why is that?'

Sandy suddenly grew cold. 'There was a lot of reasons for me to leave,' she said. 'That church saw the best and the worst of me, and I'd rather leave it at that.'

Stuart looked curiously at us both. It seemed as though every Went had a secret.

'But the Light Within still exists?' I asked.

'For now,' Sandy said. 'If I had to guess, it won't completely die until Reverend Creech does.'

'I met Dale Creech yesterday,' I said. 'He was very nice, but he also seemed a little ...'

'Intense?'

'Exactly,' I said. 'I can see how he'd make a good preacher.'

'Amen,' she said. 'Dale could be addressing a room fulla people and you'd be certain he was talking only to you, and you could guarantee everyone in the room would be thinking the same thing. He was always passionate, even as a child.'

'Some people think he had something to do with the kidnapping.'

'What people?'

'Just ... people,' I said.

Sandy frowned. 'You might have noticed I'm getting on in years, Kim. I ain't got a great deal of time left, so when people skirt around a subject instead of coming right out and saying what they mean, I'm likely to get cranky. Stu can attest to that.'

Stuart sighed and asked the question I'd been avoiding: 'Gran, do you think he could have had something to do with Sammy's disappearance?'

She waved a dismissive hand as if she were swatting a mosquito. 'Dale's an honest, God-fearing man. He's troubled, perhaps. Maybe even a little lonely. But he doesn't have it in him to harm a child. He's not Catholic.'

'Troubled, how?' I asked.

'Nobody's perfect, Kim. The trick is having plenty more good on the scale than bad.'

'But there was *some* bad in Reverend Creech?'

Sandy eased back in the porch swing. 'She's relentless, this one, ain't she? There's plenty of your daddy in her.'

Stuart frowned.

'Dale's *bad* was that he cared too much. He has a sister, Becky. She must be … oh, six or seven years younger. As kids they were inseparable. You know how people say some twins have an almost paranormal connection? You pinch one and the other feels it, stuff like that? Well it was just about like that with those two.'

She dabbed her eyes with the handkerchief again. I had assumed Sandy was emotional, but now I saw that her watering eyes were a side effect of the cataracts.

'But Dale and Becky grew into vastly different people. Dale was charismatic and passionate – and I suppose Becky was too, in her own way, but something about her always made it seem like she was phoning it in. He was hard on her when he didn't have to be. But it was only because he cared.'

'How do you mean?'

'Becky had something of a rebellious side. She danced to the beat of her own drum. Dale read that as *troubled*, so, as the old chestnut goes, she *became* troubled. She played the part her brother cast her in, and she played it well. Her skirt got a little higher and her blouse got a little tighter. Dale was young. He was just trying to be true to his faith. But when you push too hard, sometimes you push 'em away.'

'Is that what Dale did? Did he push too hard?'

'Look, I still have a good relationship with God, a darn good one, but the trouble with fundamentalism is, if you're not one of us, you're one of them. A lost soul. And for a while there, that's how Dale saw her.'

'She left the Church?'

'Not officially, but we didn't see her for a while. People talked. Now, if you ask me, rumour is the one thing that gets *thicker* when you spread it, but some of the Light Withiners said she got knocked up.'

'By who?'

She shrugged. 'Anyone's guess.'

The black-and-brown bird returned, chirped and began digging around in the dirt a couple of metres from where we sat. Puffy clouds rolled across the sky. A dog barked in the distance. Coffee brewed in a loud percolator inside the house.

'What happened to her?' I asked.

Sandy smiled. 'Dale brought her back into the Light. It might have been that the man who put a child in her didn't want to stick around, or it might have been the fact she never brought any baby to term, but somewhere along the way she hit rock bottom. She was ready to step out of the darkness and her brother was there to show her the path. He reminded her of God's plan and soon her skirt grew long again, and she carved a new role for herself in her brother's eyes: that of loyal servant to God. She prayed, she snake-handled, and she wore her snake bite like a badge of honour.'

'She got bit?'

'Oh yes, most did. People have a misconception about snake-handling. They think it's a trick. They think the snakes are drugged. But they bite, and when they do they bite hard.'

'Stuart told me a little bit about that.'

'Told you about his uncle Clyde, I bet,' she said smiling. 'He got bit by a handful of rattlers and passed with a smile on his face. To be bit was to be touched by God, and to survive was to be saved. Sixty-three years of worship and I never once got bit, mind you. But Becky was given a good one, right here on her hand.'

She touched the webbing between her left thumb and forefinger, and all the air suddenly left my body.

'Her left hand?' I said loudly. 'The scar was on her left hand? Are you sure?'

'Pretty sure,' she said. 'Are you alright? I feel like a rush of cold air just came through.'

My mind raced back to that afternoon in Amy's garage, rummaging through old boxes, cringing my way through my old photography project – *Scars: physical and emotional.* I remembered the nick on my pinkie toe, the scar on Amy's thigh, the burn on my mother's hand.

The burn on my mother's hand.

It was a small, knotted mark at the base of her left thumb. The fingers on her right hand would often find the scar, press it and poke it, especially when she was deep in thought. She claimed to have got it as a teenager, when the fan in her bedroom had shorted out and she had tried to fix it without turning the power off at the wall first. It was a lumpy, jagged thing shaped like a barbell – large at both ends. Just like a snake bite.

'Does Becky Creech still live in Manson?' I asked.

'No,' she said. 'She moved away a long time back.'

'How long ago did she move? Where did she go?'

'I can't quite remember. Maybe Mississippi. I'm not sure. You'd have to ask her brother. Why?'

Stuart stepped forward. 'Kim, what's wrong?'

I didn't answer. I was already on my feet and running for the car.

MANSON, KENTUCKY

Then

Emma ate dinner with her brother, aunts and cousin a little after seven pm. She tried not to think about Travis and her dad, about the way her mother did get a little too angry at Sammy sometimes, about the man shot dead at the gristmill and about her baby sister who was either *out there* and scared or *out there* and dead.

Dead. Never had that word felt more total and complete.

She thought about Sammy's name on the mill wall. Even after the sheriff had told her the vet probably had nothing to do with Sammy's disappearance, she couldn't stop picturing him reading her sister's name aloud. In Emma's mind he looked just like the police sketch, only even darker around the eyes – more monstrous, somehow. His face was emotionless and nondescript, a blank canvas onto which Emma could project her deepest fears: a mad child killer, an unhinged psychopath, a sex pervert or some wild combination of all three.

'—Emma, did you hear what I said?'

She looked up from her food. All three of her aunts were staring at her. Todd, her cousin, sat next to Stuart and watched his food silently.

'What?'

'I was asking about school,' Aunt Tillie said, sipping from a tall glass of non-alcoholic cider. 'You don't want to get left behind. Have you spoken to your teachers? Maybe they can send some work home.'

'Falling behind in school is at the bottom of a very long list of things to worry about, Aunt Tillie,' Emma said.

'No need to bite your aunt's head off,' Pauline said. 'She's only trying to help.'

'That's all any of us are trying to do,' said Anne, the third head on the three-headed beast at the table. 'Mind yourself, now. Just 'cause you're going through Hell doesn't mean you have to act like the Devil. Your father could take the same advice, truth be told.'

Emma wanted to throw her plate against the wall – or even better, at one of her aunts. She wanted to leave the table, or perhaps help herself to a glass of Scotch. She knew where her father kept it, right at the back of the pantry behind the breadbox.

As the Brides of Dracula went on talking, she looked over the table at Stu.

He met her eyes. 'Hey, Em?'

'Yeah, Piss-Shit?'

'Where's Sammy's chair?'

She glanced up and down the table. Stu was right. Sammy's high chair was conspicuously absent. 'Yeah, where is it?'

'I put it out in the hall,' Anne said. 'We had to clear some space if we were all gonna fit 'round this table.'

'But where will she sit?' Stu asked.

'What's that, Stewey?'

He hated being called Stewey.

'Where will Sammy sit when she comes home?'

'Let's just worry about that when the time comes, shall we?' Tillie said in a soft, condescending tone.

Stu looked across the table at Emma. She wanted to tell him Sammy was coming home, but that might be a lie. There was only one thing she could give him in this moment.

'He's right,' Emma said, climbing to her feet.

'Where are you going?' Anne said.

'To get Sammy's goddamn high chair.'

'And I'll put it right back out in the hall,' Tillie said. 'You have to find your strength now, Emma. You can't act like a child. You need to focus on what's here, not who isn't.'

'God, you're ridiculous,' Emma said. She marched out of the room, found the red-and-blue high chair and dragged it back to the kitchen. Its rear legs squeaked along the floorboards.

'Sit down and finish your meal right now, Emma. Don't make me tell your mother and add to her—'

Suddenly the front door banged open. A tall figure appeared on the stoop, and for a moment Emma thought it was the man from the police sketch, back from the dead and here to finish off the family. But as the figure stepped into the light of the hallway, she saw it was her father.

'Where's your mother?' he said coldly. Jack was reeling, red-faced and furious. He swept into the house like a hurricane. 'Where is she? Molly? MOLLY?'

'Dad, what's happened? Is it something to do with Sammy?'

Ignoring her, Emma's father started up the stairs. 'Molly, are you here?'

Anne, Pauline and Tillie all poked their heads out from the kitchen doorway, like some ludicrous sitcom scene.

'MOLLY!?'

Emma followed her father up the stairs. 'She's not here, Dad.'

He spun on one foot. His hands had clenched into tight fists. 'Where is she?'

'Tell me what's going on.'

'Jesus, Em. Just tell me where your fucking mother is.'

She had rarely seen him this angry, and when she had it had never been directed at her. It was usually in traffic, when someone cut him off – a flash of anger that was gone just as fast as it had appeared, and usually followed by a quick apology. But this was something else. He wasn't thinking straight. If he had been, he would have remembered exactly where her mother was at this time each week.

'She's at church.'

He shoved Emma to one side and hurried back down the

stairs, taking three steps at a time. Emma watched him go, a sick horror rising in the back of her throat.

Jack reached the front door and stopped. He took a deep breath and turned back. 'Sorry, Em. I didn't mean to yell. I'm not mad at you. This … this isn't about you.'

Emma came back down the stairs and put a hand on her father's wrist. 'What's happened?'

'I just really need to talk to your mother.'

'Then let me come with you,' she said. 'You can explain on the way.'

'Emma—'

'Let me come with you.'

'Your brother—'

'The aunts will take care of Stu. You're pissed, Dad. I don't want you doing something you'll regret.'

'No.'

'I know about Travis.'

Jack froze. For a moment it seemed he might collapse on the doorstep and cry.

'What's going on, Jack?' came Tillie's shrill voice from the kitchen.

'For Christ's sake, Tillie, mind your own fucking business.' He turned to Emma. 'Get your coat.'

For a while they didn't talk. The silence between them was so complete, in fact, that when they stopped at the traffic light between Otter Street and Herbert Avenue, Emma could hear her dad's teeth grinding. Finally, as Jack stared mournfully over the highway ahead, he said, 'How did you find out?'

'His brother told me,' Emma said.

'Patrick? Why?'

'Are you in love with Travis, Dad?'

'... When I was twelve years old,' he said in a slow, crackly voice. 'I was—'

'Don't change the subject. I asked you a question.'

'I'm trying my best to answer it, Em. When I was twelve, I was taken from my bed in the middle of the night. Four men crept into the house, up the stairs and into the bedroom. They were wearing black ski masks. One of the men put a hand over my mouth while the other three dragged me outside and into an unmarked white van.'

'Jesus, I ... what ...? Why didn't you tell us?'

'I kept thinking about my parents, about how devastated they would be if I just disappeared. When they put me in the van, one of the men let me go for a second. He might have been reaching out to pull the sliding door shut, or he might have let his guard down. All I remember is I took that fraction of a second and I ran. I found my way out of the van and onto the front lawn. I was screaming at the top of my lungs. I got about halfway across the lawn before I saw my mother. Your gran. She was standing in the front doorway in her pyjamas. My dad was behind her. And I thought, thank God. I'm saved. But they were just ... standing there.'

His voice became infused with rage, deep and raw. 'I screamed out to them. "Mommy, Daddy, help me, the bad men are trying to get me." But they didn't move. They just watched me. I didn't … I didn't understand. I couldn't. As I got closer, just as I reached the front door, they closed it. They closed it in my face, and I heard it lock. They locked me out.'

'I don't get it,' Emma said. She was trying desperately not to cry. 'Why didn't they help you?'

'Because they'd arranged it, Em. They had organised the whole thing. The men were from the Church. I never found out who they were – that was part of it. That's why they wore the masks.'

'What do you mean Gran and Gramps *arranged* it?' Emma said. 'Dad, you must be remembering it wrong.'

'They had me reprogrammed, Em. That's what they called it. Somehow, my mother had figured out I was … *different*, that instead of girls I liked … boys. She had figured it out and thought the Devil was in me.'

'Shit, Dad.'

'The men dragged me back into the van, drove me out to an old farmhouse in Coleman, and *reprogrammed* me.'

'What does that mean?'

'They performed an exorcism.'

Emma's muscles stiffened. 'What does that mean?'

'It doesn't matter.'

'What did they do to you?'

'You don't want to know, Em,' he said.

'I do, Dad. Please. I can handle it.'

His hands clenched tight around the steering wheel. 'There were more men waiting at the farmhouse. They took me to a room. They held me down against a stained old box-spring with no mattress. They pressed the Bible against my forehead and took turns screaming scripture into my ears. When one got too red-faced and worn out, the next would take over. It lasted for hours. Next, they dragged me into a deep bathtub filled to the brim with holy water. They held me under. For ten seconds, thirty, a minute. Over and over.'

'My God,' Emma said. It took everything she had not to burst into tears.

'They put me in the basement overnight. They took away my clothes, my shoes, and let a rattlesnake loose. It went on like that for three days.'

'I'm so sorry, Dad.'

'Growing up like me, in a place like Manson, under the eyes of *their* God … I never stood a chance, Em. I do love Travis. I love him, but I hate the part of myself that does.'

They came to an unsealed road with no name. Where the road met the highway was a sign that read, *This way to The Light*. At the end of the road was the Church of the Light Within, a low concrete building with a flat corrugated roof. There was no steeple and no stained-glass window. The only thing that gave it away as a church was the small, hand-painted crucifix above the entrance.

They pulled into a lot packed with parked cars, pickup trucks and motorcycles. Thumping music was coming from within.

'Wait in the car,' Jack said.

'No, Dad.'

'There'll be snakes. Snakes, maybe scorpions – and worse, a whole lot of people filled with the Holy Spirit. I'll be right out. I'm just going to find your mother and bring her home. That's all.'

'What did you find out about her?' Emma asked.

He didn't answer her question. Instead, he got out of the car and walked into the church. Emma waited less than a minute before following.

There were close to a hundred truebelievers gathered in the Church of the Light Within. The building was alive with what her mother would call the Holy Spirit and her father would call mass hysteria.

On a table by the front door was a large wooden donation box. Engraved on the side was, *Give your whole self to God, give what you can afford to the Light Within.* The slot on the lid was stuffed with cash.

A six-piece bluegrass band was playing a lightning-paced number at the back of the church. The band was dressed all in white, and none of them were wearing shoes. Stencilled in a banner over their heads was, *The Barefoot Prophets.*

In front of the band, some of the aisles had been cleared to make a dance floor. On it, Billy Wayne, who Emma saw walking his French poodle along the firebreak most mornings, was dancing barefoot around a copperhead. His white cotton trousers were rolled up to the knees and he was laughing madly. Every now and then the snake struck lazily at Billy, but this just got him laughing more. He held his hands tight by his side and gyrated in place.

Startled, Emma stepped backwards. She hated snakes and always had. When she was younger, ten or eleven, she was curious about the church, and had asked her mother what it felt like to hold a snake.

'Their skin is stiff and leathery,' Molly had told her. 'First you get a gust of nerves, like sitting in a rollercoaster as it climbs to the first drop. Then, you feel a flush of heat, as if you're being bathed in God's own hot breath. You feel alive. You feel close to God, so close you could just about reach out and touch him. That's how it feels to me, anyway.'

Being here in her mother's world, pressing through the jostling crowd in search of her father, Emma felt terrified.

She recognised many faces – from the drugstore where Emma worked the register over summer, from Christmases at her gran's house, from walking around Manson – but there were many more she didn't. It was like walking through a bad dream: familiar and jarringly wrong.

Patsy Halcomb, a regular at Went Drugs, held a four-foot diamondback above her head and was shaking it wildly in the aisles. At the far end of the church a massive man with a stylish red goatee was setting up shots of some kind of milky liquid like a seasoned bartender. He took the first shot himself, convulsing at the taste. A couple were next in line, and both slammed back the poison like sailors. Two men were up next. The first got his down with a yelp; the second immediately fell to his knees, gasping.

There were too many people and too much noise.

A big man – Emma thought his name was Hershel something – was speaking in tongues. A string of gibberish slipped quickly from his mouth. '*Dutchie no no highbalmo, chu chu mana.* Jesus His name Jesus His name!'

Suzie Litterback, who Emma knew from Home Foods, the grocery store across the street from her father's pharmacy, spun past her, a rattlesnake clenched firmly in her hands.

Emma pushed forward. She caught a glimpse of her father through the crowd and quickened her pace, until a hand clapped onto her arm. It was a fat man in a white linen shirt and a white fedora. She didn't know his name, but he had come to the house a few days earlier. She had assumed he was a friend of her father's, but seeing him here made her doubt that.

'Emma?' he said. 'Does your mother know you're here?'

Without a word, she shook herself loose of the man's grip and pushed through a wall of people, out onto the dance floor.

Someone dropped a rattlesnake less than six feet from where she stood and it took everything she had not to scream. Not that anyone would have heard: the bluegrass band was too loud, and too relentless.

She scanned the faces for her father, even her mother, but couldn't find them. It didn't matter. Jack was about to make his presence known.

'Creech!' Her father's voice echoed against the ceiling of the church.

She saw Reverend Dale Creech first. He was standing by a long glass terrarium, now empty of snakes. He wore a casually rebellious leather jacket and a startled expression. Then she saw her dad. Jack appeared from her left, crossed the floor, cocked his fist, and punched Creech hard across his jaw.

The preacher spun backwards and slumped to his knees. His hand rushed to his jaw and his eyes bulged.

Jack stood over the reverend. Veins were throbbing along his forehead. 'What did you do, you goddamn fanatic?'

A collective courtroom gasp swept around the room. The Barefoot Prophets abruptly stopped playing, and a hush fell over the room.

'Jack?' Creech said, flexing out the pain in his jaw. 'This is a place of worship. I can see you're angry about something. Why don't we talk about it outside?'

'Did something go wrong during her reprogramming, is that it?'

'I can assure you, I have no idea what you're talking about.'

'Did you push the Bible so hard against her little skull that it cracked?'

The crowd around them swelled with shouts and chatter. They were completely outnumbered. Emma wanted to stop him, to take him by the arm and yank him out of there. But her feet refused to move. She was paralysed – not with fear, but with rage.

If what her father was saying was true: if this man and his church had something to do with Sammy's disappearance …

Then Mom is in on it too, Emma thought.

Creech stood and held his ground. 'Jack, please, you're not making any sense.'

'Did you hold her head under holy water a few seconds too long? When you locked her in a room full of snakes in bare feet and no lights, did she—'

'Judge him not,' Creech said, raising his voice above Jack's to address the truebelievers. They had circled in and were growing restless. 'This man is going through dark times. And while his accusations are unfounded and misdirected, we must put ourselves in his shoes and consider the pain of—'

Jack swung at him again. His fist struck Creech hard across the face. Creech absorbed the blow, held his hand up to the crowd to silence them, and spat blood on the hardwood floor. Emma thought she heard the *tink-tink* of a broken tooth.

'Judge him not,' Creech said again, a trail of blood spilling down his chin. 'For he knows not—'

Her father moved to hit him again, but the man in the white fedora struck Jack from behind. Suddenly Jack was on his belly, face pressed against the floor. He fought and flailed, managed to turn himself around. But the big man's knee pressed hard against Jack's back, pinning him.

'Get off me, Buddy!' Jack cried.

'This ain't right, Jack.'

'He killed her, Buddy! He killed my little girl! Let me up! Let me—'

'Get the fuck off my dad!' Emma yelled. Now her feet were moving and moving fast. She sprung from the crowd, screaming wildly, charged forward and leaped onto the man's back. Her skinny arms were wrapped around his neck. The man – Buddy – rose, then dropped to one knee.

Jack scrambled to his feet. 'Emma, wait, stop!'

But Emma didn't stop. She squeezed her arms tight around Buddy's neck and clamped her legs around his considerable stomach. Worshippers poured over her, grabbed at her, clamped on and dragged her off him, kicking and screaming.

She screamed again, felt rage surging through her body. It was hot and intense.

She struggled against the fundies, elbowing and slapping her way from their grip – and tripped backwards. She landed hard, looked to her right and spotted a rattlesnake less than three feet away. It had pulled itself into a tight, panicked coil and was sounding its rattle. 'Fucking Jesus—'

'Enough!'

Her mother exploded through the wall of people, nostrils flaring, eyes darting between Jack and Emma. 'What's going on? What are you doing here? How dare you come to *my* church and—'

'Oh, for God's sake, Mom, this isn't a church,' Emma yelled. Only it wasn't her speaking, not truly. It was the rage. *The Devil.* 'This is a cult! You're in a cult, Mom! Look at this place! You're in a cult! You're all in a cult! YOU'RE ALL IN A CULT!'

Molly spun toward Jack. 'Get her out of here, Jack. Get …'

Molly paused when she saw that Jack was sobbing.

Emma stopped too. All at once the rage drained away. Her father looked suddenly very small, very soft.

'What are you doing here, Jack?' Molly said, her face flushed with embarrassment.

'Just tell me,' he said. 'Please. Just tell me what happened.'

'Tell you what?'

'Tell me if she's dead. Tell me if Sammy is gone.'

It was quieter outside. Creech stood with two men by the church doors, keeping watch. Emma sat down at one of the picnic tables with her father, who had turned sullen and silent. Her mother stood over them, hands on hips.

For a long time nobody talked. A gust of wind that sounded like whispers moved through the Virginia pines. It stirred up a meat-rot smell that made Emma think of dead things. Molly noticed the smell too. She turned and sniffed the air sharply.

Jack massaged his right hand, which had seen a lot of action over the past few days. He wet his lips and spoke softly. 'You can't truly believe the Devil is in our little girl.'

'The Church didn't take her, Jack,' Molly said, rubbing her face and moving her fingers through her hair. In the dull moonlight she somehow looked both old and young. 'You've been away from the Light for too long.'

'What does that mean?'

'It means I only wanted to help her. To heal her. But someone else took her first. You would have seen … I would have fixed her and we'd all go back to being happy. You would have seen.'

'It's my fault,' he said. 'I've spent so much time being mad at you, Molly. For changing. For embracing this place. But it's my fault. You would never have known about the Church if you hadn't met me, and even if you had, you wouldn't have opened up so goddamn wide to let it in.'

They weren't yelling at each other. It didn't even feel to Emma like an argument. Their tones were soft and steady.

This is the end of them, Emma thought. *The fight has left them. This is the end of my family.*

'You showed me the Light, Jack,' she said, her voice barely louder than the wind. 'This is my home, my support network. You gave me that. These people are my family.'

'We're supposed to be your family, Mom,' Emma said.

'I'm sorry, Emma,' Molly said. 'You shouldn't have to be here for this.'

'Why did you go to Creech?' Jack asked. 'Why didn't you come to me?'

'Because you didn't want to hear it.'

'Creech is—'

'Dale has been there for me in my darkest moments.'

'He manipulated you.'

'Please don't tell me how it is,' she said. 'We all take our own bucket down the well.'

Emma tried to talk again but her mouth was too dry. Tears were streaming freely down her face. She looked skyward. The universe felt smaller.

'This is the end of us,' Jack said. 'If we were alone right now I might murder you, Molly. I wouldn't care if they saw.' He gestured to Creech and his two sentries watching them. 'But I'd care if our daughter did.'

'Go home, Jack,' came a voice from the church. A small

woman strutted across the grass toward them. It was Emma's grandmother, Sandy. Emma considered charging across the yard to beat her. She might have too, if she weren't so damn tired all of a sudden.

Her father stood up. 'I should have fought harder for you, Molly, but they have you now. You're too far gone.'

'Goodbye, Jack,' she said.

'Goodbye, Molly.' He turned to Emma. 'Come on. It's time to go home.'

MANSON, KENTUCKY

Now

As I paced back and forth across Stuart's hotel room, I caught myself chewing my nails – a habit I'd not had before arriving in Manson. 'Becky Creech and Carol Leamy are the same person. It makes sense. It feels right.'

'We'll drive over to Dale Creech's place tomorrow and show him a photo of Carol,' Stuart said. 'But don't get too ahead of yourself, Kim. This isn't a slam dunk.'

He was sitting on the bed with his legs crossed like a sage, his face white in the glow of his laptop.

'It has to be her,' I said, pacing, pacing, pacing. 'There are no photos of Becky Creech online. That's strange, right?'

'Not necessarily. She might have married and taken her husband's name well before the internet.'

'But what about the scar?'

'People have scars, Kim.'

'In the same spot? That's a pretty big coincidence.'

'I don't disagree with you. All I'm saying is, watch your pace. I've learned the hard way not to get too excited too early. Do you have any idea how many times I thought I'd found Sammy before you?'

I caught myself gnawing at my nails again and forced myself to stop. I fetched a beer from Stuart's minibar and went over to the glass sliding doors that led to the balcony. Full dark had crept in over Manson, catching me by surprise. Just ten minutes earlier I'd looked through these same windows and seen a wild, brutal mountain range. Now, all I saw was my own reflection.

'Besides,' Stuart said. 'There's no motive. Why would Becky Creech kidnap Sammy? Actually scratch that. Why would Becky Creech kidnap Sammy, move to Australia, adopt a false identity and raise you as her own?'

He was right. Mum was grounded and down to earth, and, as far as I knew, she was a long way from crazy. But how well did I really know her? It takes a kind of certain person to keep a secret as big as the one she kept until the day she died.

'Maybe she had a good reason,' I said.

'Like what?'

'I don't know.'

'Like, maybe she wanted to save you from our mother?'

'I didn't say that.'

'You're trying to invent scenarios that could justify Carol's actions,' he said. 'That's fine. I get that. But just because you're trying to make her a hero, doesn't mean you get to make our mother a villain.' He slammed his laptop shut.

Sipping my beer, I sat down on the edge of the bed. 'Sorry. I've only met the woman once. Once that I can remember. She just seemed so …'

'Bat-shit crazy?'

'*Sad.*'

Stuart eyed my beer. 'Can you get me one of those?'

I did. He drank and unfolded his legs. 'Try to understand, Kim, Mom wasn't always like this. She used to be full of life. She was funny, patient, kind, beautiful. There was even a time the Light Within added to her life, before it started to control it.'

'But all that changed after I disappeared?'

'Actually, all that changed after you were born. Look, I don't know for sure, but I'm fairly certain Mom suffered from postnatal depression. I didn't know that's what it was at the time because I was a kid, and it's not like she ever got diagnosed, but it was obvious something wasn't right, even to a nine-year-old.'

Stuart took a moment and sipped his beer. When he spoke again it was almost as if he were talking to himself. 'Dad must have seen it too. I'm pretty sure he just ignored it – or worse, resented her for it. If he had just tried to talk to her, to help her, then everything might have turned out different. I might have grown up with a little sister.'

'Stuart, postnatal depression is a horrible thing for someone to go through, but it's a mood disorder. I'm sure therapy or antidepressants or a more present husband would have helped, but it wouldn't have stopped someone coming into your house and taking me—'

Turning back to face him, I saw that he was crying.

'Stuart, what's wrong?'

He wiped his eyes with the heels of his hands. He swung his legs over the end of the bed and sat up, draining the last of his beer in two big gulps.

'Nobody came into the house,' he said quietly.

'… What?'

'I've never told anyone this, Kim,' he said, taking a deep breath and blinking away fresh tears. 'Not even Claire.'

'Stuart, what are you talking about? What do you mean nobody came into the house?'

'… On Tuesday, April 3rd, 1990, the day you disappeared, I was home sick, getting over a cold. I really could have gone to school, but I was milking it for one more day off. I loved being home when Emma was at school and Dad was at the store. There weren't so many people to share Mom with.'

I grew up with a sister, so I knew exactly what he meant.

'Of course, I still had to share her with you, but that was fine. I loved you – honestly. And you won't remember this, but you idolised me. You'd follow me around from room to room, and most of the time I could keep you from …'

'Keep me from what?'

'Getting in Mom's way. You were a handful. I mean, you were two, but you were fussy. You needed attention. And once in a while, like all toddlers do, you'd have a bad day.'

'Was that day one of those times?'

Turning away from me, he tore the label from his bottle of beer and traced the rim with his finger. 'That day, you were being a brat. You were tired or cranky, and I tried to play interference, as usual. But Mom was at the end of her rope. She'd get so mad at you sometimes. And when she got mad at you she turned cold on me. She took you upstairs and shut you in your bedroom. You hated it when your bedroom door was shut. Mom put herself to bed, but you wouldn't stop crying. I didn't want you to wake her.'

He put the empty bottle down. 'Mom had told me to leave you be, to let you tire yourself out, but you were screaming blue murder, Sammy … So I snuck into your room. Tried to calm you down. It was spring so all the baby birds were out. There was a big sweetgum right outside your bedroom window with a bird nest in it. Northern cardinals. They were your favourite.'

The image of a small red bird flashed into my mind. Was I simply recalling what a northern cardinal looked like, or was I remembering that day?

'I opened your window so we could hear them sing a little better, but you wanted to get closer. So I …' He paused to inhale. His bottom lip was quivering. '… So I took you outside, into the front yard, to the sweetgum. You wanted to look at the bird nest through Dad's binoculars. You called them "Daddy's long glasses". But they were inside.'

He couldn't look at me, and if he had, I doubt he'd be able to make much out through the tears gliding down his chin, catching on the stubble. 'I was only gone for five minutes, Kim. I swear to God. Five fucking minutes. And when I came back …'

'... I was gone,' I said. 'Why didn't you tell anyone?'

'Because I was nine, and scared, and I didn't want to get into trouble and ... part of me was actually *relieved*.'

The last word broke the dam. His head dropped between his knees and he sobbed loudly, vulnerably. Like a child. He'd been holding onto that guilt for twenty-eight years. I could only imagine how it had grown and festered within.

'I'm so sorry, Sammy,' he said, trying to catch his breath. Snot fell from his nose. He slid onto the floor and held his hands over his face. He looked nine years old again.

'It's okay,' I tried to say, but the words turned to sludge in my mouth. I slid down beside him and put a hand on his shoulder. He flinched, then shuddered. I put my arms around him and pulled him close. '... It's okay, Stu. It's over. You were just a kid, you were—'

'Don't,' he said, pulling away from me and climbing quickly to his feet. 'It's not okay, Kim. It's pretty fucking far from okay.'

'It was a long time ago, Stuart,' I said.

'Stop.'

'You were nine.'

'Don't.'

'Stuart—'

'Don't you dare, Kim,' he said. 'Don't you dare let me off the hook.'

'Look—'

'That's not what I'm looking for. I don't want your forgiveness and I won't take it.'

He went into the bathroom and slammed the door shut behind him. I thought about the people my absence had hurt, the people whose lives had been wrecked, the tears that had been shed, all because of one person. Carol Leamy. *Becky Creech.*

The key to Stuart's Prius was in a silver bowl on the dresser by the door. I grabbed it on my way out.

The Church of the Light Within was outside Manson town limits and not easy to find on a map, let alone in real life and in the dark. The GPS on my phone showed a blue ball in the middle of a field of black. I'd been driving around for fifteen minutes without spotting another car on the road.

I came to an unsealed road without a name. A hand-painted sign had been stuck in the dirt on the corner that read, *This Way to the Light.* I turned down the road and followed it for half a mile. Trees formed an arch overhead, meeting in the centre and blocking out the sky. Even in the middle of the day, the road to the light must have been paved with darkness.

As the Prius broke into a wide clearing, moonlight spilled into the cab and an eerie familiarity took over. The church, a large, low building with a red crucifix painted above the front door, stood in the middle of the clearing. About a hundred feet from the church was a second building with no windows. A light was on inside.

I pulled in to a muddy parking lot, parked nose-out, and got out of the car. The only other vehicle in the lot was a sleek black Yamaha motorbike. Its engine was still warm and ticking.

'Evening, stranger.' Dale Creech must have heard my arrival. He had ducked out of the smaller building and was walking across the grass to meet me, carrying a snake in his left hand.

Taking an instinctive step backwards, I nearly knocked over Creech's motorbike. It wobbled, then corrected itself.

He laughed. 'Oh, don't mind Annie here. She might look like a snake but inside she's a kitten. Wanna hold?'

He held the snake out the way an older brother might taunt a younger sibling with a spider. The creature coiled lazily in his hand. It was fat and short, patterned with different shades of tan that looked grey in the moonlight. I couldn't see its head – it was somewhere behind Creech's thumb – but I could see its rattle, which was, thankfully, still.

'No,' I said.

Stroking the snake with his free hand, he said, 'It's good to see you again, Kim. Or are you going by Sammy now?'

'Still Kim,' I said.

He took a step forward and I took another back, eyeing the rattlesnake in his hand. 'Let me put Annie back to bed and see about fixing you some coffee.' He gestured at the church. 'Go on inside now, I'll be right with you.'

He walked back into the darkness toward the smaller building, which I assumed was where he kept the snakes. His feet left shallow indentations in the damp grass. He wasn't wearing any shoes.

The church looked yellow under bright fluorescent lights. I'd been expecting a dimly lit place of worship filled with candles and shadows, but it looked more like a community centre: stark, clean and modern. About a hundred plastic chairs were stacked against the far wall. All those chairs used to be filled, I guessed, but if Sandy Went was right, the Church now had only a handful of members.

A long glass terrarium stood at the front of the church in lieu of a pulpit. The floor of the terrarium was dusted with red sand. Thankfully there were no snakes inside. I stood with my hand on the lip of the tank and tried to imagine what it must be like to dance around with venomous snakes in the name of God.

The church door opened behind me. Turning, I expected to see Reverend Creech standing in the doorway. Instead, I saw the shadow man. The thing from my nightmare stood just outside the church door, its long, narrow arms hung slack and sickening by its side.

My lungs constricted.

But as the shadow man stepped into the light of the church, it became Dale Creech again, barefoot in dusty jeans, with a steaming glass coffeepot in his hand. I was suddenly aware that nobody knew I was here, not even Stuart.

Creech smiled. 'I hope decaf is alright?'

We sat down at a table in the corner of the room. Creech filled two cups of coffee. The church had fallen unnaturally silent, as if he had told the crickets to stop cricking and the wind to stop blowing.

'So,' Creech said. 'To what do I owe the pleasure of this visit?'

'I was hoping you could look at something for me.' I took a passport-sized photo of Carol Leamy from my wallet. It had been taken in the snow some time around 2007, in the pre-cancer days. It showed Carol smiling, a red woollen hat pulled down over her hair. A heavy green parka puffed around her torso like a formless blob, but she looked happy and very much alive. She looked like *Mum*.

Handing Creech the picture felt like one of the last pieces of the puzzle was about to fall into place. Any moment now, he would recognise Carol as his sister, Becky, and everything would click into place like the final turn of a Rubik's Cube. I wondered if this was how Stuart felt when he approached me back in Australia, when he opened his manila folder and slid a photo of Sammy Went across the table for me to see.

'Do you recognise her?' I asked.

Creech looked at the photo. I examined his reaction, but he gave nothing away. 'No. I don't know her. Sorry.'

'Are you sure?'

He looked again. 'I'm positive. And by the look on your face that's not the answer you were looking for.'

'Would you mind looking again?' I asked.

'I've already looked twice.'

'Look a third time.'

He looked at the photo once more, shaking his head. 'I've never seen this woman before in my life.' There wasn't a flicker of doubt in his voice. He handed the photo back and held my gaze easily. If he was lying, he had somehow convinced even himself. 'I'm sorry I couldn't help. Is this about the kidnapping?'

'Do you still see your sister, Reverend?'

There it was: a flinch. Barely perceptible, but a flinch all the same. 'My sister?'

'Becky,' I said.

'How do you know Becky?'

'Do you see her much?'

'… No.'

'When was the last time you spoke to her?'

'Why are you asking about my sister?'

'Does she still live in Manson?' I asked. 'I heard that she moved away.'

'Where did you hear that?'

'Is it true?'

He sipped his coffee, cracked his knuckles, and composed himself. When he spoke again it was with the light, singsong tone he'd used when we first met outside Molly's apartment. 'Becky is a long way from here.'

'Where's that?' I asked.

'Do you remember anything?' He asked. 'Do you remember anything from before?'

'Not much,' I said.

'Do you remember coming here?'

'I …'

'Do you remember that day?' Creech suddenly stood up. Even without shoes he was tall, his chest wide, his arms strong. 'Are you a religious woman, Sammy?'

Fear crept up the back of my spine, leaving gooseflesh. 'No. And my name is *Kim*.'

'Do you believe in the Devil?'

'No.'

He topped up his coffee. 'To move through life without being accountable to a higher power is to drift unanchored through a dark ocean full of monsters.'

'The deeper you go,' Dean's voice whispered in my head. *'The darker the water becomes.'*

'God is my rudder, Sammy,' Creech said. 'And whether you believe it or not don't change the facts. God is real and so is the Devil. And just as strong as I feel God in the room, I feel the Devil too. I've seen it take many forms, as I suspect you have too.'

He took a step around the table and blew steam from his coffee cup. 'Have you ever seen the Devil, Sammy?'

'My name is Kim.'

'Have you ever *felt* it?'

'No.'

'Oh, I doubt that's true. If you've known anyone who hit the bottle too hard, to whom the term "drink responsibly" meant don't spill a drop, then you've seen the Devil.'

My lips turned dry.

'If you've known those who read horoscopes and *Harry Potter*, those who consult a ouija board and have abortions and premarital sex, those who play video games and celebrate films with satanic overtones, those who lay with their own sex, the way your daddy does … If you've known them, Sammy, then you've felt the Devil.'

Creech's eyes widened and I saw panic in them – panic and rage. 'I know why you're here, Sammy.'

'Wait—'

But I was too late. In one fluid motion, Creech slid his fingers around the coffeepot and brought it hard against the side of my head.

REDWATER, KENTUCKY

Then

Ellis arrived in Redwater at six-thirty, half an hour early for his date. He parked the car – his civilian ride, a dusty yellow Datsun – across the street from Barracuda: Italian Cuisine, and waited.

He had every reason to cancel on Sue Beady, the sandy-haired woman who found him through his personal ad, and he suspected a few of his deputies were sorry that he didn't. He'd left a huge mess back in Manson, but he would help clean it up tomorrow. Tonight he would go on a date with Sue Beady, dine on fancy pizza and drive her home afterwards. He would kiss her goodnight, on the lips if she'd allow it, and then he'd drive himself home.

If nothing else, it was just nice to spend a few hours away from Manson. Redwater was Kentucky's seventh-largest city, thirty miles east of Manson. Ellis knew it well. He'd had an aunt who lived here once: Ida, who would sit on a rickety old rocking chair on a rickety old porch and watch the world go by. She was buried in Redwater Cemetery now.

The city wasn't how he remembered it from his monthly visits as a child.

It had been a flourishing place back then. But a sawmill closure in 1966 triggered a severe economic downturn. Then, in '72, two major neighbourhoods were the site of a huge government buyout and a mass-eviction of its citizens. Aunty Ida managed to keep her house, but many of her friends weren't so lucky.

The bought-up houses were intended to be torn down and the land absorbed by the surrounding national park, which Ellis always thought sounded okay. But instead the plans languished in bureaucratic limbo until '86, when, for reasons that weren't quite clear, the government released the land back to the city. Now that side of Redwater sat largely unoccupied, aside from a handful of tramps and junkies.

Progress, Ellis thought, and checked his watch. Eight minutes had crawled by.

He adjusted the rear-view mirror to examine his reflection. It was familiarly disappointing, but he was making the best of what he had. At least he smelled good, having doused himself with something called *Aquatic Mist* he'd pulled out of the station's Lost'n'Found.

He checked his watch again. It had been one minute since he last checked, so he got out of the car and took a stroll along a busy street. His legs creaked as he walked. His body felt tired – because it was – yet his mind felt oddly sharp and awake.

Do I have Sue Beady to thank for that? he wondered. *Or John Regler?* Military records had confirmed his identity and hospital logs confirmed his alibi, which meant he was lying on a slab in the basement of Manson Mercy for no good reason Ellis could think of.

'Leave us alone,' the man had screamed. In that moment Ellis had been sure he was talking about Sammy. Now it seemed more likely he was talking about the voices in his head – or maybe to them.

In an effort to kill time and distract himself from the shadow of Manson, he went into a small grocery store. He remembered it as Gerry's Local, but having changed owners countless times, it was now just called The Local.

The cashier was watching a small black-and-white television by the front counter. A news story was running about Sammy Went. Terry Beaumont's police sketch flashed across the screen. Information about John Regler and the circumstances surrounding his death hadn't hit the media yet. Ellis would need to call another press conference. The thought made him nauseous.

He wandered the store, drawn to a display of colourful flowers. He wondered if bringing flowers to a date was considered corny, or just corny enough. Beyond the display – *50% off assorted day-old Roses!* – stood a tall, lean man with short-cropped hair and matching stubble. He wore a cheap suit but wore it well. A shopping basket was hanging under one long arm, and he had stopped in the candy section. He couldn't seem to decide between Jujyfruits and the Blue Raspberry Airheads. He looked back and forth with a graceful urgency, until he settled on a pack of each.

Ellis wasn't sure why he was watching the man at first. He just seemed like someone to watch. It worked that way for him sometimes: his body knew first what the mind knew later. Then it dawned on him.

That's Patrick Eckles.

The last time he'd seen Patrick was at his sentence hearing. He briefly considered going over to make his presence known, but hesitated when Patrick moved to the toy section. Below a shelf of dolls and action figures was a large crate filled to the brim with stuffed toys.

Candy and a stuffed toy, Ellis thought. *Not exactly what you'd expect an ex-con to be shopping for. But, hell, each to their own. Maybe he got addicted to candy in Greenwood and maybe he wanted a stuffed toy to remind himself of simpler times.*

But there was more to it than that. Ellis just knew it. No, more than knew it, he *felt* it.

Patrick pulled a bright-green stuffed turtle from the crate, smiled at his choice, then headed for the counter. Ellis slipped into the frozen food isle to keep from being seen. He checked his watch. It was seven forty-five. He still had fifteen minutes before his date, so he decided to follow Patrick.

Patrick drove a maroon '85 AMC Eagle station wagon. Ellis slipped into his Datsun and followed from a safe distance. Patrick headed west, not toward Manson, as Ellis had expected.

He was heading for the dead side of town, where the streets were lined with boarded-up businesses, ramshackle homes and dilapidated buildings. A burned-out car sat half-on, half-off the curb. Garbage bins had been upended in the street. The road was peppered with potholes.

Patrick was probably on his way to score some dope, Ellis decided. He wouldn't bust him for it, partly because he didn't want to miss his date with Sue Beady, and partly because he just couldn't handle the hassle. In the pre-Sammy days, a dope bust on an ex-con would be something to write home about. Now, Ellis simply couldn't be bothered.

Still, he'd at least get a good look at where the dope-selling might take place, something to pass on to the Redwater Police. Then it would become their problem.

Patrick pulled up on a darkened street, outside an old apartment building with rows of broken windows. Ellis eased over to the curb and sat low in the car, watching as Patrick collected his groceries from the back of the Eagle and carried them toward the apartment building.

This was all dead land. There was no power in this street, and certainly no tenants, yet Patrick moved with the ease of a man coming home after a day's work.

Ellis checked his watch; it was right on eight. If he hurried he could make it back to the restaurant by ten-past. Late, but not too late. He jotted down the address of the apartment building.

There, you've got what you came for, he thought. *Don't you know it's rude to leave a lady waiting?*

Yet he found himself killing the engine, getting out of the car and walking up the street toward the apartment building.

Broken glass cracked beneath his feet as he crossed the sidewalk and approached the entrance to the apartment building. Both front doors were broken. Ellis had to lift and drag the left one to make enough room to slip inside.

He entered a dark hallway littered with shards of glass and nearly a dozen used syringes. At the end of the hall, light flickered from beneath one of the apartment doors. It was too strong to be candlelight. Ellis guessed someone had started a fire, perhaps in a rusted-out old oil drum, the kind hobos stood around in movies.

Fine, Ellis thought. *You have the address of the drug den, and now you have the apartment number too. If you leave right now you can still be fashionably late.*

He sighed and continued down the hall.

As he neared the apartment door, he heard the fire crackling and murmured conversation. A woman's voice. Perhaps Patrick was here to see a hooker. The more he thought about it the more it made sense. Patrick had served three years of his sentence, and he was only human. Ellis hadn't heard anything about prostitution in Redwater, but in a city this size it was likely. Besides, where there were drugs and poverty, there were usually whores too.

But then he heard a third voice. A child's voice. Yes, here it came again: a sleepy child's voice.

Before his mind could catch up, Ellis was barging through the door and into the apartment. Flickering firelight gave a disjointed view of the interior: an old sofa, an army cot, fire in an old oil drum – just as Ellis had envisioned.

Then he saw Patrick kneeling on the floor of the apartment, staring back at him with a stunned expression. There was a child in his arms, a chubby two-year-old girl with a mop of thick black hair and eyes that shone yellow in the firelight.

'No,' Patrick said.

'Sammy.' Ellis reached for his .45, but it wasn't there. He had left it at home. Bringing a gun to a date was a sure-fire way not to get a second one. '… Sammy Went.'

Patrick rose quickly to his feet, pulling Sammy tight into his chest. She started to cry. 'Please, wait—'

But Ellis wouldn't wait. 'It's over, Patrick.'

'No, hold up, just wait, don't—'

It was then Ellis realised Patrick wasn't talking to him, but to someone over his left shoulder. He spun, saw a slight woman with dark hair, saw the hunting rifle in her arms.

'Becky, wait—' Patrick moved toward her, pulling Sammy tight with one arm and reaching out for the gun with the other.

Ellis didn't hear the shot ring out, and he felt no pain. He simply was, and then he wasn't.

Sue Beady had a good feeling about Chester. They'd only talked once, and the conversation had been brief, but he sounded good and honest. He might even turn out to be someone to spend a life with, although she wouldn't tell him that on a first date. She knew all about coming on too strong.

She sat in the window of the restaurant and watched cars pass in the street. The waiter appeared and she ordered a white wine. The wine arrived, so she drank it and ordered another.

She waited for a long time. Longer than she should have. She waited until the dinner rush had eased, until the restaurant staff began their nightly cleaning ritual, until the hostess flipped the sign on the back of the door from *OPEN* to *CLOSED.*

Finally, Sue stood up, gathered her things and, embarrassed and crestfallen, paid the bill. It was a shame. A damn shame. She'd had such a good feeling about Chester.

MANSON, KENTUCKY

Now

Lights flickered on overhead, slowly drawing me into semi-consciousness. It was impossible to tell how much time had passed. The pain in my head was intense. My face was hot and wet, my right ear was completely numb and my vision was blurred, like trying to look through a rain-streaked window.

My phone was gone and my feet were bare.

I tried to move my head but couldn't. I managed to prop myself up onto my elbows but immediately collapsed. I focused on my breathing and tried to get a sense of the space I was in. It was a windowless room with a low ceiling, unnaturally hot.

Foggy, fragmented memories came back. The coffeepot. The shadow man.

Reverend Creech slipped in and out of my field of vision as he moved busily around the room.

Slowly, my focus began to sharpen. I saw that the walls were lined with small glass tanks. *Snakes*, I thought.

Something buzzed to my right. It might have been a heat lamp.

Creech stepped over me, his dirty feet landing either side of my head. He was holding a plastic bucket. There was a strip of tape on the side with something written on it. My vision strained and shifted focus, and finally the word appeared: *Supper.*

Looking from the bucket, to the underside of Creech's dusty jeans, I tried to say, 'please', but it came out, '*pleh*'.

Without a word, Creech flicked the lid off the bucket and turned it upside down. A dozen shapes tumbled out, falling against my chest and face. Mice. One of them squeaked in fright and darted over my left eye, leaving sticky tracks of warm blood across my forehead.

I tried to swat it but I wasn't fast enough. I was hardly strong enough to lift my arm.

More mice scattered and others remained where they were. One snuck under the folds of my T-shirt and onto the skin of my belly.

'No,' I managed to say.

Creech ignored me. He went to one of the glass tanks, lifted the lid and produced a stubby, three-foot rattlesnake. He tossed it over his shoulder with sickening confidence. It landed someplace near my feet. I heard it slither across the room.

The hot air smelled sweet and beefy.

Creech moved to the next tank and removed the lid. He took out another snake. This one had no rattle but looked fiercely alien, with bands of blue running the length of its body. It flipped and flopped in Creech's grip, aggressively fast. He dropped it onto the leg of my jeans, where its sickening weight remained.

Clarity crawled into my mind as I moved closer toward full consciousness, and with it came fear. A deep, brutal, primal fear like nothing I'd ever felt before. Creech moved around the small room, pulling snakes from their tanks and dropping them onto the floor. Most were rattlesnakes, but there were more species I didn't recognise. One was completely black with beady yellow eyes. It moved fast when it hit the floor, slithering up and over my right arm and resting there.

Then the rattling started. Stimulated by the mice, or my fear, or Creech's madness – or perhaps all three – the rattlesnakes sounded their warning rattles and the room filled with their chorus.

My hands lay slack by my sides. I might have been able to move them, but I was too afraid to try. Long dark shapes shifted around the periphery of my vision.

When all the tanks were empty, Creech returned. He planted one dirty bare foot against my chest and shifted his weight against my lungs, making it difficult to breathe. Almost as an afterthought, he plucked the black snake from my leg and dangled it over my head. It thrashed against him at first, but when he wedged his thumb and forefinger against the base of the snake's head, it fell deathly still.

He looked me in the eyes and said, 'As Saint Peter writ in the Holy Scripture, *Our adversary the Devil goes about seeking whom he may devour.*'

He wasn't talking to me now, but *through* me. His eyes were those of a man far gone. 'The Devil visited and possessed this girl, but now let the serpents drive it out.'

He dropped the snake onto the crotch of my jeans. It circled, gave my belly an exploratory nudge, then pulled itself into a coil.

'*And we shall speak with new tongues,*' Creech said, his voice deep and hollow. '*We shall take up serpents and if we drink any deadly thing it shall not hurt us.* Amen. *And we shall lay hands on the sick and they shall recover.* Amen.'

He brushed aside a thick, sandy-coloured snake and kneeled beside me. 'Can you feel Him in the room, Sammy? God arises. Can you feel the Light?'

He looked at the fluorescent lights overhead. They pulsed once. 'He's here. Don't you feel Him, Sammy?'

A fat old rattlesnake struck lazily for Creech's knee. Creech struck it back with the flat of his hand. The noisy rattling sound grew louder and echoed off the low ceiling.

My lips felt taut and dry, but I could speak again. '... No,' I managed, and, '*please*.'

'Let me hear you say it, Sammy,' Creech said. 'Let me hear you say amen.'

'Please ... I won't tell anyone anything.'

He took my chin between his fingers and squeezed. 'The only way out of this room is if God wills it. I am but an instrument. Now let me hear you say amen.'

'I ...'

He flicked me on the forehead. Fresh pain vibrated through

my skull. 'I'm not leaving here without an amen, and neither are you.'

'... Amen.'

'Louder now.'

'Amen.'

Creech grinned. He strolled casually toward the shed door, minding the snakes the way a man might mind puddles on a drizzly Sunday afternoon walk.

A furry mass slipped from my sleeve and hurried away.

Creech swung the door wide open and stepped outside. A cool breeze swept in, momentarily relieving the sick, artificial humidity. Over his shoulder I saw the night and wanted badly to be out in it.

'May the Light always find you,' Creech said. 'And may you always find the Light.'

Creech reached in, switched off the lights and closed the door behind him. *I'm going to die in this room*, I had time to think, before darkness enveloped me.

MANSON, KENTUCKY

Then

Travis stood in the offices of Miller & Associates, looking out over Manson. The roads were quiet. A faulty streetlight on Womack Street was blinking on and off. A billboard on the corner of Streng and Collins advertised a new burger place. It showed a giant pair of woman's lips wrapped around a cartoon burger. It was only a matter of time before someone spray-painted a penis on it.

I need to get out of Manson, he thought.

Miller & Associates occupied the whole top floor of the three-storey Manson Business Park. It shared the building with several mid-sized commercial companies, such as the law firm of Brown & Still, Dripping Tap Pool & Spa Installations, Ace Air Conditioning and Ray's Security Doors.

He liked it here alone after dark. It was fun to imagine what it would be like to work here during the day. The design was open-plan, with long white desks in place of cubicles. The walls were painted a pastel blue and possessed an oddly soothing quality. Of course, it wasn't doing much to sooth Travis tonight. The medication Dr Redmond had prescribed was wearing off, and now blasts of pain throbbed in his head.

He found the bottle of painkillers in the pocket of his baggy coveralls, dropped two tablets into his mouth and dry swallowed, rubbing his temples.

At the end of the floor stood a large office with a glass wall separating it from the floor. Travis imagined that was where the boss might stand, hands on hips, keeping watch over his accounting minions. Feeling like a trespasser, he went into the office now to run a vacuum across the floor. The noise of the SuckDuck sent shuddering waves of pain through his skull, but he'd run out of sick days, and all those tiny plastic wastebaskets weren't going to empty themselves.

When the pain became too much, he switched off the vacuum, dropped the pack down from his back and sat in the boss's deep leather chair. Being in places like this – offices, schools, the roller rink his second cousin ran in Arlington – outside of business hours always filled him with a very particular kind of melancholy. These places were designed to be full of people, and when those people went home, it felt eerily empty.

The blast of a car horn outside sent a fresh dart of agony through his head. He dry swallowed another two painkillers, stood up and told himself to get to work. The sooner he got through the carpets, the quicker he'd get to the kitchen, bathrooms, surfaces … Sighing, he fell back down into the chair.

The car horn sounded once more. It was coming from the parking lot. Travis went to the window and looked down into the lot. There below the big white *Manson Business Park* sign was Jack Went. He was standing beside his car, looking up. When he spotted Travis at the window, he reached into the car and honked a third time.

'What the hell do you want, Jack?' Travis told the glass. Shifting focus, he looked at his reflection. What wasn't bandaged was bloody.

Another honk. Jack waved him down. Reluctantly, Travis left his cleaning equipment and went downstairs to meet him.

Jack was leaning against Travis's cleaning van when Travis stepped off the elevators and into the lobby. He went to the front door but didn't open it. Jack met him on the other side. He flinched when he saw the blood-matted bandages on Travis's face.

'Does it hurt?' Jack asked.

'Only when I'm awake,' Travis said. 'It's been a long day, Jack. What do you want?'

'To talk. To apologise. To beg your forgiveness, actually.'

Travis massaged the bridge of his busted nose. It hurt in a morbidly addictive way, like picking a scab or tonguing a mouth ulcer.

'There's no excuse for what I did to you,' Jack said. 'I've made a lot of bad choices, Travis. A lot. All I can say is that I'm sorry. I'm sorry for everything.'

'That's not enough, Jack.'

'But it's a start, right?'

Travis looked at Jack for a long moment. He seemed older. 'You wanna come upstairs?'

'Not tonight,' Jack said. 'When's your next break? Feel like going out for a burger or something? Just to talk.'

'Aren't you worried someone'll see us?'

'Not anymore, Travis.'

He got home after eleven that night and was surprised to find his mother awake. She had heaped herself in the dusty sofa on the front porch, sat in a sea of beer cans and cigarette butts. Ava had positioned herself away from the porch light so she could watch Cromdale Street from the shadows, but a lone bug-zapper cracked and popped a few feet to her left, and each time it did, her weathered old face was illuminated.

'Hi, Mom,' Travis said.

'What's new, honey-pie?'

'What are you doing out here?'

'Minding my own, Travis.' She said, and burped. 'That, and waiting for the rain to reach us.'

He sat down on the front porch step and looked at the sky. Storm clouds were gathering.

He found two more painkillers in the pockets of his baggy coveralls, then found a dollar bill. He handed it to his mother. In return she gave him a beer, which he used to wash down the medication.

'Is Patrick home?' he asked.

'Not yet.'

'Did he call?'

'Nope.'

Travis had been thinking a lot about Patrick lately. He'd been thinking about Jack too, and Sammy, but mostly Patrick. He was beginning to fathom Patrick's relationship with Becky Creech and, eventually, he might even fathom his relationship to the Church of the Light Within. Everyone chose their own path, and if Patrick's path happened to be lined with snakes and a fundie with perfect ears, then who was Travis to judge? If anyone knew a thing or two about falling in love with the wrong person, it was him.

Ava chugged a beer. The bug zapper sparked, and for a flash Travis saw a look of concern on her face. Then the porch was dark again, and she burped from the shadows.

He sat in stillness with his mother, watching Cromdale Street, still thinking about Patrick, about Jack, about Sammy, and waiting for the rain to reach him.

MANSON, KENTUCKY

Now

Complete darkness. Not even a pencil-thin sliver of light creeping in under the door. Full, complete and total dark. In that darkness, snakes. I heard them shifting in the corners of the room, across the concrete floor around my feet. I felt the weight of the black snake. It had moved from my belly and settled between my breasts.

I lay motionless on my back, too afraid to move, but knowing that if I didn't I might get bit.

I heard rattling, and the short, sharp squeal of a mouse meeting its end. The air was hot. Sweat beaded on my forehead, under my arms, on the small of my back.

Something moved over my hand. Instinctively, I struck at it, and was relieved to feel fur and not scales.

The snake on my chest began to move again, this time toward my neck. Its tongue flicked against the underside of my chin. If I was going to move, it had to be now.

Bracing my hand against the concrete floor, I took three deep breaths, then swung my body onto my side. My head rung with pain.

The snake slid off me, landing somewhere in the dark with an angry hiss. Climbing quickly to my feet, panting against the fear, I scrambled backwards through black. The ball of my foot landed on a short, stubby shape. It moved away from me with the sound of a sausage being dragged over concrete.

Where's the fucking door? I thought. I'd managed to get myself turned around and cursed myself.

'Help!' I cried. The sound came back to me, and a fresh spasm of pain seared behind my eyes. 'Stuart! Help! Help!'

But there was no help coming.

A mouse ran up the leg of my jeans. I slapped at it, swatting it away. A long, narrow shape slithered between my feet. I kicked it, sent it flopping backwards.

Snakes hissed. Snakes rattled.

Stumbling blindly into the dark, my left foot fell against a tight, leathery coil. The snake sounded its rattle, so close I could feel the vibrations in my toes. Afraid that it might turn savage if I kicked it or tried to move, I remained perfectly still. Even if I could charge forward, I didn't know which direction to head. And even if I managed to avoid the reptile at my foot, the floor was peppered with rattling landmines.

Slithering, scurrying, nightmarish shapes moved all around me in the dark.

Move, I told myself. *You have to swim toward something.*

A force slammed against my right leg, and something flailed against me. I screamed. The sound echoed and came back to me tenfold.

The *thing* was still thrashing wildly against my leg. I reached toward it. My fingers closed around a pulsing snake. I tried yanking it away but it was stuck. It had struck me, I realised, and caught its fangs in the denim of my jeans.

It flailed, more violently now, as panic seized it. I yanked harder this time and the snake came loose. Extending my hand as far away from my body as possible, I dropped it.

I wasn't fast enough. It spun around and clamped down hard around the knuckles on my right hand.

I've been bit, I had time to think, before a searing hot pain pounded through my hand, as if I'd just stuck it in a bear trap.

The snake fell heavily and, thankfully, slithered away.

Tucking my injured hand under my arm, I cried out in fear and agony. The pain was getting steadily worse, moving from my hand up into my forearm.

I remembered what Stuart had told me about his uncle Clyde. '*It would have been a horrific way to go,*' he had said. '*A bite from a rattler destroys nerves, tissue, even bone.*'

I took another blind step forward and landed gingerly on the body of another snake. It struck at my bare foot. Another bite. More searing hot pain.

I stumbled to my knees and threw up. The smell of my own vomit filled the room and made me vomit again.

My hand was beginning to swell. Breathing was becoming extremely difficult. Intense pain swept through me. My mind fogged over and soon my thoughts became fragmented and distant.

I tried to stand but stumbled, grabbed the lip of a terrarium for balance but instead brought it crashing down to the floor. There was broken glass underfoot now, cracking and shredding the bare soles of my feet, but I hardly felt it. I could hardly sense anything now. The humidity, the smell of mice and vomit, the sound of shapes moving around my feet, even the fear was gone.

I reached out through the dark, hoping to find the door handle, expecting to find nothing, but instead found a … *thread.*

While there was no way of knowing what colour the thread was in the dark, somehow I knew it was red, like the one I imagined tied around Sammy Went's waist in the nowhere place of my mind. It was soft and silky. As my fingers closed around it a voice whispered, *This isn't real, you're in shock or hallucinating from the extreme pain.*

Ignoring the voice, I followed the thread through the darkness. Hand over hand, through broken glass and shifting snakes, it led me directly to the door. It was locked, but after two or three solid shoves it swung open.

I stumbled out into the cold air and collapsed in the damp grass.

Rolling onto my back I saw a vast starscape. For a second I was taken back to before my mother – *she's not your mother* – died, sitting on the little balcony outside her hospice room, looking at the stars. In a morphine daze she said the sky was a big black sheet with hundreds, thousands, millions of tiny pinpricks poked in it, letting in light from the Great Beyond. I'd half-ignored her. I hadn't cared about the stars. How could I? She was dying.

But the sky looked that way to me now.

Red and blue lights began to dance over the landscape, through the trees and across the wall of the church. Then there were footsteps behind me.

'She's here,' a voice called out. 'She's over here.'

A man approached. 'Jesus, she's been bit.'

Someone strong pulled me into their arms, stroked my hair, told me over and over that everything was going to be alright. Help was on the way. Hold on. Just hold on.

'Stuart …' I whispered. 'You found me.'

'You're goddamn right I found you,' he said. 'But it's not Stuart.'

'… Who?'

I blinked blood from my eyes and shifted to see the man's face. It was Jack Went.

MANSON, KENTUCKY

Then

Becky Creech sat in the passenger side of Patrick's Eagle as they turned off the highway and started up the long road to the church.

'This is a bad idea,' Patrick said. 'We should be past state lines by now.'

'We wouldn't get far without cash, darling,' Becky said. She rested her hand on his knee. That seemed to calm him. 'You'll see an opening to the left just up ahead. It's an old firebreak. It's mostly overgrown now, but there'll be enough room for you guys to wait.'

'Let *me* go.'

'You don't know where my brother keeps the donation box. It's easier this way.'

She stretched out her neck with a crack and a pop, first left, then right. They'd slept in the car last night, and now her muscles were paying for it. She craned her head – wincing at fresh pain in her neck – to look into the back seat. Sammy was asleep. Morning light filtered through the trees lining the unsealed road and fell over her face. Her eyes were closed but moving beneath the lids. She must have been dreaming. Her thumb was wedged firmly between her lips and she had pulled a tight woollen blanket halfway over her face. Her brand-new stuffed turtle sat beside her.

She had cried blue murder when Patrick took away the gorilla, but it had been a good plan to plant it in the woods. They had made a lot of good plans, but none of them mattered anymore. As dawn crept in over the road ahead, the events of last night crept into Becky's mind. Pulling the trigger. The gunshot. The sheriff folding in on himself like a suitcase, then falling limp against the chipped tile floor of that abandoned old apartment that had, for a brief time, been home.

Block it out, she told herself. *There will be plenty of time to repent when this is all done. Maybe God will never forgive me, but what I do now, I do for that little girl.*

Patrick eased the Eagle off the road and onto the old firebreak. It hadn't been cleared for years, but it was well hidden. Patrick and Sammy would be safe here, wouldn't they? She tried to keep it from her voice.

'I'll walk the rest of the way,' she said. 'I won't be long.'

'What if your brother's there?'

'He won't be,' she said. 'It's not even six am. He held Sunday service yesterday, so he won't be up before noon. Trust me.'

He took her hand in his, then kissed her.

'I love you,' he said. But his eyes said something different. His eyes said, *Damn you, Becky*. She'd seen that same look before, on the day he returned home from prison.

Damn you, Becky.

She and Patrick were meant to move away after his release. Becky had been saving, and it wouldn't take long for Patrick to find a job if he wasn't too fussy. As soon as they scraped together enough cash they would move away, find their own quiet place away from Manson and away from the Church, somewhere they could make up for lost time, somewhere they could just *be*. It was a good dream, sweet and simple. One she had clung to on the longest, darkest nights while Patrick was at Greenwood.

Instead, he had arrived home to find the town in chaos. A little girl was missing and his brother seemed to be a prime suspect. Then he had arrived at Becky's little rental in Old Commons and found the missing girl bundled up asleep in the spare bedroom.

He could have left her then.

'Just give me five minutes,' she had said. She was shocked, shaken, confused and pacing. 'Five minutes to explain this and then you can call the cops or my brother, or whoever the heck you want.'

He had flown briefly into a macho rage, and Becky couldn't blame him. But when the child stirred and Becky calmed her, he had agreed. 'Five minutes, then I'm gone.'

Becky had used her five minutes to state her case the best she could. She had discovered Sammy Went was to be reprogrammed, which was fundie speak for *exorcised*. It was sanctioned by her brother, Dale, and Sammy's own mother, Molly. Becky didn't know when or where the reprogramming was to take place, but knew it would be brutal, traumatic and, possibly, fatal.

Patrick listened.

She told him about a case in Floyd, Virginia, in November of 1973, when four-year-old Jocelyn Rice was fatally smothered by her mother's church during a botched exorcism.

In March of 1978, Evangelist preacher Neil Haleck claimed Satan was shifting between two children of one of the members of his church. The children were aged three and one. An exorcism was performed to drive out the Devil. When the three-year-old started to fight back, Haleck proclaimed it was Satan and drove a dagger into the child's chest.

In July of 1980, somewhere in Louisiana, a mother ripped the tongue and intestines out of her two-year-old son during a home exorcism.

In January 1984—

'Stop,' he said. She had made her point.

'All I wanted was to talk Molly out of it,' Becky said. 'To tell her what I just told you, to tell her what I've been through and what it cost me ... What it cost *us*. But when I turned into their street I saw that poor, sweet little girl was out there in the front yard all alone. To them she was something to discard, left out front like the trash on garbage day. But to me, for us, she could be a gift from God.'

'Becky.'

'I couldn't leave her, Patrick. Before I even knew what I was doing I'd bundled her into the car and brought her here.'

So their simple plan became a complicated one. They would hide out in Redwater long enough to avoid suspicion. Patrick knew a place. They would take it in turns watching over Sammy, making sure they were both seen around town. Becky would be seen at Sammy's search party. Patrick would be seen looking for work in Coleman. When the timing was right, they would slip out of Manson and into the night, and they could be sure nobody would be looking for them.

That changed last night, after the gunshot.

She went around to the back of the Eagle and popped the rear door open. She pulled up the square of carpet covering the spare tyre well and took from it her father's hunting rifle.

Just in case.

She closed the door gently. She didn't want to wake Sammy. Then she went back around to the driver's side window and kissed Patrick once more.

'If anything happens,' she said.

'Don't.'

'If anything happens, you look after Sammy, okay?'

'Becky.'

'Promise me, Patrick,' she said. 'I lost the light a long time ago, but found it again in you, and in that little girl. If anything happens, keep driving. Keep both those lights burning. Don't look back.'

He glanced into the back seat, then looked back at Becky. 'I promise.'

'I'll be right back,' she said.

As she walked up the dirt road toward the church, a cold breeze whipped through the trees and lashed her bare legs. She looked down at them and remembered she was wearing denim cut-offs. It had been a long time since she left the house without wearing a skirt to the ankles, and never had she set foot in the church dressed like this.

She'd never be able to come back to Manson after all that had happened. It would be hard saying goodbye to a lot of things, but the church wasn't one of them. Not anymore. When she thought of the Light Within now, she thought of what happened in that rundown old farmhouse in Coleman.

When she reached the end of the clearing she stopped in her tracks, feeling uneasy. The parking lot was empty, and there was nothing to suggest she wasn't alone. She had been here a million times before, but today something was different.

The sun had risen behind the Appalachian Mountains. Backlit, they bled together like giant still waves. The forest wall, which formed a natural barrier between the church compound and the outside world, felt thicker today, like the mile-long perimeter fence that surrounded Greenwood Corrections. The old community garden and chicken coop – neither used since Becky was a child – stood quiet against the treeline. The snake hutch looked haunted; the church itself looked positively ominous.

When she moved again she moved fast, walking in a straight line for the church. With each step, the rifle slung over her shoulder slapped against her left thigh. She held the strap firmly with both hands, doubly glad she brought the gun with her.

There was a lock on the front door of the church, but it had never been used. She pushed it open and stepped inside. The smell of sawdust, snake shit and sweat hit her hard, but wasn't altogether unpleasant. It was the smell of the church, the smell of childhood.

It was dark, but she didn't turn on the lights. Instead, she crossed the room with her arms outstretched, relying on muscle memory to keep from tripping and breaking her neck, or knocking the glass terrarium off its table.

Behind a door at the back of the church was a narrow hallway, at the end of which was a small supply closet and a humming bar fridge where Dale kept antivenin. The supply closet door was locked, but Becky knew where Dale kept the key. She dropped to one knee, felt for the loose length of baseboard beside the closet door and yanked it out. The key lay in the one-inch space beyond.

When the door was open, she went up on tiptoes to reach the top shelf, slid aside an old mop bucket and brought down the donation box from its hiding place. Engraved on the side of the box was, *Give your whole self to God, give what you can afford to the Light Within*. It was full of cash.

If someone had told Becky a year before that she'd be sneaking into the church to empty the donation box, she would have laughed. Yet here she was. Lately her relationship with God had become increasingly complicated – especially after last night. Stealing money now sat low on a long list of sins.

The lid of the box was fastened with a small silver padlock. She set it down between her feet, took the butt of the rifle, lined it up with the padlock and—

She froze, hearing the steady whir of an engine. She listened. The engine grew louder, coming closer. It was a motorbike. Dale's motorbike. As the sound exploded into the clearing, Becky brought the butt of the rifle down against the silver padlock, pulverising it.

She set the rifle aside and slid quickly to her knees, heaping out handfuls of cash and jamming it into an old vacuum bag she'd found wedged between cleaning products in the supply closet. When the bag was full she tied it off, then stuffed the rest of the cash deep into the pockets of her cut-offs.

The engine idled out front and fell silent.

With hands that simply wouldn't move fast enough, Becky returned the donation box to the top shelf, locked the supply closet door and returned the key to its hiding place behind the baseboard. She grabbed the bag with one hand, the rifle with the other, and hurried out of the hallway.

Too late. Dale was standing just inside the church door. He flicked on the light switch, revealing a bruised face and bloody lip.

Becky flinched. 'Dale, gosh, what happened to your face?'

'Eventful service last night,' he said, touching a golfball-sized welt under his right eye. 'I didn't see your car. How did you get here?'

'Hitched some. Walked some.'

'More importantly, what are you doing with Daddy's gun?'

He looked from the gun to the stuffed vacuum bag in her arm. There was no lie that would get her out of this.

'What's going on, Becky?'

'Get out of my way, Dale,' she said, taking a step forward.

He took a step forward too, cocking his head, flashing a curious smile. One of his teeth was missing. With the lights on, she could see a faint pink bloodstain right where her brother was standing. Eventful service indeed.

'Is it true what they say about churches?' Becky asked. 'If I claim sanctuary, would you be bound by God to protect me?'

'Who would you be claiming sanctuary from?'

'Take a wild guess, Dale,' she said.

'What have you done, Becky? Does it have something to do with Sammy Went?'

She raised the rifle in his direction. That wiped the smile from his face. He stiffened, raised his hands.

'Don't do that which cannot be undone,' Dale said.

'We're way beyond that now, Dale,' Becky whispered. 'I took her. I took Sammy Went.'

'Why?'

'To save her from you,' she said, tucking the bag of cash under her arm and letting her finger settle on the rifle trigger. 'To save her from her mother, and from this goddamned church.'

'Becky.'

'I know what you were going to do to her, *Reverend*,' Becky said, 'I know about the exorcism. You were going to do to that child what you did to me.'

'Where is she?' Dale said, his voice deep and somehow confident.

'It would have killed her, Dale. Are you so blindly devoted that you couldn't see that? You would have killed that child like you killed mine.'

'What happened to you wasn't my fault.'

'What did you think was going to happen to my baby when you shouted scripture in my face, when you held me underwater, when you locked me in a basement with—'

'We were trying to save you.'

'Save me from what, you stupid asshole?'

'From the Devil!'

She wedged the butt of the gun against her shoulder and raised it, aiming for Dale's neck. 'Tell me something, Dale, do you think it worked? Do you think any of that bad you saved me from would be worse than losing an unborn child?'

Dale wet his lips and said, 'The baby would have lived if it were God's will. I didn't take that child, Becky. The Lord did. He pulled it from your womb because it was impure. Because it was spawned from sin, by a criminal. Worse, by a non-believer. All you had to do was keep your damn legs shut!'

Spittle flew from his mouth.

'You can pass the buck to God,' Becky said. 'And maybe you can even sell yourself on your own line of bullshit, but you knew exactly what you were doing. You wanted to avoid a scandal. You wanted to protect your reputation, the Church's reputation, you wanted—'

'I wanted to protect *you*.'

Her finger pressed against the trigger. 'How do you think that worked out? You think the exorcism worked, or is the Devil still in me?'

'It's not too late, Becky,' he said. 'You're lost. That's all. Come on back now. Come on back to the Light.'

'I killed the sheriff,' she said.

'What?'

'It's over for me, Dale. And if it's over for me, it's over for us. I didn't come here to kill you. You weren't supposed to be here. Yet here we are. Maybe it was God's will.'

Dale linked his fingers, bowed his head, and whispered, '*Behold, I give unto you power to tread on serpents and scorpions*.'

'Are you praying?'

'*And over all the power over my enemy*.'

'Are you actually praying?'

'*And nothing shall by any means hurt—*'

She pulled the trigger. For a moment all she could hear was a sharp ringing in her ears.

She waited for her brother to collapse in on himself. Instead, he looked down at his body and saw nothing. A thin beam of light fell in through a perfect, round bullet hole in the wall. She had missed.

Dale screamed and charged at her.

Panicked, Becky lifted the rifle to fire again, but she wasn't fast enough. Dale reached her and yanked the gun away, grabbing it by the barrel and searing his flesh. He yelped at the pain, then scowled. He struck his sister across the face.

She slopped backwards in a heap, flailing and screaming. He climbed on top of her and hit her again.

And again. And again.

Becky clawed at him, shredded a slice of skin from his chin. Hot blood drenched her face, but she felt no pain. Adrenalin shot through her system and she felt filled up. She struggled against him, but God had given him complete power over her.

Just as darkness was closing in around the corners of her vision, Becky heard the rev of Patrick's Eagle thumping into the church parking lot.

MANSON, KENTUCKY

Now

An ambulance rushed me to Manson Mercy Hospital, where doctors fed nineteen vials of antivenin into my system. Had I arrived an hour later my hand would likely have needed to be amputated. Had the bites gone untreated, I would have died a slow and painful death. I was treated for second-degree burns on my left ear, where Creech had struck me with the coffee pot. They treated abrasions on my face and stitched up deep cuts on my feet.

I was on a lot of pain medication, so I spent the next two days slipping in and out of consciousness. I don't remember much. I do remember salivating a lot, which a nurse told me was normal after a rattlesnake bite. And I remember Dean. He and Amy must have arrived sometime on the second day. At various points I woke to find him by my bed, running his fingers through my hair, or sitting in the seat by the window reading the paper.

When I woke on the morning of the third day, Dean was gone. In his place were Stuart and Amy. Stuart rose from the chair by the window when he saw I was awake. Amy was already sitting on the foot of my bed. Having them both in the same room at the same time felt surreal. The worlds of Kim Leamy and Sammy Went had officially collided.

'How's the pain?' Amy asked.

'I'm on morphine, I think, so I can't feel a whole lot.'

'Does that mean I can hug you?'

'If you promise to be gentle.'

She collapsed into the bed beside me. It was an awkward, uncomfortable embrace. It didn't matter. I'd never been so happy to see anyone in my life.

'Did you meet my brother?' I asked.

'Yeah, we've met,' Amy said.

Stuart blushed. He came to my side and took hold of my good hand – the other was wrapped in bandages – and smiled. 'That's the first time you've called me that.'

'How did you find me?'

'Dad turned up not long after you left,' he said. 'When we couldn't find you and the car was gone, it was a pretty safe bet you were at the church. You shouldn't have gone there alone.'

'I know,' I said. 'I'm sorry.'

'Me too. For everything. Claire's on her way.'

'Good.'

There was a knock on the door. Detective Burkhart had brought a bouquet of flowers from the gift shop downstairs. 'Do you have some time to talk?'

'We'll give you some space,' Amy said, climbing off the bed.

'Don't go too far, either of you.'

Stuart gave my hand a squeeze and left the room with Amy. When Burkhart and I were alone, he set the flowers down on the side table, dragged the plastic chair closer to the bed and sat down in it.

'How's the pain?'

'They have me on a lot of drugs,' I said. 'So I'm actually feeling pretty groovy.'

'Groovy, huh?' He smiled and scratched his beard. Then his smiled faded. 'We haven't got Creech yet.'

I could have cried. Creech had fled, most likely immediately after locking me in with the snakes, and while my head told me he was a thousand miles away, my heart worried he was much closer than that.

'What happened out there, Kim?' Burkhart asked. 'Your brother said you went to question Creech about his sister.'

Nodding, I eased myself up and wiped my mouth. I was still salivating. Burkhart passed me a cup of water, and I sipped it. 'I think Carol Leamy and Becky Creech are the same person. When I asked Creech about her he just … flipped. Something happened out at the church a long time ago, something to do with his sister, and I think I was there.'

Burkhart looked curious, as if he were digesting something. He then reached into his pocket and took out a folded square of paper. He turned it over a few times in his hands. 'We're in the middle of searching Creech's house. I found something there that might interest you.' He unfolded the paper and handed it to me, face down. 'A photo of Becky Creech. Take a look. Tell me if it's the woman who raised you.'

I turned the page over, took one look at the picture of Becky Creech, and immediately burst into tears. My hand swelled with pain. I pressed the button for a fresh hit of morphine, but I had already reached the maximum dose.

'Sandy was wrong,' I said. 'The scar isn't even on the same hand.'

'What?'

I folded the page, handed it back to Burkhart and said, 'It's not her.'

My next visitor was Jack Went. He was a tall man with a balding swatch of white-grey hair. His smile was as warm as it was sad. 'I don't know what to call you. Sammy or Kim?'

'I think I'll have to start going by both,' I said. 'It'll take a while for me to get used to.'

'It'll take a while for me to get used to *that accent*.'

He sat down beside me on the bed. We were unmistakably related. I saw my own face in his; the same eyes. How could Molly not have seen it?

'I should never have stopped looking for you,' Jack said. 'I should never have let you go in the first place. It was my job to protect you. I'm so sorry, Sammy.'

'For what it's worth,' I said. 'I've had a good life so far.'

He didn't bother trying to dry his tears. A man appeared in the doorway. He was dressed well, somewhere in his late forties or early fifties. He formed a steeple below his chin with his hands and was smiling broadly. Jack waved him in.

'This is my husband, Travis,' Jack said.

Travis took slow, steady steps toward the bed. 'Is it really you?'

'Yep,' I said. 'It's really me.'

As one father stood over my bed, a second one strolled in the door. Dean was holding a *Get Well Soon* balloon that floated above him like a buoy. He skidded to a stop when he saw Jack and Travis by my bed. He seemed shocked at first, but then his expression relaxed. He looked first to Jack, then to his husband.

'Hello, Travis,' he said.

Travis looked like he'd seen a ghost. '… Patrick?'

MANSON, KENTUCKY

Then

The scene revealed itself slowly to Patrick Eckles, as if too much sensory input too fast would flood his system and shut him down. The hunting rifle lay on a bloodstained floor. Beside it, an old vacuum bag, torn roughly open down the middle, spilling cash like intestines in a zombie movie.

Next he saw Dale Creech. He had expected this, after hearing the preacher's bike roar up the road to the church. After the gunshot rang through the woods, a small part of him had expected to see Creech dead. In truth, Patrick had no real idea what he would find when he stepped through the open door of the church, but he certainly hadn't expected to see Creech like this: pink-cheeked, bleeding, crying. Slowly removing his big hands from Becky's neck and rushing for the rifle.

Patrick didn't move. He was staring at the woman he loved. She was still. Too still. Spread out on the church floor like a ragdoll, her left arm stretched out at an unnatural angle. There was blood on her face, but with no heartbeat to disturb it, that was still too.

She's dead, he thought as Creech reached the hunting rifle, almost tripping on Becky's foot. Creech raised the barrel of the gun toward him. Patrick had never had a gun pointed at him before. That may have surprised some people. But right now he hardly registered it. *Becky is dead. This is happening.*

'No,' he said, whispering now.

Creech was saying something – shouting it. But his words sounded distant and foreign to Patrick. The world seemed distant and foreign. He might have stayed in his trance forever, if not for the squeal. It was high-pitched, like a train whistle, reverberating through his brain.

Becky is dead. You're here. This is happening. That man has a gun on you and is likely to pull the trigger.

The whistle sharpened and became the sound of a child crying. Sammy. She stood behind him in the doorway of the church, sobbing hard enough to force snot from her nose. Patrick's eyes shifted from the little girl, to Becky's body, to Creech and the rifle. Similarly, Creech's eyes shifted from Patrick, to his sister, to the little girl screaming in the doorway.

Becky spoke suddenly, not from her mouth, but from Patrick's memory. *'If anything happens, you look after Sammy, okay?'*

Sammy was still crying. She reached out to Patrick, tiny fingers clasping the air.

'Promise me, Patrick … Keep both those lights burning. Don't look back.'

He spun to face Sammy, lifted her tightly into his arms. She buried her face into his shoulder, shuddered violently for a second, and then started to quieten.

He looked at Creech.

Creech lowered the rifle and pointed to the door. 'Go.'

'Don't look back,' Becky had told him, and he didn't.

He drove all day, looking in the rear-view mirror every thirty seconds to make sure Sammy was still there, as if she might somehow disappear from the back seat while he was doing sixty miles an hour on the highway. The empty passenger seat brought a fresh gush of tears, so he tried not to look at it.

He pulled into a rest stop about six miles short of the state line. He found a smelly old baseball cap jammed under the driver's seat and put it on, pulling the peak down low. There were a handful of trucks parked at forty-five-degree angles by a big concrete gas station. The station was covered in chipped blue paint and graffiti. A faded sign hanging above the door read, *Bob's Stop. Gas! Donuts! Hotdogs! Pop!*

After filling the car with gas and stocking up on road snacks, his wallet was startlingly light. He thought about the bag of cash on the floor of the church and for a moment felt like howling. He took a quarter from his pocket and found a payphone at the back of the station.

'Yeah?' his mother answered on the tenth ring.

'It's me, Mom,' Patrick said. 'Is Travis around?'

'Nope.'

'Any idea when he'll be back?'

'Nope,' she said. 'That it?'

'Yeah. No. Mom, I'm in trouble.'

A truck rolled up outside in a cloud of diesel fumes.

'Where are you?' Ava asked.

'It don't matter,' he said. 'I need help.'

'How much *help*?'

'How much can you spare?'

'If you wanna keep a friend, never borrow, never lend.'

'Mom, please.'

Patrick heard the spark of a match on the other end of the line, followed by the wet sucking sound of Ava lighting a cigarette.

'Tell me how much and where you need it wired,' she said.

Tears of relief spilled out. He looked out into the lot and saw Sammy in the back seat of the Eagle. 'Thank you.'

'Uh huh,' Ava said. 'You need me to pass anything on to your brother?'

'No,' Patrick said. 'Just keep an eye on him for me.'

On Monday 9 April 1990, six days after Becky Creech took Sammy Went from her home, Patrick Eckles crossed Kentucky state lines for what he hoped would be the last time. He and Sammy drove all day and all night, stopping only for gas and food. When they slept, it was in the back of the Eagle or in cheap, cash-only motels. There was a swimming pool at one of the hotels. Patrick bought Sammy a pair of too-big yellow trunks from a local department store and waded into the deep end with her on his shoulders.

Sammy was confused for a long time. She'd get sad sometimes, and Patrick wondered how much she remembered and how much was already gone. But as the miles blew away beneath the Eagle, Sammy began to accept her new reality and grew attached to Patrick, just as he grew more attached to her. He felt her light, just as Becky Creech had, and that was all that mattered.

Patrick bought a newspaper everywhere they stopped. The body of Sheriff Ellis was found in the slum in Redwater, right where he and Becky had left it. There were rumblings about a connection to Sammy's kidnapping, at first, and theories he might have been killed while visiting a prostitute, who were known to frequent that part of the city. But as weeks drifted past without any evidence, news of his unsolved murder got smaller and deeper in the pages of the newspapers, then disappeared altogether.

There was nothing in the papers about Becky. Patrick assumed her brother covered up the murder and likely buried her body somewhere in the woods around the church. He hoped Creech had been gentle with her, and that he had said a prayer by her grave before he started filling in the dirt. He also hoped Creech hadn't said anything about seeing them at the church that day, and that he never would. It would be mutually assured destruction, but nobody could predict what a mind like the reverend's might do.

Eight months later, Patrick paid a man to forge a passport

for Sammy, and they disappeared to Australia. He changed his name from Patrick Eckles to Dean Leamy. There was no deep significance to his new name: he came up with it on the spur of the moment. It didn't matter. The important thing was, he wasn't Patrick Eckles anymore.

He found work in Melbourne and assimilated as quickly as he could. It took him a long time to neutralise his accent, so in the early days he didn't talk much. But becoming Dean was easier than he expected, like slipping into a warm bathtub or pulling on a crisp new pair of jeans.

He never planned to meet anyone, and certainly didn't plan on falling in love. But, as he'd learned the hard way in Manson, his plans had a knack of falling through. A woman named Carol fell right back in love with Dean, and she fell even harder in love with Sammy.

Sammy was called Kim then.

For a time, Carol believed Kim was Dean's daughter, but as convincing as Dean's lie had become, she soon began noticing inconsistencies in his story. At times, Dean thought she was like a human lie detector.

Eventually, he told her the truth. Eventually, Carol made her peace with it. They both agreed that Kim could never know. To strengthen the lie and further distance themselves from Sammy Went, Carol raised her under the pretence she was biologically hers.

Years passed.

Dean and Carol had a daughter, Amy. Kim had a new baby sister to boss around. They grew up believing they were half-sisters. Dean and Carol grew old and the lie became something buried. The past became a deep, dark ocean full of sharks and monsters.

Carol got sick. Lost her battle with cancer. Stuart Went approached Kim, now a grown woman, at Northampton Community TAFE, where she taught photography three nights a week.

SOMEWHERE OVER THE PACIFIC OCEAN

Now

The 787 cruised along at forty thousand feet above sea level, halfway between Manson and Melbourne, between the past and the present, between Sammy's world and mine.

The cabin lights had been dimmed, and most of the other passengers were asleep. Sipping a bourbon and coke, I stared out the window of the plane. It was too dark to see much, aside from my ghostly reflection.

Dean and I had made this trip together once. Back when he was Patrick and I was Sammy. He wouldn't be making it again, not for a long while at least.

I hadn't spoken to him since the day at Manson Mercy, when he had opened the Patrick Eckles door and invited me in. I had sat in stunned silence afterwards, my head pounding with anger, my mind spinning with questions. Had he rescued me or stolen me? Did he want my forgiveness or my thanks? Was he Dean or Patrick?

In the end, all I had managed to say was, 'I wish Mum was here.'

'Yeah,' Dean said. 'Me too.'

A small red bird had landed nervously on the windowsill then. I think it was a northern cardinal.

Dean was formally charged with kidnapping and accessory to murder under the name Patrick Eckles. They hadn't set a date for his trial yet, but I knew I would go back for it. What choice did I have? He was family.

It would be a long time before I could forgive Dean – if I ever could – and a long time before I could reconcile Sammy Went and Kim Leamy into something whole. But you've got to swim toward something, right?

On my final night in Manson, I received two phone calls. The first was from Detective Burkhart. In his charming Southern drawl he told me that Dale Creech had been arrested by state police at a truck stop somewhere near the Kentucky state line. He had confessed to the murder of Becky Creech, and claimed to have buried her body somewhere in the woods surrounding the church compound.

Finally, the shadow man was gone.

The second call was from Molly Went. She got my number from Stuart. She wasn't calling to apologise or to make a weeping declaration or anything quite so cathartic. She was just calling to shoot the breeze. She asked me how long my flight was and couldn't imagine ever sitting on a plane for that long. She wanted to know what Australia was like, if our snakes were really as deadly as everyone said they were, if kangaroos hopped around our streets. As the conversation wrapped up, she gave me her number and told me if I ever wanted to call, that would be fine.

'I'll think about it,' I'd said. And I would.

As the 787 descended over Melbourne, I looked out over the city. It was flat and grey, familiar yet somehow different.

This place hasn't changed, I decided. *But the woman coming back here has.*

Amy, Wayne and Lisa were waiting for me in the airport. My niece was the first to spot me. She shouted my name and ran toward me. I hoisted her up by the armpits and pulled her into a hug, squeezing her tight. Amy threw her arms around us both. Wayne watched from a respectful distance and offered to take my bag, but when I was done hugging Amy and Lisa, I hugged him too.

There was a lot to come, and a lot to figure out, but I wasn't thinking about any of that. I was thinking about Sammy Went, the nowhere child in my dark memory place. I could see the red thread tied around her waist. I could see her tugging at it, expecting to bring it back slack, but this time it pulled taut. She stood and followed it, hand over hand, through the darkness and into the light.

Author's Note

Writing is a solitary job, which, for the most part, is just how I like it. Working four metres from my bed and one from my dog means that at least some of the decisions I made over the years must have been good ones. But now that the book is out, I actually get to talk to people.

With that in mind, this is a note to say thank you, and to start a conversation with you, dear reader. If you feel like reaching out to share your thoughts or just to say hello, I'd love to hear from you. You can contact me through my website (christian-white.com) or hit me up on social media. I promise to up my Twitter game. With any luck, by the time you're reading this I'll have more than six followers.

While you're here, I thought I'd share the inspiration behind the book and how I went about writing it. You're under no obligation to read on, but if you're the sort of person who sits in the cinema until the credits have rolled and the lights have come up, or if you're someone who just likes knowing the story *behind* the story, stick around. Or, if you're a completionist like my wife, who feels compelled to read every single word in a book, sorry, I'll try to make this brief.

I wrote this book, first and foremost, to get it out of my head. Anyone with a story thumping around their mind (I suspect there are a lot of you out there) will know that getting it onto the page, or the screen, or the canvas, or whatever medium takes your fancy, is like an itch that must be scratched. A muscle that needs to be flexed. A scab you can't help but pick.

I had no real idea how to write a novel when I got started. I had tried and failed before and didn't want to fail again. So for guidance, as I so often do in an hour of need, I turned to Stephen King. If you've ever thought about writing a novel of your own, stop what you're doing right now and go buy, borrow or steal a copy of *On Writing*. Part memoir part how-to-guide, it gives you a clear roadmap to turning your nugget of an idea into a manuscript. I can now tell you from personal experience, the roadmap works. You're holding the proof in your hands.

When the central idea for *The Nowhere Child* came to me – *what if you discovered you were abducted as a child and the people you think are your parents are in fact your kidnappers?* – I knew it was interesting enough to generate a big story, but it was also generic enough to make me cautious. A million kidnap stories have already been told, so this one had to be different. It needed something else. It needed … Kentucky.

When I was a teenager, my family and I took a Griswoldian road trip across the United States. Starting in Wilkes-Barre, Pennsylvania (where my sister was living at the time), we drove all the way down to Florida and back again. Along the way we stopped in Kentucky, where I formed two very clear memories. One: my dad getting really excited when a local told us, 'Y'all come back now.' And two: Mammoth Cave.

In case you didn't guess by the name, Mammoth Cave is just that: a vast system of subterranean passageways and cavernous chambers. We stopped there for the afternoon and took a walking tour through the cave. It was stunning and overwhelming in a way that only naturally formed landmarks can be.

We walked beneath ancient stalactites, our path lined with small yellow lamps. When we reached a particularly gigantic cavern, our tour guide had us stand in place while he turned out all the lights. The darkness that rolled over us was like nothing I'd ever felt before or have felt since. It was heavy and total and complete. I held my hand out an inch in front of my face and couldn't see a thing. There was something spiritual about that darkness, something primal, powerful and universally binding.

Long after the tour guide turned the lights back on, that darkness lingered with me, like a strange sort of trauma. When I wrote *The Nowhere Child*, I wanted to tap into that feeling somehow, which is why I set most of it in Kentucky. When I picture Kim Leamy's dark memory place, where little Sammy Went is doomed to wander, I picture that cavern inside Mammoth Cave, with all the lights turned out.

Well, that's it for me. From the bottom of my heart, thank you for reading my book. Honestly, it means the world to me. I can't remember if I read this someplace or made it up myself, but the relationship between the author and reader is like a sacred pact. The reader gives the author a dozen or so hours of their life, and in return, hopefully, the author gives them a story worth their time. Sometimes the reader is left feeling short-changed, but more often than not, in my experience, it's a good and fair exchange. Over the years I've read a ton of books and have always expected a lot from whoever I was giving my time. Now that I'm on the other side of the pact, I want you to know that I take this shit seriously.

I sincerely hope you enjoyed *The Nowhere Child* and if you do feel short-changed, I hope you give me a second chance. I'm only just getting started.

Acknowledgements

Stephen King makes it look pretty easy, but writing a novel is tough, and requires the support of many amazing people. Come to think of it, support might not be the right word. Love might be more accurate. Patience also works. With that in mind, here's a list of some of the amazing people who helped in the creation of this book.

Everyone at Affirm Press. What can I say? Your passion is contagious and I love you all. Special thanks goes to Martin Hughes and Ruby Ashby-Orr, who taught me how to be a better writer; and Keiran Rogers, Grace Breen and Emily Ashenden, who make me look like one.

All of my overseas publishers, who overwhelmed me with support and provided invaluable insight. I hope to meet you all in real life and buy you a drink. Particular thanks to Julia Wisdom at HarperCollins, who came up with the title.

My agents at RGM, Jennifer Naughton and Candice Thom, who always have my back.

The Wheeler Centre and the Victorian Premier's Literary Award for an Unpublished Manuscript: without you, this book would still be just a Word document on my computer.

My parents, Ivan and Keera White. You taught me to find my own path and walk it. Dad, you always handed me the movie section of the newspaper on our secret McDonald's breakfasts. Mum, you taught me how to tell a story on our long walks. It was the combination of these two things that made me a writer.

My siblings, Niki (the strongest woman I know), Peter (who has life figured out), Jamie, (who torments me and makes me laugh in equal measure) and the partners that put up with them.

All of the DeRoches, with a special shout-out to Torre, who inspired me with her own writing success; and Chris, who has the best laugh I've ever heard.

My closest friends, Jon and Sophie Asquith, who continuously impress me with their creativity; Chris Dignum, the funniest man I know, and who will blow everyone away one day if he gets off his arse and writes something; Angie Sperling-Bruch, my oldest and oldest friend, who still owes me $90; and of course, Big Daz.

My dog, Issy, who will never read this (because she's too lazy) but who will forever be my sweet, furry daughter. Every time I look into your eyes I hear that Cat Stevens song playing ('I Love My Dog'). We thought we were rescuing you, but it was the other way around.

And finally, my wife, Summer DeRoche, my best friend and first reader. Everyone on this list helped create this book, but it truly wouldn't exist without you, Sum. You helped guide it from a cool-sounding logline into a bona fide manuscript, but more importantly, you kept me going with your belief. I'm in awe of your humour, inspired by your creativity, and jealous of the beautiful films you make. Thanks for being you and choosing me.